THE PE

TALES OF
SECO

ANTHONY TROLLOPE, the fourth of six surviving children, was born on 24 April 1815 in London. As he describes in his *Autobiography*, poverty and debt made his childhood acutely unhappy and disrupted his education: his school fees at Harrow and Winchester were frequently unpaid. His family attempted to restore their fortunes by going to America, leaving the young Anthony alone in England, but it was not until his mother, Frances, began to write that there was any improvement in the family's finances. Her success came too late for her husband, who died in exile in Belgium in 1835. Trollope was unable to afford a university education, and in 1834 he became a junior clerk in the Post Office. He achieved little until he was appointed Surveyor's Clerk in Ireland in 1841. There he worked hard, travelled widely, took up hunting and still found time for his literary career. He married Rose Heseltine, the daughter of a bank manager, in 1844; they had two sons, one of whom emigrated to Australia. Trollope frequently went abroad for the Post Office and did not settle in England again until 1859. He is still remembered as the inventor of the letter-box. In 1867 he resigned from the Post Office and became the editor of *St Paul's Magazine* for the next three years. He failed in his attempt to enter Parliament as a Liberal in 1868. Trollope took his place among London literary society and counted William Thackeray, George Eliot and G. H. Lewes among his friends. He died on 6 December 1882 as the result of a stroke.

Anthony Trollope wrote forty-seven novels and five volumes of short stories as well as travel books, biographies and collections of sketches. The Barsetshire series and the six Palliser or 'political' books were the first novel-sequences to be written in English. His works offer an unsurpassed portrait of the professional and landed classes of Victorian England. In his *Autobiography* (published posthumously in 1883) Trollope describes the self-discipline that enabled his prolific output: he would produce a given number of words per hour in the early morning, before work; he always wrote while travelling by rail or sea, and as soon as he finished one novel he began another. His efforts resulted in his becoming one of England's most successful and popular writers.

Tales of All Countries: Second Series was first published in book form in 1863, two years after the appearance of the *First Series*. It is the second of five volumes of Trollope's short stories and, like its predecessor, is largely drawn from the author's travels abroad on behalf of the Post Office. Many of the stories had originally been printed in the *Cornhill Magazine* under the editorship of Thackeray but he rejected 'Mrs General Talboys' on the grounds that it referred to 'a woman not as pure as she should be'.

TALES OF ALL COUNTRIES
SECOND SERIES

ANTHONY
TROLLOPE

PENGUIN BOOKS

PENGUIN BOOKS

Published by the Penguin Group
Penguin Books Ltd, 27 Wrights Lane, London W8 5TZ, England
Penguin Books USA Inc., 375 Hudson Street, New York, New York 10014, USA
Penguin Books Australia Ltd, Ringwood, Victoria, Australia
Penguin Books Canada Ltd, 10 Alcorn Avenue, Toronto, Ontario, Canada M4V 3B2
Penguin Books (NZ) Ltd, 182–190 Wairau Road, Auckland 10, New Zealand

Penguin Books Ltd, Registered Offices: Harmondsworth, Middlesex, England

First published 1863
Published in Penguin Books 1993
1 3 5 7 9 10 8 6 4 2

Printed in England by Clays Ltd, St Ives plc

CONTENTS.

REPUBLISHED FROM VARIOUS PERIODICALS.

TALES OF ALL COUNTRIES.

AARON TROW.

I WOULD wish to declare, at the beginning of this story, that I shall never regard that cluster of islets which we call Bermuda as the Fortunate Islands of the Ancients. Do not let professional geographers take me up, and say that no one has so accounted them, and that the ancients have never been supposed to have gotten themselves so far westwards. What I mean to assert is this—that, had any ancient been carried thither by enterprise or stress of weather, he would not have given those islands so good a name. That the Neapolitan sailors of King Alonzo should have been wrecked here, I consider to be more likely. The vexed Bermoothes is a good name for them. There is no getting in or out of them without the greatest difficulty, and a patient, slow navigation, which is very heart-rending. That Caliban should have lived here I can imagine; that

B

Ariel would have been sick of the place is certain; and that Governor Prospero should have been willing to abandon his governorship, I conceive to have been only natural. When one regards the present state of the place, one is tempted to doubt whether any of the governors have been conjurors since his days.

Bermuda, as all the world knows, is a British colony at which we maintain a convict establishment. Most of our outlying convict establishments have been sent back upon our hands from our colonies, but here one is still maintained. There is also in the islands a strong military fortress, though not a fortress looking magnificent to the eyes of civilians as do Malta and Gibraltar. There are also here some six thousand white people and some six thousand black people, eating, drinking, sleeping, and dying.

The convict establishment is the most notable feature of Bermuda to a stranger, but it does not seem to attract much attention from the regular inhabitants of the place. There is no intercourse between the prisoners and the Bermudians. The convicts are rarely seen by them, and the convict islands are rarely visited. As to the prisoners themselves, of course it is not open to them—or should not be open to them—to have intercourse with any but the prison authorities.

There have, however, been instances in which convicts have escaped from their confinement, and made

their way out among the islands. Poor wretches!
As a rule, there is but little chance for any that can
so escape. The whole length of the cluster is but
twenty miles, and the breadth is under four. The
prisoners are, of course, white men, and the lower
orders of Bermuda, among whom alone could a runa-
gate have any chance of hiding himself, are all
negroes; so that such a one would be known at
once. Their clothes are all marked. Their only
chance of a permanent escape would be in the
hold of an American ship; but what captain of an
American or other ship would willingly encumber
himself with an escaped convict? But, nevertheless, men have escaped; and in one instance, I
believe, a convict got away, so that of him no further tidings were ever heard.

For the truth of the following tale I will not by
any means vouch. If one were to inquire on the
spot one might probably find that the ladies all
believe it, and the old men; that all the young
men know exactly how much of it is false and
how much true; and that the steady, middle-aged,
well-to-do islanders are quite convinced that it is
romance from beginning to end. My readers may
range themselves with the ladies, the young men, or
the steady, well-to-do, middle-aged islanders, as they
please.

Some years ago, soon after the prison was first established on its present footing, three men did escape
from it, and among them a certain notorious prisoner

named Aaron Trow. Trow's antecedents in England had not been so villanously bad as those of many of his fellow-convicts, though the one offence for which he was punished had been of a deep dye : he had shed man's blood. At a period of great distress in a manufacturing town he had led men on to riot, and with his own hand had slain the first constable who had endeavoured to do his duty against him. There had been courage in the doing of the deed, and probably no malice ; but the deed, let its moral blackness have been what it might, had sent him to Bermuda, with a sentence against him of penal servitude for life. Had he been then amenable to prison discipline,—even then, with such a sentence against him as that,—he might have won his way back, after the lapse of years, to the children, and, perhaps, to the wife, that he had left behind him ; but he was amenable to no rules—to no discipline. His heart was sore to death with an idea of injury, and he lashed himself against the bars of his cage with a feeling that it would be well if he could so lash himself till he might perish in his fury.

And then a day came in which an attempt was made by a large body of convicts, under his leadership, to get the better of the officers of the prison. It is hardly necessary to say that the attempt failed. Such attempts always fail. It failed on this occasion signally, and Trow, with two other men, were condemned to be scourged terribly, and then kept in solitary confinement for some lengthened term of months. Before, however, the day of scourging came, Trow and his two associates had escaped.

I have not the space to tell how this was effected, nor the power to describe the manner. They did escape from the establishment into the islands, and though two of them were taken after a single day's run at liberty, Aaron Trow had not been yet retaken even when a week was over. When a month was over he had not been retaken, and the officers of the prison began to say that he had got away from them in a vessel to the States. It was impossible, they said, that he should have remained in the islands and not been discovered. It was not impossible that he might have destroyed himself, leaving his body where it had not yet been found. But he could not have lived on in Bermuda during that month's search. So, at least, said the officers of the prison. There was, however, a report through the islands that he had been seen from time to time; that he had gotten bread from the negroes at night, threatening them with death if they told of his whereabouts; and that all the clothes of the mate of a vessel had been stolen while the man was bathing, including a suit of dark blue cloth, in which suit of clothes, or in one of such a nature, a stranger had been seen skulking about the rocks near St. George. All this the governor of the prison affected to disbelieve, but the opinion was becoming very rife in the islands that Aaron Trow was still there.

A vigilant search, however, is a task of great

labour, and cannot be kept up for ever. By degrees it was relaxed. The warders and gaolers ceased to patrol the island roads by night, and it was agreed that Aaron Trow was gone, or that he would be starved to death, or that he would in time be driven to leave such traces of his whereabouts as must lead to his discovery; and this at last did turn out to be the fact.

There is a sort of prettiness about these islands which, though it never rises to the loveliness of romantic scenery, is nevertheless attractive in its way. The land breaks itself into little knolls, and the sea runs up, hither and thither, in a thousand creeks and inlets; and then, too, when the oleanders are in bloom, they give a wonderfully bright colour to the landscape. Oleanders seem to be the roses of Bermuda, and are cultivated round all the villages of the better class through the islands. There are two towns, St. George and Hamilton, and one main high road, which connects them; but even this high road is broken by a ferry, over which every vehicle going from St. George to Hamilton must be conveyed. Most of the locomotion in these parts is done by boats, and the residents look to the sea with its narrow creeks, as their best highway from their farms to their best market. In those days—and those days were not very long since—the building of small ships was their chief trade, and they valued their land mostly for the small scrubby cedar-trees with which this trade was carried on.

As one goes from St. George to Hamilton the road runs between two seas; that to the right is the ocean; that on the left is an inland creek, which runs up through a large portion of the islands, so that the land on the other side of it is near to the traveller. For a considerable portion of the way there are no houses lying near the road, and there is one residence, some way from the road, so secluded that no other house lies within a mile of it by land. By water it might probably be reached within half a mile. This place was called Crump Island, and here ived, and had lived for many years, an old gentleman, a native of Bermuda, whose business it had been to buy up cedar wood and sell it to the ship-builders at Hamilton. In our story we shall not have very much to do with old Mr. Bergen, but it will be necessary to say a word or two about his house.

It stood on what would have been an island in the creek, had not a narrow causeway, barely broad enough for a road, joined it to that larger island on which stands the town of St. George. As the main road approaches the ferry it runs through some rough, hilly, open ground, which on the right side towards the ocean has never been cultivated. The distance from the ocean here may, perhaps, be a quarter of a mile, and the ground is for the most part covered with low furze. On the left of the road the land is cultivated in patches, and here, some half mile or more from the ferry, a path turns away to Crump Island. The house cannot be seen from the road, and, indeed, can hardly be seen at all, except from the sea. It lies, perhaps, three furlongs from the high road, and the path to it is but little used, as the passage to and from it is chiefly made by water.

Here, at the time of our story, lived Mr. Bergen, and here lived Mr. Bergen's daughter. Miss Bergen was well known at St. George as a steady, good girl, who spent her time in looking after her father's household matters, in managing his two black maid-servants and the black gardener, and who did her duty in that sphere of life to which she had been called. She was a comely, well-shaped young woman, with a sweet countenance, rather large in size, and very quiet in demeanour. In her earlier years, when young girls usually first bud forth into womanly beauty, the neighbours had not thought much of Anastasia Bergen, nor had the young men of St. George been wont to stay their boats under the window of Crump Cottage in order that they might listen to her voice or feel the light of her eye; but slowly, as years went by, Anastasia Bergen became a woman that a man might well love; and a man learned to love her who was well worthy of a woman's heart. This was Caleb Morton, the Presbyterian minister of St. George; and Caleb Morton had been engaged to marry Miss Bergen for the last two years past, at the period of Aaron Trow's escape from prison.

Caleb Morton was not a native of Bermuda, but

had been sent thither by the synod of his church from Nova Scotia. He was a tall, handsome man, at this time of some thirty years of age, of a presence which might almost have been called commanding. He was very strong, but of a temperament which did not often give him opportunity to put forth his strength; and his life had been such that neither he nor others knew of what nature might be his courage. The greater part of his life was spent in preaching to some few of the white people around him, and in teaching as many of the blacks as he could get to hear him. His days were very quiet, and had been altogether without excitement until he had met with Anastasia Bergen. It will suffice for us to say that he did meet her, and that now, for two years past, they had been engaged as man and wife.

Old Mr. Bergen, when he heard of the engagement, was not well pleased at the information. In the first place, his daughter was very necessary to him, and the idea of her marrying and going away had hardly as yet occurred to him; and then he was by no means inclined to part with any of his money. It must not be presumed that he had amassed a fortune by his trade in cedar wood. Few tradesmen in Bermuda do, as I imagine, amass fortunes. Of some few hundred pounds he was possessed, and these, in the course of nature, would go to his daughter when he died; but he had no inclination to hand any portion of them over to his daughter before they did go to her in the course of nature. Now, the income which Caleb Morton earned as a Presbyterian clergyman was not large, and, therefore, no day had been fixed as yet for his marriage with Anastasia.

But, though the old man had been from the first averse to the match, his hostility had not been active. He had not forbidden Mr. Morton his house, or affected to be in any degree angry because his daughter had a lover. He had merely grumbled forth an intimation that those who marry in haste repent at leisure,—that love kept nobody warm if the pot did not boil; and that, as for him, it was as much as he could do to keep his own pot boiling at Crump Cottage. In answer to this Anastasia said nothing. She asked him for no money, but still kept his accounts, managed his household, and looked patiently forward for better days.

Old Mr. Bergen himself spent much of his time at Hamilton, where he had a woodyard with a couple of rooms attached to it. It was his custom to remain here three nights of the week, during which Anastasia was left alone at the cottage ; and it happened by no means seldom that she was altogether alone, for the negro whom they called the gardener would go to her father's place at Hamilton, and the two black girls would crawl away up to the road, tired with the monotony of the sea at the cottage. Caleb had more than once told her that she was too much alone, but she had laughed at him, saying that solitude in Bermuda was not dangerous. Nor, indeed, was it; for the people are quiet and well-mannered, lacking much energy, but being, in the same degree, free from any propensity to violence.

"So you are going," she said to her lover, one evening, as he rose from the chair on which he had been swinging himself at the door of the cottage which looks down over the creek of the sea. He had sat there for an hour talking to her as she worked, or watching her as she moved about the place. It was a beautiful evening, and the sun had been falling to rest with almost tropical glory before his feet. The bright oleanders were red with their blossoms all around him, and he had thoroughly enjoyed his hour of easy rest. "So you are going," she said to him, not putting her work out of her hand as he rose to depart.

"Yes; and it is time for me to go. I have still work to do before I can get to bed. Ah, well; I suppose the day will come at last when I need not leave you as soon as my hour of rest is over."

"Come; of course it will come. That is, if your reverence should choose to wait for it another ten years or so."

"I believe you would not mind waiting twenty years."

"Not if a certain friend of mine would come down and see me of evenings when I'm alone after the day. It seems to me that I shouldn't mind waiting as long as I had that to look for."

"You are right not to be impatient," he said to her, after a pause, as he held her hand before he went. "Quite right. I only wish I could school myself to be as easy about it."

"I did not say I was easy," said Anastasia. "People are seldom easy in this world, I take it. I said I could be patient. Do not look in that way, as though you pretended that you were dissatisfied with me. You know that I am true to you, and you ought to be very proud of me."

"I am proud of you, Anastasia——" on hearing which she got up and curtseyed to him. "I am proud of you; so proud of you that I feel you should not be left here all alone, with no one to help you if you were in trouble."

"Women don't get into trouble as men do, and do not want any one to help them. If you were alone in the house you would have to go to bed without your supper, because you could not make a basin of boiled milk ready for your own meal. Now, when your reverence has gone, I shall go to work and have my tea comfortably." And then he did go, bidding God bless her as he left her. Three hours after that he was disturbed in his own lodgings by one of the negro girls from the cottage rushing to his door, and begging him in Heaven's name to come down to the assistance of her mistress.

When Morton left her, Anastasia did not proceed to do as she had said, and seemed to have forgotten her evening meal. She had been working sedulously with

her needle during all that last conversation; but when
her lover was gone, she allowed the work to fall from
her hands, and sat motionless for awhile, gazing at
the last streak of colour left by the setting sun; but
there was no longer a sign of its glory to be traced
in the heavens around her. The twilight in Bermuda is not long and enduring as it is with us,
though the daylight does not depart suddenly, leaving
the darkness of night behind it without any inter-
mediate time of warning, as is the case farther south,
down among the islands of the tropics. But the soft,
sweet light of the evening had waned and gone, and
night had absolutely come upon her, while Anastasia
was still seated before the cottage with her eyes
fixed upon the white streak of motionless sea which
was still visible through the gloom. She was thinking of him, of his ways of life, of his happiness, and
of her duty towards him. She had told him, with
her pretty feminine falseness, that she could wait
without impatience; but now she said to herself that
it would not be good for him to wait longer. He
lived alone and without comfort, working very hard
for his poor pittance, and she could see and feel and
understand that a companion in his life was to him
almost a necessity. She would tell her father that
all this must be brought to an end. She would not
ask him for money, but she would make him understand that her services must, at any rate in part, be
transferred. Why should not she and Morton still
live at the cottage when they were married? And

so thinking, and at last resolving, she sat there till the dark night fell upon her.

She was at last disturbed by feeling a man's hand upon her shoulder. She jumped from her chair and faced him,— not screaming, for it was especially within her power to control herself, and to make no utterance except with forethought. Perhaps it might have been better for her had she screamed, and sent a shrill shriek down the shore of that inland sea. She was silent, however, and with awe-struck face and outstretched hands gazed into the face of him who still held her by the shoulder. The night was dark; but her eyes were now accustomed to the darkness, and she could see indistinctly something of his features. He was a low-sized man, dressed in a suit of sailor's blue clothing, with a rough cap of hair on his head, and a beard that had not been clipped for many weeks. His eyes were large, and hollow, and frightfully bright, so that she seemed to see nothing else of him; but she felt the strength of his fingers as he grasped her tighter and more tightly by the arm.

"Who are you?" she said, after a moment's pause.

"Do you know me?" he asked.

"Know you! No." But the words were hardly out of her mouth before it struck her that the man was Aaron Trow, of whom every one in Bermuda had been talking.

"Come into the house," he said, "and give me

food." And he still held her with his hand as though he would compel her to follow him.

She stood for a moment thinking what she would say to him; for even then, with that terrible man standing close to her in the darkness, her presence of mind did not desert her, "Surely," she said, "I will give you food if you are hungry. But take your hand from me. No man would lay his hands on a woman."

"A woman!" said the stranger. "What does the starved wolf care for that? A woman's blood is as sweet to him as that of a man. Come into the house, I tell you." And then she preceded him through the open door into the narrow passage, and thence to the kitchen. There she saw that the back door, leading out on the other side of the house, was open, and she knew that he had come down from the road and entered on that side. She threw her eyes round, looking for the negro girls; but they were away, and she remembered that there was no human being within sound of her voice but this man who had told her that he was as a wolf thirsty after her blood!

"Give me food at once," he said.

"And will you go if I give it you?" she asked.

"I will knock out your brains if you do not," he replied, lifting from the grate a short, thick poker which lay there. "Do as I bid you at once. You also would be like a tiger if you had fasted for two days, as I have done."

She could see, as she moved across the kitchen, that he had already searched there for something that he might eat, but that he had searched in vain. With the close economy common among his class in the islands, all comestibles were kept under close lock and key in the house of Mr. Bergen. Their daily allowance was given day by day to the negro servants, and even the fragments were then gathered up and locked away in safety. She moved across the kitchen to the accustomed cupboard, taking the keys from her pocket, and he followed close upon her. There was a small oil lamp hanging from the low ceiling which just gave them light to see each other. She lifted her hand to this to take it from its hook, but he prevented her. "No, by Heaven!" he said, "you don't touch that till I've done with it. There's light enough for you to drag out your scraps."

She did drag out her scraps and a bowl of milk, which might hold perhaps a quart. There was a fragment of bread, a morsel of cold potato-cake, and the bone of a leg of kid. "And is that all?" said he. But as he spoke he fleshed his teeth against the bone as a dog would have done.

"It is the best I have," she said; "I wish it were better, and you should have had it without violence, as you have suffered so long from hunger."

"Bah! Better; yes! You would give the best no doubt, and set the hell hounds on my track the moment I am gone. I know how much I might expect from your charity."

"I would have fed you for pity's sake," she answered.

"Pity! Who are you, that you should dare to pity me! By —— my young woman, it is I that pity you. I must cut your throat unless you give me money. Do you know that?"

"Money! I have got no money."

"I'll make you have some before I go. Come; don't move till I have done." And as he spoke to her he went on tugging at the bone, and swallowing the lumps of stale bread. He had already finished the bowl of milk. "And, now," said he, "tell me who I am."

"I suppose you are Aaron Trow," she answered, very slowly.

He said nothing on hearing this, but continued his meal, standing close to her so that she might not possibly escape from him out into the darkness. Twice or thrice in those few minutes she made up her mind to make such an attempt, feeling that it would be better to leave him in possession of the house, and make sure, if possible, of her own life. There was no money there; not a dollar! What money her father kept in his possession was locked up in his safe at Hamilton. And might he not keep to his threat, and murder her, when he found that she could give him nothing? She did not tremble outwardly, as she stood there watching him as he

ate, but she thought how probable it might be that
her last moments were very near. And yet she could
scrutinise his features, form, and garments, so as to
carry away in her mind a perfect picture of them.
Aaron Trow,—for of course it was the escaped convict,
—was not a man of frightful, hideous aspect. Had
the world used him well, giving him when he was
young ample wages and separating him from turbu-
lent spirits, he also might have used the world well ;
and then women would have praised the brightness
of his eye and the manly vigour of his brow. But
things had not gone well with him. He had been
separated from the wife he had loved, and the children who had been raised at his knee,—separated by
his own violence ; and now, as he had said of himself, he was a wolf rather than a man. As he
stood there satisfying the craving of his appetite,
breaking up the large morsels of food, he was an
object very sad to be seen. Hunger had made him
gaunt and yellow, he was squalid with the dirt of his
hidden lair, and he had the look of a beast ;—that
look to which men fall when they live like the brutes
of prey, as outcasts from their brethren. But still
there was that about his brow which might have redeemed him,—which might have turned her horror
into pity, had he been willing that it should be so.

" And now give me some brandy," he said.

There was brandy in the house,—in the sitting-
room which was close at their hand, and the key of
the little press which held it was in her pocket. It

was useless, she thought, to refuse him; and so she told him that there was a bottle partly full, but that she must go to the next room to fetch it him.

"We'll go together, my darling," he said. "There's nothing like good company." And he again put his hand upon her arm as they passed into the family sitting-room.

"I must take the light," she said. But he unhooked it himself, and carried it in his own hand.

Again she went to work without trembling. She found the key of the side cupboard, and unlocking the door, handed him a bottle which might contain about half-a-pint of spirits. "And is that all?" he said.

"There is a full bottle here," she answered, handing him another; "but if you drink it, you will be drunk, and they will catch you."

"By Heavens, yes; and you would be the first to help them; would you not?"

"Look here," she answered. "If you will go now, I will not say a word to any one of your coming, nor set them on your track to follow you. There, take the full bottle with you. If you will go, you shall be safe from me."

"What, and go without money!"

"I have none to give you. You may believe me when I say so. I have not a dollar in the house."

Before he spoke again he raised the half empty bottle to his mouth, and drank as long as there was a drop to drink. "There," said he, putting the bottle down, "I am better after that. As to the other you are right, and I will take it with me. And now, young woman, about the money?"

"I tell you that I have not a dollar."

"Look here," said he, and he spoke now in a softer voice, as though he would be on friendly terms with her. "Give me ten sovereigns, and I will go. I know you have it, and with ten sovereigns it is possible that I may save my life. You are good, and would not wish that a man should die so horrid a death. I know you are good. Come, give me the money." And he put his hands up, beseeching her. and looked into her face with imploring eyes.

"On the word of a Christian woman I have not got money to give you," she replied.

"Nonsense!" And as he spoke he took her by the arm and shook her. He shook her violently so that he hurt her, and her breath for a moment was all but gone from her. "I tell you you must make dollars before I leave you, or I will so handle you that it would have been better for you to coin your very blood."

"May God help me at my need," she said, "as I have not above a few penny pieces in the house."

"And you expect me to believe that! Look here! I will shake the teeth out of your head, but I will have it from you." And he did shake her again, using both his hands and striking her against the wall.

"Would you—murder me?" she said, hardly able now to utter the words.

"Murder you, yes; why not? I cannot be worse than I am, were I to murder you ten times over. But with money I may possibly be better."

"I have it not."

"Then I will do worse than murder you. I will make you such an object that all the world shall loathe to look on you." And so saying he took her by the arm and dragged her forth from the wall against which she had stood.

Then there came from her a shriek that was heard far down the shore of that silent sea, and away across to the solitary houses of those living on the other side,—a shriek very sad, sharp, and prolonged,—which told plainly to those who heard it of woman's woe when in her extremest peril. That sound was spoken of in Bermuda for many a day after that, as something which had been terrible to hear. But then, at that moment, as it came wailing through the dark, it sounded as though it were not human. Of those who heard it, not one guessed from whence it came, nor was the hand of any brother put forward to help that woman at her need.

"Did you hear that?" said the young wife to her husband, from the far side of the arm of the sea.

"Hear it! Oh Heaven, yes! Whence did it come?" The young wife could not say from whence it came, but clung close to her husband's breast, comforting herself with the knowledge that that terrible sorrow was not hers.

But aid did come at last, or rather that which seemed as aid. Long and terrible was the fight between that human beast of prey and the poor victim which had fallen into his talons. Anastasia Bergen was a strong, well-built woman, and now that the time had come to her when a struggle was necessary, a struggle for life, for honour, for the happiness of him who was more to her than herself, she fought like a tigress attacked in her own lair. At such a moment as this she also could become wild and savage as the beast of the forest. When he pinioned her arms with one of his, as he pressed her down upon the floor, she caught the first joint of the forefinger of his other hand between her teeth till he yelled in agony, and another sound was heard across the silent water. And then, when one hand was loosed in the struggle, she twisted it through his long hair, and dragged back his head till his eyes were nearly starting from their sockets. Anastasia Bergen had hitherto been a sheer woman, all feminine in her nature. But now the foam came to her mouth, and fire sprang from her eyes, and the muscles of her body worked as though she had been trained to deeds of violence. Of violence, Aaron Trow had known much in his rough life, but never had he combated with harder antagonist than her whom he now held beneath his breast.

"By —— I will put an end to you," he exclaimed,

in his wrath, as he struck her violently across the face with his elbow. His hand was occupied, and he could not use it for a blow, but, nevertheless, the violence was so great that the blood gushed from her nostrils, while the back of her head was driven with violence against the floor. But yet she did not lose her hold of him. Her hand was still twined closely through his thick hair, and in every move he made she clung to him with all her might. "Leave go my hair," he shouted at her, but she still kept her hold, though he again dashed her head against the floor.

There was still light in the room, for when he first grasped her with both his hands, he had put the lamp down on a small table. Now they were rolling on the floor together, and twice he had essayed to kneel on her that he might thus crush the breath from her body, and deprive her altogether of her strength; but she had been too active for him, moving herself along the ground, though in doing so she dragged him with her. But by degrees he got one hand at liberty, and with that he pulled a clasp knife out of his pocket and opened it. "I will cut your head off, if you do not let go my hair," he said. But still she held fast by him. He then stabbed at her arm, using his left hand and making short ineffectual blows. Her dress partly saved her, and partly also the continual movement of all her limbs; but, nevertheless, the knife wounded her. It wounded her in several places about the arm,

covering them both with blood ;—but still she hung
on. So close was her grasp in her agony, that, as
she afterwards found, she cut the skin of her own
hand with her own nails. Had the man's hair been
less thick or strong, or her own tenacity less stead-
fast, he would have murdered her before any inter-
ruption could have saved her..

And yet he had not purposed to murder her, or
even, in the first instance, to inflict on her any
bodily harm. But he had been determined to get
money. With such a sum of money as he had
named, it might, he thought, be possible for him to
win his way across to America. He might bribe
men to hide him in the hold of a ship, and thus
there might be for him, at any rate, a possibility of
escape. That there must be money in the house,
he had still thought when first he laid hands on the
poor woman ; and then, when the struggle had once
begun, when he had felt her muscles contending
with his, the passion of the beast was aroused within
him, and he strove against her as he would have
striven against a dog. But yet, when the knife was
in his hand, he had not driven it against her heart.

Then suddenly, while they were yet rolling on the
floor, there was a sound of footsteps in the passage.
Aaron Trow instantly leaped to his feet, leaving his
victim on the ground, with huge lumps of his thick
clotted hair in her hand. Thus, and thus only,
could he have liberated himself from her grasp. He
rushed at the door with the open knife still in his

hand, and there he came against the two negro servant-girls who had returned down to their kitchen from the road on which they had been straying. Trow, as he half saw them in the dark, not knowing how many there might be, or whether there was a man among them, rushed through them, upsetting one scared girl in his passage. With the instinct and with the timidity of a beast, his impulse now was to escape, and he hurried away back to the road and to his lair, leaving the three women together in the cottage. Poor wretch! As he crossed the road, not skulking in his impotent haste, but running at his best, another pair of eyes saw him, and when the search became hot after him, it was known that his hiding-place was not distant.

It was some time before any of the women were able to act, and when some step was taken, Anastasia was the first to take it. She had not absolutely swooned, but the reaction, after the violence of her efforts, was so great, that for some minutes she had been unable to speak. She had risen from the floor when Trow left her, and had even followed him to the door; but since that she had fallen back into her father's old armchair, and there she sat gasping not only for words, but for breath also. At last she bade one of the girls to run into St. George, and beg Mr. Morton to come to her aid. The girl would not stir without her companion; and even then, Anastasia, covered as she was with blood, with dishevelled hair and her clothes half torn from her body, accompanied them as far as the road. There they found a negro lad still hanging about the place, and he told them that he had seen the man cross the road, and run down over the open ground towards the rocks of the sea-coast. "He must be there," said the lad, pointing in the direction of a corner of the rocks ; "unless he swim across the mouth of the ferry." But the mouth of that ferry is an arm of the sea, and it was not probable that a man would do that when he might have taken the narrow water by keeping on the other side of the road.

At about one that night Caleb Morton reached the cottage breathless with running, and before a word was spoken between them, Anastasia had fallen on his shoulder and had fainted. As soon as she was in the arms of her lover, all her power had gone from her. The spirit and passion of the tiger had gone, and she was again a weak woman shuddering at the thought of what she had suffered. She remembered that she had had the man's hand between her teeth, and by degrees she found his hair still clinging to her fingers ; but even then she could hardly call to mind the nature of the struggle she had undergone. His hot breath close to her own cheek she did remember, and his glaring eyes, and even the roughness of his beard as he pressed his face against her own ; but she could not say whence had come the blood, nor till her arm became stiff and motionless did she know that she had been wounded.

It was all joy with her now, as she sat motionless without speaking, while he administered to her wants and spoke words of love into her ears. She remembered the man's horrid threat, and knew that by God's mercy she had been saved. And *he* was there caressing her, loving her, comforting her! As she thought of the fate that had threatened her, of the evil that had been so imminent, she fell forward on her knees, and with incoherent sobs uttered her thanksgivings, while her head was still supported on his arms.

It was almost morning before she could induce herself to leave him and lie down. With him she seemed to be so perfectly safe; but the moment he was away she could see Aaron Trow's eyes gleaming at her across the room. At last, however, she slept; and when he saw that she was at rest, he told himself that his work must then begin. Hitherto Caleb Morton had lived in all respects the life of a man of peace; but now, asking himself no questions as to the propriety of what he would do, using no inward arguments as to this or that line of conduct, he girded the sword on his loins, and prepared himself for war. The wretch who had thus treated the woman whom he loved should be hunted down like a wild beast, as long as he had arms and legs with which to carry on the hunt. He would pursue the miscreant with any weapons that might come to his hands; and might Heaven help him at his need, as he dealt forth punishment to that man, if he caught him within his

grasp. Those who had hitherto known Morton in
the island, could not recognise the man as he came
forth on that day, thirsty after blood, and desirous to
thrust himself into personal conflict with the wild
ruffian who had injured him. The meek Presbyterian minister had been a preacher, preaching ways of
peace, and living in accordance with his own doctrines. The world had been very quiet for him, and
he had walked quietly in his appointed path. But
now the world was quiet no longer, nor was there any
preaching of peace. His cry was for blood; for the
blood of the untamed savage brute who had come
upon his young doe in her solitude, and striven with
such brutal violence to tear her heart from her
bosom.

He got to his assistance early in the morning
some of the constables from St. George, and before
the day was over, he was joined by two or three of
the warders from the convict establishment. There
was with him also a friend or two, and thus a party
was formed, numbering together ten or twelve persons. They were of course all armed, and therefore
it might be thought that there would be but small
chance for the wretched man if they should come
upon his track. At first they all searched together,
thinking, from the tidings which had reached them,
that he must be near to them; but gradually they
spread themselves along the rocks between St. George
and the ferry, keeping watchmen on the road, so that
he should not escape unnoticed into the island.

Ten times during the day did Anastasia send from the cottage up to Morton, begging him to leave the search to others, and come down to her. But not for a moment would he lose the scent of his prey. What! should it be said that she had been so treated, and that others had avenged her? He sent back to say that her father was with her now, and that he would come when his work was over. And in that job of work the life-blood of Aaron Trow was counted up.

Towards evening they were all congregated on the road near to the spot at which the path turns off towards the cottage, when a voice was heard hallooing to them from the summit of a little hill which lies between the road and the sea on the side towards the ferry, and presently a boy came running down to them full of news. "Danny Lund has seen him," said the boy, "he has seen him plainly in among the rocks." And then came Danny Lund himself, a small negro lad about fourteen years of age, who was known in those parts as the idlest, most dishonest, and most useless of his race. On this occasion, however, Danny Lund became important, and every one listened to him. He had seen, he said, a pair of eyes moving down in a cave of the rocks which he well knew. He had been in the cave often, he said, and could get there again. But not now; not while that pair of eyes was moving at the bottom of it. And so they all went up over the hill, Morton leading the way with hot haste. In his waistband he held a

pistol, and his hand grasped a short iron bar with
which he had armed himself. They ascended the top
of the hill, and when there, the open sea was before
them on two sides, and on the third was the narrow
creek over which the ferry passed. Immediately beneath their feet were the broken rocks ; for on that
side, towards the sea, the earth and grass of the hill
descended but a little way towards the water. Down
among the rocks they all went, silently, Caleb Morton
leading the way, and Danny Lund directing him from
behind.

"Mr. Morton," said an elderly man from St.
George, "had you not better let the warders of the
gaol go first ; he is a desperate man, and they will
best understand his ways ?"

In answer to this Morton said nothing, but he
would let no one put a foot before him. He still
pressed forward among the rocks, and at last came to
a spot from whence he might have sprung at one
leap into the ocean. It was a broken cranny on the
sea-shore into which the sea beat, and surrounded on
every side but the one by huge broken fragments of
stone, which at first sight seemed as though they
would have admitted of a path down among them
to the water's edge ; but which, when scanned more
closely, were seen to be so large in size, that no man
could climb from one to another. It was a singularly
romantic spot, but now well known to them all there,
for they had visited it over and over again that
morning.

"In there," said Danny Lund, keeping well behind Morton's body, and pointing at the same time to a cavern high up among the rocks, but quite on the opposite side of the little inlet of the sea. The mouth of the cavern was not twenty yards from them where they stood, but at the first sight it seemed as though it must be impossible to reach it. The precipice on the brink of which they all now stood, ran down sheer into the sea, and the fall from the mouth of the cavern on the other side was as steep. But Danny solved the mystery by pointing upwards, and showing them how he had been used to climb to a projecting rock over their heads, and from thence creep round by certain vantages of the stone till he was able to let himself down into the aperture. But now, at the present moment, he was unwilling to make essay of his prowess as a cragsman. He had, he said, been up on that projecting rock thrice, and there had seen the eyes moving in the cavern. He was quite sure of that fact of the pair of eyes, and declined to ascend the rock again.

Traces soon became visible to them by which they knew that some one had passed in and out of the cavern recently The stone, when examined, bore those marks of friction which passage and repassage over it will always give. At the spot from whence the climber left the platform and commenced his ascent, the side of the stone had been rubbed by the close friction of a man's body. A light boy like Danny Lund might find his way in and out without leaving such marks behind him, but no heavy man could do so. Thus before long they all were satisfied that Aaron Trow was in the cavern before them.

Then there was a long consultation as to what they would do to carry on the hunt, and how they would drive the tiger from his lair. That he should not again come out, except to fall into their hands, was to all of them a matter of course. They would keep watch and ward there, though it might be for days and nights. But that was a process which did not satisfy Morton, and did not indeed well satisfy any of them. It was not only that they desired to inflict punishment on the miscreant in accordance with the law, but also that they did not desire that the miserable man should die in a hole like a starved dog, and that then they should go after him to take out his wretched skeleton. There was something in that idea so horrid in every way, that all agreed that active steps must be taken. The warders of the prison felt that they would all be disgraced if they could not take their prisoner alive. Yet who would get round that perilous ledge in the face of such an adversary? A touch to any man while climbing there would send him headlong down among the waves! And then his fancy told to each what might be the nature of an embrace with such an animal as that, driven to despair, hopeless of life, armed, as they knew, at any rate, with a knife! If the first adventurous spirit should succeed in crawling round that ledge, what would be the reception which he might expect in the terrible depth of that cavern?

They called to their prisoner, bidding him come out, and telling him that they would fire in upon him if he did not show himself; but not a sound was heard. It was indeed possible that they should send their bullets to, perhaps, every corner of the cavern; and if so, in that way they might slaughter him; but even of this they were not sure. Who could tell that there might not be some protected nook in which he could lay secure? And who could tell when the man was struck, or whether he were wounded?

"I will get to him," said Morton, speaking with a low dogged voice, and so saying he clambered up to the rock to which Danny Lund had pointed. Many voices at once attempted to restrain him, and one or two put their hands upon him to keep him back, but he was too quick for them, and now stood upon the ledge of rock. "Can you see him?" they asked below.

"I can see nothing within the cavern," said Morton.

"Look down very hard, Massa," said Danny, "very hard indeed, down in deep dark hole, and then see him big eyes moving!"

Morton now crept along the ledge, or rather he was beginning to do so, having put forward his shoulders and arms to make a first step in advance from the spot on which he was resting, when a hand was put forth from one corner of the cavern's mouth, —a hand armed with a pistol;—and a shot was fired.

D

There could be no doubt now but that Danny
Lund was right, and no doubt now as to the whereabouts of Aaron Trow.

A hand was put forth, a pistol was fired, and Caleb
Morton still clinging to a corner of the rock with
both his arms, was seen to falter. " He is wounded,"
said one of the voices from below ; and then they all
expected to see him fall into the sea. But he did
not fall, and after a moment or two, he proceeded
carefully to pick his steps along the ledge. The ball
had touched him, grazing his cheek and cutting
through the light whiskers that he wore ; but he had
not felt it, though the blow had nearly knocked him
from his perch. And then four or five shots were
fired from the rocks into the mouth of the cavern.
The man's arm had been seen, and indeed one or two
declared that they had traced' the dim outline of his
figure. But no sound was heard to come from the
cavern, except the sharp crack of the bullets against
the rock, and the echo of the gunpowder. There had
been no groan as of a man wounded, no sound of a
body falling, no voice wailing in despair. For a few
seconds all was dark with the smoke of the gunpowder, and then the empty mouth of the cave was
again yawning before their eyes. Morton was now
near it, still cautiously creeping. The first danger
to which he was exposed was this ; that his enemy
within the recess might push him down from the
rocks with a touch. But on the other hand, there
were three or four men ready to fire, the moment

that a hand should be put forth ; and then Morton
could swim,—was known to be a strong swimmer ;—
whereas of Aaron Trow it was already declared by
the prison gaolers that he could not swim. Two of
the warders had now followed Morton on the rocks,
so that in the event of his making good his entrance
into the cavern, and holding his enemy at bay for a
minute, he would be joined by aid.

It was strange to see how those different men
conducted themselves as they stood on the opposite
platform watching the attack. The officers from the
prison had no other thought but of their prisoner,
and were intent on taking him alive or dead. To
them it was little or nothing what became of Morton.
It was their business to encounter peril, and they
were ready to do so ;—feeling, however, by no means
sorry to have such a man as Morton in advance of
them. Very little was said by them. They had
their wits about them, and remembered that every
word spoken for the guidance of their ally would be
heard also by the escaped convict. Their prey was
sure, sooner or later, and had not Morton been so
eager in his pursuit, they would have waited till
some plan had been devised of trapping him without
danger. But the townsmen from St. George, of
whom some dozen were now standing there, were
quick and eager and loud in their counsels. "Stay
where you are, Mr. Morton,—stay awhile for the love
of God,—or he'll have you down." "Now's your
time, Caleb ; in on him now, and you'll have him."

" Close with him, Morton, close with him at once; it's your only chance." "There's four of us here; we'll fire on him if he as much as shows a limb." All of which words as they were heard by that poor wretch within, must have sounded to him as the barking of a pack of hounds thirsting for his blood. For him at any rate there was no longer any hope in this world.

My reader, when chance has taken you into the hunting-field, has it ever been your lot to sit by on horseback, and watch the digging out of a fox? The operation is not an uncommon one, and in some countries it is held to be in accordance with the rules of fair sport. For myself, I think that when the brute has so far saved himself, he should be entitled to the benefit of his cunning; but I will not now discuss the propriety or impropriety of that practice in venery. I can never, however, watch the doing of that work without thinking much of the agonising struggles of the poor beast whose last refuge is being torn from over his head. There he lies within a few yards of his arch enemy, the huntsman. The thick breath of the hounds make hot the air within his hole. The sound of their voices is close upon his ears. His breast is nearly bursting with the violence of that effort which at last has brought him to his retreat. And then pickaxe and mattock are plied above his head, and nearer and more near to him press his foes,—his double foes, human and canine,— till at last a huge hand grasps him, and he is dragged forth among his enemies. Almost as soon as his eyes have seen the light the eager noses of a dozen hounds have moistened themselves in his entrails. Ah me! I know that he is vermin, the vermin after whom I have been risking my neck, with a bold ambition that I might ultimately witness his death-struggles; but, nevertheless, I would fain have saved him that last half hour of gradually diminished hope.

And Aaron Trow was now like a hunted fox, doomed to be dug out from his last refuge, with this addition to his misery, that these hounds when they caught their prey, would not put him at once out of his misery. When first he saw that throng of men coming down from the hill top and resting on the platform, he knew that his fate was come. When they called to him to surrender himself he was silent, but he knew that his silence was of no avail. To them who were so eager to be his captors the matter seemed to be still one of considerable difficulty; but, to his thinking, there was no difficulty. There were there some score of men, fully armed, within twenty yards of him. If he but showed a trace of his limbs he would become a mark for their bullets. And then if he were wounded, and no one would come to him! If they allowed him to lie there without food till he perished! Would it not be well for him to yield himself? Then they called again and he was still silent. That idea of yielding is very terrible to the heart of a man. And when the worst had come to the worst, did not the ocean run deep beneath his cavern's mouth?

But as they yelled at him and halloa-ed, making their preparations for his death, his presence of mind deserted the poor wretch. He had stolen an old pistol on one of his marauding expeditions, of which one barrel had been loaded. That in his mad despair he had fired; and now, as he lay near the mouth of the cavern, under the cover of the projecting stone, he had no weapon with him but his hands. He had had a knife, but that had dropped from him during the struggle on the floor of the cottage. He had now nothing but his hands, and was considering how he might best use them in ridding himself of the first of his pursuers. The man was near him, armed, with all the power and majesty of right on his side; whereas on his side, Aaron Trow had nothing,—not a hope. He raised his head that he might look forth, and a dozen voices shouted as his face appeared above the aperture. A dozen weapons were levelled at him, and he could see the gleaming of the muzzles of the guns. And then the foot of his pursuer was already on the corner stone at the cavern's mouth. "Now, Caleb, on him at once!" shouted a voice. Ah me! it was a moment in which to pity even such a man as Aaron Trow.

"Now, Caleb, at him at once!" shouted the voice. No, by heavens; not so, even yet! The sound of triumph in those words roused the last burst of energy in the breast of that wretched man; and he sprang forth, head foremost, from his prison house. Forth he came, manifest enough before the eyes of

them all, and with head well down, and hands outstretched, but with his wide glaring eyes still turned
towards his pursuers as he fell, he plunged down into
the waves beneath him. Two of those who stood by,
almost unconscious of what they did, fired at his
body as it made its rapid way to the water; but, as
they afterwards found, neither of the bullets struck
him. Morton, when his prey thus leaped forth,
escaping him for awhile, was already on the verge of
the cavern,—had even then prepared his foot for that
onward spring which should bring him to the throat
of his foe. But he arrested himself, and for a moment stood there watching the body as it struck the
water, and hid itself at once beneath the ripple.
He stood there for a moment watching the deed and
its effect, and then, leaving his hold upon the rock,
he once again followed his quarry. Down he went,
head foremost, right on to the track in the waves
which the other had made; and when the two rose
to the surface together, each was struggling in the
grasp of the other.

It was a foolish, nay, a mad deed to do. The poor
wretch who had first fallen could not have escaped.
He could not even swim, and had therefore flung
himself to certain destruction when he took that
leap from out of the cavern's mouth. It would have
been sad to see him perish beneath the waves,—to
watch him as he rose gasping for breath, and then to
see him sinking again, to rise again and then to go
for ever. But his life had been fairly forfeit,—and

why should one so much more precious have been
flung after it ? It was surely with no view of saving
that pitiful life that Caleb Morton had leaped after
his enemy. But the hound, hot with the chace, will
follow the stag over the precipice and dash himself
to pieces against the rocks. The beast thirsting for
blood, will rush in even among the weapons of men.
Morton in his fury had felt but one desire, burned
with but one passion. If the Fates would but grant
him to fix his clutches in the throat of the man who
had ill-used his love ;—for the rest it might all go as
it would !

In the earlier part of the morning, while they
were all searching for their victim, they had brought
a boat up into this very inlet among the rocks ; and
the same boat had been at hand during the whole
day. Unluckily, before they had come hither, it had
been taken round the headland to a place among the
rocks at which a government skiff is always moored.
The sea was still so quiet that there was hardly a
ripple on it, and the boat had been again sent for
when first it was supposed that they had at last
traced Aaron Trow to his hiding-place. Anxiously
now were all eyes turned to the headland, but as yet
no boat was there.

The two men rose to the surface, each struggling in
the arms of the other. Trow, though he was in an
element to which he was not used, though he had
sprung thither as another suicide might spring
to certain death beneath a railway engine, did not

altogether lose his presence of mind. Prompted by a double instinct, he had clutched hold of Morton's body when he encountered it beneath the waters. He held on to it, as to his only protection, and he held on to him also as to his only enemy. If there was a chance for a life struggle, they would share that chance together; and if not, then together would they meet that other fate.

Caleb Morton was a very strong man, and though one of his arms was altogether encumbered by his antagonist, his other arm and his legs were free. With these he seemed to succeed in keeping his head above the water, weighted as he was with the body of his foe. But Trow's efforts were also used with the view of keeping himself above the water. Though he had purposed to destroy himself in taking that leap, and now hoped for nothing better than that they might both perish together, he yet struggled to keep his head above the waves. Bodily power he had none left to him, except that of holding on to Morton's arm and plunging with his legs; but he did hold on, and thus both their heads remained above the surface.

But this could not last long. It was easy to see that Trow's strength was nearly spent, and that when he went down Morton must go with him. If indeed they could be separated,—if Morton could once make himself free from that embrace into which he had been so anxious to leap,—then indeed there might be a hope. All round that little inlet the rock fell sheer down into the deep sea, so that there was no resting place for a foot; but round the headlands on either side, even within forty or fifty yards of that spot, Morton might rest on the rocks, till a boat should come to his assistance. To him that distance would have been nothing, if only his limbs had been at liberty.

Upon the platform of rock they were all at their wit's ends. Many were anxious to fire at Trow; but even if they hit him, would Morton's position have been better? Would not the wounded man have still clung to him who was not wounded? And then there could be no certainty that any one of them would hit the right man. The ripple of the waves, though it was very slight, nevertheless sufficed to keep the bodies in motion; and then, too, there was not among them any marksman peculiar for his skill.

Morton's efforts in the water were too severe to admit of his speaking, but he could hear and understand the words which were addressed to him. "Shake him off, Caleb." "Strike him from you with your foot." "Swim to the right shore; swim for it, even if you take him with you." Yes; he could hear them all; but hearing and obeying were very different. It was not easy to shake off that dying man; and as for swimming with him, that was clearly impossible. It was as much as he could do to keep his head above water, let alone any attempt to move in one settled direction.

For some four or five minutes they lay thus battling on the waves before the head of either of them went

down. Trow had been twice below the surface, but
it was before he had succeeded in supporting himself by Morton's arm. Now it seemed as though he
must sink again,—as though both must sink. His
mouth was barely kept above the water, and as
Morton shook him with his arm, the tide would pass
over him. It was horrid to watch from the shore the
glaring upturned eyes of the dying wretch, as his
long streaming hair lay back upon the wave. "Now,
Caleb, hold him down. Hold him under," was
shouted in the voice of some eager friend. Rising
up on the water, Morton made a last effort to do as
he was bid. He did press the man's head down,—
well down below the surface,—but still the hand clung
to him, and as he struck out against the water, he
was powerless against that grasp.

Then there came a loud shout along the shore, and
all those on the platform, whose eyes had been fixed
so closely on that terrible struggle beneath them,
rushed towards the rocks on the other coast. The
sound of oars was heard close to them,—an eager
pressing stroke, as of men who knew well that they
were rowing for the salvation of a life. On they
came, close under the rocks, obeying with every
muscle of their bodies the behests of those who
called to them from the shore. The boat came with
such rapidity,—was so recklessly urged,—that it was
driven somewhat beyond the inlet ; but in passing, a
blow was struck which made Caleb Morton once more
the master of his own life. The two men had been

carried out in their struggle towards the open sea;
and as the boat curved in, so as to be as close as the
rocks would allow, the bodies of the men were
brought within the sweep of the oars. He in the
bow—for there were four pulling in the boat—had
raised his oar as he neared the rocks,—had raised it
high above the water; and now, as they passed close
by the struggling men, he let it fall with all its force
on the upturned face of the wretched convict. It
was a terrible, frightful thing to do,—thus striking
one who was so stricken; but who shall say that the
blow was not good and just? Methinks, however, that
the eyes and face of that dying man will haunt for
ever the dreams of him who carried that oar!

Trow never rose again to the surface. Three days
afterwards his body was found at the ferry, and then
they carried him to the convict island and buried
him. Morton was picked up and taken into the boat.
His life was saved; but it may be a question how the
battle might have gone had not that friendly oar
been raised in his behalf. As it was, he lay at the
cottage for days before he was able to be moved, so
as to receive the congratulations of those who had
watched that terrible conflict from the shore. Nor
did he feel that there had been anything in that
day's work of which he could be proud;—much
rather of which it behoved him to be thoroughly
ashamed. Some six months after that he obtained
the hand of Anastasia Bergen, but they did not
remain long in Bermuda. "He went away, back to

his own country," my informant told me; "because he could not endure to meet the ghost of Aaron Trow, at that point of the road which passes near the cottage." That the ghost of Aaron Trow may be seen there and round the little rocky inlet of the sea, is part of the creed of every young woman in Bermuda.

MRS. GENERAL TALBOYS.

WHY Mrs. General Talboys first made up her mind to pass the winter of 1859 at Rome I never clearly understood. To myself she explained her purposes, soon after her arrival at the Eternal City, by declaring, in her own enthusiastic manner, that she was inspired by a burning desire to drink fresh at the still living fountains of classical poetry and sentiment. But I always thought that there was something more than this in it. Classical poetry and sentiment were doubtless very dear to her; but so also, I imagine, were the substantial comforts of Hardover Lodge, the General's house in Berkshire; and I do not think that she would have emigrated for the winter had there not been some slight domestic misunderstanding. Let this, however, be fully made clear,—that such misunderstanding, if it existed, must have been simply an affair of temper. No impropriety of conduct has, I am very sure, ever been imputed to the lady. The General, as all the world knows, is hot; and Mrs. Talboys, when the sweet rivers of her enthusiasm are unfed by congenial waters, can, I believe, make herself disagreeable.

But be this as it may, in November, 1859, Mrs. Talboys came among us English at Rome, and soon succeeded in obtaining for herself a comfortable footing in our society. We all thought her more remarkable for her mental attributes than for physical perfection ; but, nevertheless, she was, in her own way, a sightly woman. She had no special brilliance, either of eye or complexion, such as would produce sudden flames in susceptible hearts ; nor did she seem to demand instant homage by the form and step of a goddess ; but we found her to be a good-looking woman of some thirty or thirty-three years of age, with soft peach-like cheeks,—rather too like those of a cherub, with sparkling eyes which were hardly large enough, with good teeth, a white forehead, a dimpled chin and a full bust. Such, outwardly, was Mrs. General Talboys. The description of the inward woman is the purport to which these few pages will be devoted.

There are two qualities to which the best of mankind are much subject, which are nearly related to each other, and as to which the world has not yet decided whether they are to be classed among the good or evil attributes of our nature. Men and women are under the influence of them both, but men oftenest undergo the former, and women the latter. They are ambition and enthusiasm. Now Mrs. Talboys was an enthusiastic woman.

As to ambition, generally as the world agrees with
Mark Antony in stigmatising it as a grievous fault,
I am myself clear that it is a virtue ; but with ambition at present we have no concern. Enthusiasm
also, as I think, leans to virtue's side ; or, at least,
if it be a fault, of all faults it is the prettiest. But
then, to partake at all of virtue, or even to be in
any degree pretty, the enthusiasm must be true.

Bad coin is known from good by the ring of it ;
and so is bad enthusiasm. Let the coiner be ever
so clever at his art, in the coining of enthusiasm the
sound of true gold can never be imparted to the
false metal. And I doubt whether the cleverest she
in the world can make false enthusiasm palatable
to the taste of man. To the taste of any woman
the enthusiasm of another woman is never very
palatable.

We understood at Rome that Mrs. Talboys had a
considerable family,—four or five children, we were
told ; but she brought with her only one daughter, a
little girl about twelve years of age. She had torn
herself asunder, as she told me, from the younger
nurslings of her heart, and had left them to the
care of a devoted female attendant, whose love was all
but maternal. And then she said a word or two
about the General, in terms which made me almost
think that this quasi-maternal love extended itself
beyond the children. The idea, however, was a mistaken one, arising from the strength of her language,
to which I was then unaccustomed. I have since

become aware that nothing can be more decorous than old Mrs. Upton, the excellent head-nurse at Hardover Lodge ; and no gentleman more discreet in his conduct than General Talboys.

And I may as well here declare, also, that there could be no more virtuous woman than the General's wife. Her marriage vow was to her paramount to all other vows and bonds whatever. The General's honour was quite safe when he sent her off to Rome by herself ; and he no doubt knew that it was so. *Illi robur et æs triplex*, of which I believe no weapons of any assailant could get the better. But, nevertheless, we used to fancy that she had no repugnance to impropriety in other women,—to what the world generally calls impropriety. Invincibly attached herself to the marriage tie, she would constantly speak of it as by no means necessarily binding on others ; and, virtuous herself as any griffin of propriety, she constantly patronised, at any rate, the theory of infidelity in her neighbours. She was very eager in denouncing the prejudices of the English world, declaring that she had found existence among them to be no longer possible for herself. She was hot against the stern unforgiveness of British matrons, and equally eager in reprobating the stiff conventionalities of a religion in which she said that none of its votaries had faith, though they all allowed themselves to be enslaved.

We had at that time a small set at Rome, consist-

ing chiefly of English and Americans, who habitu-
ally met at each other's rooms, and spent many of
our evening hours in discussing Italian politics. We
were, most of us, painters, poets, novelists, or sculptors ;—perhaps I should say would-be painters, poets,
novelists, and sculptors,—aspirants, hoping to become
some day recognised ; and among us Mrs. Talboys
took her place, naturally enough, on account of a
very pretty taste she had for painting. I do not
know that she ever originated anything that was
grand ; but she made some nice copies, and was
fond, at any rate, of art conversation. She wrote
essays, too, which she showed in confidence to various
gentlemen, and had some idea of taking lessons in
modelling.

In all our circle Conrad Mackinnon, an American,
was, perhaps, the person most qualified to be styled
its leader. He was one who absolutely did gain his
living, and an ample living too, by his pen, and was
regarded on all sides as a literary lion, justified by
success in roaring at any tone he might please. His
usual roar was not exactly that of a sucking-dove or
a nightingale ; but it was a good-humoured roar, not
very offensive to any man, and apparently acceptable
enough to some ladies. He was a big burly man,
near to fifty as I suppose, somewhat awkward in his
gait, and somewhat loud in his laugh. But though
nigh to fifty, and thus ungainly, he liked to be smiled
on by pretty women, and liked, as some said, to be
flattered by them also. If so, he should have been

happy, for the ladies at Rome at that time made much of Conrad Mackinnon.

Of Mrs. Mackinnon no one did make very much, and yet she was one of the sweetest, dearest, quietest, little creatures that ever made glad a man's fireside. She was exquisitely pretty, always in good humour, never stupid, self-denying to a fault, and yet she was generally in the background. She would seldom come forward of her own will, but was contented to sit behind her teapot and hear Mackinnon do his roaring. He was certainly much given to what the world at Rome called flirting, but this did not in the least annoy her. She was twenty years his junior, and yet she never flirted with any one. Women would tell her—good-natured friends—how Mackinnon went on; but she received such tidings as an excellent joke, observing that he had always done the same, and no doubt always would till he was ninety. I do believe that she was a happy woman; and yet I used to think that she should have been happier. There is, however, no knowing the inside of another man's house, or reading the riddles of another man's joy and sorrow.

We had also there another lion,—a lion cub,—entitled to roar a little, and of him also I must say something. Charles O'Brien was a young man, about twenty-five years of age, who had sent out from his studio in the preceding year a certain bust, supposed by his admirers to be unsurpassed by any effort of ancient or modern genius. I am no judge of sculp-

ture, and will not, therefore, pronounce an opinion;
but many who considered themselves to be judges,
declared that it was a "goodish head and shoulders,"
and nothing more. I merely mention the fact, as it
was on the strength of that head and shoulders that
O'Brien separated himself from a throng of others
such as himself in Rome, walked solitary during the
days, and threw himself at the feet of various
ladies when the days were over. He had ridden
on the shoulders of his bust into a prominent
place in our circle, and there encountered much
feminine admiration—from Mrs. General Talboys and
others.

Some eighteen or twenty of us used to meet every
Sunday evening in Mrs. Mackinnon's drawing-room.
Many of us, indeed, were in the habit of seeing each
other daily, and of visiting together the haunts in
Rome which are best loved by art-loving strangers;
but here, in this drawing-room, we were sure to
come together, and here before the end of November
Mrs. Talboys might always be found, not in any
accustomed seat, but moving about the room as
the different male mental attractions of our society
might chance to move themselves. She was at first
greatly taken by Mackinnon,—who also was, I think,
a little stirred by her admiration, though he stoutly
denied the charge. She became, however, very dear
to us all before she left us, and certainly we owed to
her our love, for she added infinitely to the joys of
our winter.

"I have come here to refresh myself," she said to Mackinnon one evening,—to Mackinnon and myself, for we were standing together.

"Shall I get you tea?" said I.

"And will you have something to eat?" Mackinnon asked.

"No, no, no;" she answered. "Tea, yes; but for heaven's sake let nothing solid dispel the associations of such a meeting as this."

"I thought you might have dined early," said Mackinnon. Now Mackinnon was a man whose own dinner was very dear to him. I have seen him become hasty and unpleasant, even under the pillars of the Forum, when he thought that the party were placing his fish in jeopardy by their desire to linger there too long.

"Early! Yes: No; I know not when it was. One dines and sleeps in obedience to that dull clay which weighs down so generally the particle of our spirit. But the clay may sometimes be forgotten. Here I can always forget it."

"I thought you asked for refreshment," I said. She only looked at me, whose small attempts at prose composition had, up to that time, been altogether unsuccessful, and then addressed herself in reply to Mackinnon.

"It is the air which we breathe that fills our lungs and gives us life and light. It is that which refreshes us if pure, or sinks us into stagnation if it be foul. Let me for awhile inhale the breath of an invigorating literature. Sit down, Mr. Mackinnon; I have a question that I must put to you." And then she succeeded in carrying him off into a corner. As far as I could see he went willingly enough at that time, though he soon became averse to any long retirement in company with Mrs. Talboys.

We none of us quite understood what were her exact ideas on the subject of revealed religion. Somebody, I think, had told her that there were among us one or two whose opinions were not exactly orthodox according to the doctrines of the established English church. If so, she was determined to show us that she also was advanced beyond the prejudices of an old and dry school of theology. "I have thrown down all the barriers of religion," she said to poor Mrs. Mackinnon, "and am looking for the sentiments of a pure Christianity."

"Thrown down all the barriers of religion!" said Mrs. Mackinnon, in a tone of horror which was not appreciated.

"Indeed, yes," said Mrs. Talboys, with an exulting voice. "Are not the days for such trammels gone by?"

"But yet you hold by Christianity?"

"A pure Christianity, unstained by blood and perjury, by hypocrisy and verbose genuflection. Can I not worship and say my prayers among the clouds?" And she pointed to the lofty ceiling and the handsome chandelier.

"But Ida goes to church," said Mrs. Mackinnon.

Ida Talboys was her daughter. Now, it may be observed that many who throw down the barriers of religion, so far as those barriers may affect themselves, still maintain them on behalf of their children. "Yes," said Mrs. Talboys; "dear Ida! her soft spirit is not yet adapted to receive the perfect truth. We are obliged to govern children by the strength of their prejudices." And then she moved away, for it was seldom that Mrs. Talboys remained long in conversation with any lady.

Mackinnon, I believe, soon became tired of her. He liked her flattery, and at first declared that she was clever and nice; but her niceness was too purely celestial to satisfy his mundane tastes. Mackinnon himself can revel among the clouds in his own writings, and can leave us sometimes in doubt whether he ever means to come back to earth; but when his foot is on *terra firma*, he loves to feel the earthly substratum which supports his weight. With women he likes a hand that can remain an unnecessary moment within his own, an eye that can glisten with the sparkle of champagne, a heart weak enough to make its owner's arm tremble within his own beneath the moonlight gloom of the Coliseum arches. A dash of sentiment the while makes all these things the sweeter; but the sentiment alone will not suffice for him. Mrs. Talboys did, I believe, drink her glass of champagne, as do other ladies; but with her it had no such pleasing effect. It loosened only her tongue, but never her eye. Her arm, I think, never trembled, and her hand never lingered. The General was always safe, and happy, perhaps, in his solitary safety.

It so happened that we had unfortunately among us two artists who had quarrelled with their wives. O'Brien, whom I have before mentioned, was one of them. In his case, I believe him to have been almost as free from blame as a man can be, whose marriage was in itself a fault. However, he had a wife in Ireland, some ten years older than himself; and though he might sometimes almost forget the fact, his friends and neighbours were well aware of it. In the other case the whole fault probably was with the husband. He was an ill-tempered, bad-hearted man, clever enough, but without principle; and he was continually guilty of the great sin of speaking evil of the woman whose name he should have been anxious to protect. In both cases our friend Mrs. Talboys took a warm interest, and in each of them she sympathised with the present husband against the absent wife.

Of the consolation which she offered in the latter instance we used to hear something from Mackinnon. He would repeat to his wife, and to me and my wife, the conversations which she had with him. "Poor Brown;" she would say, "I pity him, with my very heart's blood."

"You are aware that he has comforted himself in his desolation," Mackinnon replied.

"I know very well to what you allude. I think

I may say that I am conversant with all the circumstances of this heart-blighting sacrifice." Mrs. Talboys was apt to boast of the thorough confidence reposed in her by all those in whom she took an interest. " Yes, he has sought such comfort in another love as the hard cruel world would allow him."

" Or perhaps something more than that," said Mackinnon. " He has a family here in Rome, you know ; two little babies."

"I know it, I know it," she said. "Cherub angels!" and as she spoke, she looked up into the ugly face of Marcus Aurelius ; for they were standing at the moment under the figure of the great horseman on the Campidoglio. " I have seen them, and they are the children of innocence. If all the blood of all the Howards ran in their veins it could not make their birth more noble ! "

" Not if the father and mother of all the Howards had never been married," said Mackinnon.

" What ; that from you, Mr. Mackinnon ! " said Mrs. Talboys, turning her back with energy upon the equestrian statue, and looking up into the faces, first of Pollux and then of Castor, as though from them she might gain some inspiration on the subject which Marcus Aurelius in his coldness had denied to her. " From you, who have so nobly claimed for mankind the divine attributes of free action ! From you, who have taught my mind to soar above the petty bonds which one man in his littleness contrives for the subjection of his brother. Mackinnon! you who are so great!" And she now looked up into his face. "Mackinnon, unsay those words."

"They *are* illegitimate," said he; "and if there was any landed property——"

"Landed property! and that from an American!"

"The children are English, you know."

"Landed property! The time will shortly come— ay, and I see it coming—when that hateful word shall be expunged from the calendar; when landed property shall be no more. What! shall the free soul of a God-born man submit itself for ever to such trammels as that? Shall we never escape from the clay which so long has manacled the subtler particles of the divine spirit? Ay, yes, Mackinnon;" and then she took him by the arm, and led him to the top of the huge steps which lead down from the Campidoglio into the streets of modern Rome. "Look down upon that countless multitude." Mackinnon looked down, and saw three groups of French soldiers, with three or four little men in each group; he saw, also, a couple of dirty friars, and three priests very slowly beginning the side ascent to the church of the Ara Cœli. "Look down upon that countless multitude," said Mrs. Talboys, and she stretched her arms out over the half-deserted city. "They are escaping now from these trammels,—now, now,—now that I am speaking."

"They have escaped long ago from all such trammels as that of landed property,' said Mackinnon.

" Ay, and from all terrestrial bonds," she continued, not exactly remarking the pith of his last observation ; "from bonds quasi-terrestrial and quasi-celestial. The full-formed limbs of the present age, running with quick streams of generous blood, will no longer bear the ligatures which past times have woven for the decrepit. Look down upon that multitude, Mackinnon ; they shall all be free." And then, still clutching him by the arm, and still standing at the top of those stairs, she gave forth her prophecy with the fury of a Sibyl.

"They shall all be free. Oh, Rome, thou eternal one, thou who hast bowed thy neck to imperial pride and priestly craft ; thou who hast suffered sorely, even to this hour, from Nero down to Pio Nono,—the days of thine oppression are over. Gone from thy enfranchised ways for ever is the clang of Prætorian cohorts, and the more odious drone of meddling monks !" And yet, as Mackinnon observed, there still stood the dirty friars and the small French soldiers ; and there still toiled the slow priests, wending their tedious way up to the church of the Ara Cœli. But that was the mundane view of the matter, —a view not regarded by Mrs. Talboys in her ecstasy. " O Italia," she continued," " O Italia una, one and indivisible in thy rights, and indivisible also in thy wrongs ! to us is it given to see the accomplishment of thy glory. A people shall arise around thine altars greater in the annals of the world than thy Scipios, thy Gracchi, or thy Cæsars. Not in torrents of blood, or with screams of bereaved mothers, shall thy new triumphs be stained. But mind shall dominate over matter; and doomed, together with Popes and Bourbons, with cardinals, diplomatists, and police spies, ignorance and prejudice shall be driven from thy smiling terraces. And then Rome shall again become the fair capital of the fairest region of Europe. Hither shall flock the artisans of the world, crowding into thy marts all that God and man can give. Wealth, beauty, and innocence shall meet in thy streets——"

"There will be a considerable change before that takes place," said Mackinnon.

"There shall be a considerable change," she answered. "Mackinnon, to thee it is given to read the signs of the time; and hast thou not read? Why have the fields of Magenta and Solferino been piled with the corpses of dying heroes? Why have the waters of the Mincio ran red with the blood of martyrs? That Italy might be united and Rome immortal. Here, standing on the Capitolium of the ancient city, I say that it shall be so; and thou, Mackinnon, who hearest me, knowest that my words are true."

There was not then in Rome,—I may almost say there was not in Italy, an Englishman or an American who did not wish well to the cause for which Italy was and is still contending; as also there is hardly one who does not now regard that cause as well nigh triumphant; but, nevertheless, it was almost impossible to sympathise with Mrs. Talboys. As Mackinnon said, she flew so high that there was no comfort in flying with her.

"Well," said he, "Brown and the rest of them are down below. Shall we go and join them?"

"Poor Brown! How was it that, in speaking of his troubles, we were led on to this heart-stirring theme? Yes, I have seen them, the sweet angels; and I tell you also that I have seen their mother. I insisted on going to her when I heard her history from him."

"And what is she like, Mrs. Talboys?"

"Well; education has done more for some of us than for others; and there are those from whose morals and sentiments we might thankfully draw a lesson, whose manners and outward gestures are not such as custom has made agreeable to us. You, I know, can understand that. I have seen her, and feel sure that she is pure in heart and high in principle. Has she not sacrificed herself, and is not self-sacrifice the surest guarantee for true nobility of character? Would Mrs. Mackinnon object to my bringing them together?"

Mackinnon was obliged to declare that he thought his wife would object; and from that time forth he and Mrs. Talboys ceased to be very close in their friendship. She still came to the house every Sunday evening, still refreshed herself at the fountains of his literary rills; but her special prophecies from henceforth were poured into other ears. And it so

happened that O'Brien now became her chief ally.
I do not remember that she troubled herself much
further with the cherub angels or with their mother;
and I am inclined to think that, taking up warmly,
as she did, the story of O'Brien's matrimonial wrongs,
she forgot the little history of the Browns. Be that
as it may, Mrs. Talboys and O'Brien now became
strictly confidential, and she would enlarge by the
half-hour together on the miseries of her friend's
position, to any one whom she could get to hear her.

"I'll tell you what, Fanny," Mackinnon said to his
wife one day,—to his wife and to mine, for we were all
together; "we shall have a row in the house if we
don't take care. O'Brien will be making love to
Mrs. Talboys."

"Nonsense," said Mrs. Mackinnon. "You are always thinking that somebody is going to make love
to some one."

"Somebody always is," said he.

"She's old enough to be his mother," said Mrs.
Mackinnon.

"What does that matter to an Irishman?" said
Mackinnon. "Besides, I doubt if there is more than
five years' difference between them."

"There must be more than that," said my wife.
"Ida Talboys is twelve, I know, and I am not quite
sure that Ida is the eldest."

"If she had a son in the Guards, it would make no
difference," said Mackinnon. "There are men who
consider themselves bound to make love to a woman

under certain circumstances, let the age of the lady be what it may. O'Brien is such a one; and if she sympathises with him much oftener, he will mistake the matter, and go down on his knees. You ought to put him on his guard," he said, addressing himself to his wife.

"Indeed I shall do no such thing," said she; "if they are two fools, they must, like other fools, pay the price of their folly." As a rule there could be no softer creature than Mrs. Mackinnon; but it seemed to me that her tenderness never extended itself in the direction of Mrs. Talboys.

Just at this time, towards the end, that is, of November, we made a party to visit the tombs which lie along the Appian Way, beyond that most beautiful of all sepulchres, the tomb of Cecilia Metella. It was a delicious day, and we had driven along this road for a couple of miles beyond the walls of the city, enjoying the most lovely view which the neighbourhood of Rome affords,—looking over the wondrous ruins of the old aqueducts, up towards Tivoli and Palestrina. Of all the environs of Rome this is, on a fair clear day, the most enchanting; and here perhaps, among a world of tombs, thoughts and almost memories of the old, old days come upon one with the greatest force. The grandeur of Rome is best seen and understood from beneath the walls of the Coliseum, and its beauty among the pillars of the Forum and the arches of the Sacred Way; but its history and fall become more palpable to the mind, and more clearly realised, out here among the tombs, where the eyes rest upon the mountains whose shades were cool to the old Romans as to us,—than anywhere within the walls of the city. Here we look out at the same Tivoli and the same Præneste, glittering in the sunshine, embowered among the far-off valleys, which were dear to them; and the blue mountains have not crumbled away into ruins. Within Rome itself we can see nothing as they saw it.

Our party consisted of some dozen or fifteen persons, and as a hamper with luncheon in it had been left on the grassy slope at the base of the tomb of Cecilia Metella, the expedition had in it something of the nature of a picnic. Mrs. Talboys was of course with us, and Ida Talboys. O'Brien also was there. The hamper had been prepared in Mrs. Mackinnon's room, under the immediate eye of Mackinnon himself, and they therefore were regarded as the dominant spirits of the party. My wife was leagued with Mrs. Mackinnon, as was usually the case; and there seemed to be a general opinion among those who were closely in confidence together, that something would happen in the O'Brien-Talboys matter. The two had been inseparable on the previous evening, for Mrs. Talboys had been urging on the young Irishman her counsels respecting his domestic troubles. Sir Cresswell Cresswell, she had told him, was his refuge. "Why should his soul submit to bonds which the world had now declared to be intolerable ? Divorce was not now the privilege of the dissolute rich. Spirits which were incompatible need no longer be compelled to fret beneath the same couples." In short she had recommended him to go to England and get rid of his wife, as she would, with a little encouragement, have recommended any man to get rid of anything. I am sure that, had she been skilfully brought on to the subject, she might have been induced to pronounce a verdict against such ligatures for the body as coats, waistcoats, and trowsers. Her aspirations for freedom ignored all bounds, and, in theory, there were no barriers which she was not willing to demolish.

Poor O'Brien, as we all now began to see, had taken the matter amiss. He had offered to make a bust of Mrs. Talboys, and she had consented, expressing a wish that it might find a place among those who had devoted themselves to the enfranchisement of their fellow-creatures. I really think she had but little of a woman's customary personal vanity. I know she had an idea that her eye was lighted up in her warmer moments by some special fire, that sparks of liberty shone round her brow, and that her bosom heaved with glorious aspirations ; but all these feelings had reference to her inner genius, not to any outward beauty. But O'Brien misunderstood the woman, and thought it necessary to gaze into her face, and sigh as though his heart were breaking. Indeed he declared to a young friend that Mrs. Talboys was perfect in her style of beauty,

F

and began the bust with this idea. It was gradually
becoming clear to us all that he would bring himself to grief ; but in such a matter who can caution
a man ?

Mrs. Mackinnon had contrived to separate them in
making the carriage arrangements on this day, but
this only added fuel to the fire which was now burning within O'Brien's bosom. I believe that he really
did love her, in his easy, eager, susceptible Irish way.
That he would get over the little episode without
any serious injury to his heart no one doubted ; but
then, what would occur when the declaration was
made ? How would Mrs. Talboys bear it ?

"She deserves it," said Mrs. Mackinnon.

"And twice as much," my wife added. Why is it
that women are so spiteful to each other ?

Early in the day Mrs. Talboys clambered up to the
top of a tomb, and made a little speech, holding a
parasol over her head. Beneath her feet, she said,
reposed the ashes of some bloated senator, some
glutton of the empire, who had swallowed into his
maw the provision necessary for a tribe. Old Rome
had fallen through such selfishness as that ; but new
Rome would not forget the lesson. All this was very
well, and then O'Brien helped her down ; but after
this there was no separating them. For her own
part she would sooner have had Mackinnon at her
elbow. But Mackinnon now had found some other
elbow. "Enough of that was as good as a feast," he
had said to his wife. And therefore Mrs. Talboys,

quite unconscious of evil, allowed herself to be engrossed by O'Brien.

And then, about three o'clock, we returned to the hamper. Luncheon under such circumstances always means dinner, and we arranged ourselves for a very comfortable meal. To those who know the tomb of Cecilia Metella no description of the scene is necessary, and to those who do not, no description will convey a fair idea of its reality. It is itself a large low tower of great diameter, but of beautiful proportion, standing far outside the city, close on to the side of the old Roman way. It has been embattled on the top by some latter-day baron, in order that it might be used for protection to the castle, which has been built on and attached to it. If I remember rightly, this was done by one of the Frangipani, and a very lovely ruin he has made of it. I know no castellated old tumble-down residence in Italy more picturesque than this baronial adjunct to the old Roman tomb, or which better tallies with the ideas engendered within our minds by Mrs. Radcliffe and the Mysteries of Udolpho. It lies along the road, protected on the side of the city by the proud sepulchre of the Roman matron, and up to the long ruined walls of the back of the building stretches a grassy slope, at the bottom of which are the remains of an old Roman circus. Beyond that is the long, thin, graceful line of the Claudian aqueduct, with Soracte in the distance to the left, and Tivoli, Palestrina, and Frascati lying among the hills which bound the view. That Frangipani baron was in the right of it, and I hope he got the value of his money out of the residence which he built for himself. I doubt, however, that he did but little good to those who lived in his close neighbourhood.

We had a very comfortable little banquet seated on the broken lumps of stone which lie about under the walls of the tomb. I wonder whether the shade of Cecilia Metella was looking down upon us. We have heard much of her in these latter days, and yet we know nothing about her, nor can conceive why she was honoured with a bigger tomb than any other Roman matron. There were those then among our party who believed that she might still come back among us, and with due assistance from some cognate susceptible spirit, explain to us the cause of her widowed husband's liberality. Alas, alas! if we may judge of the Romans by ourselves, the true reason for such sepulchral grandeur would redound little to the credit of the lady Cecilia Metella herself, or to that of Crassus, her bereaved and desolate lord.

She did not come among us on the occasion of this banquet, possibly because we had no tables there to turn in preparation for her presence; but, had she done so, she could not have been more eloquent of things of the other world than was Mrs. Talboys. I have said that Mrs. Talboys' eye never glanced more brightly after a glass of champagne, but I am inclined to think that on this occasion it may have done so. O'Brien enacted Ganymede, and was, per-

haps, more liberal than other latter-day Ganymedes,
to whose services Mrs. Talboys had been accustomed.
Let it not, however, be suspected by any one that she
exceeded the limits of a discreet joyousness. By no
means! The generous wine penetrated, perhaps, to
some inner cells of her heart, and brought forth
thoughts in sparkling words, which otherwise might
have remained concealed; but there was nothing
in what she thought or spoke calculated to give
umbrage either to an anchorite or to a vestal. A
word or two she said or sung about the flowing bowl,
and once she called for Falernian; but beyond this
her converse was chiefly of the rights of man and
the weakness of women; of the iron ages that were
past, and of the golden time that was to come.

She called a toast and drank to the hopes of the
latter historians of the nineteenth century. Then it
was that she bade O'Brien "Fill high the bowl with
Samian wine." The Irishman took her at her word,
and she raised the bumper, and waved it over her
head before she put it to her lips. I am bound to
declare that she did not spill a drop. "The true
'Falernian grape,'" she said, as she deposited the
empty beaker on the grass beneath her elbow. Viler
champagne I do not think I ever swallowed; but it was
the theory of the wine, not its palpable body present
there, as it were, in the flesh, which inspired her.
There was really something grand about her on that
occasion, and her enthusiasm almost amounted to
reality.

Mackinnon was amused, and encouraged her, as, I must confess, did I also. Mrs. Mackinnon made useless little signs to her husband, really fearing that the Falernian would do its good offices too thoroughly. My wife, getting me apart as I walked round the circle distributing viands, remarked that "the woman was a fool, and would disgrace herself." But I observed that after the disposal of that bumper she worshipped the rosy god in theory only, and therefore saw no occasion to interfere. "Come, Bacchus," she said; "and come, Silenus, if thou wilt; I know that ye are hovering round the graves of your departed favourites. And ye, too, nymphs of Egeria," and she pointed to the classic grove which was all but close to us as we sat there. "In olden days ye did not always despise the abodes of men. But why should we invoke the presence of the gods,—we, who can become godlike ourselves! We ourselves are the deities of the present age. For us shall the tables be spread with ambrosia; for us shall the nectar flow."

Upon the whole it was very good fooling,—for awhile; and as soon as we were tired of it we arose from our seats, and began to stroll about the place. It was beginning to be a little dusk, and somewhat cool, but the evening air was pleasant, and the ladies, putting on their shawls, did not seem inclined at once to get into the carriages. At any rate, Mrs. Talboys was not so inclined, for she started down the hill towards the long low wall of the old Roman circus at the bottom; and O'Brien, close at her elbow, started with her.

"Ida, my dear, you had better remain here," she said to her daughter; "you will be tired if you come as far as we are going."

"Oh, no, mamma, I shall not," said Ida. "You get tired much quicker than I do."

"Oh, yes, you will; besides, I do not wish you to come." There was an end of it for Ida, and Mrs. Talboys and O'Brien walked off together, while we all looked into each other's faces.

"It would be a charity to go with them," said Mackinnon.

"Do you be charitable, then," said his wife.

"It should be a lady," said he.

"It is a pity that the mother of the spotless cherubim is not here for the occasion," said she. "I hardly think that any one less gifted will undertake such a self-sacrifice." Any attempt of the kind would, however, now have been too late, for they were already at the bottom of the hill. O'Brien certainly had drunk freely of the pernicious contents of those long-necked bottles; and though no one could fairly accuse him of being tipsy, nevertheless that which might have made others drunk had made him bold, and he dared to do—perhaps more than might become a man. If under any circumstances he could be fool enough to make an avowal of love to Mrs. Talboys, he might be expected, as we all felt, to do it now.

We watched them as they made for a gap in the wall which led through into the large enclosed space of the old circus. It had been an arena for chariot games, and they had gone down with the avowed purpose of searching where might have been the meta, and ascertaining how the d ivers could have turned when at their full speed. For awhile we had heard their voices,—or rather her voice especially. "The heart of a man, O'Brien, should suffice for all emergencies," we had heard her say. She had assumed a strange habit of calling men by their simple names, as men address each other. When she did this to Mackinnon, who was much older than herself, we had been all amused by it, and other ladies of our party had taken to call him "Mackinnon" when Mrs. Talboys was not by ; but we had felt the comedy to be less safe with O'Brien, especially when, on one occasion, we heard him address her as Arabella. She did not seem to be in any way struck by his doing so, and we supposed, therefore, that it had become frequent between them. What reply he made at the moment about the heart of a man I do not know ;— and then in a few minutes they disappeared through the gap in the wall.

None of us followed them, though it would have seemed the most natural thing in the world to do so had nothing out of the way been expected. As it was we remained there round the tomb quizzing the little foibles of our dear friend, and hoping that O'Brien would be quick in what he was doing.

That he would undoubtedly get a slap in the face—
metaphorically—we all felt certain, for none of us
doubted the rigid propriety of the lady's intentions.
Some of us strolled into the buildings, and some of
us got out on to the road; but we all of us were thinking that O'Brien was very slow a considerable time
before we saw Mrs. Talboys reappear through the gap.

At last, however, she was there, and we at once
saw that she was alone. She came on, breasting the
hill with quick steps, and when she drew near we
could see that there was a frown as of injured majesty on her brow. Mackinnon and his wife went
forward to meet her. If she were really in trouble
it would be fitting in some way to assist her; and
of all women Mrs. Mackinnon was the last to see
another woman suffer from ill usage without attempting to aid her. "I certainly never liked her,"
Mrs. Mackinnon said afterwards; "but I was bound
to go and hear her tale, when she really had a tale
to tell."

And Mrs. Talboys now had a tale to tell,—if she
chose to tell it. The ladies of our party declared
afterwards that she would have acted more wisely
had she kept to herself both O'Brien's words to her
and her answer. "She was well able to take care
of herself," Mrs. Mackinnon said; "and, after all,
the silly man had taken an answer when he got it."
Not, however, that O'Brien had taken his answer
quite immediately, as far as I could understand
from what we heard of the matter afterwards.

At the present moment Mrs. Talboys came up the rising ground all alone, and at a quick pace. "The man has insulted me," she said aloud, as well as her panting breath would allow her, and as soon as she was near enough to Mrs. Mackinnon to speak to her.

"I am sorry for that," said Mrs. Mackinnon. "I suppose he has taken a little too much wine."

"No; it was a premeditated insult. The base-hearted churl has failed to understand the meaning of true, honest sympathy."

"He will forget all about it when he is sober," said Mackinnon, meaning to comfort her.

"What care I what he remembers or what he forgets!" she said, turning upon poor Mackinnon indignantly. "You men grovel so in your ideas——" "And yet," as Mackinnon said afterwards, "she had been telling me that I was a fool for the last three weeks."—— "You men grovel so in your ideas, that you cannot understand the feelings of a true-hearted woman. What can his forgetfulness or his remembrance be to me? Must not I remember this insult? Is it possible that I should forget it?"

Mr. and Mrs. Mackinnon only had gone forward to meet her; but, nevertheless, she spoke so loud that all heard her who were still clustered round the spot on which we had dined.

"What has become of Mr. O'Brien?" a lady whispered to me.

I had a field-glass with me, and, looking round, I

saw his hat as he was walking inside the walls of
the circus in the direction towards the city. "And
very foolish he must feel," said the lady.

"No doubt he's used to it," said another.

"But considering her age, you know," said the
first, who might have been perhaps three years
younger than Mrs. Talboys, and who was not
herself averse to the excitement of a moderate flir-
tation. But then why should she have been averse,
seeing that she had not as yet become subject to the
will of any imperial lord ?

"He would have felt much more foolish," said the
third, "if she had listened to what he said to
her."

"Well I don't know," said the second ; "nobody
would have known anything about it then, and in a
few weeks they would have gradually become tired
of each other in the ordinary way."

But in the meantime Mrs. Talboys was among
us. There had been no attempt at secresy, and she
was still loudly inveighing against the grovelling pro-
pensities of men. "That's quite true, Mrs. Talboys,"
said one of the elder ladies ; "but then women
are not always so careful as they should be. Of
course I do not mean to say that there has been any
fault on your part."

"Fault on my part ! Of course there has been
fault on my part. No one can make any mistake
without fault to some extent. I took him to be a man
of sense, and he is a fool. Go to Naples indeed !"

"Did he want you to go to Naples?"asked Mrs. Mackinnon.

"Yes; that was what he suggested. We were to leave by the train for Civita Vecchia at six to-morrow morning, and catch the steamer which leaves Leghorn to-night. Don't tell me of wine. He was prepared for it!" And she looked round about on us with an air of injured majesty in her face which was almost insupportable.

"I wonder whether he took the tickets over-night," said Mackinnon.

"Naples!" she said, as though now speaking exclusively to herself, "the only ground in Italy which has as yet made no struggle on behalf of freedom;— a fitting residence for such a dastard!"

"You would have found it very pleasant at this season," said the unmarried lady, who was three years her junior.

My wife had taken Ida out of the way when the first complaining note from Mrs. Talboys had been heard ascending the hill. But now, when matters began gradually to become quiescent, she brought her back, suggesting, as she did so, that they might begin to think of returning.

"It is getting very cold, Ida, dear, is it not?" said she. "But where is Mr. O'Brien?" said Ida.

"He has fled,—as poltroons always fly," said Mrs. Talboys. I believe in my heart that she would have been glad to have had him there in the middle of the circle, and to have triumphed over him publicly among us all. No feeling of shame would have kept her silent for a moment.

"Fled!" said Ida, looking up into her mother's face.

"Yes, fled, my child." And she seized her daughter in her arms, and pressed her closely to her bosom. "Cowards always fly."

"Is Mr. O'Brien a coward?" Ida asked.

"Yes, a coward, a very coward! And he has fled before the glance of an honest woman's eye. Come, Mrs. Mackinnon, shall we go back to the city? I am sorry that the amusement of the day should have received this check." And she walked forward to the carriage and took her place in it with an air that showed that she was proud of the manner in which she had conducted herself.

"She is a little conceited about it after all," said that unmarried lady. "If poor Mr. O'Brien had not shown so much premature energy with reference to that little journey to Naples, things might have gone quietly after all."

But the unmarried lady was wrong in her judgment. Mrs. Talboys was proud and conceited in the matter,—but not proud of having excited the admiration of her Irish lover. She was proud of her own subsequent conduct, and gave herself credit for coming out strongly as a noble-minded matron. "I believe she thinks," said Mrs. Mackinnon, "that her virtue is quite Spartan and unique; and if she remains in Rome she'll boast of it through the whole winter."

" If she does, she may be certain that O'Brien will
do the same," said Mackinnon. "And in spite of
his having fled from the field, it is upon the cards
that he may get the best of it. Mrs. Talboys is a
very excellent woman. She has proved her excellence
beyond a doubt. But, nevertheless, she is susceptible
of ridicule."

We all felt a little anxiety to hear O'Brien's account of the matter, and after having deposited the
ladies at their homes, Mackinnon and I went off to
his lodgings. At first he was denied to us, but after
awhile we got his servant to acknowledge that he
was at home, and then we made our way up to his
studio. We found him seated behind a half-formed
model, or rather a mere lump of clay punched into
something resembling the shape of a head, with a
pipe in his mouth and a bit of stick in his hand.
He was pretending to work, though we both knew
that it was out of the question that he should do anything in his present frame of mind.

"I think I heard my servant tell you that I was
not at home," said he.

"Yes, he did," said Mackinnon, "and would have
sworn to it too if we would have let him. Come,
don't pretend to be surly."

"I am very busy, Mr. Mackinnon."

"Completing your head of Mrs. Talboys, I suppose,
before you start for Naples."

"You don't mean to say that she has told you all
about it," and he turned away from his work, and

looked up into our faces with a comical expression, half of fun and half of despair.

"Every word of it," said I. "When you want a lady to travel with you, never ask her to get up so early in winter."

"But, O'Brien, how could you be such an ass?" said Mackinnon. "As it has turned out, there is no very great harm done. You have insulted a respectable middle-aged woman, the mother of a family, and the wife of a general officer, and there is an end of it;—unless, indeed, the general officer should come out from England to call you to account."

"He is welcome," said O'Brien, haughtily.

"No doubt, my dear fellow," said Mackinnon; "that would be a dignified and pleasant ending to the affair. But what I want to know is this,—what would you have done if she had agreed to go?"

"He never calculated on the possibility of such a contingency," said I.

"By heavens, then, I thought she would like it," said he.

"And to oblige her you were content to sacrifice yourself," said Mackinnon.

"Well, that was just it. What the deuce is a fellow to do when a woman goes on in that way. She told me down there, upon the old race course you know, that matrimonial bonds were made for fools and slaves. What was I to suppose that she meant by that? But to make all sure, I asked her what sort of a fellow the General was. 'Dear old man,' she said, clasping her hands together. 'He might, you know, have been my father.' 'I wish he were,' said I, 'because then you'd be free.' 'I am free,' said she, stamping on the ground, and looking up at me as much as to say that she cared for no one. 'Then,' said I, 'accept all that is left of the heart of Wenceslaus O'Brien,' and I threw myself before her in her path. 'Hand,' said I, 'I have none to give, but the blood which runs red through my veins is descended from a double line of kings.' I said that because she is always fond of riding a high horse. I had gotten close under the wall, so that none of you should see me from the tower."

"And what answer did she make?" said Mackinnon.

"Why she was pleased as Punch;—gave me both her hands, and declared that we would be friends for ever. It is my belief, Mackinnon, that that woman never heard anything of the kind before. The General, no doubt, did it by letter."

"And how was it that she changed her mind."

"Why; I got up, put my arm round her waist, and told her that we would be off to Naples. I'm blest if she didn't give me a knock in the ribs that nearly sent me backwards. She took my breath away, so that I couldn't speak to her."

"And then——"

"Oh, there was nothing more. Of course I saw how it was. So she walked off one way and I the other. On the whole I consider that I am well out of it."

"And so do I," said Mackinnon, very gravely "But if you will allow me to give you my advice, I would suggest that it would be well to avoid such mistakes in future."

"Upon my word," said O'Brien, excusing himself, "I don't know what a man is to do under such circumstances. I give you my honour that I did it all to oblige her."

We then decided that Mackinnon should convey to the injured lady the humble apology of her late admirer. It was settled that no detailed excuses should be made. It should be left to her to consider whether the deed which had been done might have been occasioned by wine, or by the folly of a moment, —or by her own indiscreet enthusiasm. No one but the two were present when the message was given, and therefore we were obliged to trust to Mackinnon's accuracy for an account of it.

She stood on very high ground indeed, he said, at first refusing to hear anything that he had to say on the matter. "The foolish young man," she declared, "was below her anger, and below her contempt."

"He is not the first Irishman that has been made indiscreet by beauty," said Mackinnon.

"A truce to that," she replied, waving her hand with an air of assumed majesty. "The incident, contemptible as it is, has been unpleasant to me. It will necessitate my withdrawal from Rome."

"Oh, no, Mrs. Talboys; that will be making too much of him."

"The greatest hero that lives," she answered, "may have his house made uninhabitable by a very small insect." Mackinnon swore that those were her own words. Consequently a *sobriquet* was attached to O'Brien of which he by no means approved. And from that day we always called Mrs. Talboys "the hero."

Mackinnon prevailed at last with her, and she did not leave Rome. She was even induced to send a message to O'Brien, conveying her forgiveness. They shook hands together with great *éclat* in Mrs. Mackinnon's drawing-room; but I do not suppose that she ever again offered to him sympathy on the score of his matrimonial troubles.

THE PARSON'S DAUGHTER OF OXNEY COLNE.

THE prettiest scenery in all England—and if I am contradicted in that assertion, I will say in all Europe —is in Devonshire, on the southern and south-eastern skirts of Dartmoor, where the rivers Dart, and Avon, and Teign form themselves, and where the broken moor is half cultivated, and the wild-looking upland fields are half moor. In making this assertion I am often met with much doubt, but it is by persons who do not really know, the locality. Men and women talk to me on the matter, who have travelled down the line of railway from Exeter to Plymouth, who have spent a fortnight at Torquay, and perhaps made an excursion from Tavistock to the convict prison on Dartmoor. But who knows the glories of Chagford? Who has walked through the parish of Manaton? Who is conversant with Lustleigh Cleeves and Withycombe in the moor? Who has explored Holne Chase? Gentle reader, believe me that you will be rash in contradicting me, unless you have done these things.

There or thereabouts—I will not say by the waters

of which little river it is washed—is the parish of
Oxney Colne.   And for those who would wish to see
all the beauties of this lovely country, a sojourn in
Oxney Colne would be most desirable, seeing that the
sojourner would then be brought nearer to all that he
would wish to visit, than at any other spot in the
country.   But there is an objection to any such
arrangement.   There are only two decent houses in
the whole parish, and these are—or were when I
knew the locality—small and fully occupied by their
possessors.   The larger and better is the parsonage,
in which lived the parson and his daughter ; and the
smaller is the freehold residence of a certain Miss Le
Smyrger, who owned a farm of a hundred acres,
which was rented by one Farmer Cloysey, and who
also possessed some thirty acres round her own house,
which she managed herself, regarding herself to be
quite as great in cream as Mr. Cloysey, and altogether
superior to him in the article of cider.   " But yeu has
to pay no rent, Miss," Farmer Cloysey would say,
when Miss Le Smyrger expressed this opinion of her
art in a manner too defiant.   " Yeu pays no rent, or
yeu couldn't do it."   Miss Le Smyrger was an old
maid, with a pedigree and blood of her own, a hundred and thirty acres of fee-simple land on the borders of Dartmoor, fifty years of age, a constitution of
iron, and an opinion of her own on every subject
under the sun.

And now for the parson and his daughter.   The
parson's name was Woolsworthy—or Woolathy as it

was pronounced by all those who lived around him—
the Rev. Saul Woolsworthy; and his daughter was
Patience Woolsworthy, or Miss Patty, as she was
known to the Devonshire world of those parts. That
name of Patience had not been well chosen for her,
for she was a hot-tempered damsel, warm in her con-
victions, and inclined to express them freely. She
had but two closely intimate friends in the world,
and by both of them this freedom of expression had
now been fully permitted to her since she was a child.
Miss Le Smyrger and her father were well accustomed
to her ways, and on the whole well satisfied with
them. The former was equally free and equally
warm-tempered as herself, and as Mr. Woolsworthy
was allowed by his daughter to be quite paramount
on his own subject—for he had a subject—he did not
object to his daughter being paramount on all others.
A pretty girl was Patience Woolsworthy at the time
of which I am writing, and one who possessed much
that was worthy of remark and admiration, had she
lived where beauty meets with admiration, or where
force of character is remarked. But at Oxney Colne,
on the borders of Dartmoor, there were few to appreciate her, and it seemed as though she herself had
but little idea of carrying her talent further afield, so
that it might not remain for ever wrapped in a
blanket.

She was a pretty girl, tall and slender, with dark
eyes and black hair. Her eyes were perhaps too
round for regular beauty, and her hair was perhaps

too crisp ; her mouth was large and expressive ; her
nose was finely formed, though a critic in female form
might have declared it to be somewhat broad.   But
her countenance altogether was wonderfully attractive
—if only it might be seen without that resolution for
dominion which occasionally marred it, though sometimes it even added to her attractions.

It must be confessed on behalf of Patience Woolsworthy, that the circumstances of her life had peremp-
torily called upon her to exercise dominion.   She had
lost her mother when she was sixteen, and had had
neither brother nor sister.   She had no neighbours
near her fit either from education or rank to interfere
in the conduct of her life, excepting always Miss Le
Smyrger.   Miss Le Smyrger would have done anything for her, including the whole management of
her morals and of the parsonage household, had
Patience been content with such an arrangement.
But much as Patience had ever loved Miss Le Smyrger, she was not content with this, and therefore she
had been called on to put forth a strong hand of her
own.   She had put forth this strong hand early, and
hence had come the character which I am attempting
to describe.   But I must say on behalf of this girl,
that it was not only over others that she thus exercised
dominion.   In acquiring that power she had also ac-
quired the much greater power of exercising rule over
herself.

But why should her father have been ignored in
these family arrangements ?   Perhaps it may almost

suffice to say, that of all living men her father was the man best conversant with the antiquities of the county in which he lived. He was the Jonathan Oldbuck of Devonshire, and especially of Dartmoor, without that decision of character which enabled Oldbuck to keep his womenkind in some kind of subjection, and probably enabled him also to see that his weekly bills did not pass their proper limits. Our Mr. Oldbuck, of Oxney Colne, was sadly deficient in these. As a parish pastor with but a small cure, he did his duty with sufficient energy to keep him, at any rate, from reproach. He was kind and charitable to the poor, punctual in his services, forbearing with the farmers around him, mild with his brother clergymen, and indifferent to aught that bishop or archdeacon might think or say of him. I do not name this latter attribute as a virtue, but as a fact. But all these points were as nothing in the known character of Mr. Woolsworthy, of Oxney Colne. He was the antiquarian of Dartmoor. That was his line of life. It was in that capacity that he was known to the Devonshire world; it was as such that he journeyed about with his humble carpet-bag, staying away from his parsonage a night or two at a time; it was in that character that he received now and again stray visitors in the single spare bedroom—not friends asked to see him and his girl because of their friendship—but men who knew something as to this buried stone, or that old land-mark. In all these things his daughter let him have his own way, assisting and encouraging him. That was his line of life, and therefore she respected it. But in all other matters she chose to be paramount at the parsonage.

Mr. Woolsworthy was a little man, who always wore, except on Sundays, grey clothes—clothes of so light a grey that they would hardly have been regarded as clerical in a district less remote. He had now reached a goodly age, being full seventy years old; but still he was wiry and active, and shewed but few symptoms of decay. His head was bald, and the few remaining locks that surrounded it were nearly white. But there was a look of energy about his mouth, and a' humour in his light grey eye, which forbade those who knew him to regard him altogether as an old man. As it was, he could walk from Oxney Colne to Priestown, fifteen long Devonshire miles across the moor; and he who could do that could hardly be regarded as too old for work.

But our present story will have more to do with his daughter than with him. A pretty girl, I have said, was Patience Woolsworthy; and one, too, in many ways remarkable. She had taken her outlook into life, weighing the things which she had and those which she had not, in a manner very unusual, and, as a rule, not always desirable for a young lady. The things which she had not were very many. She had not society; she had not a fortune; she had not any assurance of future means of livelihood; she had not high hope of procuring for herself a position in life by marriage; she had not that excitement and pleasure in life which she read of in such books as found their way down to Oxney Colne Parsonage.. It would be easy to add to the list of the things which she had not; and this list against herself she made out with the utmost vigour. The things which she had, or those rather which she assured herself of having, were much more easily counted. She had the birth and education of a lady, the strength of a healthy woman, and a will of her own. Such was the list as she made it out for herself, and I protest that I assert no more than the truth in saying that she never added to it either beauty, wit, or talent.

I began these descriptions by saying that Oxney Colne would, of all places, be the best spot from which a tourist could visit those parts of Devonshire, but for the fact that he could obtain there none of the accommodation which tourists require. A brother antiquarian might, perhaps, in those days have done so, seeing that there was, as I have said, a spare bedroom at the parsonage. Any intimate friend of Miss Le Smyrger's might be as fortunate, for she was equally well provided at Oxney Combe, by which name her house was known. But Miss Le Smyrger was not given to extensive hospitality, and it was only to those who were bound to her, either by ties of blood or of very old friendship, that she delighted to open her doors. As her old friends were very few in number, as those few lived at a distance, and as her nearest relations were higher in the world than

she was, and were said by herself to look down upon
her, the visits made to Oxney Combe were few and
far between.

But now, at the period of which I am writing,
such a visit was about to be made. Miss Le Smyrger
had a younger sister, who had inherited a property
in the parish of Oxney Colne equal to that of the
lady who now lived there; but this the younger
sister had inherited beauty also, and she therefore,
in early life, had found sundry lovers, one of whom
became her husband. She had married a man even
then well to do in the world, but now rich and
almost mighty; a Member of Parliament, a Lord of
this and that board, a man who had a house in
Eaton-square, and a park in the north of England;
and in this way her course of life had been very
much divided from that of our Miss Le Smyrger.
But the Lord of the Government board had been
blessed with various children; and perhaps it was
now thought expedient to look after Aunt Penelope's
Devonshire acres. Aunt Penelope was empowered
to leave them to whom she pleased; and though it
was thought in Eaton-square that she must, as a
matter of course, leave them to one of the family,
nevertheless a little cousinly intercourse might make
the thing more certain. I will not say that this was
the sole cause for such a visit, but in these days a
visit was to be made by Captain Broughton to his
aunt. Now Captain John Broughton was the second
son of Alfonso Broughton, of Clapham Park and

Eaton-square, Member of Parliament, and Lord of the aforesaid Government Board.

"And what do you mean to do with him?" Patience Woolsworthy asked of Miss Le Smyrger when that lady walked over from the Combe to say that her nephew John was to arrive on the following morning.

"Do with him? Why, I shall bring him over here to talk to your father."

"He'll be too fashionable for that, and papa won't trouble his head about him if he finds that he doesn't care for Dartmoor."

"Then he may fall in love with you, my dear."

"Well, yes; there's that resource at any rate, and for your sake I dare say I should be more civil to him than papa. But he'll soon get tired of making love, and what you'll do then I cannot imagine."

That Miss Woolsworthy felt no interest in the coming of the Captain I will not pretend to say. The advent of any stranger with whom she would be called on to associate must be matter of interest to her in that secluded place; and she was not so absolutely unlike other young ladies that the arrival of an unmarried young man would be the same to her as the advent of some patriarchal paterfamilias. In taking that outlook into life of which I have spoken she had never said to herself that she despised those things from which other girls received the excitement, the joys, and the disappointment of their lives. She had simply given herself to under-

stand that very little of such things would come her
way, and that it behoved her to live—to live happily
if such might be possible—without experiencing the
need of them. She had heard, when there was no
thought of any such visit to Oxney Colne, that John
Broughton was a handsome, clever man—one who
thought much of himself, and was thought much of
by others—that there had been some talk of his
marrying a great heiress, which marriage, however,
had not taken place through unwillingness on his
part, and that he was on the whole a man of more
mark in the world than the ordinary captain of
ordinary regiments.

Captain Broughton came to Oxney Combe, stayed
there a fortnight,—the intended period for his projected visit having been fixed at three or four days—
and then went his way. He went his way back to
his London haunts, the time of the year then being
the close of the Easter holydays ; but as he did so
he told his aunt that he should assuredly return to
her in the autumn.

"And assuredly I shall be happy to see you, John
—if you come with a certain purpose. If you have
no such purpose, you had better remain away."

"I shall assuredly come," the Captain had replied,
and then he had gone on his journey.

The summer passed rapidly by, and very little was
said between Miss Le Smyrger and Miss Woolsworthy
about Captain Broughton. In many respects—nay,
I may say, as to all ordinary matters, no two

women could well be more intimate with each other than they were,—and more than that, they had the courage each to talk to the other with absolute truth as to things concerning themselves—a courage in which dear friends often fail. But, nevertheless, very little was said between them about Captain John Broughton. All that was said may be here repeated.

"John says that he shall return here in August," Miss Le Smyrger said, as Patience was sitting with her in the parlour at Oxney Combe, on the morning after that gentleman's departure.

"He told me so himself," said Patience; and as she spoke her round dark eyes assumed a look of more than ordinary self-will. If Miss Le Smyrger had intended to carry the conversation any further, she changed her mind as she looked at her companion. Then, as I said, the summer ran by, and towards the close of the warm days of July, Miss Le Smyrger, sitting in the same chair in the same room, again took up the conversation.

"I got a letter from John this morning. He says that he shall be here on the third."

"Does he?"

"He is very punctual to the time he named."

"Yes; I fancy that he is a punctual man," said Patience.

"I hope that you will be glad to see him," said Miss Le Smyrger.

"Very glad to see him," said Patience, with a

bold clear voice; and then the conversation was again dropped, and nothing further was said till after Captain Broughton's second arrival in the parish.

Four months had then passed since his departure, and during that time Miss Woolsworthy had performed all her usual daily duties in their accustomed course. No óne could discover that she had been less careful in her household matters than had been her wont, less willing to go among her poor neighbours, or less assiduous in her attentions to her father. But not the less was there a feeling in the minds of those around her that some great change had come upon her. She would sit during the long summer evenings on a certain spot outside the parsonage orchard, at the top of a small sloping field in which their solitary cow was always pastured, with a book on her knees before her, but rarely reading. There she would sit, with the beautiful view down to the winding river below her, watching the setting sun, and thinking, thinking, thinking—thinking of something of which she had never spoken. Often would Miss Le Smyrger come upon her there, and sometimes would pass by her even without a word; but never—never once did she dare to ask her of the matter of her thoughts. But she knew the matter well enough. No confession was necessary to inform her that Patience Woolsworthy was in love with John Broughton—ay, in love, to the full and entire loss of her whole heart.

On one evening she was so sitting till the July sun had fallen and hidden himself for the night, when her father came upon her as he returned from one of his rambles on the moor. "Patty," he said, "you are always sitting there now. Is it not late? Will you not be cold?"

"No, papa," she said, "I shall not be cold."

"But won't you come to the house? I miss you when you come in so late that there's no time to say a word before we go to bed."

She got up and followed him into the parsonage, and when they were in the sitting-room together, and the door was closed, she came up to him and kissed him. "Papa," she said, "would it make you very unhappy if I were to leave you?"

"Leave me!" he said, startled by the serious and almost solemn tone of her voice. "Do you mean for always?"

"If I were to marry, papa?"

"Oh, marry! No; that would not make me unhappy. It would make me very happy, Patty, to see you married to a man you would love—very, very happy; though my days would be desolate without you."

"That is it, papa. What would you do if I went from you?"

"What would it matter, Patty? I should be free, at any rate, from a load which often presses heavy on me now. What will you do when I shall leave you? A few more years and all will be over with

me.　But who is it, love?　Has anybody said anything to you?"

"It was only an idea, papa.　I don't often think
of such a thing; but I did think of it then."　And
so the subject was allowed to pass by.　This had
happened before the day of the second arrival had
been absolutely fixed and made known to Miss
Woolsworthy.

And then that second. arrival took place.　The
reader may have understood from the words with
which Miss Le Smyrger authorised her nephew to
make his second visit to Oxney Combe that Miss
Woolsworthy's passion was not altogether unautho-
rised.　Captain Broughton had been told that he
was not to come unless he came with a certain
purpose; and having been so told, he still persisted
in coming.　There can be no doubt but that he well
understood the purport to which his aunt alluded.
"I shall assuredly come," he had said.　And true to
his word, he was now there.

Patience knew exactly the hour at which he must
arrive at the station at Newton Abbot, and the time
also which it would take to travel over those twelve up-
hill miles from the station to Oxney.　It need hardly
be said that she paid no visit to Miss Le Smyrger's
house on that afternoon; but she might have known
something of Captain Broughton's approach without
going thither.　His road to the Combe passed by
the parsonage-gate, and had Patience sat even at
her bedroom window she must have seen him.　But

on such a morning she would not sit at her bedroom window—she would do nothing which would force her to accuse herself of a restless longing for her lover's coming. It was for him to seek her. If he chose to do so, he knew the way to the parsonage.

Miss Le Smyrger—good, dear, honest, hearty Miss Le Smyrger, was in a fever of anxiety on behalf of her friend. It was not that she wished her nephew to marry Patience—or rather that she had entertained any such wish when he first came among them. She was not given to match-making, and moreover thought, or had thought within herself, that they of Oxney Colne could do very well without any admixture from Eaton-square. Her plan of life had been that, when old Mr. Woolsworthy was taken away from Dartmoor, Patience should live with her; and that when she also shuffled off her coil, then Patience Woolsworthy should be the maiden mistress of Oxney Combe—of Oxney Combe and Mr. Cloysey's farm—to the utter detriment of all the Broughtons. Such had been her plan before nephew John had come among them—a plan not to be spoken of till the coming of that dark day which should make Patience an orphan. But now her nephew had been there, and all was to be altered. Miss Le Smyrger's plan would have provided a companion for her old age; but that had not been her chief object. She had thought more of Patience than of herself, and now it seemed that a prospect of a higher happiness was opening for her friend.

H

"John," she said, as soon as the first greetings were over, "do you remember the last words that I said to you before you went away?" Now, for myself, I much admire Miss Le Smyrger's heartiness, but I do not think much of her discretion. It would have been better, perhaps, had she allowed things to take their course.

"I can't say that I do," said the Captain. At the same time the Captain did remember very well what those last words had been.

"I am so glad to see you, so delighted to see you, if—if—if—," and then she paused, for with all her courage she hardly dared to ask her nephew whether he had come there with the express purpose of asking Miss Woolsworthy to marry him.

To tell the truth—for there is no room for mystery within the limits of this short story,—to tell, I say, at a word the plain and simple truth, Captain Broughton had already asked that question. On the day before he left Oxney Colne, he had in set terms proposed to the parson's daughter, and indeed the words, the hot and frequent words, which previously to that had fallen like sweetest honey into the ears of Patience Woolsworthy, had made it imperative on him to do so. When a man in such a place as that has talked to a girl of love day after day, must not he talk of it to some definite purpose on the day on which he leaves her? Or if he do not, must he not submit to be regarded as false, selfish, and almost fraudulent? Captain Broughton, however, had asked the question honestly and truly. He had done so honestly and truly, but in words, or, perhaps, simply with a tone, that had hardly sufficed to satisfy the proud spirit of the girl he loved. She by that time had confessed to herself that she loved him with all her heart ; but she had made no such confession to him. To him she had spoken no word, granted no favour, that any lover might rightfully regard as a token of love returned. She had listened to him as he spoke, and bade him keep such sayings for the drawing-rooms of his fashionable friends. Then he had spoken out and had asked for that hand,—not, perhaps, as a suitor tremulous with hope,—but as a rich man who knows that he can command that which he desires to purchase.

"You should think more of this," she had said to him at last. "If you would really have me for your wife, it will not be much to you to return here again when time for thinking of it shall have passed by." With these words she had dismissed him, and now he had again come back to Oxney Colne. But still she would not place herself at the window to look for him, nor dress herself in other than her simple morning country dress, nor omit one item of her daily work. If he wished to take her at all, he should wish to take her as she really was, in her plain country life, but he should take her also with full observance of all those privileges which maidens are allowed to claim from their lovers. He should contract no ceremonious observance because she was

the daughter of a poor country parson who would
come to him without a shilling, whereas he stood
high in the world's books. He had asked her to
give him all that she had, and that all she was ready
to give, without stint. But the gift must be valued
before it could be given or received. He also was to
give her as much, and she would accept it as being
beyond all price. But she would not allow that that
which was offered to her was in any degree the more
precious because of his outward worldly standing.

She would not pretend to herself that she thought
he would come to her that day, and therefore she
busied herself in the kitchen and about the house,
giving directions to her two maids as though the
afternoon would pass as all other days did pass in
that household. They usually dined at four, and she
rarely, in these summer months, went far from the
house before that hour. At four precisely she sat
down with her father, and then said that she was going
up as far as Helpholme after dinner. Helpholme
was a solitary farmhouse in another parish, on the
border of the moor, and Mr. Woolsworthy asked her
whether he should accompany her.

" Do, papa," she said, " if you are not too tired."
And yet she had thought how probable it might be
that she should meet John Broughton on her walk.
And so it was arranged ; but, just as dinner was
over, Mr. Woolsworthy remembered himself.

" Gracious me," he said, " how my memory is
going. Gribbles, from Ivybridge, and old John

Poulter, from Bovey, are coming to meet here by appointment. You can't put Helpholme off till to-morrow?"

Patience, however, never put off anything, and therefore at six o'clock, when her father had finished his slender modicum of toddy, she tied on her hat and went on her walk. She started forth with a quick step, and left no word to say by which route she would go. As she passed up along the little lane which led towards Oxney Combe, she would not even look to see if he was coming towards her; and when she left the road, passing over a stone stile into a little path which ran first through the upland fields, and then across the moor ground towards Helpholme, she did not look back once, or listen for his coming step.

She paid her visit, remaining upwards of an hour with the old bedridden mother of the tenant of Helpholme. "God bless you, my darling!" said the old woman as she left her; "and send you some one to make your own path bright and happy through the world." These words were still ringing in her ears with all their significance as she saw John Broughton waiting for her at the first stile which she had to pass after leaving the farmer's haggard.

"Patty," he said, as he took her hand, and held it close within both his own, "what a chase I have had after you!"

"And who asked you, Captain Broughton?" she

answered, smiling. "If the journey was too much for your poor London strength, could you not have waited till to-morrow morning, when you would have found me at the parsonage?" But she did not draw her hand away from him, or in any way pretend that he had not a right to accost her as a lover.

"No, I could not wait. I am more eager to see those I love than you seem to be."

"How do you know whom I love, or how eager I might be to see them? There is an old woman there whom I love, and I have thought nothing of this walk with the object of seeing her." And now, slowly drawing her hand away from him, she pointed to the farmhouse which she had left.

"Patty," he said, after a minute's pause, during which she had looked full into his face with all the force of her bright eyes; "I have come from London to-day, straight down here to Oxney, and from my aunt's house close upon your footsteps after you, to ask you that one question. Do you love me?"

"What a Hercules!" she said, again laughing. "Do you really mean that you left London only this morning? Why, you must have been five hours in a railway carriage and two in a postchaise, not to talk of the walk afterwards. You ought to take more care of yourself, Captain Broughton!"

He would have been angry with her—for he did not like to be quizzed—had she not put her hand on his arm as she spoke, and the softness of her touch had redeemed the offence of her words.

"All that have I done," said he, "that I may hear one word from you."

"That any word of mine should have such potency! But let us walk on, or my father will take us for some of the standing stones of the moor. How have you found your aunt? If you only knew the cares that have sat on her dear shoulders for the last week past, in order that your high mightiness might have a sufficiency to eat and drink in these desolate half-starved regions."

"She might have saved herself such anxiety. No one can care less for such things than I do."

"And yet I think I have heard you boast of the cook of your club." And then again there was silence for a minute or two.

"Patty," said he, stopping again in the path; "answer my question. I have a right to demand an answer. Do you love me?"

"And what if I do? What if I have been so silly as to allow your perfections to be too many for my weak heart? What then, Captain Broughton?"

"It cannot be that you love me, or you would not joke now."

"Perhaps not, indeed," she said. It seemed as though she were resolved not to yield an inch in her own humour. And then again they walked on.

"Patty," he said once more, "I shall get an answer from you to-night,—this evening; now, during this walk, or I shall return to-morrow, and never revisit this spot again."

"Oh, Captain Broughton, how should we ever manage to live without you?"

"Very well," he said; "up to the end of this walk I can bear it all;—and one word spoken then will mend it all."

During the whole of this time she felt that she was ill-using him. She knew that she loved him with all her heart; that it would nearly kill her to part with him; that she had heard his renewed offer with an ecstacy of joy. She acknowledged to herself that he was giving proof of his devotion as strong as any which a girl could receive from her lover. And yet she could hardly bring herself to say the word he longed to hear. That word once said, and then she knew that she must succumb to her love for ever! That word once said, and there would be nothing for her but to spoil him with her idolatry! That word once said, and she must continue to repeat it into his ears, till perhaps he might be tired of hearing it! And now he had threatened her, and how could she speak it after that? She certainly would not speak it unless he asked her again without such threat. And so they walked on again in silence.

"Patty," he said at last. "By the heavens above us you shall answer me. Do you love me?"

She now stood still, and almost trembled as she looked up into his face. She stood opposite to him for a moment, and then placing her two hands on his shoulders, she answered him. "I do, I do, I do," she said, "with all my heart; with all my heart—

with all my heart and strength." And then her head fell upon his breast.

———

Captain Broughton was almost as much surprised as delighted by the warmth of the acknowledgment made by the eager-hearted passionate girl whom he now held within his arms. She had said it now ; the words had been spoken ; and there was nothing for her but to swear to him over and over again with her sweetest oaths, that those words were true—true as her soul. And very sweet was the walk down from thence to the parsonage gate. He spoke no more of the distance of the ground, or the length of his day's journey. But he stopped her at every turn that he might press her arm the closer to his own, that he might look into the brightness of her eyes, and prolong his hour of delight. There were no more gibes now on her tongue, no raillery at his London finery, no laughing comments on his coming and going. With downright honesty she told him everything : how she had loved him before her heart was warranted in such a passion ; how, with much thinking, she had resolved that it would be unwise to take him at his first word, and had thought it better that he should return to London, and then think over it ; how she had almost repented of her courage when she had feared, during those long summer days, that he would forget her ; and how her heart had leapt for joy when her old friend had told her that he was coming.

"And yet," said he, "you were not glad to see me!"

"Oh, was I not glad? You cannot understand the feelings of a girl who has lived secluded as I have done. Glad is no word for the joy I felt. But it was not seeing you that I cared for so much. It was the knowledge that you were near me once again. I almost wish now that I had not seen you till to-morrow." But as she spoke she pressed his arm, and this caress gave the lie to her last words.

" No, do not come in to-night," she said, when she reached the little wicket that led up to the parsonage. "Indeed, you shall not. I could not behave myself properly if you did."

"But I don't want you to behave properly."

"Oh! I am to keep that for London, am I? But, nevertheless, Captain Broughton, I will not invite you either to tea or to supper to-night."

"Surely I may shake hands with your father."

"Not to night—not till—. John, I may tell him, may I not? I must tell him at once."

"Certainly," said he.

"And then you shall see him to-morrow. Let me see—at what hour shall I bid you come?"

"To breakfast."

"No, indeed. What on earth would your aunt do with her broiled turkey and the cold pie? I have got no cold pie for you."

"I hate cold pie."

"What a pity! But, John, I should be forced to

have you directly after breakfast. Come down—
come down at two, or three; and then I will go back
with you to Aunt Penelope. I must see her to-
morrow;" and so at last the matter was settled, and
the happy Captain, as he left her, was hardly resisted
in his attempt to press her lips to his own.

When she entered the parlour in which her father
was sitting, there still were Gribbles and Poulter
discussing some knotty point of Devon lore. So
Patience took off her hat, and sat herself down,
waiting till they should go. For full an hour she
had to wait, and then Gribbles and Poulter did go
But it was not in such matters as this that Patience
Woolsworthy was impatient. She could wait, and
wait, and wait, curbing herself for weeks and months,
while the thing waited for was in her eyes good;
but she could not curb her hot thoughts or her hot
words when things came to be discussed which she
did not think to be good.

"Papa," she said, when Gribbles' long-drawn last
word had been spoken at the door. "Do you remember how I asked you the other day what you would
say if I were to leave you?"

"Yes, surely," he replied, looking up at her in
astonishment.

"I am going to leave you now," she said. "Dear,
dearest father, how am I to go from you?"

"Going to leave me," said he, thinking of her visit
to Helpholme, and thinking of nothing else.

Now, there had been a story about Helpholme.

That bed-ridden old lady there had a stalwart son, who was now the owner of the Helpholme pastures. But though owner in fee of all those wild acres, and of the cattle which they supported, he was not much above the farmers around him, either in manners or education. He had his merits, however; for he was honest, well-to-do in the world, and modest withal. How strong love had grown up, springing from neighbourly kindness, between our Patience and his mother, it needs not here to tell; but rising from it had come another love—or an ambition which might have grown to love. The young man, after much thought, had not dared to speak to Miss Woolsworthy, but he had sent a message by Miss Le Smyrger. If there could be any hope for him, he would present himself as a suitor—on trial. He did not owe a shilling in the world, and had money by him—saved. He wouldn't ask the parson for a shilling of fortune. Such had been the tenor of his message, and Miss Le Smyrger had delivered it faithfully. "He does not mean it," Patience had said with her stern voice. "Indeed he does, my dear. You may be sure he is in earnest," Miss Le Smyrger had replied; "and there is not an honester man in these parts."

"Tell him," said Patience, not attending to the latter portion of her friend's last speech, "that it cannot be—make him understand, you know—and tell him also that the matter shall be thought of no more." The matter had, at any rate, been spoken of no more, but the young farmer still remained a bachelor, and Helpholme still wanted a mistress. But all this came back upon the parson's mind when his daughter told him that she was about to leave him.

"Yes, dearest," she said; and as she spoke she now knelt at his knees. "I have been asked in marriage, and I have given myself away."

"Well, my love, if you will be happy——"

"I hope I shall; I think I shall. But you, papa?"

"You will not be far from us."

"Oh, yes; in London."

"In London?"

"Captain Broughton lives in London generally."

"And has Captain Broughton asked you to marry him?"

"Yes, papa—who else? Is he not good? Will you not love him? Oh, papa, do not say that I am wrong to love him?"

He never told her his mistake, or explained to her that he had not thought it possible that the high-placed son of the London great man should have fallen in love with his undowered daughter; but he embraced her, and told her, with all his enthusiasm, that he rejoiced in her joy, and would be happy in her happiness. "My own Patty," he said, "I have ever known that you were too good for this life of ours here." And then the evening wore away into the night, with many tears, but still with much happiness.

Captain Broughton, as he walked back to Oxney

Combe, made up his mind that he would say nothing on the matter to his aunt till the next morning. He wanted to think over it all, and to think it over, if possible, by himself. He had taken a step in life, the most important that a man is ever called on to take, and he had to reflect whether or no he had taken it with wisdom.

"Have you seen her?" said Miss Le Smyrger, very anxiously, when he came into the drawing-room.

"Miss Woolsworthy you mean," said he. "Yes, I've seen her. As I found her out, I took a long walk, and happened to meet her. Do you know, aunt, I think I'll go to bed; I was up at five this morning, and have been on the move ever since."

Miss Le Smyrger perceived that she was to hear nothing that evening, so she handed him his candle-stick and allowed him to go to his room.

But Captain Broughton did not immediately retire to bed, nor when he did so was he able to sleep at once. Had this step that he had taken been a wise one? He was not a man who, in worldly matters, had allowed things to arrange themselves for him, as is the case with so many men. He had formed views for himself, and had a theory of life. Money for money's sake he had declared to himself to be bad. Money, as a concomitant to things which were in themselves good, he had declared to himself to be good also. That concomitant in this affair of his marriage, he had now missed. Well; he had made up his mind to that, and would put up with the loss.

He had means of living of his own, the means not so extensive as might have been desirable. That it would be well for him to become a married man, looking merely to that state of life as opposed to his present state, he had fully resolved. On that point, therefore, there was nothing to repent. That Patty Woolsworthy was good, affectionate, clever, and beautiful he was sufficiently satisfied. It would be odd indeed if he were not so satisfied now, seeing that for the last four months he had so declared to himself daily with many inward asseverations. And yet though, he repeated, now again that he was satisfied, I do not think that he was so fully satisfied of it as he had been throughout the whole of those four months. It is sad to say so, but I fear—I fear that such was the case. When you have your plaything, how much of the anticipated pleasure vanishes, especially if it be won easily.

He had told none of his family what were his intentions in this second visit to Devonshire, and now he had to bethink himself whether they would be satisfied. What would his sister say, she who had married the Honourable Augustus Gumbleton, gold-stick-in-waiting to Her Majesty's Privy Council? Would she receive Patience with open arms, and make much of her about London? And then how far would London suit Patience, or would Patience suit London? There would be much for him to do in teaching her, and it would be well for him to set about the lesson without loss of time. So far he got

that night, but when the morning came he went a
step further, and began mentally to criticise her
manner to himself. It had been very sweet, that
warm, that full, that ready declaration of love.
Yes; it had been very sweet; but—but—; when,
after her little jokes, she did confess her love, had
she not been a little too free for feminine excellence? A man likes to be told that he is loved, but
he hardly wishes that the girl he is to marry should
fling herself at his head!

Ah me! yes; it was thus he argued to himself as
on that morning he went through the arrangements of
his toilet. "Then he was a brute," you say, my
pretty reader. I have never said that he was not a
brute. But this I remark, that many such brutes are
to be met with in the beaten paths of the world's high
highway. When Patience Woolsworthy had answered
him coldly, bidding him go back to London and
think over his love; while it seemed from her manner
that at any rate as yet she did not care for him;
while he was absent from her, and, therefore, longing for her, the possession of her charms, her talent
and bright honesty of purpose had seemed to him a
thing most desirable. Now they were his own. They
had, in fact, been his own from the first. The heart
of this country-bred girl had fallen at the first word
from his mouth. Had she not so confessed to him?
She was very nice—very nice indeed. He loved
her dearly. But had he not sold himself too cheaply?

I by no means say that he was not a brute. But

whether brute or no he was an honest man, and had no remotest dream, either then, on that morning, or during the following days on which such thoughts pressed more thickly on his mind—of breaking away from his pledged word. At breakfast on that morning he told all to Miss Le Smyrger, and that lady, with warm and gracious intentions, confided to him her purpose regarding her property. " I have always regarded Patience as my heir," she said, " and shall do so still."

" Oh, indeed," said Captain Broughton.

" But it is a great, great pleasure to me to think that she will give back the little property to my sister's child. You will have your mother's, and thus it will all come together again."

" Ah !" said Captain Broughton. He had his own ideas about property, and did not, even under existing circumstances, like to hear that his aunt considered herself at liberty to leave the acres away to one who was by blood quite a stranger to the family.

" Does Patience know of this ? " he asked.

" Not a word," said Miss Le Smyrger. And then nothing more was said upon the subject.

On that afternoon he went down and received the parson's benediction and congratulations with a good grace. Patience said very little on the occasion, and indeed was absent during the greater part of the interview. The two lovers then walked up to Oxney Combe, and there were more benedictions and more

congratulations. "All went merry as a marriage
bell," at any rate as far as Patience was concerned.
Not a word had yet fallen from that dear mouth, not
a look had yet come over that handsome face, which
tended in any way to mar her bliss. Her first day
of acknowledged love was a day altogether happy,
and when she prayed for him as she knelt beside her
bed there was no feeling in her mind that any fear
need disturb her joy.

I will pass over the next three or four days very
quickly, merely saying that Patience did not find
them so pleasant as that first day after her engagement. There was something in her lover's manner
—something which at first she could not define—
which by degrees seemed to grate against her feelings. He was sufficiently affectionate, that being a
matter on which she did not require much demon-
stration; but joined to his affection there seemed to
be——; she hardly liked to suggest to herself a
harsh word, but could it be possible that he was
beginning to think that she was not good enough for
him? And then she asked herself the question—was
she good enough for him? If there were doubt
about that, the match should be broken off, though
she tore her own heart out in the struggle. The
truth, however, was this—that he had begun that
teaching which he had already found to be so necessary. Now, had any one essayed to teach Patience
German or mathematics, with that young lady's free
consent, I believe that she would have been found a

meek scholar. But it was not probable that she would ' be meek when she found a self-appointed tutor teaching her manners and conduct without her consent.

So matters went on for four or five days, and on the evening of the fifth day, Captain Broughton and his aunt drank tea at the parsonage. Nothing very especial occurred; but as the parson and Miss Le Smyrger insisted on playing backgammon with devoted perseverance during the whole evening, Broughton had a good opportunity of saying a word or two about those changes in his lady-love which a life in London would require—and some word he said also—some single slight word as to the higher station in life to which he would exalt his bride. Patience bore it—for her father and Miss Le Smyrger were in the room—she bore it well, speaking no syllable of anger, and enduring, for the moment, the implied scorn of the old parsonage. Then the evening broke up, and Captain Broughton walked back to Oxney Combe with his aunt. "Patty," her father said to her before they went to bed, "he seems to me to be a most excellent young man." "Dear papa," she answered, kissing him. "And terribly deep in love," said Mr. Woolsworthy. "Oh, I don't know about that," she answered, as she left him with her sweetest smile. But though she could thus smile at her father's joke, she had already made up her mind that there was still something to be learned as to her promised husband before she could place herself alto-

gether in his hands. She would ask him whether he
thought himself liable to injury from this proposed
marriage; and though he should deny any such
thought, she would know from the manner of his
denial what his true feelings were.

And he, too, on that night, during his silent walk
with Miss Le Smyrger, had entertained some similar
thoughts. "I fear she is obstinate," he had said to
himself, and then he had half accused her of being
sullen also. "If that be her temper, what a life of
misery I have before me!"

"Have you fixed a day yet?" his aunt asked him
as they came near to her house.

"No, not yet: I don't know whether it will suit
me to fix it before I leave."

"Why, it was but the other day you were in such
a hurry."

"Ah—yes—I have thought more about it since
then."

"I should have imagined that this would depend
on what Patty thinks," said Miss Le Smyrger, stand-
up for the privileges of her sex. "It is presumed
that the gentleman is always ready as soon the lady
will consent."

"Yes, in ordinary cases it is so; but when a girl is
taken out of her own sphere—"

"Her own sphere! Let me caution you, Master
John, not to talk to Patty about her own sphere."

"Aunt Penelope, as Patience is to be my wife and
not yours, I must claim permission to speak to her

on such subjects as may seem suitable to me." And then they parted—not in the best humour with each other.

On the following day Captain Broughton and Miss Woolsworthy did not meet till the evening. She had said, before those few ill-omened words had passed her lover's lips, that she would probably be at Miss Le Smyrger's house on the following morning. Those ill-omened words did pass her lover's lips, and then she remained at home. This did not come from sullenness, nor even from anger, but from a conviction that it would be well that she should think much before she met him again. Nor was he anxious to hurry a meeting. His thought—his base thought —was this; that she would be sure to come up to the Combe after him; but she did not come, and therefore in the evening he went down to her, and asked her to walk with him.

They went away by the path that led to Helpholme, and little was said between them till they had walked some mile together. Patience, as she went along the path, remembered almost to the letter the sweet words which had greeted her ears as she came down that way with him on the night of his arrival; but he remembered nothing of that sweetness then. Had he not made an ass of himself during these last six months? That was the thought which very much had possession of his mind.

" Patience," he said at last, having hitherto spoken only an indifferent word now and again since they had left the parsonage, "Patience, I hope you realise the importance of the step which you and I are about to take?"

"Of course I do," she answered: "what an odd question that is for you to ask!"

"Because," said he, "sometimes I almost doubt it. It seems to me as though you thought you could remove yourself from here to your new home with no more trouble than when you go from home up to the Combe."

"Is that meant for a reproach, John?"

"No, not for a reproach, but for advice. Certainly not for a reproach."

"I am glad of that."

"But I should wish to make you think how great is the leap in the world which you are about to take." Then again they walked on for many steps before she answered him.

"Tell me then, John," she said, when she had sufficiently considered what words she would speak; and as she spoke a bright colour suffused her face, and her eyes flashed almost with anger. "What leap do you mean? Do you mean a leap upwards?"

"Well, yes; I hope it will be so."

"In one sense, certainly, it would be a leap upwards. To be the wife of the man I loved; to have the privilege of holding his happiness in my hand; to know that I was his own—the companion whom he had chosen out of all the world—that would, indeed, be a leap upwards; a leap almost to heaven, if all that were so. But if you mean upwards in any other sense——"

"I was thinking of the social scale."

"Then, Captain Broughton, your thoughts were doing me dishonour."

"Doing you dishonour!"

"Yes, doing me dishonour. That your father is, in the world's esteem, a greater man than mine is doubtless true enough. That you, as a man, are richer than I am as a woman, is doubtless also true. But you dishonour me, and yourself also, if these things can weigh with you now."

"Patience,—I think you can hardly know what words you are saying to me."

"Pardon me, but I think I do. Nothing that you can give me—no gifts of that description—can weigh aught against that which I am giving you. If you had all the wealth and rank of the greatest lord in the land, it would count as nothing in such a scale. If—as I have not doubted—if in return for my heart you have given me yours, then—then—then you have paid me fully. But when gifts such as those are going, nothing else can count even as a make-weight."

"I do not quite understand you," he answered, after a pause. "I fear you are a little high-flown." And then, while the evening was still early, they walked back to the parsonage almost without another word.

Captain Broughton at this time had only one full

day more to remain at Oxney Colne. On the afternoon following that he was to go as far as Exeter, and
thence return to London. Of course, it was to be
expected that the wedding day would be fixed before
he went, and much had been said about it during the
first day or two of his engagement. Then he had
pressed for an early time, and Patience, with a girl's
usual diffidence, had asked for some little delay. But
now nothing was said on the subject; and how was
it probable that such a matter could be settled after
such a conversation as that which I have related?
That evening, Miss Le Smyrger asked whether the
day had been fixed. "No," said Captain Broughton
harshly; "nothing has been fixed." "But it will be
arranged before you go." "Probably not," he said;
and then the subject was dropped for the time.

"John," she said, just before she went to bed, "if
there be anything wrong between you and Patience,
I conjure you to tell me."

"You had better ask her," he replied. "I can tell
you nothing."

On the following morning he was much surprised
by seeing Patience on the gravel path before Miss
Le Smyrger's gate immediately after breakfast. He
went to the door to open it for her, and she, as she
gave him her hand, told him that she came up to
speak to him. There was no hesitation in her
manner, nor any look of anger in her face. But
there was in her gait and form, in her voice and
countenance, a fixedness of purpose which he had

never seen before, or at any rate had never acknowledged.

"Certainly," said he. "Shall I come out with you, or will you come up stairs?"

"We can sit down in the summer-house," she said; and thither they both went.

"Captain Broughton," she said—and she began her task the moment that they were both seated—"You and I have engaged ourselves as man and wife, but perhaps we have been over rash."

"How so?" said he.

"It may be—and indeed I will say more—it is the case that we have made this engagement without knowing enough of each other's character."

"I have not thought so."

"The time will perhaps come when you will so think, but for the sake of all that we most value, let it come before it is too late. What would be our fate—how terrible would be our misery—if such a thought should come to either of us after we have linked our lots together."

There was a solemnity about her as she thus spoke which almost repressed him,—which for a time did prevent him from taking that tone of authority which on such a subject he would choose to adopt. But he recovered himself. "I hardly think that this comes well from you," he said.

"From whom else should it come? Who else can fight my battle for me; and, John, who else can fight that same battle on your behalf? I tell you this, that with your mind standing towards me as it does stand at present, you could not give me your hand at the altar with true words and a happy conscience. Am I not true? You have half repented of your bargain already. Is it not so?"

He did not answer her; but getting up from his seat walked to the front of the summer-house, and stood there with his back turned upon her. It was not that he meant to be ungracious, but in truth he did not know how to answer her. He had half repented of his bargain.

"John," she said, getting up and following him, so that she could put her hand upon his arm, "I have been very angry with you."

"Angry with me!" he said, turning sharp upon her.

"Yes, angry with you. You would have treated me like a child. But that feeling has gone now. I am not angry now. There is my hand;—the hand of a friend. Let the words that have been spoken between us be as though they had not been spoken. Let us both be free."

"Do you mean it?" he asked.

"Certainly I mean it." As she spoke these words her eyes were filled with tears, in spite of all the efforts she could make; but he was not looking at her, and her efforts had sufficed to prevent any sob from being audible.

"With all my heart," he said; and it was manifest from his tone that he had no thought of her happiness as he spoke. It was true that she had been angry with him—angry, as she had herself declared; but nevertheless, in what she had said and what she had done, she had thought more of his happiness than of her own. Now she was angry once again.

"With all your heart, Captain Broughton! Well, so be it. If with all your heart, then is the necessity so much the greater. You go to-morrow. Shall we say farewell now?"

"Patience, I am not going to be lectured."

"Certainly not by me. Shall we say farewell now?"

"Yes, if you are determined."

"I am determined. Farewell, Captain Broughton. You have all my wishes for your happiness." And she held out her hand to him.

"Patience!" he said. And he looked at her with a dark frown, as though he would strive to frighten her into submission. If so, he might have saved himself any such attempt.

"Farewell, Captain Broughton. Give me your hand, for I cannot stay." He gave her his hand, hardly knowing why he did so. She lifted it to her lips and kissed it, and then, leaving him, passed from the summer-house down through the wicket-gate, and straight home to the parsonage.

During the whole of that day she said no word to anyone of what had occurred. When she was once more at home she went about her household affairs as she had done on that day of his arrival. When she sat down to dinner with her father he observed nothing to make him think that she was unhappy; nor during the evening was there any expression in her face, or any tone in her voice, which excited his attention. On the following morning Captain Broughton called at the parsonage, and the servant-girl brought word to her mistress that he was in the parlour. But she would not see him. "Laws, miss, you ain't a quarrelled with your beau?" the poor girl said. "No, not quarrelled," she said; "but give him that." It was a scrap of paper, containing a word or two in pencil. "It is better that we should not meet again. God bless you." And from that day to this, now more than ten years, they never have met.

"Papa," she said to her father that afternoon, "dear papa, do not be angry with me. It is all over between me and John Broughton. Dearest, you and I will not be separated."

It would be useless here to tell how great was the old man's surprise and how true his sorrow. As the tale was told to him no cause was given for anger with anyone. Not a word was spoken against the suitor who had on that day returned to London with a full conviction that now at least he was relieved from his engagement. "Patty, my darling child," he said, "may God grant that it be for the best!"

"It is for the best," she answered stoutly. "For this place I am fit; and I much doubt whether I am fit for any other."

On that day she did not see Miss Le Smyrger, but on the following morning, knowing that Captain

Broughton had gone off, having heard the wheels of the carriage as they passed by the parsonage gate on his way to the station,—she walked up to the Combe.

"He has told you, I suppose?" said she.

"Yes," said Miss Le Smyrger. "And I will never see him again unless he asks your pardon on his knees. I have told him so. I would not even give him my hand as he went."

"But why so, thou kindest one? The fault was mine more than his."

"I understand. I have eyes in my head," said the old maid. "I have watched him for the last four or five days. If you could have kept the truth to yourself and bade him keep off from you, he would have been at your feet now, licking the dust from your shoes."

"But, dear friend, I do not want a man to lick dust from my shoes."

"Ah, you are a fool. You do not know the value of your own wealth."

"True ; I have been a fool. I was a fool to think that one coming from such a life as he has led could be happy with such as I am. I know the truth now. I have bought the lesson dearly,—but perhaps not too dearly, seeing that it will never be forgotten."

There was but little more said about the matter between our three friends at Oxney Colne. What, indeed, could be said? Miss Le Smyrger for a year or two still expected that her nephew would return and claim his bride ; but he has never done so, nor has there been any correspondence between them. Patience Woolsworthy had learned her lesson dearly. She had given her whole heart to the man; and, though she so bore herself that no one was aware of the violence of the struggle, nevertheless the struggle within her bosom was very violent. She never told herself that she had done wrong; she never regretted her loss; but yet—yet!—the loss was very hard to bear. He also had loved her, but he was not capable of a love which could much injure his daily peace. Her daily peace was gone for many a day to come.

Her father is still living; but there is a curate now in the parish. In conjunction with him and with Miss Le Smyrger she spends her time in the concerns of the parish. In her own eyes she is a confirmed old maid; and such is my opinion also. The romance of her life was played out in that summer. She never sits now lonely on the hill-side thinking how much she might do for one whom she really loved. But with a large heart she loves many, and, with no romance, she works hard to lighten the burdens of those she loves.

As for Captain Broughton, all the world knows that he did marry that great heiress with whom his name was once before connected, and that he is now a useful member of Parliament, working on committees three or four days a week with a zeal that is indefatigable. Sometimes, not often, as he thinks of Patience Woolsworthy, a gratified smile comes across his face.

GEORGE WALKER AT SUEZ.

Of all the spots on the world's surface that I, George Walker, of Friday Street, London, have ever visited, Suez in Egypt at the head of the Red Sea is by far the vilest, the most unpleasant, and the least interesting. There are no women there, no water, and no vegetation. It is surrounded, and indeed often filled, by a world of sand. A scorching sun is always overhead; and one is domiciled in a huge cavernous hotel, which seems to have been made purposely destitute of all the comforts of civilised life. Nevertheless, in looking back upon the week of my life which I spent there I always enjoy a certain sort of triumph;—or rather, upon one day of that week, which lends a sort of halo not only to my sojourn at Suez, but to the whole period of my residence in Egypt.

I am free to confess that I am not a great man, and that, at any rate in the earlier part of my career, I had a hankering after the homage which is paid to greatness. I would fain have been a popular orator, feeding myself on the incense tendered to me by thousands; or failing that, a man born to power, whom those around him were compelled to respect, and perhaps to fear. I am not ashamed to acknowledge this, and I believe that most of my neighbours in Friday Street would own as much were they as candid and open hearted as myself.

It is now some time since I was recommended to pass the first four months of the year in Cairo because I had a sore-throat. The doctor may have been right, but I shall never divest myself of the idea that my partners wished to be rid of me while they made certain changes in the management of the firm. They would not otherwise have shown such interest every time I blew my nose or relieved my huskiness by a slight cough;—they would not have been so intimate with that surgeon from St. Bartholomew's who dined with them twice at the Albion; nor would they have gone to work directly that my back was turned, and have done those very things which they could not have done had I remained at home. Be that as it may, I was frightened and went to Cairo, and while there I made a trip to Suez for a week.

I was not happy at Cairo, for I knew nobody there and the people at the hotel were as I thought uncivil. It seemed to me as though I were allowed to go in and out merely by sufferance; and yet I paid my bill regularly every week. The house was full of company, but the company was made up of parties of twos and threes, and they all seemed to have their own friends. I did make attempts to overcome that terrible British exclusiveness, that *noli me tangere* with which an Englishman arms himself, and in which he thinks it necessary to envelop his wife; but it was in vain, and I found myself sitting down to breakfast and dinner, day after day, as much alone as I should do if I called for a chop at a separate table in the Cathedral Coffee-house. And yet at breakfast and dinner I made one of an assemblage of thirty or forty people. That I thought dull.

But as I stood one morning on the steps before the hotel, bethinking myself that my throat was as well as ever I remembered it to be, I was suddenly slapped on the back. Never in my life did I feel a more pleasant sensation, or turn round with more un-affected delight to return a friend's greeting. It was as though a cup of water had been handed to me in the desert. I knew that a cargo of passengers for Australia had reached Cairo that morning, and were to be passed on to Suez as soon as the railway would take them, and did not therefore expect that the greeting had come from any sojourner in Egypt. I should perhaps have explained that the even tenor of our life at the hotel was disturbed some four times a month by a flight through Cairo of a flock of travellers, who like locusts eat up all that there was eatable at the Inn for the day. They sat down at the same tables with us, never mixing with us, having their separate interests and hopes, and being often, as I thought, somewhat loud and almost selfish in the expression of them. These flocks consisted of passen-

K

gers passing and repassing by the overland route to and from India and Australia; and had I nothing else to tell, I should delight to describe all that I watched of their habits and manners—the outward bound being so different in their traits from their brethren on their return. But I have to tell of my own triumph at Suez, and must therefore hasten on to say that on turning round quickly with my outstretched hand, I found it clasped by John Robinson.

"Well, Robinson, is this you?" "Holloa, Walker, what are you doing here?" That of course was the style of greeting. Elsewhere I should not have cared much to meet John Robinson, for he was a man who had never done well in the world. He had been in business and connected with a fairly good house in Size Lane, but he had married early, and things had not exactly gone well with him. I don't think the house broke, but he did; and so he was driven to take himself and five children off to Australia. Elsewhere I should not have cared to come across him, but I was positively glad to be slapped on the back by anybody on that landing-place in front of Shepperd's Hotel at Cairo.

I soon learned that Robinson with his wife and children, and indeed with all the rest of the Australian cargo, were to be passed on to Suez that afternoon, and after awhile I agreed to accompany their party. I had made up my mind, on coming out from England, that I would see all the wonders of Egypt, and hitherto I had seen nothing. I did ride on one day some fifteen miles on a donkey to see the petrified forest ; but the guide, who called himself a dragoman, took me wrong or cheated me in some way. We rode half the day over a stony, sandy plain, seeing nothing, with a terrible wind that filled my mouth with grit, and at last the dragoman got off. "Dere," said he, picking up a small bit of stone, " Dis is de forest made of stone. Carry that home." Then we turned round and rode back to Cairo. My chief observation as to the country was this—that whichever way we went, the wind blew into our teeth. The day's work cost me five-and-twenty shillings, and since that I had not as yet made any other expedition. I was therefore glad of an opportunity of going to Suez, and of making the journey in company with an acquaintance.

At that time the railway was open, as far as I remember, nearly half the way from Cairo to Suez. It did not run four or five times a day, as railways do in other countries, but four or five times a month. In fact, it only carried passengers on the arrival of these flocks passing between England and her Eastern possessions. There were trains passing backwards and forwards constantly, as I perceived in walking to and from the station ; but, as I learned, they carried nothing but the labourers working on the line, and the water sent into the Desert for their use. It struck me forcibly at the time that I should not have liked to have money in that investment.

Well; I went with Robinson to Suez. The journey,

like everything else in Egypt, was sandy, hot, and
unpleasant. The railway carriages were pretty fair,
and we had room enough ; but even in them the dust
was a great nuisance. We travelled about ten miles
an hour, and stopped about an hour at every ten
miles. This was tedious, but we had cigars with us
and a trifle of brandy and water ; and in this manner the railway journey wore itself away. In the
middle of the night, however, we were moved from
the railway carriages into omnibuses, as they were
called, and then I was not comfortable. These omnibuses were wooden boxes, placed each upon a pair
of wheels, and supposed to be capable of carrying six
passengers. I was thrust into one with Robinson,
his wife and five children, and immediately began to
repent of my good-nature in accompanying them.
To each vehicle were attached four horses or mules,
and I must acknowledge that as on the railway they
went as slow as possible, so now in these conveyances,
dragged through the sand, they went as fast as the
beasts could be made to gallop. I remember the
Fox Tally-ho coach on the Birmingham road when
Boyce drove it, but as regards pace the Fox Tally-ho
was nothing to these machines in Egypt. On the
first going off I was jolted right on to Mrs. R.
and her infant ; and for a long time that lady thought
that the child had been squeezed out of its proper
shape ; but at last we arrived at Suez, and the baby
seemed to me to be all right when it was handed
down into the boat at Suez.

The Robinsons were allowed time to breakfast at that cavernous hotel—which looked to me like a scheme to save the expense of the passengers' meal on board the ship—and then they were off. I shook hands with him heartily as I parted with him at the quay, and wished him well through all his troubles. A man who takes a wife and five young children out into a colony, and that with his pockets but indifferently lined, certainly has his troubles before him. So he has at home, no doubt; but, judging for myself, I should always prefer sticking to the old ship as long as there is a bag of biscuits in the locker. Poor Robinson! I have never heard a word of him or his since that day, and sincerely trust that the baby was none the worse for the little accident in the box.

And now I had the prospect of a week before me at Suez, and the Robinsons had not been gone half an hour before I began to feel that I should have been better off even at Cairo. I secured a bedroom at the hotel—I might have secured sixty bedrooms had I wanted them—and then went out and stood at the front door, or gate. It is a large house, built round a quadrangle, looking with one front towards the head of the Red Sea, and with the other into and on a sandy, dead-looking, open square. There I stood for ten minutes, and finding that it was too hot to go forth, returned to the long cavernous room in which we had breakfasted. In that long cavernous room I was destined to eat all my meals for the next six

days. Now at Cairo I could, at any rate, see my
fellow-creatures at their food. So I lit a cigar,
and began to wonder whether I could survive the
week. It was now clear to me that I had done a
very rash thing in coming to Suez with the Robinsons.

Somebody about the place had asked me my
name, and I had told it plainly—George Walker. I
never was ashamed of my name yet, and never had
cause to be. I believe at this day it will go as far
in Friday Street as any other. A man may be
popular, or he may not. That depends mostly on
circumstances which are in themselves trifling. But
the value of his name depends on the way in which
he is known at his bank. I have never dealt in tea
spoons or gravy spoons, but my name will go as far
as another name. "George Walker," I answered,
therefore, in a tone of some little authority, to the
man who asked me, and who sat inside the gate of
the hotel in an old dressing gown and slippers.

That was a melancholy day with me, and twenty
times before dinner did I wish myself back at Cairo.
I had been travelling all night, and therefore hoped
that I might get through some little time in sleeping, but the mosquitoes attacked me the moment I
laid myself down. In other places mosquitoes
torment you only at night, but at Suez they buzz
around you, without ceasing, at all hours. A scorching sun was blazing overhead, and absolutely forbade
me to leave the house. I stood for awhile in the
verandah, looking down at the few small vessels

which were moored to the quay, but there was no life in them ; not a sail was set, not a boatman or a sailor was to be seen, and the very water looked as though it were hot. I could fancy the glare of the sun was cracking the paint on the gunwales of the boats. I was the only visitor in the house, and during all the long hours of the morning it seemed as though the servants had deserted it.

I dined at four ; not that I chose that hour, but because no choice was given to me. At the hotels in Egypt one has to dine at an hour fixed by the landlord, and no entreaties will suffice to obtain a meal at any other. So at four I dined, and after dinner was again reduced to despair.

I was sitting in the cavernous chamber almost mad at the prospect of the week before me, when I heard a noise as of various feet in the passage leading from the quadrangle. Was it possible that other human beings were coming into the hotel—Christian human beings at whom I could look, whose voices I could hear, whose words I could understand, and with whom I might possibly associate ? I did not move, however, for I was still hot, and I knew that my chances might be better, if I did not show myself over-eager for companionship at the first moment. The door, however, was soon opened, and I saw that at least in one respect I was destined to be disappointed. The strangers who were entering the room were not Christians—if I might judge by the nature of the garments in which they were clothed.

The door had been opened by the man in an old dressing gown and slippers, whom I had seen sitting inside the gate.   He was the Arab porter of the hotel, and as he marshalled the new visitors into the room, I heard him pronounce some sound similar to my own name, and perceived that he pointed me out to the most prominent person of those who then entered the apartment. This was a stout, portly man, dressed from head to foot in Eastern costume of the brightest colours.   He wore, not only the red fez cap which everybody wears—even I had accustomed myself to a fez cap—but a turban round it, of which the voluminous folds were snowy white.   His face was fat, but not the less grave, and the lower part of it was enveloped in a magnificent beard, which projected round it on all sides, and touched his breast as he walked.   It was a grand grizzled beard, and I acknowledged at a moment that it added a singular dignity to the appearance of the stranger. His flowing robe was of bright colours, and the under garment which fitted close round his breast, and then descended, becoming beneath his sash a pair of the loosest pantaloons—I might, perhaps, better describe them as bags—was a rich tawny silk.   These loose pantaloons were tied close round his legs, above the ankle, and over a pair of scrupulously white stockings, and on his feet he wore a pair of yellow slippers.   It was manifest to me at a glance that the Arab gentleman was got up in his best raiment, and that no expense had been spared on the suit.

And here I cannot but make a remark on the
personal bearing of these Arabs. Whether they be
Arabs, or Turks, or Copts, it is always the same.
They are a mean, false, cowardly race, I believe.
They will bear blows, and respect the man who gives
them. Fear goes further with them than love, and
between man and man they understand nothing of
forbearance. He who does not exact from them all
that he can exact is simply a fool in their estimation,
to the extent of that which he loses. In all this,
they are immeasurably inferior to us who have had
Christian teaching. But in one thing they beat us.
They always know how to maintain their personal
dignity.

Look at my friend and partner Judkins, as he
stands with his hands in his trousers pockets at the
door of our house in Friday Street. What can be
meaner than his appearance? He is a stumpy, short,
podgy man; but then so also was my Arab friend at
Suez. Judkins is always dressed from head to foot
in a decent black cloth suit; his coat is ever a dress
coat, and is neither old nor shabby. On his head he
carries a shining new silk hat, such as fashion in our
metropolis demands. Judkins is rather a dandy than
otherwise, piquing himself somewhat on his apparel.
And yet how mean is his appearance, as compared
with the appearance of that Arab;—how mean also
is his gait, how ignoble his step! Judkins could
buy that Arab out four times over, and hardly feel
the loss; and yet were they to enter a room together,

Judkins would know and acknowledge by his look that he was the inferior personage. Not the less, should a personal quarrel arise between them, would Judkins punch the Arab's head ; ay, and reduce him to utter ignominy at his feet. Judkins would break his heart in despair, rather than not return a blow ; whereas the Arab would put up with any indignity of that sort. Nevertheless Judkins is altogether deficient in personal dignity. I often thought, as the hours hung in Egypt, whether it might not be practicable to introduce an oriental costume into Friday Street.

At this moment, as the Arab gentleman entered the cavernous coffee-room, I felt that I was greatly the inferior personage. He was followed by four or five others, dressed somewhat as himself, though by no means in such magnificent colours, and by one gentleman in a coat and trowsers. The gentleman in the coat and trowsers came last, and I could see that he was one of the least of the number. As for myself, I felt almost overawed by the dignity of the stout party in the turban, and seeing that he came directly across the room to the place where I was seated, I got upon my legs and made him some sign of Christian obeisance. I am a little man, and not podgy, as is Judkins, and I flatter myself that I showed more deportment, at any rate, than he would have exhibited.

I made, as I have said, some Christian obeisance. I bobbed my head, that is, rubbing my hands together the while, and expressed an opinion that it was a fine day. But if I was civil, as I hope I was, the Arab was much more so. He advanced till he was about six paces from me, then placed his right hand open upon his silken breast, and inclining forward with his whole body, made to me a bow which Judkins never could accomplish. The turban and flowing robe might be possible in Friday Street, but of what avail would be the outer garments and mere symbols, if the inner sentiment of personal dignity were wanting? I have often since tried it when alone, but I could never accomplish anything like that bow. The Arab with the flowing robe bowed, and then the other Arabs all bowed also; and after that the Christian gentleman with the coat and trowsers made a leg. I made a leg also, rubbing my hands again, and added to my former remarks that it was rather hot.

"Dat berry true," said the porter in the dirty dressing gown, who stood by. I could see at a glance that the manner of that porter towards me was greatly altered, and I began to feel comforted in my wretchedness. Perhaps a Christian from Friday Street, with plenty of money in his pockets, would stand in higher esteem at Suez than at Cairo. If so, that alone would go far to atone for the apparent wretchedness of the place. At Cairo I had not received that attention which had certainly been due to me as the second partner in the flourishing Manchester house of Grimes, Walker, and Judkins.

But now, as my friend with the beard again bowed to me, I felt that this deficiency was to be made up. It was clear, however, that this new acquaintance, though I liked the manner of it, would be attended with considerable inconvenience, for the Arab gentleman commenced an address to me in French. It has always been to me a source of sorrow that my parents did not teach me the French language, and this deficiency on my part has given rise to an incredible amount of supercilious overbearing pretension on the part of Judkins—who after all can hardly do more than translate a correspondent's letter. I do not believe that he could have understood a word of that Arab's oration, but at any rate I did not. He went on to the end, however, speaking for some three or four minutes, and then again he bowed. If I could only have learned that bow, I might still have been greater than Judkins with all his French.

"I am very sorry," said I, "but I don't exactly follow the French language—when it is spoken."

"Ah! no French!" said the Arab in very broken English, "dat is one sorrow." How is it that these fellows learn all languages under the sun? I afterwards found that this man could talk Italian and Turkish and Armenian fluently, and say a few words in German, as he could also in English. I could not ask for my dinner in any other language than English, if it were to save me from starvation. Then he called to the Christian gentleman in the pantaloons, and, as far as I could understand, made over to him the duty of interpreting between us. There seemed, however, to be one difficulty in the way of this being carried on with efficiency. The Christian gentleman could not speak English himself. He knew of it, perhaps, something more than did the Arab, but by no means enough to enable us to have a fluent conversation.

And had the interpreter—who turned out to be an Italian from Trieste, attached to the Austrian Consulate at Alexandria—had the interpreter spoken English with the greatest ease, I should have had considerable difficulty in understanding, and digesting in all its bearings, the proposition made to me. But before I proceed to the proposition, I must describe a ceremony which took place previous to its discussion. I had hardly observed, when first the procession entered the room, that one of my friend's followers—my friend's name, as I learned afterwards, was Mahmoud al Ackbar, and I will therefore call him Mahmoud—that one of Mahmoud's followers bore in his arms a bundle of long sticks, and that another carried an iron pot and a tray. Such was the case, and these two followers came forward to perform their services, while I, having been literally pressed down on to the sofa by Mahmoud, watched them in their progress. Mahmoud also sat down, and not a word was spoken while the ceremony went on. The man with the sticks first placed on the ground two little pans—one at my feet, and then one at the feet of his master. After that he loosed an ornamented bag which he carried round his neck, and producing from it tobacco, proceeded to fill two pipes. This he did with the utmost gravity, and apparently with very peculiar care. The pipes had been already fixed at one end of the stick, and to the other end the man had fastened two large yellow balls. These, as I afterwards perceived, were mouth-pieces made of amber. Then he lit the pipes, drawing up the difficult smoke by long painful suckings at the mouthpiece, and then, when the work had become apparently easy, he handed one pipe to me, and the other to his master. The bowls he had first placed in the little pans on the ground.

During all this time no word was spoken, and I was left altogether in the dark as to the cause which had produced this extraordinary courtesy. There was a stationary sofa—they called it there a divan—which was fixed into the corner of the room, and on one side of the angle sat Mahmoud al Ackbar, with his feet tucked under him, while I sat on the other. The remainder of the party stood around, and I felt so little master of the occasion, that I did not know whether it would become me to bid them be seated. I was not master of the entertainment. They were not my pipes. Nor was it my coffee, which I saw one of the followers preparing in a distant part of the room. And, indeed, I was much confused as to the management of the stick and amber mouth-piece with which I had been presented. With a cigar I am as much at home as any man in the city. I can nibble off the end of it, and smoke it to the last ash, when I am three parts asleep. But I had never before been invited to regale myself with such an instrument as this. What was I to do with that huge yellow ball? So I watched my new friend closely.

It had manifestly been a part of his urbanity not to commence till I had done so, but seeing my difficulty he at last raised the ball to his mouth and sucked at it. I looked at him, and envied the gravity of his countenance, and the dignity of his demeanour. I sucked also, but I made a sputtering noise, and must confess that I did not enjoy it. The smoke curled gracefully from his mouth and nostrils as he sat there in mute composure. I was mute as regarded speech, but I coughed as the smoke came from me in convulsive puffs. And then the attendant brought us coffee in little tin cups—black coffee, without sugar and full of grit, of which the berries had been only bruised, not ground. I took the cup and swallowed the mixture, for I could not refuse, but I wish that I might have asked for some milk and sugar. Nevertheless there was something very pleasing in the whole ceremony, and at last I began to find myself more at home with my pipe.

When Mahmoud had exhausted his tobacco, and perceived that I also had ceased to puff forth smoke, he spoke in Italian to the interpreter, and the interpreter forthwith proceeded to explain to me the purport of this visit. This was done with much difficulty, for the interpreter's stock of English was very scanty—but after awhile I understood, or thought I understood, as follows : — At some previous period of my existence I had done some deed which had given infinite satisfaction to Mahmoud al Ackbar. Whether, however, I had done it myself, or whether my father had done it, was not quite clear to me. My father, then some time deceased, had been a wharfinger at Liverpool, and it was quite possible that Mahmoud might have found himself at that port. Mahmoud had heard of my arrival in Egypt, and had been given to understand that I was coming to Suez—to carry myself away in the ship, as the interpreter phrased it. This I could not understand, but I let it pass. Having heard these agreeable tidings—and Mahmoud, sitting in the corner, bowed low to me as this was said—he had prepared for my acceptance a slight refection for the morrow, hoping that I would not carry myself away in the ship till this had been eaten. On this subject I soon made him quite at ease, and he then proceeded to explain that as there was a point of interest at Suez, Mahmoud was anxious that I should partake of the refection somewhat in the guise of a picnic, at the Well of Moses, over in Asia, on the other side of the head of the Red Sea. Mahmoud would provide a boat to take across the party in the morning, and camels on which we would return after sunset. Or else we would go and return on camels, or go on camels and return in the boat. Indeed any arrangement would be made that I preferred. If I was afraid of the heat, and disliked the open boat, I could be carried round in a litter. The provisions had already been sent over to the Well of Moses in the anticipation that I would not refuse this little request.

I did not refuse it. Nothing could have been more agreeable to me than this plan of seeing something of the sights and wonders of this land,—and of this seeing them in good company. I had not heard of the Well of Moses before, but now that I learned that it was in Asia,—in another quarter of the globe, to be reached by a transit of the Red Sea, to be returned from by a journey on camels' backs,— I burned with anxiety to visit its waters. What a story would this be for Judkins ! This was, no doubt, the point at which the Israelites had passed. Of those waters had they drunk. I almost felt that I had already found one of Pharaoh's chariot wheels. I readily gave my assent, and then, with much ceremony and many low salaams, Mahmoud and his attendant left me. " I am very glad that I came to Suez," said I to myself.

I did not sleep much that night, for the mosquitoes of Suez are very persevering ; but I was saved from the agonising despair which these animals so frequently produce, by my agreeable thoughts as to Mahmoud al Ackbar. I will put it to any of my readers who have travelled, whether it is not a painful thing to find one's-self regarded among strangers

L

without any kindness or ceremonious courtesy. I had on this account been wretched at Cairo, but all this was to be made up to me at Suez. Nothing could be more pleasant than the whole conduct of Mahmoud al Ackbar, and I determined to take full advantage of it, not caring overmuch what might be the nature of those previous favours to which he had alluded. That was his look-out, and if he was satisfied, why should not I be so also?

On the following morning I was dressed at six, and, looking out of my bed-room, I saw the boat in which we were to be wafted into Asia being brought up to the quay close under my window. It had been arranged that we should start early, so as to avoid the mid-day sun, breakfast in the boat,— Mahmoud in this way engaged to provide me with two refections,—take our rest at noon in a pavilion which had been built close upon the well of the patriarch, and then eat our dinner, and return riding upon camels in the cool of the evening. Nothing could sound more pleasant than such a plan ; and, knowing as I did that the hampers of provisions had already been sent over, I did not doubt that the table arrangements would be excellent. Even now, standing at my window, I could see a basket laden with long-necked bottles going into the boat, and became aware that we should not depend altogether for our morning repast on that gritty coffee which my friend Mahmoud's followers prepared.

I had promised to be ready at six, and having

carefully completed my toilet, and put a clean collar and comb into my pocket ready for dinner, I descended to the great gateway and walked slowly round to the quay. As I passed out, the porter greeted me with a low obeisance, and walking on, I felt that I stepped the ground with a sort of dignity of which I had before been ignorant. It is not, as a rule, the man who gives grace and honour to the position, but the position which confers the grace and honour upon the man. I have often envied the solemn gravity and grand demeanour of the Lord Chancellor, as I have seen him on the bench; but I almost think that even Judkins would look grave and dignified under such a wig. Mahmoud al Ackbar had called upon me and done me honour, and I felt myself personally capable of sustaining before the people of Suez the honour which he had done me.

As I walked forth with a proud step from beneath the portal, I perceived, looking down from the square along the street, that there was already some commotion in the town. I saw the flowing robes of many Arabs, with their backs turned towards me, and I thought that I observed the identical gown and turban of my friend Mahmoud on the back and head of a stout short man, who was hurrying round a corner in the distance. I felt sure that it was Mahmoud. Some of his servants had failed in their preparations, I said to myself, as I made my way round to the water's edge. This was only another testimony how anxious he was to do me honour.

I stood for awhile on the edge of the quay looking into the boat, and admiring the comfortable cushions which were luxuriously arranged around the seats. The men who were at work did not know me, and I was unnoticed, but I should soon take my place upon the softest of those cushions. I walked slowly backwards and forwards on the quay, listening to a hum of voices that came to me from a distance. There was clearly something stirring in the town, and I felt certain that all the movement and all those distant voices were connected in some way with my expedition to the Well of Moses. At last there came a lad upon the walk dressed in Frank costume, and I asked him what was in the wind. He was a clerk attached to an English warehouse, and he told me that there had been an arrival from Cairo. He knew no more than that, but he had heard that the omnibuses had just come in. Could it be possible that Mahmoud al Ackbar had heard of another old acquaintance, and had gone to welcome him also?

At first my ideas on the subject were altogether pleasant. I by no means wished to monopolise the delights of all those cushions, nor would it be to me a cause of sorrow that there should be some one to share with me the conversational powers of that interpreter. Should another guest be found, he might also be an Englishman, and I might thus form an acquaintance which would be desirable. Thinking of these things, I walked the quay for some minutes in a happy state of mind; but by

degrees I became impatient, and by degrees also
disturbed in my spirit. I observed that one of the
Arab boatmen walked round from the vessel to the
front of the hotel, and that on his return he looked
at me—as I thought, not with courteous eyes. Then
also I saw, or rather heard, some one in the verandah
of the hotel above me, and was conscious that I was
being viewed from thence. I walked and walked,
and nobody came to me, and I perceived by my
watch that it was seven o'clock. The noise, too, had
come nearer and nearer, and I was now aware that
wheels had been drawn up before the front door of
the hotel, and that many voices were speaking there.
It might be that Mahmoud should wait for some
other friend, but why did he not send some one to
inform me? And then, as I made a sudden turn at
the end of the quay, I caught sight of the retreating
legs of the Austrian interpreter, and I became aware
that he had been sent down, and had gone away,
afraid to speak to me. "What can I do?" said I
to myself, "I can but keep my ground." I own that
I feared to go round to the front of the hotel. So
I still walked slowly up and down the length of the
quay, and began to whistle to show that I was not
uneasy. The Arab sailors looked at me uncomfortably, and from time to time some one peered at me
round the corner. It was now fully half-past seven,
and the sun was becoming hot in the heavens. Why
did we not hasten to place ourselves beneath the
awning in that boat?

I had just made up my mind that I would go round to the front and penetrate this mystery, when, on turning, I saw approaching to me a man dressed at any rate like an English gentleman. As he came near to me, he raised his hat, and accosted me in our own language. "Mr. George Walker, I believe?" said he. "Yes," said I, with some little attempt at a high demeanour, "of the firm of Grimes, Walker, and Judkins, Friday Street, London."

"A most respectable house, I am sure," said he. "I'm afraid there has been a little mistake here."

"No mistake as to the respectability of that house," said I. I felt that I was again alone in the world, and that it was necessary that I should support myself. Mahmoud al Ackbar had separated himself from me for ever. Of that I had no longer a doubt.

"Oh, none at all," said he. "But about this little expedition over the water;" and he pointed contemptuously to the boat. "There has been a mistake about that, Mr. Walker; I happen to be the English Vice-Consul here."

I took off my hat and bowed. It was the first time I had ever been addressed civilly by any English consular authority.

"And they have made me get out of bed to come down here and explain all this to you."

"All what?" said I.

"You are a man of the world, I know, and I'll just tell it you plainly. My old friend, Mahmoud al

Ackbar, has mistaken you for Sir George Walker, the new Lieutenant-Governor of Pegu. Sir George Walker is here now; he has come this morning; and Mahmoud is ashamed to face you after what has occurred. If you won't object to withdraw with me into the hotel, I'll explain it all."

I felt as though a thunderbolt had fallen; and I must say, that even up to this day I think that the Consul might have been a little less abrupt. "We can get in here," said he, evidently in a hurry, and pointing to a small door which opened out from one corner of the house to the quay. What could I do but follow him? I did follow him, and in a few words learned the remainder of the story. When he had once withdrawn me from the public walk he seemed but little anxious about the rest, and soon left me again alone. The facts, as far as I could learn them, were simply these.

Sir George Walker, who was now going out to Pegu as Governor, had been in India before, commanding an army there. I had never heard of him before, and had made no attempt to pass myself off as his relative. Nobody could have been more innocent than I was—or have received worse usage. I have as much right to the name as he has. Well; when he was in India before, he had taken the city of Begum after a terrible siege—Begum, I think the Consul called it; and Mahmoud had been there, having been, it seems, a great man at Begum, and Sir George had spared him and his money; and in this

way the whole thing had come to pass. There was
no further explanation than that. The rest of it was
all transparent. Mahmoud, having heard my name
from the porter, had hurried down to invite me to his
party. So far so good. But why had he been afraid
to face me in the morning? And, seeing that the
fault had all been his, why had he not asked me
to join the expedition? Sir George and I may, after
all, be cousins. But, coward as he was, he had been
afraid of me. When they found that I was on the
quay, they had been afraid of me, not knowing how
to get rid of me. I wish that I had kept the quay
all day, and stared them down one by one as they
entered the boat. But I was down in the mouth, and
when the Consul left me, I crept wearily back to my
bed-room.

And the Consul did leave me almost immediately.
A faint hope had, at one time, come upon me that he
would have asked me to breakfast. Had he done so,
I should have felt it as a full compensation for all
that I had suffered. I am not an exacting man, but
I own that I like civility. In Friday Street I can
command it, and in Friday Street for the rest of my
life will I remain. From this Consul I received no
civility. As soon as he had got me out of the way
and spoken the few words which he had to say, he
again raised his hat and left me. I also again raised
mine, and then crept up to my bed-room.

From my window, standing a little behind the
white curtain, I could see the whole embarkation.

There was Mahmoud al Ackbar, looking indeed a little hot, but still going through his work with all that excellence of deportment which had graced him on the preceding evening. Had his foot slipped, and had he fallen backwards into that shallow water, my spirit would, I confess, have been relieved. But, on the contrary, everything went well with him. There was the real Sir George, my namesake and perhaps my cousin, as fresh as paint, cool from the bath which he had been taking while I had been walking on that terrace. How is it that these governors and commanders-in-chief ·go through such a deal of work without fagging? It was not yet two hours since he was jolting about in that omnibus-box, and there he had been all night. I could not have gone off to the Well of Moses immediately on my arrival. It's the dignity of the position that does it. I have long known that the head of a firm must never count on a mere clerk to get through as much work as he could do himself. It's the interest in the matter that supports the man.

There they went, and Sir George, as I was well assured, had never heard a word about me. Had he done so, is it not probable that he would have requested my attendance?

But Mahmoud and his followers no doubt kept their own counsel as to that little mistake. There they went, and the gentle rippling breeze filled their sail pleasantly, as the boat moved away into the bay. I felt no spite against any of them but Mahmoud.

Why had he avoided me with such cowardice? I could still see them when the morning tchibouk was handed to Sir George; and, though I wished him no harm, I did envy him as he lay there reclining luxuriously upon the cushions.

A more wretched day than that, I never spent in my life. As I went in and out, the porter at the gate absolutely scoffed at me. Once I made up my mind to complain within the house. But what could I have said of the dirty Arab? They would have told me that it was his religion, or a national observance, or meant for a courtesy. What can a man do, in a strange country, when he is told that a native spits in his face by way of civility? I bore it, I bore it—like a man; and sighed for the comforts of Friday Street.

As to one matter, I made up my mind on that day, and I fully carried out my purpose on the next: I would go across to the Well of Moses in a boat. I would visit the coasts of Asia. And I would ride back into Africa on a camel. Though I did it alone, I would have my day's pleasuring. I had money in my pocket, and, though it might cost me £20, I would see all that my namesake had seen. It did cost me the best part of £20; and as for the pleasuring, I cannot say much for it.

I went to bed early that night, having concluded my bargain for the morrow with a rapacious Arab who spoke English. I went to bed early in order to escape the returning party, and was again on the

quay at six the next morning. On this occasion, I
stepped boldly into the boat the very moment that I
came along the shore. There is nothing in the world
like paying for what you use. I saw myself to the
bottle of brandy and the cold meat, and acknowledged
that a cigar out of my case would suit me better than
that long stick. The long stick might do very well
for a Governor of Pegu, but would be highly inconvenient in Friday Street.

Well, I am not going to give an account of my
day's journey here, though perhaps I may do so
some day. I did go to the Well of Moses—if
a small dirty pool of salt water, lying high above
the sands, can be called a well; I did eat my
dinner in the miserable ruined cottage which they
graced by the name of a pavilion; and, alas for
my poor bones! I did ride home upon a camel.
If Sir George did so early, and started for Pegu
the next morning—and I was informed such was
the fact—he must have been made of iron. I
laid in bed the whole day suffering grievously;
but I was told that on such a journey I should
have slakened my throat with oranges, and not
with brandy.

I survived those four terrible days which remained
to me at Suez, and after another month was once
again in Friday Street. I suffered greatly on the
occasion; but it is some consolation to me to reflect
that I smoked a pipe of peace with Mahmoud al
Ackbar; that I saw the hero of Begum while

journeying out to new triumphs at Pegu ; that I sailed into Asia in my own yacht—hired for the occasion ; and that I rode back into Africa on a camel. Nor can Judkins, with all his ill-nature, rob me of these remembrances.

THE MISTLETOE BOUGH.

"LET the boys have it if they like it," said Mrs. Garrow, pleading to her only daughter on behalf of her two sons.

"Pray don't, mamma," said Elizabeth Garrow. "It only means romping. To me all that is detestable, and I am sure it is not the sort of thing that Miss Holmes would like."

"We always had it at Christmas when we were young."

"But, mamma, the world is so changed."

The point in dispute was one very delicate in its nature, hardly to be discussed in all its bearings, even in fiction, and the very mention of which between a mother and daughter showed a great amount of close confidence between them. It was no less than this. Should that branch of mistletoe which Frank Garrow had brought home with him out of the Lowther woods be hung up on Christmas Eve in the dining-room at Thwaite Hall, according to his wishes; or should permission for such hanging be positively refused? It was clearly a thing not to be done after such a discussion, and therefore the decision given by Mrs. Garrow was against it.

I am inclined to think that Miss Garrow was right in saying that the world is changed as touching mistletoe boughs. Kissing, I fear, is less innocent now than it used to be when our grandmothers were alive, and we have become more fastidious in our amusements. Nevertheless, I think that she made herself fairly open to the raillery with which her brothers attacked her.

"Honi soit qui mal y pense," said Frank, who was eighteen.

"Nobody will want to kiss you, my lady Fineairs," said Harry, who was just a year younger.

"Because you choose to be a Puritan, there are to be no more cakes and ale in the house," said Frank.

"Still waters run deep; we all know that," said Harry.

The boys had not been present when the matter was decided between Mrs. Garrow and her daughter, nor had the mother been present when these little amenities had passed between the brothers and sister.

"Only that mamma has said it, and I wouldn't seem to go against her," said Frank, "I'd ask my father. He wouldn't give way to such nonsense, I know."

Elizabeth turned away without answering, and left the room. Her eyes were full of tears, but she would not let them see that they had vexed her. They were only two days home from school, and for the

last week before their coming, all her thoughts had
been to prepare for their Christmas pleasures. She
had arranged their rooms, making everything warm
and pretty. Out of her own pocket she had bought
a shot-belt for one, and skates for the other. She
had told the old groom that her pony was to belong
exclusively to Master Harry for the holidays, and
now Harry told her that still waters ran deep. She
had been driven to the use of all her eloquence in
inducing her father to purchase that gun for Frank,
and now Frank called her a Puritan. And why?
She did not choose that a mistletoe bough should be
hung in her father's hall, when Godfrey Holmes was
coming to visit him. She could not explain this to
Frank, but Frank might have had the wit to understand it. But Frank was thinking only of Patty
Coverdale, a blue-eyed little romp of sixteen, who,
with her sister Kate, was coming from Penrith to
spend the Christmas at Thwaite Hall. Elizabeth
left the room with her slow, graceful step, hiding her
tears,—hiding all emotion, as latterly she had taught
herself that it was feminine to do. "There goes my
lady Fineairs," said Harry, sending his shrill voice
after her.

Thwaite Hall was not a place of much pretension.
It was a moderate-sized house, surrounded by pretty
gardens and shrubberies, close down upon the river
Eamont, on the Westmoreland side of the river, look-
ing over to a lovely wooded bank in Cumberland.
All the world knows that the Eamont runs out of

Ulleswater, dividing the two counties, passing under
Penrith Bridge and by the old ruins of Brougham
Castle, below which it joins the Eden. Thwaite
Hall nestled down close upon the clear rocky stream
about half way between Ulleswater and Penrith, and
had been built just at a bend of the river. The
windows of the dining-parlour and of the drawing-
room stood at right angles to each other, and yet
each commanded a reach of the stream. Immediately
from a side door of the house steps were cut down
through the red rock to the water's edge, and here a
small boat was always moored to a chain. The chain
was stretched across the river, fixed to the staples
driven into the rock on either side, and the boat was
pulled backwards and forwards over the stream without aid from oars or paddles. From the opposite side
a path led through the woods and across the fields to
Penrith, and this was the route commonly used
between Thwaite Hall and the town.

Major Garrow was a retired officer of Engineers, who
had seen service in all parts of the world, and who
was now spending the evening of his days on a small
property which had come to him from his father.
He held in his own hands about twenty acres of land,
and he was the owner of one small farm close by,
which was let to a tenant. That, together with his
half-pay, and the interest of his wife's thousand
pounds, sufficed to educate his children and keep
the wolf at a comfortable distance from his door.
He himself was a spare thin man, with quiet, lazy,

literary habits.   He had done the work of life, but had
so done it as to permit of his enjoying that which
was left to him.   His sole remaining care was the
establishment of his children ; and, as far as he could
see, he had no ground for anticipating disappointment.   They were clever, good-looking, well-disposed
young people, and upon the whole it may be said
that the sun shone brightly on Thwaite Hall.   Of
Mrs. Garrow it may suffice to say that she always
deserved such sunshine.

For years past it had been the practice of the
family to have some sort of gathering at Thwaite
Hall during Christmas.   Godfrey Holmes had been
left under the guardianship of Major Garrow, and, as
he had always spent his Christmas holidays with his
guardian, this, perhaps, had given rise to the practice.
Then the Coverdales were cousins of the Garrows,
and they had usually been there as children.   At
the Christmas last past the custom had been broken,
for young Holmes had been abroad.   Previous to
that, they had all been children, excepting him.   But
now that they were to meet again, they were no
longer children.   Elizabeth, at any rate, was not so,
for she had already counted nineteen winters.   And
Isabella Holmes was coming.   Now Isabella was two
years older than Elizabeth, and had been educated in
Brussels ; moreover she was comparatively a stranger
at Thwaite Hall, never having been at those early
Christmas meetings.

And now I must take permission to begin my

story by telling a lady's secret. Elizabeth Garrow had already been in love with Godfrey Holmes, or perhaps it might be more becoming to say that Godfrey Holmes had already been in love with her. They had already been engaged ; and, alas ! they had already agreed that that engagement should be broken off !

Young Holmes was now twenty-seven years of age, and was employed in a bank at Liverpool, not as a clerk, but as assistant manager, with a large salary. He was a man well to do in the world, who had money also of his own, and who might well afford to marry. Some two years since, on the eve of leaving Thwaite Hall, he had with low doubting whisper told Elizabeth that he loved her, and she had flown trembling to her mother. "Godfrey, my boy," the father said to him, as he parted with him the. next morning, " Bessy is only a child, and too young to think of this yet." At the next Christmas Godfrey was in Italy, and the thing was gone by,—so at least the father and mother said to each other. But the young people had met in the summer, and one joyful letter had come from the girl home to her mother. " I have accepted him. Dearest, dearest mamma, I do love him. But don't tell papa yet, for I have not quite accepted him. I think I am sure, but I am not quite sure. I am not quite sure about him."

And then, two days after that, there had come a letter that was not at all joyful. " Dearest Mamma,— It is not to be. It is not written in the book. We have both agreed that it will not do. I am so glad that you have not told dear papa, for I could never make him understand. You will understand, for I shall tell you everything, down to his very words. But we have agreed that there shall be no quarrel. It shall be exactly as it was, and he will come at Christmas all the same. It would never do that he and papa should be separated, nor could we now put off Isabella. It is better so in every way, for there is and need be no quarrel. We still like each other. I am sure I like him, but I know that I should not make him happy as his wife. He says it is my fault. I, at any rate, have never told him that I thought it his." From all which it will be seen that the confidence between the mother and daughter was very close.

Elizabeth Garrow was a very good girl, but it might almost be a question whether she was not too good. She had learned, or thought that she had learned, that most girls are vapid, silly, and useless,—given chiefly to pleasure-seeking and a hankering after lovers ; and she had resolved that she would not be such a one. Industry, self-denial, and a religious purpose in life, were the tasks which she set herself ; and she went about the performance of them with much courage. But such tasks, though they are excellently well adapted to fit a young lady for the work of living, may also be carried too far, and thus have the effect of unfitting her for that work. When Elizabeth Garrow made up her mind that the finding of a husband was not the only purpose of life, she did very well. It is very well that a young lady should feel herself capable of going through the world happily without one. But in teaching herself this she also taught herself to think that there was a certain merit in refusing herself the natural delight of a lover, even though the possession of the lover were compatible with all her duties to herself, her father and mother, and the world at large. It was not that she had determined to have no lover. She made no such resolve, and when the proper lover came he was admitted to her heart. But she declared to herself unconsciously that she must put a guard upon herself, lest she should be betrayed into weakness by her own happiness. She had resolved that in loving her lord she would not worship him, and that in giving her heart she would only so give it as it should be given to a human creature like herself. She had acted on these high resolves, and hence it had come to pass,—not unnaturally,—that Mr. Godfrey Holmes had told her that it was " her fault."

She was a pretty, fair girl, with soft dark-brown hair, and soft long dark eyelashes. Her grey eyes, though quiet in their tone, were tender and lustrous. Her face was oval, and the lines of her cheek and chin perfect in their symmetry. She was generally quiet in her demeanour, but when moved she could rouse herself to great energy, and speak with feeling and almost with fire. Her fault was a reverence for martyrdom in general, and a feeling, of which she

was unconscious, that it became a young woman to be
unhappy in secret ;—that it became a young woman
I might rather say, to have a source of unhappiness
hidden from the world in general, and endured without any detriment to her outward cheerfulness. We
know the story of the Spartan boy who held the fox
under his tunic. The fox was biting into him,—into
the very entrails ; but the young hero spake never a
word. Now Bessy Garrow was inclined to think that
it was a good thing to have a fox always biting, so
that the torment caused no ruffling to her outward
smiles. Now at this moment the fox within her
bosom was biting her sore enough, but she bore it
without flinching.

"If you would rather that he should not come I
will have it arranged," her mother had said to her.

"Not for worlds," she had answered. "I should
never think well of myself again."

Her mother had changed her own mind more than
once as to the conduct in this matter which might be
best for her to follow, thinking solely of her daughter's welfare. "If he comes they will be reconciled,
and she will be happy," had been her first idea. But
then there was a stern fixedness of purpose in
Bessy's words when she spoke of Mr. Holmes,
which had expelled this hope, and Mrs. Garrow had
for awhile thought it better that the young man
should not come. But Bessy would not permit this.
It would vex her father, put out of course the arrangements of other people, and display weakness on her

own part. He should come, and she would endure without flinching while the fox gnawed at her.

That battle of the mistletoe had been fought on the morning before Christmas-day, and the Holmes's came on Christmas-eve. Isabella was comparatively a stranger, and therefore received at first the greater share of attention. She and Elizabeth had once seen each other, and for the last year or two had corresponded, but personally they had never been intimate. Unfortunately for the latter, that story of Godfrey's offer and acceptance had been communicated to Isabella, as had of course the immediately subsequent story of their separation. But now it would be almost impossible to avoid the subject in conversation. "Dearest Isabella, let it be as though it had never been," she had said in one of her letters. But sometimes it is very difficult to let things be as though they had never been.

The first evening passed over very well. The two Coverdale girls were there, and there had been much talking and merry laughter, rather juvenile in its nature, but on the whole none the worse for that. Isabella Holmes was a fine, tall, handsome girl ; good-humoured, and well disposed to be pleased ; rather Frenchified in her manners, and quite able to take care of herself. But she was not above round games, and did not turn up her nose at the boys. Godfrey behaved himself excellently, talking much to the Major, but by no means avoiding Miss Garrow. Mrs. Garrow, though she had known him since he was a

boy, had taken an aversion to him since he had quarrelled with her daughter; but there was no room on
this first night for showing such aversion, and everything went off well.

"Godfrey is very much improved," the Major said
to his wife that night.

"Do you think so?"

"Indeed I do. He has filled out and become a
fine man."

"In personal appearance, you mean. Yes, he is
well-looking enough."

"And in his manner too. He is doing uncommonly
well in Liverpool, I can tell you; and if he should
think of Bessy—"

"There is nothing of that sort," said Mrs. Garrow.

"He did speak to me, you know,—two years ago.
Bessy was too young then, and so indeed was he.
But if she likes him—"

"I don't think she does."

"Then there's an end of it." And so they went to
bed.

"Frank," said the sister to her elder brother,
knocking at his door when they had all gone up stairs,
"may I come in,—if you are not in bed?"

"In bed," said he, looking up with some little pride
from his Greek book; "I've one hundred and fifty
lines to do before I can get to bed. It'll be two, I
suppose. I've got to mug uncommon hard these
holidays. I have only one more half, you know, and
then—"

" Don't overdo it, Frank."

" No ; I won't overdo it. I mean to take one
day a week, and work eight hours a day on the other
five. That will be forty hours a week, and will give
me just two hundred hours for the holidays. I have
got it all down here on a table. That will be a hundred
and five for Greek play, forty for Algebra—" and so
he explained to her the exact destiny of all his long
hours of proposed labour. He had as yet been home
a day and a half, and had succeeded in drawing out
with red lines and blue figures the table which he
showed her. " If I can do that, it will be pretty well ;
won't it ? "

" But, Frank, you have come home for your holidays,—to enjoy yourself ? "

" But a fellow must work now-a-days."

" Don't overdo it, dear ; that's all. But, Frank, I
could not rest if I went to bed without speaking to
you. You made me unhappy to-day."

" Did I, Bessy ? "

" You called me a Puritan, and then you quoted
that ill-natured French proverb at me. Do you
really believe your sister thinks evil, Frank ? " and as
she spoke she put her arm caressingly round his neck.

" Of course I don't."

" Then why say so ? Harry is so much younger
and so thoughtless that I can bear what he says without so much suffering. But if you and I are not
friends I shall be very wretched. If you knew how I
have looked forward to your coming home ! "

"I did not mean to vex you, and I won't say such things again."

"That's my own Frank. What I said to mamma, I said because I thought it right; but you must not say that I am a Puritan. I would do anything in my power to make your holidays bright and pleasant. I know that boys require so much more to amuse them than girls do. Good night, dearest; pray don't over-do yourself with work, and do take care of your eyes." So saying she kissed him and went her way In twenty minutes after that, he had gone to sleep over his book; and when he woke up to find the candle guttering down, he resolved that he would not begin his measured hours till Christmas-day was fairly over.

The morning of Christmas-day passed very quietly. They all went to church, and then sat round the fire chatting until the four-o'clock dinner was ready. The Coverdale girls thought it was rather more dull than former Thwaite Hall festivities, and Frank was seen to yawn. But then everybody knows that the real fun of Christmas never begins till the day itself be passed. The beef and pudding are ponderous, and unless there be absolute children in the party, there is a difficulty in grafting any special afternoon amusements on the Sunday pursuits of the morning, In the evening they were to have a dance;—that had been distinctly promised to Patty Coverdale; but the dance would not commence till eight. The beef and pudding were ponderous, but with due efforts they were overcome and disappeared. The glass of port was sipped, the almonds and raisins were nibbled, and then the ladies left the room. Ten minutes after that Elizabeth found herself seated with Isabella Holmes over the fire in her father's little book-room. It was not by her that this meeting was arranged, for she dreaded such a constrained confidence; but of course it could not be avoided, and perhaps it might be as well now as hereafter.

"Bessy," said the elder girl, "I am dying to be alone with you for a moment."

"Well, you shall not die; that is, if being alone with me will save you."

"I have so much to say to you. And if you have any true friendship in you, you also will have so much to say to me." Miss Garrow perhaps had no true friendship in her at that moment, for she would gladly have avoided saying anything, had that been possible. But, in order to prove that she was not deficient in friendship, she gave her friend her hand.

"And now tell me everything about Godfrey," said Isabella.

"Dear Bella, I have nothing to tell;—literally nothing."

"That is nonsense. Stop a moment, dear, and understand that I do not mean to offend you. It cannot be that you have nothing to tell, if you choose to tell it. You are not the girl to have accepted Godfrey without loving him, nor is he the man to have asked you without loving you. When you write me word that you have changed your mind, as you might about a dress, of course I know you have not told me all. Now I insist upon knowing it,—that is, if we are to be friends. I would not speak a word to Godfrey till I had seen you, in order that I might hear your story first."

"Indeed, Bella, there is no story to tell."

"Then I must ask him."

"If you wish to play the part of a true friend to me, you will let the matter pass by and say nothing. You must understand that, circumstanced as we are, your brother's visit here,—what I mean is, that it is very difficult for me to act and speak exactly as I should do, and a few unfortunate words spoken may make my position unendurable."

"Will you answer me one question?"

"I cannot tell. I think I will."

"Do you love him?" For a moment or two Bessy remained silent, striving to arrange her words so that they should contain no falsehood, and yet betray no truth. "Ah, I see you do," continued Miss Holmes. "But of course you do. Why else did you accept him?"

"I fancied that I did, as young ladies do sometimes fancy."

"And will you say that you do not, now?" Again Bessy was silent, and then her friend rose from her seat. "I see it all," she said. "What a pity it was that you both had not some friend like me by you at the time! But perhaps it may not be too late."

I need not repeat at length all the protestations
which upon this were poured forth with hot energy
by poor Bessy. She endeavoured to explain how
great had been the difficulty of her position. This
Christmas visit had been arranged before that unhappy affair at Liverpool had occurred. Isabella's
visit had been partly one of business, it being necessary that certain money affairs should be arranged
between her, her brother, and the Major. "I determined," said Bessy, "not to let my feelings stand in
the way ; and hoped that things might settle down
to their former friendly footing. I already fear that
I have been wrong, but it will be ungenerous in you
to punish me." Then she went on to say that if anybody attempted to interfere with her, she should at
once go away to her mother's sister, who lived at
Hexham, in Northumberland.

Then came the dance, and the hearts of Kate and
Patty Coverdale were at last happy. But here again
poor Bessy was made to understand how terribly
difficult was this experiment of entertaining on a
footing of friendship a lover with whom she had
quarrelled only a month or two before. That she must
as a necessity become the partner of Godfrey Holmes
she had already calculated, and so much she was prepared to endure. Her brothers would of course dance
with the Coverdale girls, and her father would of
course stand up with Isabella. There was no other
posssible arrangement, at any rate as a beginning.
She had schooled herself too as to the way in which

she would speak to him on the occasion, and how she would remain mistress of herself and of her thoughts. But when the time came the difficulty was almost too much for her.

"You do not care much for dancing, if I remember?" said he.

"Oh yes, I do. Not as Patty Coverdale does. It's a passion with her. But then I am older than Patty Coverdale." After that he was silent for a minute or two.

"It seems so odd to me to be here again," he said. It was odd;—she felt that it was odd. But he ought not to have said so.

"Two years make a great difference. The boys have grown so much."

"Yes, and there are other things," said he.

"Bella was never here before ; at least not with you."

"No. But I did not exactly mean that. All that would not make the place so strange. But your mother seems altered to me. She used to be almost like my own mother."

"I suppose she finds that you are a more formidable person as you grow older. It was all very well scolding you when you were a clerk in the bank, but it does not do to scold the manager. These are the penalties men pay for becoming great."

"It is not my greatness that stands in my way, but—"

"Then I'm sure I cannot say what it is. But

Patty will scold you if you do not mind the figure, though you were the whole Board of Directors packed into one. She won't respect you if you neglect your present work."

When Bessy went to bed that night she began to feel that she had attempted too much. "Mamma," she said, "could I not make some excuse and go away to Aunt Mary?"

"What, now?"

"Yes, mamma; now; to-morrow. I need not say that it will make me very unhappy to be away at such a time, but I begin to think that it will be better."

"What will papa say?"

"You must tell him all."

"And Aunt Mary must be told also. You would not like that. Has he said anything?"

"No, nothing;—very little, that is. But Bella has spoken to me. Oh, mamma, I think we have been very wrong in this. That is, I have been wrong. I feel as though I should disgrace myself, and turn the whole party here into a misfortune."

It would be dreadful, that telling of the story to her father and to her aunt, and such a necessity must, if possible, be avoided. Should such a necessity actually come, the former task would, no doubt, be done by her mother, but that would not lighten the load materially. After a fortnight she would again meet her father, and would be forced to discuss it. "I will remain if it be possible," she

said ; "but, mamma, if I wish to go, you will not
stop me ?." Her mother promised that she would
not stop her, but strongly advised her to stand her
ground.

On the following morning, when she came down
stairs before breakfast, she found Frank standing in
the hall with his gun of which he was trying the
lock. "It is not loaded, is it, Frank ? " said she.

"Oh dear, no ; no one thinks of loading now-a-
days till he has got out of the house. Directly after
breakfast I am going across with Godfrey to the
back of Greystock, to see after some moor-fowl. He
asked me to go, and I couldn't well refuse."

"Of course not. Why should you ? "

"It will be deuced hard work to make up the
time. I was to have been up at four this morning,
but that alarum went off and never woke me. However, I shall be able to do something to-night."

"Don't make a slavery of your holidays, Frank.
What's the good of having a new gun if you're not
to use it ? "

"It's not the new gun. I'm not such a child as
that comes to. But, you see, Godfrey is here, and
one ought to be civil to him. I'll tell you what I
want you girls to do, Bessy. You must come and
meet us on our way home. Come over in the boat
and along the path to the Patterdale road. We'll
be there under the hill at about five."

"And if you are not, we are to wait in the
snow ? "

"Don't make difficulties, Bessy. I tell you we will be there. We are to go in the cart, and so shall have plenty of time."

"And how do you know the other girls will go ?"

"Why, to tell you the truth, Patty Coverdale has promised. As for Miss Holmes, if she won't, why you must leave her at home with mamma. But Kate and Patty can't come without you."

"Your discretion has found that out, has it ?"

"They say so. But you will come; won't you Bessy? As for waiting, it's all nonsense. Of course you can walk on. But we'll be at the stile by five. I've got my watch, you know." And then Bessy promised him. What would she not have done for him that was in her power to do ?

"Go ! Of course I'll go," said Miss Holmes. "I'm up to anything. I'd have gone with them this morning, and have taken a gun if they'd asked me. But, by the bye, I'd better not."

"Why not ?" said Patty, who was hardly yet without fear lest something should mar the expedition.

"What will three gentlemen do with four ladies ?"

"Oh, I forgot," said Patty innocently.

"I'm sure I don't care," said Kate; "you may have Harry if you like."

"Thank you for nothing," said Miss Holmes. "I want one for myself. It's all very well for you to make the offer, but what should I do if Harry wouldn't have me ? There are two sides, you know, to every bargain."

"I'm sure he isn't anything to me," said Kate. "Why, he's not quite seventeen years old yet!"

"Poor boy! What a shame to dispose of him so soon. We'll let him off for a year or two; won't we, Miss Coverdale? But as there seems by acknowledgment to be one beau with unappropriated services—"

"I'm sure I have appropriated nobody," said Patty, "and didn't intend."

"Godfrey, then, is the only knight whose services are claimed," said Miss Holmes, looking at Bessy. Bessy made no immediate answer with either her eyes or tongue; but when the Coverdales were gone, she took her new friend to task.

"How can you fill those young girls' heads with such nonsense?"

"Nature has done that, my dear."

"But nature should be trained; should it not? You will make them think that those foolish boys are in love with them."

"The foolish boys, as you call them, will look after that themselves. It seems to me that the foolish boys know what they are about better than some of their elders." And then, after a moment's pause, she added, "As for my brother, I have no patience with him."

"Pray do not discuss your brother," said Bessy. "And, Bella, unless you wish to drive me away, pray do not speak of him and me together as you did just now."

N

" Are you so bad as that,—that the slightest commonplace joke upsets you ? Would not his services be due to you as a matter of course ? If you are so sore about it, you will betray your own secret."

"I have no secret,—none at least from you, or from mamma ; and, indeed, none from him. We were both very foolish, thinking that we knew each other and our own hearts, when we knew neither."

"I hate to hear people talk of knowing their hearts. My idea is, that if you like a young man, and he asks you to marry him, you ought to have him. That is, if there is enough to live on. I don't know what more is wanted. But girls are getting to talk and think as though they were to send their hearts through some fiery furnace of trial before they may give them up to a husband's keeping. I'm not at all sure that the French fashion is not the best, and that these things shouldn't be managed by the fathers and mothers, or perhaps by the family lawyers. Girls who are so intent upon knowing their own hearts generally end by knowing nobody's heart but their own ; and then they die old maids."

" Better that than give themselves to the keeping of those they don't know and cannot esteem."

"That's a matter of taste. I mean to take the first that comes, so long as he looks like a gentleman, and has not less than eight hundred a year. Now Godfrey does look like a gentleman, and has double that. If I had such a chance I shouldn't think twice about it."

"But I have no such chance. And if you have not, you would not think of it at all. That's the way the wind blows; is it?"

"No, no. Oh, Bella, pray, pray leave me alone. Pray do not interfere. There is no wind blowing in any way. All that I want is your silence and your sympathy."

"Very well. I will be silent and sympathetic as the grave. Only don't imagine that I am cold as the grave also. I don't exactly appreciate your ideas; but if I can do no good, I will at any rate endeavour to do no harm."

After lunch, at about three, they started on their walk, and managed to ferry themselves over the river. "Oh, do let me, Bessy," said Kate Coverdale. "I understand all about it. Look here, Miss Holmes. You pull the chain through your hands—"

"And inevitably tear your gloves to pieces," said Miss Holmes. Kate certainly had done so, and did not seem to be particularly well pleased with the accident. "There's a nasty nail in the chain," she said. "I wonder those stupid boys did not tell us."

Of course they reached the trysting-place much too soon, and were very tired of walking up and down to keep their feet warm, before the sportsmen came up. But this was their own fault, seeing that they had reached the stile half an hour before the time fixed.

"I never will go anywhere to meet gentlemen again," said Miss Holmes. "It is most preposterous that ladies should be left in the snow for an hour. Well, young men, what sport have you had?"

"I shot the big black cock," said Harry.

"Did you indeed?" said Kate Coverdale.

"And here are the feathers out of his tail for you. He dropped them in the water, and I had to go in after them up to my middle. But I told you that I would, so I was determined to get them."

"Oh you silly, silly boy," said Kate. "But I'll keep them for ever. I will indeed." This was said a little apart, for Harry had managed to draw the young lady aside before he presented the feathers.

Frank had also his trophies for Patty, and the tale to tell of his own prowess. In that he was a year older than his brother, he was by a year's growth less ready to tender his present to his lady-love, openly in the presence of them all. But he found his opportunity, and then he and Patty went on a little in advance. Kate also was deep in her consolations to Harry for his ducking; and therefore the four disposed of themselves in the manner previously suggested by Miss Holmes. Miss Holmes, therefore, and her brother, and Bessy Garrow, were left together in the path, and discussed the performances of the day in a manner that elicited no very ecstatic interest. So they walked for a mile, and by degrees the conversation between them dwindled down almost to nothing.

"There is nothing I dislike so much as coming out with people younger than myself," said Miss Holmes. "One always feels so old and dull. Listen to those children there; they make me feel as though I were an old maiden aunt, brought out with them to do propriety."

"Patty won't at all approve if she hears you call her a child."

"Nor shall I approve, if she treats me like an old woman," and then she stepped on and joined the children. "I wouldn't spoil even their sport if I could help it," she said to herself. "But with them I shall only be a temporary nuisance; if I remain behind I shall become a permanent evil." And thus Bessy and her old lover were left by themselves.

"I hope you will get on well with Bella," said Godfrey, when they had remained silent for a minute or two.

"Oh, yes. She is so good-natured and light-spirited that everybody must like her. She has been used to so much amusement and active life, that I know she must find it very dull here."

"She is never dull anywhere,—even at Liverpool, which, for a young lady, I sometimes think the dullest place on earth. I know it is for a man."

"A man who has work to do can never be dull; can he?"

"Indeed he can; as dull as death. I am so often enough. I have never been very bright there, Bessy, since you left us." There was nothing in his calling her Bessy, for it had become a habit with him since they were children; and they had formerly agreed that everything between them should be as it had been before that foolish whisper of love had been spoken and received. Indeed, provision had been made by them specially on this point, so that there need be no awkwardness in this mode of addressing each other. Such provision had seemed to be very prudent, but it hardly had the desired effect on the present occasion.

"I hardly know what you mean by brightness," she said, after a pause. "Perhaps it is not intended that people's lives should be what you call bright."

"Life ought to be as bright as we can make it."

"It all depends on the meaning of the word. I suppose we are not very bright here at Thwaite Hall, but yet we think ourselves very happy."

"I am sure you are," said Godfrey. "I very often think of you here."

"We always think of places where we have been when we were young," said Bessy; and then again they walked on for some way in silence, and Bessy began to increase her pace with the view of catching the children. The present walk to her was anything but bright, and she bethought herself with dismay that there were still two miles before she reached the Ferry.

"Bessy," Godfrey said at last. And then he

stopped as though he were doubtful how to proceed. She, however, did not say a word, but walked on quickly, as though her only hope was in catching the party before her. But they also were walking quickly, for Bella had determined that she would not be caught.

"Bessy, I must speak to you once of what passed between us at Liverpool."

"Must you?" said she.

"Unless you positively forbid it."

"Stop, Godfrey," she said. And they did stop in the path, for now she no longer thought of putting an end to her embarrassment by overtaking her companions. "If any such words are necessary for your comfort, it would hardly become me to forbid them. Were I to speak so harshly you would accuse me afterwards in your own heart. It must be for you to judge whether it is well to re-open a wound that is nearly healed."

"But with me it is not nearly healed. The wound is open always."

"There are some hurts," she said, "which do not admit of an absolute and perfect cure, unless after long years." As she said so, she could not but think how much better was his chance of such perfect cure than her own. With her,—so she said to herself,— such curing was all but impossible; whereas with him, it was as impossible that the injury should last.

"Bessy," he said, and he again stopped her on the

narrow path, standing immediately before her on the way, "you remember all the circumstances that made us part?"

"Yes; I think I remember them."

"And you still think that we were right to part?"

She paused for a moment before she answered him; but it was only for a moment, and then she spoke quite firmly. "Yes, Godfrey, I do; I have thought about it much since then. I have thought, I fear, to no good purpose about aught else. But I have never thought that we had been unwise in that."

"And yet I think you loved me."

"I am bound to confess I did so, as otherwise I must confess myself a liar. I told you at the time that I loved you, and I told you so truly. But it is better, ten times better, that those who love should part, even though they still should love, than that two should be joined together who are incapable of making each other happy. Remember what you told me."

"I do remember."

"You found yourself unhappy in your engagement, and you said it was my fault."

"Bessy, there is my hand. If you have ceased to love me, there is an end of it. But if you love me still, let all that be forgotten."

"Forgotten, Godfrey! How can it be forgotten? You were unhappy, and it was my fault. My fault, as it would be if I tried to solace a sick child with arithmetic, or feed a dog with grass. I had no right to love you, knowing you as I did; and knowing also that my ways would not be your ways. My punishment I understand, and it is not more than I can bear; but I had hoped that your punishment would have been soon over."

"You are too proud, Bessy."

"That is very likely. Frank says that I am a Puritan, and pride was the worst of their sins."

"Too proud and unbending. In marriage should not the man and woman adapt themselves to each other?"

"When they are married, yes. And every girl who thinks of marrying should know that in very much she must adapt herself to her husband. But I do not think that a woman should be the ivy, to take the direction of every branch of the tree to which she clings. If she does so, what can be her own character? But we must go on, or we shall be too late."

"And you will give me no other answer?"

"None other, Godfrey. Have you not just now, at this very moment, told me that I was too proud? Can it be possible that you should wish to tie yourself for life to female pride? And if you tell me that now, at such a moment as this, what would you tell me in the close intimacy of married life, when the trifles of every day would have worn away the courtesies of guest and lover?"

There was a sharpness of rebuke in this which

Godfrey Holmes could not at the moment overcome. Nevertheless he knew the girl, and understood the workings of her heart and mind. Now, in her present state, she could be unbending, proud, and almost rough. In that she had much to lose in declining the renewed offer which he made her, she would, as it were, continually prompt herself to be harsh and inflexible. Had he been poor, had she not loved him, had not all good things seemed to have attended the promise of such a marriage, she would have been less suspicious of herself in receiving the offer, and more gracious in replying to it. Had he lost all his money before he came back to her, she would have taken him at once; or had he been deprived of an eye, or become crippled in his legs, she would have done so. But, circumstanced as he was, she had no motive to tenderness. There was an organic defect in her character, which no doubt was plainly marked by its own bump in her cranium,—the bump of philomartyrdom, it might properly be called. She had shipwrecked her own happiness in rejecting Godfrey Holmes; but it seemed to her to be the proper thing that a well-behaved young lady should shipwreck her own happiness. For the last month or two she had been tossed about by the waters and was nearly drowned. Now there was beautiful land again close to her, and a strong pleasant hand stretched out to save her. But though she had suffered terribly among the waves, she still thought it wrong to be saved. It would be so pleasant to take that hand, so sweet, so joyous, that it surely must be wrong. That was her doctrine; and Godfrey Holmes, though he hardly analyzed the matter, partly understood that it was so. And yet, if once she were landed on that green island, she would be so happy. She spoke with scorn of a woman clinging to a tree like ivy ; and yet, were she once married, no woman would cling to her husband with sweeter feminine tenacity than Bessy Garrow. He spoke no further word to her as he walked home, but in handing her down to the ferry-boat he pressed her hand. For a second it seemed as though she had returned this pressure. If so, the action was involuntary, and her hand instantly resumed its stiffness to his touch.

It was late that night when Major Garrow went to his bed-room, but his wife was still up, waiting for him. "Well," said she, "what has he said to you ? He has been with you above an hour."

"Such stories are not very quickly told ; and in this case it was necessary to understand him very accurately. At length I think I do understand him."

It is not necessary to repeat at length all that was said on that night between Major and Mrs. Garrow, as to the offer which had now for a third time been made to their daughter. On that evening after the ladies had gone, and when the two boys had taken themselves off, Godfrey Holmes told his tale to his host, and had honestly explained to him what he believed to be the state of his daughter's feelings. "Now you know all," said he. "I do believe that she loves me, and if she does, perhaps she may still listen to you." Major Garrow did not feel sure that he "knew it all." But when he had fully discussed the matter that night with his wife, then he thought that perhaps he had arrived at that knowledge.

On the following morning Bessy learned from the maid, at an early hour, that Godfrey Holmes had left Thwaite Hall and gone back to Liverpool. To the girl she said nothing on the subject, but she felt obliged to say a word or two to Bella. "It is his coming that I regret," she said;—"that he should have had the trouble and annoyance for nothing. I acknowledge that it was my fault, and I am very sorry."

"It cannot be helped," said Miss Holmes, somewhat gravely. "As to his misfortunes, I presume that his journeys between here and Liverpool are not the worst of them."

After breakfast on that day Bessy was summoned into her father's book-room, and found him there, and her mother also. "Bessy," said he, "sit down, my dear. You know, why Godfrey has left us this morning?"

Bessy walked round the room, so that in sitting she might be close to her mother and take her mother's hand in her own. "I suppose I do, papa," she said.

"He was with me late last night, Bessy; and when he told me what had passed between you I agreed with him that he had better go."

"It was better that he should go, papa."

"But he has left a message for you."

"A message, papa?"

"Yes, Bessy. And your mother agrees with me that it had better be given to you. It is this,—that if you will send him word to come again, he will be here by Twelfth-night. He came before on my invitation, but if he returns it must be on yours."

"Oh, papa, I cannot."

"I do not say that you can, but think of it calmly before you altogether refuse. You shall give me your answer on New Year's morning."

"Mamma knows that it would be impossible," said Bessy.

"Not impossible, dearest.

"In such a matter you should do what you believe to be right," said her father.

"If I were to ask him here again, it would be telling him that I would—"

"Exactly, Bessy. It would be telling him that you would be his wife. He would understand it so, and so would your mother and I. It must be so understood altogether."

"But, papa, when we were at Liverpool—"

"I have told him everything, dearest," said Mrs. Garrow.

"I think I understand the whole," said the Major; "and in such a matter as this I will not give you counsel on either side. But you must remember that in making up your mind, you must think of him as well as of yourself. If you do not love him;—if you feel that as his wife you should not love him, there is not another word to be said. I need not explain to my daughter that under such circumstances she would be wrong to encourage the visits of a suitor. But your mother says you do love him."

"Oh, mamma!"

"I will not ask you. But if you do;—if you have so told him, and allowed him to build up an idea of his life-happiness on such telling, you will, I think, sin greatly against him by allowing a false feminine pride to mar his happiness. When once a girl has confessed to a man that she loves him, the confession and the love together put upon her the burden of a duty towards him, which she cannot with impunity throw aside." Then he kissed her, and bidding her give him a reply on the morning of the new year, left her with her mother.

She had four days for consideration, and they went past her by no means easily. Could she have been alone with her mother, the struggle would not have been so painful; but there was the necessity that she should talk to Isabella Holmes, and the necessity also that she should not neglect the Coverdales. Nothing could have been kinder than Bella. She did not speak on the subject till the morning of the last day, and then only in a very few words. "Bessy," she said, "as you are great, be merciful."

"But I am not great, and it would not be mercy."

" As to that," said Bella " he has surely a right to his own opinion."

On that evening she was sitting alone in her room when her mother came to her, and her eyes were red with weeping. Pen and paper were before her, as though she were resolved to write, but hitherto no word had been written.

" Well, Bessy," said her mother, sitting down close beside her ; " is the deed done ? "

"What deed, mamma ? Who says that I am to do it?"

" The deed is not the writing, but the resolution to write. Five words will be sufficient,—if only those five words may be written."

" It is for one's whole life, mamma. For his life, as well as my own."

" True, Bessy ;—that is quite true. But equally true whether you bid him come or allow him to remain away. That task of making up one's mind for life, must at last be done in some special moment of that life."

" Mamma, mamma ; tell me what I should do."

But this Mrs. Garrow would not do. " I will write the words for you if you like," she said, " but it is you who must resolve that they shall be written. I cannot bid my darling go away and leave me for another home ;—I can only say that in my heart I do believe that home would be a happy one."

It was morning before the note was written, but when the morning came Bessy had written it and brought it to her mother. " You must take it to

papa," she said. Then she went and hid herself from
all eyes till the noon had passed. "Dear Godfrey,"
the letter ran, "Papa says that you will return on
Wednesday if I write to ask you. Do come back to
us,—if you wish it. Yours always, BESSY."

"It is as good as though she had filled the sheet,"
said the Major. But in sending it to Godfrey Holmes,
he did not omit a few accompanying remarks of his own.

An answer came from Godfrey by return of post ;
and on the afternoon of the sixth of January, Frank
Garrow drove over to the station at Penrith to meet
him. On their way back to Thwaite Hall there grew
up a very close confidence between the two future
brothers-in-law, and Frank explained with great per-
spicuity a little plan which he had arranged himself.
"As soon as it is dark, so that she won't see it, Harry
will hang it up in the dining-room," he said, "and
mind you go in there before you go anywhere else."

"I am very glad you have come back, Godfrey,"
said the Major, meeting him in the hall.

"God bless you, dear Godfrey," said Mrs. Garrow,
" you will find Bessy in the dining-room," she whispered ; but in so whispering she was quite unconscious
of the mistletoe bough.

And so also was Bessy, nor do I think that she
was much more conscious when that introduction was
over. Godfrey had made all manner of promises to
Frank, but when the moment arrived, he had found
the moment too important for any special reference to
the little bough above his head. Not so, however, Patty

Coverdale. "It's a shame," she said, bursting out of the room, "and if I'd known what you had done, nothing on earth should have induced me to go in. I won't enter the room till I know that you have taken it out." Nevertheless her sister Kate was bold enough to solve the mystery before the evening was over.

RETURNING HOME.

——◆——

IT is generally supposed that people who live at home,—good domestic people, who love tea and their arm-chairs, and who keep the parlour hearth-rug ever warm,—it is generally supposed that these are the people who value home the most, and best appreciate all the comforts of that cherished institution. I am inclined to doubt this. It is, I think, to those who live farthest away from home, to those who find the greatest difficulty in visiting home, that the word conveys the sweetest idea. In some distant parts of the world it may be that an Englishman acknowledges his permanent resting place; but there are many others in which he will not call his daily house, his home. He would, in his own idea, desecrate the word by doing so. His Home is across the blue waters, in the little northern island, which perhaps he may visit no more; which he has left, at any rate, for half his life; from which circumstances, and the necessity of living, have banished him. His home is still in England, and when he speaks of home his thoughts are there.

No one can understand the intensity of this feeling

who has not seen or felt the absence of interest in life which falls to the lot of many who have to eat their bread on distant soils. We are all apt to think that a life in strange countries will be a life of excitement, of stirring enterprise, and varied scenes;— that in abandoning the comforts of home, we shall receive in exchange more of movement and of adventure than would come in our way in our own tame country; and this feeling has, I am sure, sent many a young man roaming. Take any spirited fellow of twenty, and ask him whether he would like to go to Mexico for the next ten years! Prudence and his father may ultimately save him from such banishment, but he will not refuse without a pang of regret.

Alas; it is a mistake. Bread may be earned, and fortunes, perhaps, made in such countries; and as it is the destiny of our race to spread itself over the wide face of the globe, it is well that there should be something to gild and paint the outward face of that lot which so many are called upon to choose. But for a life of daily excitement, there is no life like life in England; and the farther that one goes from England the more stagnant, I think, do the waters of existence become.

But if it be so for men, it is ten times more so for women. An Englishman, if he be at Guatemala or Belize, must work for his bread, and that work will find him in thought and excitement. But what of his wife? Where will she find excitement? By what pursuit will she repay herself for all that she has left

o 2

behind her at her mother's fireside? She will love her husband. Yes; that at least! If there be not that, there will be a hell, indeed. Then she will nurse her children, and talk of her—home. When the time shall come that her promised return thither is within a year or two of its accomplishment, her thoughts will all be fixed on that coming pleasure, as are the thoughts of a young girl on her first ball for the fortnight before that event comes off.

On the central plain of that portion of Central America which is called Costa Rica stands the city of San José. It is the capital of the Republic,—for Costa Rica is a Republic,—and, for Central America, is a town of some importance. It is in the middle of the coffee district, surrounded by rich soil on which the sugar-cane is produced, is blessed with a climate only moderately hot, and the native inhabitants are neither cut-throats nor cannibals. It may be said, therefore, that by comparison with some other spots to which Englishmen and others are congregated for the gathering together of money, San José may be considered as a happy region; but, nevertheless, a life there is not in every way desirable. It is a dull place, with little to interest either the eye or the ear. Although the heat of the tropics is but little felt there on account of its altitude, men and women become too lifeless for much enterprise. There is no society. There are a few Germans and a few Englishmen in the place, who see each other on matters of business during the day; but, sombre as life generally is, they seem to care little for each other's company on any other footing. I know not to what point the aspirations of the Germans may stretch themselves, but to the English the one idea that gives salt to life is the idea of home. On some day, however distant it may be, they will once more turn their faces towards the little northern island, and then all will be well with them.

To a certain Englishman there, and to his dear little wife, this prospect came some few years since somewhat suddenly. Events and tidings, it matters not which or what, brought it about that they resolved between themselves that they would start immediately;—almost immediately. They would pack up and leave San José within four months of the day on which their purpose was first formed. At San José a period of only four months for such a purpose was immediately. It creates a feeling of instant excitement, a necessity for instant doing, a consciousness that there was in those few weeks ample work both for the hands and thoughts,—work almost more than ample. The dear little wife, who for the last two years had been so listless, felt herself flurried.

"Harry," she said to her husband, "How shall we ever be ready?" And her pretty face was lighted up with unusual brightness at the happy thought of so much haste with such an object. "And baby's things too," she said, as she thought of all the various little articles of dress that would be needed. A journey from San José to Southampton cannot in truth be made as easily as one from London to Liverpool. Let us think of a month to be passed without any aid from the washerwoman, and the greatest part of that month amidst the sweltering heats of the West Indian tropics !

In the first month of her hurry and flurry Mrs. Arkwright was a happy woman. She would see her mother again and her sisters. It was now four years since she had left them on the quay at Southampton, while all their hearts were broken at the parting. She was a young bride then going forth with her new lord to meet the stern world. He had then been home to look for a wife, and he had found what he looked for in the younger sister of his partner. For he, Henry Arkwright, and his wife's brother, Abel Ring, had established themselves together in San José. And now, she thought, how there would be another meting on those quays at which there should be no broken hearts ; at which there should be love without sorrow, and kisses, sweet with the sweetness of welcome, not bitter with the bitterness of parting. And people told her,—the few neighbours around her, —how happy, how fortunate she was to get home thus early in her life. They had been out some ten, —some twenty years, and still the day of their return was distant. And then she pressed her living baby to her breast, and wiped away a tear as she thought of the other darling whom she would leave beneath that distant sod.

And then came the question as to the route home.

San José stands in the middle of the high plain of Costa Rica, half way between the Pacific and the Atlantic. The journey thence down to the Pacific is, by comparison, easy. There is a road, and the mules on which the travellers must ride go steadily and easily down to Punta Arenas, the port on that ocean. There are inns too on the way,—places of public entertainment at which refreshment may be obtained, and beds, or fair substitutes for beds. But then by this route the traveller must take a long additional sea voyage. He must convey himself and his weary baggage down to that wretched place on the Pacific, there wait for a steamer to take him to Panamá, cross the isthmus, and reship himself in the other waters for his long journey home. That terrible unshipping and reshipping is a sore burden to the unaccustomed traveller. When it is absolutely necessary,—then indeed it is done without much thought ; but in the case of the Arkwrights it was not absolutely necessary. And there was another reason which turned Mrs. Arkwright's heart against that journey by Punt' Arenas. The place is unhealthy, having at certain seasons a very bad name ;—and here on their outward journey her husband had been taken ill. She had never ceased to think of the fortnight she had spent there among uncouth strangers during a portion of which his life had trembled in the balance. Early, therefore, in those four months she begged that she might not be taken round by Punt' Arenas. There was another route. " Harry, if you

love me, let me go by the Serapiqui." As to Harry's
loving her, there was no doubt about that, as she well
knew.

There was this other route by the Serapiqui river,
and by Greytown. Greytown, it is true, is quite as
unhealthy as Punt' Arenas, and by that route one's
baggage must be shipped and unshipped into small
boats. There are all manner of difficulties attached
to it. Perhaps no direct road to and from any city
on the world's surface is subject to sharper fatigue
while it lasts. Journeying by this route also, the
traveller leaves San José mounted on his mule, and
so mounted he makes his way through the vast
primeval forests down to the banks of the Serapiqui
river. That there is a track for him is of course true ;
but it is simply a track, and during nine months of
the twelve is so deep in mud that the mules sink in
it to their bellies. Then, when the river has been
reached, the traveller seats him in his canoe, and for
two days is paddled down,—down along the Serapiqui, into the San Juan river, and down along the
San Juan till he reaches Greytown, passing one night
at some hut on the river side. At Greytown he waits
for the steamer which will carry him his first stage
on his road towards Southampton. He must be a
connoisseur in disagreeables of every kind who can
say with any precision whether Greytown or Punt'
Arenas is the better place for a week's sojourn.

For a full month Mr. Arkwright would not give
way to his wife. At first he all but conquered her

by declaring that the Serapiqui journey would be dangerous for the baby; but she heard from some one that it could be made less fatiguing for the baby than the other route. A baby had been carried down in a litter strapped on to a mule's back. A guide at the mule's head would be necessary, and that was all. When once in her boat the baby would be as well as in her cradle. What purpose cannot a woman gain by perseverance? Her purpose in this instance Mrs. Arkwright did at last gain by persevering.

And then their preparations for the journey went on with much flurrying and hot haste. To us at home, who live and feel our life every day, the manufacture of endless baby-linen and the packing of mountains of clothes does not give an idea of much pleasurable excitement; but at San José, where there was scarcely motion enough in existence to prevent its waters from becoming foul with stagnation, this packing of baby-linen was delightful, and for a month or so the days went by with happy wings.

But by degrees reports began to reach both Arkwright and his wife as to this new route, which made them uneasy. The wet season had been prolonged, and even though they might not be deluged by rain themselves, the path would be in such a state of mud as to render the labour incessant. One or two people declared that the road was unfit at any time for a woman,—and then the river would be much swollen. These tidings did not reach Arkwright and his wife together, or at any rate not till late amidst their preparations, or a change might still have been made. As it was, after all her entreaties, Mrs. Arkwright did not like to ask him again to alter his plans; and he, having altered them once, was averse to change them again. So things went on till the mules and the boats had been hired, and things had gone so far that no change could then be made without much cost and trouble.

During the last ten days of their sojourn at San José Mrs. Arkwright had lost all that appearance of joy which had cheered up her sweet face during the last few months. Terror at that terrible journey obliterated in her mind all the happiness which had arisen from the hope of being soon at home. She was thoroughly cowed by the danger to be encountered, and would gladly have gone down to Punt' Arenas, had it been now possible that she could so arrange it. It rained, and rained, and still rained, when there was now only a week from the time before they started. Oh! if they could only wait for another month! But this she said to no one. After what had passed between her and her husband, she had not the heart to say such words to him. Arkwright himself was a man not given to much talking, a silent thoughtful man, stern withall in his outward bearing, but tender hearted and loving in his nature. The sweet young wife who had left all and come with him out to that dull distant place, was very dear to him,—dearer than she herself was aware, and in these days he was thinking much of her coming troubles. Why had he given way to her foolish prayers? Ah, why indeed?

And thus the last few days of their sojourn in San José passed away from them. Once or twice during these days she did speak out, expressing her fears. Her feelings were too much for her, and she could not restrain herself. "Poor mamma," she said, "I shall never see her!" And then again, "Harry, I know I shall never reach home alive."

"Fanny, my darling, that is nonsense." But in order that his spoken word might not sound stern to her, he took her in his arms and kissed her.

"You must behave well, Fanny," he said to her the day before they started. Though her heart was then very low within her, she promised him that she would do her best, and then she made a great resolution. Though she should be dying on the road, she would not complain beyond the absolute necessity of her nature. She fully recognised his thoughtful tender kindness, for though he thus cautioned her, he never told her that the dangers which she feared were the result of her own choice. He never threw in her teeth those prayers which she had made, in yielding to which he knew that he had been weak.

Then came the morning of their departure. The party of travellers consisted of four besides the baby. There was Mr. Arkwright, his wife, and an English nurse, who was going to England with them, and her brother Abel Ring, who was to accompany them

as far as the Serapiqui river. When they had
reached that, the real labour of the journey would
be over. They had eight mules : four for the four
travellers, one for the baby, a spare mule laden
simply with blankets, so that Mrs. Arkwright might
change in order that she should not be fatigued by
the fatigue of her beast, and two for their luggage.
The heavier portion of their baggage had already
been sent off by Punt' Arenas, and would meet them
at the other side of the Isthmus of Panamá.

For the last four days the rain had ceased,—had
ceased at any rate at San José. Those who knew
the country well, would know that it might still be
raining over those vast forests ; but now, as the
matter was settled, they would hope for the best.
On that morning on which they started the sun
shone fairly, and they accepted this as an omen of
good. Baby seemed to lay comfortably on her pile
of blankets on the mule's back, and the face of the
tall Indian guide who took his place at that mule's
head pleased the anxious mother.

"Not leave him ever," he said in Spanish, laying
his hand on the cord which was fastened to the
beast's head ; and not for one moment did he leave
his charge, though the labour of sticking close to
him was very great.

They had four attendants or guides, all of whom
made the journey on foot. That they were all men
of mixed race was probable ; but three of them
would have been called Spaniards, Spaniards, that is,

of Costa Rica, and the other would be called an Indian. One of the Spaniards was the leader, or chief man of the party, but the others seemed to stand on an equal footing with each other; and indeed the place of greatest care had been given to the Indian.

For the first four or five miles their route lay along the high road which leads from San José to Punt' Arenas, and so far a group of acquaintances followed them, all mounted on mules. Here, where the ways forked, their road leading through the great forests to the Atlantic, they separated, and many tears were shed on each side. What might be the future life of the Arkwrights had not been absolutely fixed, but there was a strong hope on their part that they might never be forced to return to Costa Rica. Those from whom they now parted had not seemed to be dear to them in any especial degree while they all lived together in the same small town, seeing each other day by day; but now,—now that they might never meet again, a certain love sprang up for the old familiar faces, and women kissed each other who hitherto had hardly cared to enter each other's houses.

And then the party of the Arkwrights again started, and its steady work began. In the whole of the first day the way beneath their feet was tolerably good, and the weather continued fine. It was one long gradual ascent from the plain where the roads parted, but there was no real labour in travelling. Mrs. Arkwright rode beside her baby's mule, at the head of which the Indian always walked, and the two men went together in front. The husband had found that his wife would prefer this, as long as the road allowed of such an arrangement. Her heart was too full to admit of much speaking, and so they went on in silence.

The first night was passed in a hut by the roadside, which seemed to have been deserted,—a hut or rancho, as it is called in that country. Their food they had, of course, brought with them; and here, by common consent, they endeavoured in some sort to make themselves merry.

"Fanny," Arkwright said to her, "it is not so bad after all; eh, my darling?"

"No," she answered; "only that the mule tires one so. Will all the days be as long as that?"

He had not the heart to tell her that, as regarded hours of work, that first day must of necessity be the shortest. They had risen to a considerable altitude, and the night was very cold; but baby was enveloped among a pile of coloured blankets, and things did not go very badly with them; only this, that when Fanny Arkwright rose from her hard bed, her limbs were more weary and much more stiff than they had been when Arkwright had lifted her from her mule.

On the second morning they mounted before the day had quite broken, in order that they might breakfast on the summit of the ridge which separates the two oceans. At this spot the good road comes to an end, and the forest track begins; and here, also, they would, in truth, enter the forest, though their path had for some time been among straggling trees and bushes. And now, again, they rode two and two, up to this place of halting, Arkwright and Ring well knowing that from hence their labours would in truth commence.

Poor Mrs. Arkwright, when she reached this resting-place, would fain have remained there for the rest of the day. One word, in her low, plaintive voice, she said, asking whether they might not sleep in the large shed which stands there. But this was manifestly impossible. At such a pace they would never reach Greytown; and she spoke no further word when he told her that they must go on.

At about noon that day the file of travellers formed itself into the line which it afterwards kept during the whole of the journey, and then started by the narrow path into the forest. First walked the leader of the guides, then another man following him; Abel Ring came next, and behind him the maid-servant; then the baby's mule, with the Indian ever at its head; close at his heels followed Mrs. Arkwright, so that the mother's eye might be always on her child; and after her her husband; then another guide on foot completed the number of the travellers. In this way they went on and on, day after day, till they reached the banks of the Serapiqui, never once

varying their places in the procession. As they
started in the morning, so they went on till their
noon-day's rest, and so again they made their evening
march. In that journey there was no idea of variety, no searching after the pleasures of scenery, no
attempts at conversation with any object of interest
or amusement. What words were spoken were those
simply needful, or produced by sympathy for suffering. So they journeyed, always in the same
places, with one exception. They began their work
with two guides leading them, but before the first
day was over one of them had fallen back to the side
of Mrs. Arkwright, for she was unable to sit on her
mule without support.

Their daily work was divided into two stages, so
as to give some hours for rest in the middle of the
day. It had been arranged that the distance for
each day should not be long,—should be very short
as was thought by them all when they talked it
over up at San José; but now the hours which they
passed in the saddle seemed to be endless. Their
descent began from that ridge of which I have
spoken, and they had no sooner turned their faces
down upon the mountain slopes looking towards the
Atlantic, than that passage of mud began to which
there was no cessation till they found themselves on
the banks of the Serapiqui river. I doubt whether
it be possible to convey in words an adequate idea
of the labour of riding over such a path. It is not
that any active exertion is necessary,—that there is

anything which requires doing. The traveller has before him the simple task of sitting on his mule from hour to hour, and of seeing that his knees do not get themselves jammed against the trees; but at every step the beast he rides has to drag his legs out from the deep clinging mud, and the body of the rider never knows one moment of ease. Why the mules do not die on the road, I cannot say. They live through it, and do not appear to suffer. They have their own way in everything, for no exertion on the rider's part will make them walk either faster or slower than is their wont.

On the day on which they entered the forest,—that being the second of their journey,—Mrs. Arkwright had asked for mercy, for permission to escape that second stage. On the next she allowed herself to be lifted into her saddle after her mid-day rest without a word. She had tried to sleep, but in vain; and had sat within a little hut, looking out upon the desolate scene before her, with her baby in her lap. She had this one comfort, that of all the travellers, she, the baby, suffered the least. They had now left the high grounds, and the heat was becoming great, though not as yet intense. And then, the Indian guide, looking out slowly over the forest, saw that the rain was not yet over. He spoke a word or two to one of his companions in a low voice and in a patois which Mrs. Arkwright did not understand, and then going after the husband, told him that the heavens were threatening.

P

"We have only two leagues," said Arkwright, "and it may perhaps hold up."

"It will begin in an hour," said the Indian, "and the two leagues are four hours."

"And to-morrow?" asked Arkwright.

"To-morrow, and to-morrow, and to-morrow it will still rain," said the guide, looking as he spoke up over the huge primeval forest.

"Then we had better start at once," said Arkwright, "before the first falling drops frighten the women." So the mules were brought out, and he lifted his uncomplaining wife on to the blankets which formed her pillion. The file again formed itself, and slowly they wound their way out from the small enclosure by which the hut was surrounded ;—out from the enclosure on to a rough scrap of undrained pasture ground from which the trees had been cleared. In a few minutes they were once more struggling through the mud.

The name of the spot which our travellers had just left is Carablanco. There they had found a woman living all alone. Her husband was away, she told them, at San José, but would be back to her when the dry weather came, to look up the young cattle which were straying in the forest. What a life for a woman! Nevertheless, in talking with Mrs. Arkwright she made no complaint of her own lot, but had done what little she could to comfort the poor lady who was so little able to bear the fatigues of her journey.

" Is the road very bad ?" Mrs. Arkwright asked her in a whisper.

" Ah, yes ; it is a bad road."

" And when shall we be at the river ? "

" It took me four days," said the woman.

"Then I shall never see my mother again," and as she spoke Mrs. Arkwright pressed her baby to her bosom. Immediately after that her husband came in, and they started.

Their path now led away across the slope of a mountain which seemed to fall from the very top of that central ridge in an unbroken descent down to the valley at its foot. Hitherto, since they had entered the forest, they had had nothing before their eyes but the trees and bushes which grew close around them. But now a prospect of unrivalled grandeur was opened before them, if only they had been able to enjoy it. At the bottom of the valley ran a river, which, so great was the depth, looked like a moving silver cord ; and on the other side of this there arose another mountain, steep but unbroken like that which they were passing,—unbroken, so that the eye could stretch from the river up to the very summit. Not a spot on that mountain side or on their side either was left uncovered by thick forest, which had stood there untouched by man since nature first produced it.

But all this was nothing to our travellers, nor was the clang of the macaws anything, or the roaring of the little congo ape. Nothing was gained by them from beautiful scenery, nor was there any fear from the beasts of prey. The immediate pain of each step of the journey drove all other feelings from them, and their thoughts were bounded by an intense desire for the evening halt.

And then, as the guide had prophesied, the rain began. At first it came in such small soft drops that it was found to be refreshing, but the clouds soon gathered and poured forth their collected waters as though it had not rained for months among those mountains. Not that it came in big drops, or with the violence which wind can give it, beating hither and thither, breaking branches from the trees, and rising up again as it pattered against the ground. There was no violence in the rain. It fell softly in a long, continuous, noiseless stream, sinking into everything that it touched, converting the deep rich earth on all sides into mud.

Not a word was said by any of them as it came on. The Indian covered the baby with her blanket, closer than she was covered before, and the guide who walked by Mrs. Arkwright's side drew her cloak around her knees. But such efforts were in vain. There is a rain that will penetrate everything, and such was the rain which fell upon them now. Nevertheless, as I have said, hardly a word was spoken. The poor woman, finding that the heat of her cloak increased her sufferings, threw it open again.

"Fanny," said her husband, "you had better let him protect you as well as he can."

She answered him merely by an impatient wave of her hand, intending to signify that she could not speak, but that in this matter she must have her way.

After that her husband made no further attempt to control her. He could see, however, that ever and again she would have slipped forward from her mule and fallen, had not the man by her side steadied her with his hand. At every tree he protected her knees and feet, though there was hardly room for him to move between the beast and the bank against which he was thrust.

And then, at last, that day's work was also over, and Fanny Arkwright slipped from her pillion down into her husband's arms at the door of another rancho in the forest. Here there lived a large family adding from year to year to the patch of ground which they had rescued from the wood, and valiantly doing their part in the extension of civilisation. Our party was but a few steps from the door when they left their mules, but Mrs. Arkwright did not now as heretofore hasten to receive her baby in her arms. When placed upon the ground, she still leaned against the mule, and her husband saw that he must carry her into the hut. This he did, and then wet, mud-laden, dishevelled as she was, she laid herself down upon the planks that were to form her bed, and there stretched out her arms for her infant. On that evening they undressed and tended her like a child; and then, when she was alone with her husband, she repeated to him her sad foreboding.

"Harry," she said, "I shall never see my mother again."

"Oh, yes, Fanny, you will see her and talk over all these troubles with pleasure. It is very bad, I know; but we shall live through it yet."

"You will, of course; and you will take baby home to her."

"And face her without you! No, my darling, Three more days' riding, or rather two and a half will bring us to the river, and then your trouble will be over. All will be easy after that."

"Ah, Harry, you do not know."

"I do know that it is very bad, my girl, but you must cheer up. We shall be laughing at all this in a month's time."

On the following morning she allowed herself to be lifted up, speaking no word of remonstrance. Indeed she was like a child in their hands, having dropped all the dignity and authority of a woman's demeanour. It rained again during the whole of this day, and the heat was becoming oppressive as every hour they were descending nearer and nearer to the sea level. During this first stage hardly a word was spoken by any one; but when she was again taken from her mule she was in tears. The poor servant-girl, too, was almost prostrate with fatigue, and absolutely unable to wait upon her mistress, or even to do anything for herself. Nevertheless they did make the second stage, seeing that their mid-day resting place had been under the trees of the forest. Had there been any hut there, they would have remained for the night.

On the following day they rested altogether, though the place at which they remained had but few attractions. It was another forest hut inhabited by an old Spanish couple who were by no means willing to give them room, although they paid for their accommodation at exorbitant rates. It is one singularity of places strange and out of the way like such forest tracks as these, that money in small sums is hardly valued. Dollars there were not appreciated as sixpences are in this rich country. But there they stayed for a day, and the guides employed themselves in making a litter with long poles so that they might carry Mrs. Arkwright over a portion of the ground. Poor fellows! When once she had thus changed her mode of conveyance, she never again was lifted on to the mule.

There was strong reason against this day's delay. They were to go down the Serapiqui along with the post, which would overtake them on its banks. But if the post should pass them before they got there, it could not wait; and then they would be deprived of the best canoe on the water. Then also it was possible, if they encountered further delay, that the steamer might sail from Greytown without them, and a month's residence at that frightful place be thus made necessary.

The day's rest apparently did little to relieve Mrs.

Arkwright's sufferings. On the following day she allowed herself to be put upon the mule, but after the first hour the beasts were stopped and she was taken off it. During that hour they had travelled hardly over half a league. At that time she so sobbed and moaned that Arkwright absolutely feared that she would perish in the forest, and he implored the guides to use the poles which they had prepared. She had declared to him over and over again that she felt sure that she should die, and half delirious with weariness and suffering, had begged him to leave her at the last hut. They had not yet come to the flat ground over which a litter might be carried with comparative ease ; but nevertheless the men yielded, and she was placed in a recumbent position upon blankets supported by boughs of trees. In this way she went through that day with somewhat less of suffering than before, and without that necessity for self-exertion which had been worse to her than any suffering.

There were places between that and the river at which one would have said that it was impossible that a litter should be carried, or even impossible that a mule should walk with a load on his back. But still they went on, and the men carried their burden without complaining. Not a word was said about money, or extra pay ;—not a word at least by them ; and when Arkwright was profuse in his offer, their leader told him that they would not have done it for money. But for the poor suffering Señora they would make exertions which no money would have bought from them.

On the next day about noon the post did pass them, consisting of three strong men carrying great weights on their backs, suspended by bands from their foreheads. They travelled much quicker than our friends, and would reach the banks of the river that evening. In their ordinary course they would start down the river close upon daybreak on the following day; but, after some consultation with the guides, they agreed to wait till noon. Poor Mrs. Arkwright knew nothing of hours or of any such arrangements now, but her husband greatly doubted their power of catching this mail despatch. However, it did not much depend on their exertions that afternoon. Their resting place was marked out for them, and they could not go beyond it, unless indeed they could make the whole journey, which was impossible.

But towards evening matters seemed to improve with them. They had now got on to ground which was more open, and the men who carried the litter could walk with greater ease. Mrs. Arkwright also complained less, and when they reached their resting place on that night, said nothing of a wish to be left there to her fate. This was a place called Padregal, a cacao plantation, which had been cleared in the forest with much labour. There was a house here containing three rooms, and some forty or fifty acres round it had been stripped of the forest trees. But nevertheless the adventure had not been a prosperous one, for the place was at that time deserted. There were the cacao plants, but there was no one to pick the cacao. There was a certain melancholy beauty about the place. A few grand trees had been left standing near the house, and the grass around was rich and park-like. But it was deserted, and nothing was heard but the roaring of the congos. Ah me! Indeed it was a melancholy place as it was seen by some of that party afterwards.

On the following morning they were astir very early, and Mrs. Arkwright was so much better that she offered to sit again upon her mule. The men however declared that they would finish their task, and she was placed again upon the litter. And then with slow and weary step they did make their way to the river bank. It was not yet noon when they saw the mud fort which stands there, and as they drew into the enclosure round a small house which stands close by the river side, they saw the three postmen still busy about their packages.

"Thank God," said Arkwright.

"Thank God, indeed," said his brother. "All will be right with you now."

"Well, Fanny," said her husband, as he took her very gently from the litter and seated her on a bench which stood outside the door, "It is all over now,—is it not?"

She answered him by a shower of tears, but they were tears which brought her relief. He was aware of this, and therefore stood by her, still holding her oy both her hands while her head rested against his side. " You will find the motion of the boat very gentle," he said; "indeed there will be no motion, and you and baby will sleep all the way down to Greytown." She did not answer him in words, but she looked up into his face, and he could see that her spirit was recovering itself.

There was almost a crowd of people collected on the spot, preparatory to the departure of the canoes. In the first place there was the commandant of the fort, to whom the small house belonged. He was looking to the passports of our friends, and with due diligence endeavouring to make something of the occasion, by discovering fatal legal impediments to the further prosecution of their voyage, which impediments would disappear on the payment of certain dollars. And then there were half a dozen Costa Rican soldiers, men with coloured caps and old muskets, ready to support the dignity and authority of the commandant. There were the guides taking payment from Abel Ring for their past work, and the postmen preparing their boats for the further journey. And then there was a certain German there, with a German servant, to whom the boats belonged. He also was very busy preparing for the river voyage. He was not going down with them, but it was his business to see them well started. A singular looking man was he, with a huge shaggy beard, and shaggy uncombed hair, but with bright blue eyes, which gave to his face a remarkable look of sweetness. He was an uncouth man to the eye, and yet a child would have trusted herself with him in a forest.

At this place they remained some two hours. Coffee was prepared here, and Mrs. Arkwright refreshed herself and her child. They washed and arranged their clothes, and when she stepped down the steep bank, clinging to her husband's arm as she made her way towards the boat, she smiled upon him as he looked at her.

"It is all over now,—is it not, my girl?"—he said, encouraging her.

"Oh Harry, do not talk about it," she answered, shuddering.

"But I want you to say a word to me to let me know that you are better."

"I am better,—much better."

"And you will see your mother again; will you not; and give baby to her yourself?"

To this she made no immediate answer, for she was on a level with the river, and the canoe was close at her feet. And then she had to bid farewell to her brother. He was now the unfortunate one of the party, for his destiny required that he should go back to San José alone,—go back and remain there perhaps some ten years longer before he might look for the happiness of home.

"God bless you, dearest Abel," she said, kissing him and sobbing as she spoke.

"Good-bye, Fanny," he said, "and do not let them forget me in England. It is a great comfort to think that the worst of your troubles are over."

"Oh,—she's all right now," said Arkwright. "Good-bye, old boy,"—and the two brothers-in-law grasped each other's hands heartily. "Keep up your spirits, and we'll have you home before long."

"Oh, I am all right," said the other. But from the tone of the voices, it was clear that poor Ring was despondent at the thoughts of his coming solitude, and that Arkwright was already triumphing in his emancipation.

And then, with much care, Fanny Arkwright was stowed away in the boat. There was a great contest about the baby, but at last it was arranged, that at any rate for the first few hours, she should be placed in the boat with the servant. The mother was told that by this plan she would feel herself at liberty to sleep during the heat of the day, and then she might hope to have strength to look to the child when they should be on shore during the night. In this way therefore they prepared to start, while Abel Ring stood on the bank looking at them with wishful eyes. In the first boat were two Indians paddling, and a third man steering with another paddle. In the middle there was much luggage, and near the luggage so as to be under shade, was the baby's soft bed. If nothing evil happened to the boat, the child could not be more safe in the best cradle that was ever rocked. With her was the maid servant and some stranger who was also going down to Greytown.

In the second boat were the same number of men to paddle, the Indian guide being one of them, and there were the mails placed. Then there was a seat arranged with blankets, cloaks, and cushions, for Mrs. Arkwright, so that she might lean back and sleep without fatigue, and immediately opposite to her her husband placed himself. "You all look very comfortable," said poor Abel from the bank.

"We shall do very well now," said Arkwright.

"And I do think I shall see mamma again," said his wife.

"That's right, old girl;—of course you will see her. Now then,—we are all ready." And with some little assistance from the German on the bank, the first boat was pushed off into the stream.

The river in this place is rapid, because the full course of the water is somewhat impeded by a bank of earth jutting out from the opposite side of the river into the stream; but it is not so rapid as to make any recognised danger in the embarkation. Below this bank, which is opposite to the spot at which the boats were entered, there were four or five broken trees in the water, some of the shattered boughs of which showed themselves above the surface. These are called snags, and are very dangerous if they are met with in the course of the stream; but in this instance no danger was apprehended from them, as they lay considerably to the left of the passage which

the boats would take. The first canoe was pushed off
by the German, and went rapidly away. The waters
were strong with the rain, and it was pretty to see
with what velocity the boat was carried on some
hundred of yards in advance of the other by the
force of the first effort of the paddle. The German
however from the bank holloaed to the first men in
Spanish, bidding them relax their efforts for a while;
and then he said a word or two of caution to those
who were now on the point of starting.

The boat then was pushed steadily forward, the
man at the stern keeping it with his paddle a little
further away from the bank at which they had em-
barked. It was close under the land that the stream
ran the fastest, and in obedience to the directions
given to him he made his course somewhat nearer to
the sunken trees. It was but one turn of his hand
that gave the light boat its direction, but that turn
of the hand was too strong. Had the anxious master
of the canoes been but a thought less anxious, all
might have been well; but, as it was, the prow of the
boat was caught by some slight hidden branch which
impeded its course and turned it round in the rapid
river. The whole length of the canoe was thus brought
against the sunken tree, and in half a minute the five
occupants of the boat were struggling in the stream.

Abel Ring and the German were both standing
on the bank close to the water when this happened,
and each for a moment looked into the other's face·
"Stand where you are," shouted the German, "so

that you may assist them from the shore. I will go in." And then, throwing from him his boots and coat, he plunged into the river.

The canoe had been swept round so as to be brought by the force of the waters absolutely in among the upturned roots and broken stumps of the trees which impeded the river, and thus, when the party was upset, they were at first to be seen scrambling among the branches. But unfortunately there was much more wood below the water than above it, and the force of the stream was so great, that those who caught hold of the timber were not able to support themselves by it above the surface. Arkwright was soon to be seen some forty yards down, having been carried clear of the trees, and here he got out of the river on the further bank. The distance to him was not above forty yards, but from the nature of the ground he could not get up towards his wife, unless he could have forced his way against the stream.

The Indian who had had charge of the baby rose quickly to the surface, was carried once round in the eddy, with his head high above the water, and then was seen to throw himself among the broken wood. He had seen the dress of the poor woman, and made his effort to save her. The other two men were so caught by the fragments of the boughs, that they could not extricate themselves so as to make any exertions; ultimately, however, they also got out on the further bank.

Mrs. Arkwright had sunk at once on being pre-
cipitated into the water, but the buoyancy of her
clothes had brought her for a moment again to the
surface. She had risen for a moment, and then had
again gone down, immediately below the forked
trunk of a huge tree;—had gone down, alas, alas!
never to rise again with life within her bosom.
The poor Indian made two attempts to save her,
and then came up himself, incapable of further
effort.

It was then that the German, the owner of the
canoes, who had fought his way with great efforts
across the violence of the waters, and indeed up
against the stream for some few yards, made his
effort to save the life of that poor frail creature.
He had watched the spot at which she had gone
down, and even while struggling across the river,
had seen how the Indian had followed her and had
failed. It was now his turn. His life was in his
hand, and he was prepared to throw it away in that
attempt. Having succeeded in placing himself a
little above the large tree, he turned his face towards the bottom of the river, and dived down
among the branches. And he also, after that, was
never again seen with the life-blood flowing round
his heart.

When the sun set that night, the two swollen
corpses were lying in the Commandant's hut, and
Abel Ring and Arkwright were sitting beside them.
Arkwright had his baby sleeping in his arms, but

Q

he sat there for hours,—into the middle of the long night,—without speaking a word to any one.

"Harry," said his brother at last, "come away and lay down. It will be good for you to sleep."

"Nothing ever will be good again for me," said he.

"You must bear up against your sorrow as other men do," said Ring.

"Why am I not sleeping with her as the poor German sleeps? Why did I let another man take my place in dying for her?" And then he walked away that the other might not see the tears on his face.

It was a sad sight,—that at the Commandant's hut, and a sad morning followed upon it. It must be remembered that they had there none of those appurtenances which are so necessary to make woe decent and misfortune comfortable. They sat through the night in the small hut, and in the morning they came forth with their clothes still wet and dirty, with their haggard faces, and weary stiff limbs, encumbered with the horrid task of burying that loved body among the forest trees. And then, to keep life in them till it was done, the brandy flask passed from hand to hand; and after that, with slow but resolute efforts, they reformed the litter on which the living woman had been carried thither, and took her body back to the wild plantation at Padregal. There they dug for her her grave, and repeating over her some portion of the service for the dead, left her to sleep the sleep of death. But before they left her, they erected a pallisade of timber round the grave, so that the beasts of the forest should not tear the body from its resting-place.

When that was done Arkwright and his brother made their slow journey back to San José. The widowed husband could not face his darling's mother with such a tale upon his tongue as that.

A RIDE ACROSS PALESTINE.

CIRCUMSTANCES took me to the Holy Land without a companion, and compelled me to visit Bethany, the Mount of Olives, and the Church of the Sepulchre alone. I acknowledge myself to be a gregarious animal, or, perhaps, rather one of those which Nature has intended to go in pairs. At any rate I dislike solitude, and especially travelling solitude, and was, therefore, rather sad at heart as I sat one night at Z——'s hotel, in Jerusalem, thinking over my proposed wanderings for the next few days. Early on the following morning I intended to start, of course on horseback, for the Dead Sea, the banks of Jordan, Jericho, and those mountains of the wilderness through which it is supposed that Our Saviour wandered for the forty days when the Devil tempted him. I would then return to the Holy City, and remaining only long enough to refresh my horse and wipe the dust from my hands and feet, I would start again for Jaffa, and there catch a certain Austrian steamer which would take me to Egypt. Such was my programme, and I confess that I was but ill contented with it, seeing that I was to be alone during the time.

I had already made all my arrangements, and though I had no reason for any doubt as to my personal security during the trip, I did not feel altogether satisfied with them. I intended to take a French guide, or dragoman, who had been with me for some days, and to put myself under the peculiar guardianship of two Bedouin Arabs, who were to accompany me as long as I should remain east of Jerusalem. This travelling through the desert under the protection of Bedouins was, in idea, pleasant enough; and I must here declare that I did not at all begrudge the forty shillings which I was told by our British consul that I must pay them for their trouble, in accordance with the established tariff. But I did begrudge the fact of the tariff. I would rather have fallen in with my friendly Arabs, as it were, by chance, and have rewarded their fidelity at the end of our joint journeyings by a donation of piastres to be settled by myself, and which, under such circumstances, would certainly have been as agreeable to them as the stipulated sum. In the same way I dislike having waiters put down in my bill. I find that I pay them twice over, and thus lose money; and as they do not expect to be so treated, I never have the advantage of their civility. The world, I fear, is becoming too fond of tariffs.

"A tariff!" said I to the consul, feeling that the whole romance of my expedition would be dissipated by such an arrangement. "Then I'll go alone; I'll take a revolver with me."

"You can't do it, sir," said the consul, in a dry and somewhat angry tone. "You have no more right to ride through that country without paying the regular price for protection, than you have to stop in Z——'s hotel without settling the bill."

I could not contest the point, so I ordered my Bedouins for the appointed day, exactly as I would send for a ticket-porter at home, and determined to make the best of it. The wild unlimited sands, the desolation of the Dead Sea, the rushing waters of Jordan, the outlines of the mountains of Moab;— those things the consular tariff could not alter, nor deprive them of the glories of their association.

I had submitted, and the arrangements had been made. Joseph, my dragoman, was to come to me with the horses and an Arab groom at five in the morning, and we were to encounter our Bedouins outside the gate of St. Stephen, down the hill, where the road turns, close to the tomb of the Virgin.

I was sitting alone in the public room at the hotel, filling my flask with brandy,—for matters of primary importance I never leave to servant, dragoman, or guide,—when the waiter entered, and said that a gentleman wished to speak with me. The gentleman had not sent in his card or name ; but any gentleman was welcome to me in my solitude, and I requested that the gentleman might enter. In appearance the gentleman certainly was a gentleman, for I thought that I had never before seen a young man whose looks were more in his favour, or whose face and gait and outward bearing seemed to betoken better breeding. He might be some twenty or twenty-one years of age, was slight and well made, with very black hair, which he wore rather long, very dark long bright eyes, a straight nose, and teeth that were perfectly white. He was dressed throughout in grey tweed clothing, having coat, waistcoat, and trousers of the same; and in his hand he carried a very broad-brimmed straw hat.

"Mr. Jones, I believe," he said, as he bowed to me. Jones is a good travelling name, and, if the reader will allow me, I will call myself Jones on the present occasion.

"Yes," I said, pausing with the brandy-bottle in one hand and the flask in the other. "That's my name; I'm Jones. Can I do anything for you, sir?"

"Why, yes, you can," said he. "My name is Smith,—John Smith."

"Pray sit down, Mr. Smith," I said, pointing to a chair. "Will you do anything in this way?" and I proposed to hand the bottle to him. "As far as I can judge from a short stay, you won't find much like that in Jerusalem."

He declined the Cognac, however, and immediately began his story. "I hear, Mr. Jones," said he, "that you are going to Moab to-morrow."

"Well," I replied; "I don't know whether I shall cross the water. It's not very easy, I take it, at all times; but I shall certainly get as far as Jordan. Can I do anything for you in those parts?"

And then he explained to me what was the object of his visit. He was quite alone in Jerusalem, as I was myself, and was staying at H——'s hotel. He had heard that I was starting for the Dead Sea, and had called to ask if I objected to his joining me. He had found himself, he said, very lonely ; and as he had heard that I also was alone, he had ventured to call and make his proposition. He seemed to be very bashful, and half ashamed of what he was doing; and when he had done speaking he declared himself conscious that he was intruding, and expressed a hope that I would not hesitate to say so if his suggestion were from any cause disagreeable to me.

As a rule I am rather shy of chance travelling English friends. It has so frequently happened to me that I have had to blush for the acquaintances whom I have selected, that I seldom indulge in any close intimacies of this kind. But, nevertheless, I was taken with John Smith, in spite of his name. There was so much about him that was pleasant, both to the eye and to the understanding ! One meets constantly with men from contact with whom one revolts without knowing the cause of such dislike. The cut of their beard is displeasing, or the mode in which they walk or speak. But, on the other hand, there are men who are attractive, and I must confess that I was attracted by John Smith at first sight. I hesitated, however, for a minute ; for there are sundry things of which it behoves a traveller to think before he can join a companion for such a journey as that which I was about to make. Could the young man rise early, and remain in the saddle for ten hours together? Could he live upon hard-boiled eggs and brandy-and-water? Could he take his chance of a tent under which to sleep, and make himself happy with the bare fact of being in the desert? He saw my hesitation, and attributed it to a cause which was not present in my mind at the moment, though the subject is one of the greatest importance when strangers consent to join themselves together for a time, and agree to become no strangers on the spur of the moment.

"Of course I will take half the expense," said he, absolutely blushing as he mentioned the matter.

"As to that there will be very little. You have your own horse, of course?"

"Oh, yes."

"My dragoman and groom-boy will do for both. But you'll have to pay forty shillings to the Arabs! There's no getting over that. The consul won't even look after your dead body, if you get murdered, without going through that ceremony."

Mr. Smith immediately produced his purse, which he tendered to me. "If you will manage it all," said he, "it will make it so much the easier, and I shall be infinitely obliged to you." This of course I declined to do. I had no business with his purse, and explained to him that if we went together we could settle that on our return to Jerusalem. "But could he go through really hard work?" I asked.

He answered me with an assurance that he would
and could do anything in that way that it was possible for man to perform. As for eating and drinking
he cared nothing about it, and would undertake to
be astir at any hour of the morning that might be
named. As for sleeping accommodation, he did not
care if he kept his clothes on for a week together.
He looked slight and weak ; but he spoke so well,
and that without boasting, that I ultimately agreed
to his proposal, and in a few minutes he took his
leave of me, promising to be at Z——'s door with
his horse at five o'clock on the following morning.

"I wish you'd allow me to leave my purse with
you," he said again.

"I cannot think of it. There is no possible occasion for it," I said again. "If there is anything to
pay, I'll ask you for it when the journey is over.
That forty shillings you must fork out. It's a law
of the Medes and Persians."

"I'd better give it to you at once," he said, again
offering me money. But I would not have it. It
would be quite time enough for that when the Arabs
were leaving us.

"Because," he added, "strangers, I know, are
sometimes suspicious about money ; and I would
not, for worlds, have you think that I would put you
to expense." I assured him that I did not think so,
and then the subject was dropped.

He was, at any rate, up to his time, for when I
came down on the following morning I found him in

the narrow street, the first on horseback. Joseph, the Frenchman, was strapping on to a rough pony our belongings, and was staring at Mr. Smith. My new friend, unfortunately, could not speak a word of French, and therefore I had to explain to the dragoman how it had come to pass that our party was to be enlarged.

" But the Bedouins will expect full pay for both," said he, alarmed. Men in that class, and especially Orientals, always think that every arrangement of life, let it be made in what way it will, is made with the intention of saving some expense, or cheating somebody out of some amount of money. They do not understand that men can have any other object, and are ever on their guard lest the saving should be made at their cost, or lest they should be the victims of the fraud.

" All right," said I.

" I shall be responsible, Monsieur," said the dragoman, piteously.

" It shall be all right," said I, again. " If that does not satisfy you, you may remain behind."

" If Monsieur says it is all right, of course it is so ; " and then he completed his strapping. We took blankets with us, of which I had to borrow two out of the hotel for my friend Smith, a small hamper of provisions, a sack containing forage for the horses, and a large empty jar, so that we might supply ourselves with water when leaving the neighbourhood of wells for any considerable time.

"I ought to have brought these things for myself," said Smith, quite unhappy at finding that he had thrown on me the necessity of catering for him. But I laughed at him, saying that it was nothing ; he should do as much for me another time. I am prepared to own that I do not willingly rush up-stairs and load myself with blankets out of strange rooms for men whom I do not know ; nor, as a rule, do I make all the Smiths of the world free of my canteen. But, with reference to this fellow I did feel more than ordinarily good-natured and unselfish. There was something in the tone of his voice which was satisfactory ; and I should really have felt vexed had anything occurred at the last moment to prevent his going with me.

Let it be a rule with every man to carry an English saddle with him when travelling in the East. Of what material is formed the nether man of a Turk I have never been informed, but I am sure that it is not flesh and blood. No flesh and blood,— simply flesh and blood,—could withstand the wear and tear of a Turkish saddle. This being the case, and the consequences being well known to me, I was grieved to find that Smith was not properly provided. He was seated in one of those hard, red, high-pointed machines, to which the shovels intended to act as stirrups are attached in such a manner, and hang at such an angle, as to be absolutely destructive to the leg of a Christian. There is no part of the Christian body with which the Turkish saddle comes in contact that does not become more or less macerated. I have sat in one for days, but I left it a flayed man ; and, therefore, I was sorry for Smith.

I explained this to him, taking hold of his leg by the calf to show how the leather would chafe him ; but it seemed to me that he did not quite like my interference. " Never mind," said he, twitching his leg away, " I have ridden in this way before."

" Then you must have suffered the very mischief?"

" Only a little, and I shall be used to it now. You will not hear me complain."

" By heavens, you might have heard me complain a mile off when I came to the end of a journey I once took. I roared like a bull when I began to cool. Joseph, could you not get a European saddle for Mr. Smith ?" But Joseph did not seem to like Mr. Smith, and declared such a thing to be impossible. No European in Jerusalem would think of lending so precious an article, except to a very dear friend. Joseph himself was on an English saddle, and I made up my mind that after the first stage, we would bribe him to make an exchange. And then we started. The Bedouins were not with us, but we were to meet them, as I have said before, outside St. Stephen's gate. " And if they are not there," said Joseph, " we shall be sure to come across them on the road."

" Not there !" said I. " How about the consul's tariff, if they don't keep their part of the engagement ?" But Joseph explained to me that their

part of the engagement really amounted to this,—
that we should ride into their country without moles-
tation, provided that such and such payments were
made.

It was the period of Easter, and Jerusalem was
full of pilgrims. Even at that early hour of the
morning we could hardly make our way through
the narrow streets. It must be understood that
there is no accommodation in the town for the
fourteen or fifteen thousand strangers who flock to
the Holy Sepulchre at this period of the year.
Many of them sleep out in the open air, lying on
low benches which run along the outside walls of
the houses, or even on the ground, wrapped in their
thick hoods and cloaks. Slumberers such as these
are easily disturbed, nor are they detained long at
their toilets. They shake themselves like dogs, and
growl and stretch themselves, and then they are
ready for the day.

We rode out of the town in a long file. First
went the groom-boy; I forget his proper Syrian
appellation, but we used to call him Mucherry, that
sound being in some sort like the name. Then
followed the horse with the forage and blankets,
and next to him my friend Smith in the Turkish
saddle. I was behind him and Joseph brought up
the rear. We moved slowly down the Via Dolorosa,
noting the spot at which our Saviour is said to have
fallen while bearing his cross; we passed by Pilate's
house, and paused at the gate of the Temple,—the

gate which once was beautiful,—looking down into the hole of the pool in which the maimed and halt were healed whenever the waters moved. What names they are! And yet there at Jerusalem they are bandied to and fro with as little reverence as are the fanciful appellations given by guides to rocks and stones and little lakes in all countries overrun by tourists.

"For those who would still fain believe,—let them stay at home," said my friend Smith.

"For those who cannot divide the wheat from the chaff, let *them* stay at home," I answered. And then we rode out through St. Stephen's gate, having the mountain of the men of Galilee directly before us, and the Mount of Olives a little to our right, and the Valley of Jehoshaphat lying between us and it. "Of course you know all these places now?" said Smith. I answered that I did know them well. "And was it not better for you when you knew them only in Holy Writ?" he asked.

"No, by Jove," said I. "The mountains stand where they ever stood. The same valleys are still green with the morning dew, and the water-courses are unchanged. The children of Mahomet may build their tawdry temple on the threshing-floor which David bought that there might stand the Lord's house. Man may undo what man did, even though the doer was Solomon. But here we have God's handiwork and his own evidences."

At the bottom of the steep descent from the city

gate we came to the tomb of the Virgin ; and by special agreement made with Joseph we left our horses here for a few moments, in order that we might descend into the subterranean chapel under the tomb, in which mass was at this moment being said. There is something awful in that chapel, when, as at the present moment, it is crowded with Eastern worshippers from the very altar up to the top of the dark steps by which the descent is made. It must be remembered that Eastern worshippers are not like the churchgoers of London, or even of Rome or Cologne. They are wild men of various nations and races,—Maronites from Lebanon, Roumelians, Candiotes, Copts from Upper Egypt, Russians from the Crimea, Armenians and Abyssinians. They savour strongly of Oriental life and of Oriental dirt. They are clad in skins or hairy cloaks with huge hoods. Their heads are shaved, and their faces covered with short, grisly, fierce beards. They are silent mostly, looking out of their eyes ferociously, as though murder were in their thoughts, and rapine. But they never slouch, or cringe in their bodies, or shuffle in their gait. Dirty, fierce-looking, uncouth, repellent as they are, there is always about them a something of personal dignity which is not compatible with an Englishman's ordinary hat and pantaloons.

As we were about to descend, preparing to make our way through the crowd, Smith took hold of my arm. "That will never do, my dear fellow," said I,

" the job will be tough enough for a single file, but
we should never cut our way two and two. I'm
broad-shouldered and will go first." So I did, and
gradually we worked our way into the body of the
chapel. How is it that Englishmen can push themselves anywhere? These men were fierce-looking,
and had murder and rapine, as I have said, almost
in their eyes. One would have supposed that they
were not lambs or doves, capable of being thrust
here or there without anger on their part; and they,
too, were all anxious to descend and approach the
altar. Yet we did win our way through them,
and apparently no man was angry with us. I doubt,
after all, whether a ferocious eye and a strong smell
and dirt are so efficacious in creating awe and obedience in others, as an open brow and traces of soap
and water. I know this, at least,—that a dirty
Maronite would make very little progress, if he
attempted to shove his way unfairly through a
crowd of Englishmen at the door of a London
theatre. We did shove unfairly, and we did make
progress, till we found ourselves in the centre of the
dense crowd collected in the body of the chapel.

Having got so far, our next object was to get out
again. The place was dark, mysterious, and full of
strange odours; but darkness, mystery, and strange
odours soon lose their charms when men have much
work before them. Joseph had made a point of
being allowed to attend mass before the altar of the
Virgin, but a very few minutes sufficed for his

R

prayers. So we again turned round and pushed our
way back again, Smith still following in my wake.
The men who had let us pass once let us pass again
without opposition or show of anger. To them the
occasion was very holy. They were stretching out
their hands in every direction, with long tapers, in
order that they might obtain a spark of the sacred
fire which was burning on one of the altars. As we
made our way out we passed many who, with dumb
motions, begged us to assist them in their object.
And we did assist them, getting lights for their tapers,
handing them to and fro, and using the authority
with which we seemed to be invested. But Smith,
I observed, was much more courteous in this way to
the women than to the men, as I did not forget to
remind him when we were afterwards on our road
together.

Remounting our horses we rode slowly up the
winding ascent of the Mount of Olives, turning round
at the brow of the hill to look back over Jerusalem.
Sometimes I think that of all spots in the world
this one should be the spot most cherished in the
memory of Christians. It was there that He stood
when He wept over the city. So much we do know,
though we are ignorant, and ever shall be so, of the
site of His cross and of the tomb. And then we
descended on the eastern side of the hill, passing
through Bethany, the town of Lazarus and his sisters,
and turned our faces steadily towards the mountains
of Moab.

Hitherto we had met no Bedouins, and I interrogated my dragoman about them more than once ; but he always told me that it did not signify ; we should meet them, he said, before any danger could arise. "As for danger," said I, "I think more of this than I do of the Arabs," and I put my hand on my revolver. "But as they agreed to be here, here they ought to be. Don't you carry a revolver, Smith ? "

Smith said that he never had done so, but that he would take the charge of mine if I liked. To this, however, I demurred. "I never part with my pistol to any one," I said, rather drily. But he explained that he only intended to signify that if there were danger to be encountered, he would be glad to encounter it ; and I fully believed him. "We shan't have much fighting," I replied ; "but if there be any, the tool will come readiest to the hand of its master. But if you mean to remain here long I would advise you to get one. These Orientals are a people with whom appearances go a long way, and, as a rule, fear and respect mean the same thing with them. A pistol hanging over your loins is no great trouble to you, and looks as though you could bite. Many a dog goes through the world well by merely showing his teeth."

And then my companion began to talk of himself. "He did not," he said, "mean to remain in Syria very long."

"Nor I either," said I. "I have done with this

part of the world for the present, and shall take the next steamer from Jaffa for Alexandria. I shall only have one night in Jerusalem on my return."

After this he remained silent for a few moments, and then declared that that also had been his intention. He was almost ashamed to say so, however, because it looked as though he had resolved to hook himself on to me. So he answered, expressing almost regret at the circumstance.

"Don't let that trouble you," said I; "I shall be delighted to have your company. When you know me better, as I hope you will do, you will find that if such were not the case I should tell you so as frankly. I shall remain in Cairo some little time; so that beyond our arrival in Egypt, I can answer for nothing."

He said that he expected letters at Alexandria which would govern his future movements. I thought he seemed sad as he said so, and imagined, from his manner, that he did not expect very happy tidings. Indeed I had made up my mind that he was by no means free from care or sorrow. He had not the air of a man who could say of himself that he was " totus teres atque rotundus." But I had no wish to inquire, and the matter would have dropped had he not himself added—" I fear that I shall meet acquaintances in Egypt whom it will give me no pleasure to see."

"Then," said I, "if I were you, I would go to Constantinople instead;—indeed, anywhere rather than fall among friends who are not friendly. And the nearer the friend is, the more one feels that sort of thing. To my way of thinking, there is nothing on earth so pleasant as a pleasant wife; but then, what is there so damnable as one that is unpleasant?"

"Are you a married man?" he inquired. All his questions were put in a low tone of voice which seemed to give to them an air of special interest, and made one almost feel that they were asked with some special view to one's individual welfare. Now the fact is, that I am a married man with a family; but I am not much given to talk to strangers about my domestic concerns, and, therefore, though I had no particular object in view, I denied my obligations in this respect. "No," said I; "I have not come to that promotion yet. I am too frequently on the move to write myself down as Paterfamilias."

"Then you know nothing about that pleasantness of which you spoke just now?"

"Nor of the unpleasantness, thank God; my personal experiences are all to come,—as also are yours, I presume?"

It was possible that he had hampered himself with some woman, and that she was to meet him at Alexandria. Poor fellow! thought I. But his unhappiness was not of that kind. "No," said he; "I am not married; I am all alone in the world."

"Then I certainly would not allow myself to be troubled by unpleasant acquaintances."

It was now four hours since we had left Jerusalem, and we had arrived at the place at which it was proposed that we should breakfast. There was a large well there, and shade afforded by a rock under which the water sprung; and the Arabs had constructed a tank out of which the horses could drink, so that the place was ordinarily known as the first stage out of Jerusalem.

Smith had said not a word about his saddle, or complained in any way of discomfort, so that I had in truth forgotten the subject. Other matters had continually presented themselves, and I had never even asked him how he had fared. I now jumped from my horse, but I perceived at once that he was unable to do so. He smiled faintly, as his eye caught mine, but I knew that he wanted assistance. "Ah," said I, "that confounded Turkish saddle has already galled your skin. I see how it is; I shall have to doctor you with a little brandy,—externally applied, my friend." But I lent him my shoulder, and with that assistance he got down, very gently and slowly.

We ate our breakfast with a good will; bread and cold fowl and brandy-and-water, with a hard boiled egg by way of a final delicacy; and then I began to bargain with Joseph for the loan of his English saddle. I saw that Smith could not get through the journey with that monstrous Turkish affair, and that he would go on without complaining till he fainted or came to some other signal grief. But the Frenchman, seeing the plight in which we were, was disposed to drive a very hard bargain. He wanted forty shillings, the price of a pair of live Bedouins, for the accommodation, and declared that, even then, he should make the sacrifice only out of consideration to me.

"Very well," said I. "I'm tolerably tough myself, and I'll change with the gentleman. The chances are, that I shall not be in a very liberal humour when I reach Jaffa with stiff limbs and a sore skin. I have a very good memory, Joseph."

"I'll take thirty shillings, Mr. Jones; though I shall have to groan all the way like a condemned devil."

I struck a bargain with him at last for five-and-twenty, and set him to work to make the necessary change on the horses. "It will be just the same thing to him," I said to Smith. "I find that he is as much used to one as to the other."

"But how much money are you to pay him?" he asked. "Oh, nothing," I replied. "Give him a few piastres when you part with him at Jaffa." I do not know why I should have felt thus inclined to pay money out of my pocket for this Smith,—a man whom I had only seen for the first time on the preceding evening, and whose temperament was so essentially different from my own; but so I did. I would have done almost anything in reason for his comfort; and yet he was a melancholy fellow, with good inward pluck as I believed, but without that outward show of dash and hardihood which I

confess I love to see. "Pray tell him that I'll pay
him for it," said he. "We'll make that all right," I
answered; and then we remounted,—not without
some difficulty on his part. "You should have let
me rub in that brandy," I said. "You can't conceive how efficaciously I would have done it." But
he made me no answer.

At noon we met a caravan of pilgrims coming up
from Jordan. There might be some three or four
hundred, but the number seemed to be treble that,
from the loose and straggling line in which they
journeyed. It was a very singular sight, as they
moved slowly along the narrow path through the
sand, coming out of a defile among the hills which
was perhaps a quarter of a mile in front of us, passing
us as we stood still by the wayside, and then winding
again out of sight on the track over which we had
come. Some rode on camels,—a whole family, in
many cases, being perched on the same animal. I
observed a very old man and a very old woman slung
in panniers over a camel's back,—not such panniers
as might be befitting such a purpose, but square
baskets, so that the heads and heels of each of the
old couple hung out of the rear and front. "Surely
the journey will be their death," I said to Joseph.
"Yes, it will," he replied, quite coolly; "but what
matter how soon they die now that they have bathed
in Jordan?" Very many rode on donkeys; two,
generally, on each donkey; others, who had command
of money, on horses; but the greater number walked,

toiling painfully from Jerusalem to Jericho on the
first day, sleeping there in tents and going to bathe
in Jordan on the second day, and then returning
from Jericho to Jerusalem on the third. The pilgrimage is made throughout in accordance with
fixed rules, and there is a tariff for the tent accommodation at Jericho,—so much per head per night,
including the use of hot water.

Standing there, close by the wayside, we could see
not only the garments and faces of these strange
people, but we could watch their gestures and form
some opinion of what was going on within their
thoughts. They were much quieter,—tamer, as it
were,—than Englishmen would be under such circumstances. Those who were carried seemed to sit
on their beasts in passive tranquillity, neither enjoying anything nor suffering anything. Their object
had been to wash in Jordan,—to do that once in
their lives ;—and they had washed in Jordan. The
benefit expected was not to be immediately spiritual.
No earnest prayerfulness was considered necessary
after the ceremony. To these members of the
Greek Christian Church it had been handed down
from father to son that washing in Jordan once
during life was efficacious towards salvation. And
therefore the journey had been made at terrible cost
and terrible risk ; for these people had come from
afar, and were from their habits but little capable
of long journeys. Many die under the toil ; but this
matters not if they do not die before they have

reached Jordan. Some few there are, undoubtedly, more ecstatic in this great deed of their religion. One man I especially noticed on this day. He had bound himself to make the pilgrimage from Jerusalem to the river with one foot bare. He was of a better class, and was even nobly dressed, as though it were a part of his vow to show to all men that he did this deed, wealthy and great though he was. He was a fine man, perhaps thirty years of age, with a well-grown beard descending on his breast, and at his girdle he carried a brace of pistols. But never in my life had I seen bodily pain so plainly written in a man's face. The sweat was falling from his brow, and his eyes were strained and bloodshot with agony. He had no stick, his vow, I presume, debarring him from such assistance, and he limped along, putting to the ground the heel of the unprotected foot. I could see it, and it was a mass of blood, and sores, and broken skin. An Irish girl would walk from Jerusalem to Jericho without shoes, and be not a penny the worse for it. This poor fellow clearly suffered so much that I was almost inclined to think that in the performance of his penance he had done something to aggravate his pain. Those around him paid no attention to him, and the dragoman seemed to think nothing of the affair whatever. "Those fools of Greeks do not understand the Christian religion," he said, being himself a Latin or Roman Catholic.

At the tail of the line we encountered two Be-

douins, who were in charge of the caravan, and
Joseph at once addressed them. The men were
mounted, one on a very sorry-looking jade, but the
other on a good stout Arab barb. They had guns
slung behind their backs, coloured handkerchiefs on
their heads, and they wore the striped bernouse.
The parley went on for about ten minutes, during
which the procession of pilgrims wound out of sight ;
and it ended in our being accompanied by the two
Arabs, who thus left their greater charge to take care
of itself back to the city. I understood afterwards
that they had endeavoured to persuade Joseph that
we might just as well go on alone, merely satisfying
the demand of the tariff. But he had pointed out
that I was a particular man, and that under such circumstances the final settlement might be doubtful.
So they turned and accompanied us; but, as a matter
of fact, we should have been as well without them.

The sun was beginning to fall in the heavens when
we reached the actual margin of the Dead Sea. We
had seen the glitter of its still waters for a long time
previously, shining under the sun as though it were
not real. We have often heard, and some of us have
seen, how effects of light and shade together will
produce so vivid an appearance of water where there
is no water, as to deceive the most experienced.
But the reverse was the case here. There was the
lake, and there it had been before our eyes for the
last two hours ; and yet it looked, then and now, as
though it were an image of a lake, and not real

water. I had long since made up my mind to bathe in it, feeling well convinced that I could do so without harm to myself, and I had been endeavouring to persuade Smith to accompany me; but he positively refused. He would bathe, he said, neither in the Dead Sea nor in the river Jordan. He did not like bathing, and preferred to do his washing in his own room. Of course I had nothing further to say, and begged that, under these circumstances, he would take charge of my purse and pistols while I was in the water. This he agreed to do; but even in this he was strange and almost uncivil. I was to bathe from the furthest point of a little island, into which there was a rough causeway from the land made of stones and broken pieces of wood, and I exhorted him to go with me thither; but he insisted on remaining with his horse on the mainland at some little distance from the island. He did not feel inclined to go down to the water's edge, he said.

I confess that at this I almost suspected that he was going to play me foul, and I hesitated. He saw in an instant what was passing through my mind. "You had better take your pistol and money with you; they will be quite safe on your clothes." But to have kept the things now would have shown suspicion too plainly, and as I could not bring myself to do that, I gave them up. I have sometimes thought that I was a fool to do so.

I went away by myself to the end of the island, and then I did bathe. It is impossible to conceive anything more desolate than the appearance of the place. The land shelves very gradually away to the water, and the whole margin, to the breadth of some twenty or thirty feet, is strewn with the débris of rushes, bits of timber, and old white withered reeds. Whence these bits of timber have come it seems difficult to say. The appearance is as though the water had receded and left them there. I have heard it said that there is no vegetation near the Dead Sea; but such is not the case, for these rushes do grow on the bank. I found it difficult enough to get into the water, for the ground shelves down very slowly, and is rough with stones and large pieces of half-rotten wood; moreover, when I was in nearly up to my hips, the water knocked me down; indeed, it did so when I had gone as far as my knees, but I recovered myself, and by perseverance did proceed somewhat further. It must not be imagined that this knocking down was effected by the movement of the water. There is no such movement. Everything is perfectly still, and the fluid seems hardly to be displaced by the entrance of the body; but the effect is that one's feet are tripped up, and that one falls prostrate on to the surface. The water is so strong and buoyant, that, when above a foot in depth has to be encountered, the strength and weight of the bather are not sufficient to keep down his feet and legs. I then essayed to swim; but I could not do this in the ordinary way, as I was unable to keep enough of my body below the surface; so that my head and face

seemed to be propelled down upon it. I turned
round and floated, but the glare of the sun was so
powerful that I could not remain long in that position. However, I had bathed in the Dead Sea, and
was so far satisfied.

Anything more abominable to the palate than this
water, if it be water, I never had inside my mouth.
I expected it to be extremely salt, and no doubt, if
it were analyzed, such would be the result; but
there is a flavour in it which kills the salt. No attempt can be made at describing this taste. It may
be imagined that I did not drink heartily, merely
taking up a drop or two with my tongue from the
palm of my hand; but it seemed to me as though I
had been drenched with it. Even brandy would not
relieve me from it. And then my whole body was
in a mess, and I felt as though I had been rubbed
with pitch. Looking at my limbs, I saw no sign on
them of the fluid. They seemed to dry from this as
they usually do from any other water; but still the
feeling remained. However, I was to ride from
hence to a spot on the banks of Jordan, which I
should reach in an hour, and at which I would
wash; so I clothed myself, and prepared for my
departure.

Seated in my position in the island I was unable
to see what was going on among the remainder of
the party, and therefore could not tell whether my
pistols and money were safe. I dressed, therefore,
rather hurriedly, and on getting again to the shore,

found that Mr. John Smith had not levanted. He was seated on his horse at some distance from ·Joseph and the Arabs, and had no appearance of being in league with those, no doubt, worthy guides. I certainly had suspected a ruse, and now was angry with myself that I had done so; and yet, in London, one would not trust one's money to a stranger whom one had met twenty-four hours since in a coffee-room! Why, then, do it with a stranger whom one chanced to meet in a desert?

"Thanks," I said, as he handed me my belongings. "I wish I could have induced you to come in also. The Dead Sea is now at your elbow, and, therefore, you think nothing of it; but in ten or fifteen years' time, you would be glad to be able to tell your children that you had bathed in it."

"I shall never have any children to care for such tidings," he replied.

The river Jordan, for some miles above the point at which it joins the Dead Sea, runs through very steep banks,—banks which are almost precipitous,—and is, as it were, guarded by the thick trees and bushes which grow upon its sides. This is so much the case, that one may ride, as we did, for a considerable distance along the margin, and not be able even to approach the water. I had a fancy for bathing in some spot of my own selection, instead of going to the open shore frequented by all the pilgrims; but I was baffled in this. When I did force my way down to the river side, I found that the water ran so rapidly, and that the bushes and boughs of trees grew so far over and into the stream, as to make it impossible for me to bathe. I could not have got in without my clothes, and having got in, I could not have got out again. I was, therefore, obliged to put up with the open muddy shore to which the bathers descend, and at which we may presume that Joshua passed when he came over as one of the twelve spies to spy out the land. And even here I could not go full into the stream as I would fain have done, lest I should be carried down, and so have assisted to whiten the shores of the Dead Sea with my bones. As to getting over to the Moabitish side of the river, that was plainly impossible; and, indeed, it seemed to be the prevailing opinion that the passage of the river was not practicable without going up as far as Samaria. And yet we know that there, or thereabouts, the Israelites did cross it.

I jumped from my horse the moment I got to the place, and once more gave my purse and pistols to my friend. " You are going to bathe again?" he said. " Certainly," said I; " you don't suppose that I would come to Jordan and not wash there, even if I were not foul with the foulness of the Dead Sea!" " You'll kill yourself, in your present state of heat;" he said, remonstrating just as one's mother or wife might do. But even had it been my mother or wife I could not have attended to such remonstrance then; and before he had done looking

at me with those big eyes of his, my coat and waistcoat and cravat were on the ground, and I was at
work at my braces; whereupon he turned from me
slowly, and strolled away into the wood. On this
occasion I had no base fears about my money.

And then I did bathe,—very uncomfortably. The
shore was muddy with the feet of the pilgrims, and
the river so rapid that I hardly dared to get beyond
the mud. I did manage to take a plunge in, head-
foremost, but I was forced to wade out through the dirt
and slush, so that I found it difficult to make my feet
and legs clean enough for my shoes and stockings;
and then, moreover, the flies plagued me most
unmercifully. I should have thought that the filthy
flavour from the Dead Sea would have saved me
from that nuisance; but the mosquitoes thereabouts
are probably used to it. Finding this process of
bathing to be so difficult, I inquired as to the practice of the pilgrims. I found that with them,
bathing in Jordan has come to be much the same
as baptism has with us. It does not mean immer-
sion. No doubt they do take off their shoes and
stockings; but they do not strip, and go bodily into
the water.

As soon as I was dressed I found that Smith was
again at my side with purse and pistols. We then
went up a little above the wood, and sat down together on the long sandy grass. It was now quite
evening, so that the short Syrian twilight had commenced, and the sun was no longer hot in the

s

heavens. It would be night as we rode on to the tents at Jericho; but there was no difficulty as to the way, and therefore we did not hurry the horses, who were feeding on the grass. We sat down together on a spot from which we could see the stream, —close together, so that when I stretched myself out in my weariness, as I did before we started, my head rested on his legs. Ah, me! one does not take such liberties with new friends in England. It was a place which led one on to some special thoughts. The mountains of Moab were before us, very plain in their outline. "Moab is my wash-pot, and over Edom will I cast out my shoe!" There they were before us, very visible to the eye, and we began naturally to ask questions of each other. Why was Moab the wash-pot, and Edom thus cursed with indignity? Why had the right bank of the river been selected for such great purposes, whereas the left was thus condemned? Was there, at that time, any special fertility in this land of promise which has since departed from it? We are told of a bunch of grapes which took two men to carry it; but now there is not a vine in the whole country side. Now-a-days the sandy plain round Jericho is as dry and arid as are any of the valleys of Moab. The Jordan was running beneath our feet,—the Jordan in which the leprous king had washed, though the bright rivers of his own Damascus were so much nearer to his hand. It was but a humble stream to which he was sent; but the spot, probably, was higher up, above the Sea of Galilee, where the river is narrow. But another also had come down to this river, perhaps to this very spot on its shores, and submitted himself to its waters;—as to whom, perhaps, it will better that I should not speak much in this light story.

The Dead Sea was on our right, still glittering in the distance, and behind us lay the plains of Jericho and the wretched collection of huts which still bears the name of the ancient city. Beyond that, but still seemingly within easy distance of us, were the mountains of the wilderness. The wilderness! In truth, the spot was one which did lead to many thoughts.

We talked of these things, as to many of which I found that my friend was much more free in his doubts and questionings than myself; and then our words came back to ourselves, the natural centre of all men's thoughts and words. "From what you say," I said, "I gather that you have had enough of this land?"

"Quite enough," he said. "Why seek such spots as these, if they only dispel the associations and veneration of one's childhood?"

"But with me such associations and veneration are riveted the stronger by seeing the places, and putting my hand upon the spots. I do not speak of that fictitious marble slab up there; but here, among the sandhills by this river, and at the Mount of Olives over which we passed, I do believe."

He paused a moment, and then replied: "To me

it is all nothing,—absolutely nothing. But then do we not know that our thoughts are formed, and our beliefs modelled, not on the outward signs or intrinsic evidences of things,—as would be the case were we always rational,—but by the inner workings of the mind itself? At the present turn of my life I can believe in nothing that is gracious."

"Ah, you mean that you are unhappy. You have come to grief in some of your doings or belongings, and therefore find that all things are bitter to the taste. I have had my palate out of order too; but the proper appreciation of flavours has come back to me. Bah,—how noisome was that Dead Sea water!"

"The Dead Sea waters are noisome," he said; "and I have been drinking of them by long draughts."

"Long draughts!" I answered, thinking to console him. "Draughts have not been long which can have been swallowed in your years. Your disease may be acute, but it cannot yet have become chronic. A man always thinks at the moment of each misfortune that that special misery will last his lifetime; but God is too good for that. I do not know what ails you; but this day twelvemonth will see you again as sound as a roach."

We then sat silent for a while, during which I was puffing at a cigar. Smith, among his accomplishments, did not reckon that of smoking,—which was a grief to me; for a man enjoys the tobacco doubly when another is enjoying it with him.

" No, you do not know what ails me," he said at last, " and, therefore, cannot judge."

" Perhaps not, my dear fellow. But my experience tells me that early wounds are generally capable of cure ; and, therefore, I surmise that yours may be so. The heart at your time of life is not worn out, and has strength and soundness left wherewith to throw off its maladies. I hope it may be so with you."

" God knows. I do not mean to say that there are none more to be pitied than I am; but at the present moment, I am not—not light-hearted."

" I wish I could ease your burden, my dear fellow."

" It is most preposterous in me thus to force myself upon you, and then trouble you with my cares. But I had been alone so long, and I was so weary of it ! "

" By Jove, and so had I. Make no apology. And let me tell you this,—though perhaps you will not credit me ;—that I would sooner laugh with a comrade than cry with him is true enough ; but, if occasion demands, I can do the latter also." He then put out his hand to me, and I pressed it in token of my friendship. My own hand was hot and rough with the heat and sand ; but his was soft and cool almost as a woman's. I thoroughly hate an effeminate man; but, in spite of a certain womanly softness about this fellow, I could not hate him. "Yes," I continued, "though somewhat unused to the melting mood, I also sometimes give forth my medicinal gums. I don't want to ask you any questions, and, as a rule, I hate to be told secrets, but if I can be of any service to you in any matter I will do my best. I don't say this with reference to the present moment, but think of it before we part."

I looked round at him and saw that he was in tears. " I know that you will think that I am a weak fool," he said, pressing his handkerchief to his eyes.

" By no means. There are moments in a man's life when it becomes him to weep like a woman ; but the older he grows the more seldom those moments come to him. As far as I can see of men, they never cry at that which disgraces them."

" It is left for women to do that," he answered.

" Oh, women ! A woman cries for everything and for nothing. It is the sharpest arrow she has in her quiver,—the best card in her hand. When a woman cries, what can you do but give her all she asks for ? "

" Do you—dislike women ? "

" No, by Jove ! I am never really happy unless one is near me,—or more than one. A man, as a rule, has an amount of energy within him which he cannot turn to profit on himself alone. It is good for him to have a woman by him that he may work for her, and thus have exercise for his limbs and faculties. I am very fond of women. But I always like those best who are most helpless."

We were silent again for a while, and it was during this time that I found myself lying with my head in his lap. I had slept, but it could have been but for a few minutes, and when I woke I found his hand upon my brow. As I started up he said that the

flies had been annoying me, and that he had not
chosen to waken me as I seemed weary. "It has
been that double bathing," I said, apologetically;
for I always feel ashamed when I am detected sleeping in the day. "In hot weather the water does make
one drowsy. By Jove, it's getting dark; we had
better have the horses."

"Stay half a moment," he said, speaking very
softly, and laying his hand upon my arm, "I will not
detain you a minute."

"There is no hurry in life," I said.

"You promised me just now you would assist me."

"If it be in my power, I will."

"Before we part at Alexandria I will endeavour to
tell you the story of my troubles, and then, if you can
aid me—" It struck me as he paused that I had
made a rash promise, but nevertheless I must stand
by it now—with one or two provisoes. The chances
were that the young man was short of money, or else
that he had got into a scrape about a girl. In either
case I might give him some slight assistance; but,
then, it behoved me to make him understand that I
would not consent to become a participator in mischief. I was too old to get my head willingly into a
scrape, and this I must endeavour to make him
understand.

"I will, if it be in my power," I said. "I will ask
no questions now; but if your trouble be about some
lady——"

"It is not," said he.

"Well; so be it. Of all troubles those are the most troublesome. If you are short of cash——"

"No, I am not short of cash."

"You are not. That's well too; for want of money is a sore trouble also." And then I paused before I came to the point. "I do not suspect anything bad of you, Smith. Had I done so, I should not have spoken as I have done. And if there be nothing bad——"

"There is nothing disgraceful," he said.

"That is just what I mean; and in that case I will do anything for you that may be within my power. Now let us look for Joseph and the mucherry-boy, for it is time that we were at Jericho."

I cannot describe at length the whole of our journey from thence to our tents at Jericho, nor back to Jerusalem, nor even from Jerusalem to Jaffa. At Jericho we did sleep in tents, paying so much per night, according to the tariff. We wandered out at night, and drank coffee with a family of Arabs in the desert, sitting in a ring round their coffee-kettle. And we saw a Turkish soldier punished with the bastinado,—a sight which did not do me any good, and which made Smith very sick. Indeed after the first blow he walked away. Jericho is a remarkable spot in that pilgrim week, and I wish I had space to describe it. But I have not, for I must hurry on, back to Jerusalem and thence to Jaffa. I had much to tell also of those Bedouins; how they were essentially true to us, but teased us almost to frenzy by

their continual begging. They begged for our food
and our drink, for our cigars and our gunpowder, for
the clothes off our backs, and the handkerchiefs out of
our pockets. As to gunpowder I had none to give
them, for my charges were all made up in cartridges;
and I learned that the guns behind their backs were
a mere pretence, for they had not a grain of powder
among them.

We slept one night in Jerusalem, and started early
on the following morning. Smith came to my hotel
so that we might be ready together for the move.
We still carried with us Joseph and the mucherry-
boy; but for our Bedouins, who had duly received
their forty shillings a piece, we had no further use.
On our road down to Jerusalem we had much chat together, but only one adventure. Those pilgrims, of
whom I have spoken, journey to Jerusalem in the
greatest number by the route which we were now taking from it, and they come in long droves, reaching Jaffa
in crowds by the French and Austrian steamers from
Smyrna, Damascus, and Constantinople. As their
number confers security in that somewhat insecure
country, many travellers from the west of Europe
make arrangements to travel with them. On our
way down we met the last of these caravans for the
year, and we were passing it for more than two hours.
On this occasion I rode first, and Smith was immediately behind me; but of a sudden I observed him to
wheel his horse round, and to clamber downwards
among bushes and stones towards a river that ran

below us. "Hallo, Smith," I cried, "you will destroy your horse, and yourself too." But he would not answer me, and all I could do was to draw up in the path and wait. My confusion was made the worse, as at that moment a long string of pilgrims was passing by. "Good morning, sir," said an old man to me in good English. I looked up as I answered him, and saw a grey-haired gentleman, of very solemn and sad aspect. He might be seventy years of age, and I could see that he was attended by three or four servants. I shall never forget the severe and sorrowful expression of his eyes, over which his heavy eyebrows hung low. "Are there many English in Jerusalem?" he asked. "A good many," I replied; "there always are at Easter." "Can you tell me anything of any of them?" he asked. "Not a word," said I, for I knew no one; "but our consul can." And then we bowed to each other and he passed on.

I got off my horse and scrambled down on foot after Smith. I found him gathering berries and bushes as though his very soul were mad with botany; but as I had seen nothing of this in him before, I asked what strange freak had taken him.

"You were talking to that old man," he said.

"Well, yes, I was."

"That is the relation of whom I have spoken to you."

"The d—— he is!"

"And I would avoid him, if it be possible."

I then learned that the old gentleman was his
uncle. He had no living father or mother, and he
now supposed that his relative was going to Jerusalem in quest of him. "If so," said I, "you will undoubtedly give him leg bail, unless the Austrian boat
is more than ordinarily late. It is as much as we
shall do to catch it, and you may be half over Africa,
or far gone on your way to India, before he can be
on your track again."

"I will tell you all about it at Alexandria," he
replied; and then he scrambled up again with his
horse, and we went on. That night we slept at the
Armenian convent at Ramlath, or Ramath. This
place is supposed to stand on the site of Arimathea,
and is marked as such in many of the maps. The
monks at this time of the year are very busy, as the
pilgrims all stay here for one night on their routes
backwards and forwards, and the place on such occasions is terribly crowded. On the night of our visit
it was nearly empty, as a caravan had left it that
morning; and thus we were indulged with separate
cells, a point on which my companion seemed to lay
considerable stress.

On the following day, at about noon, we entered
Jaffa, and put up at an inn there which is kept by a
Pole. The boat from Beyrout, which touches at Jaffa
on its way to Alexandria, was not yet in, nor even
sighted; we were therefore amply in time. "Shall
we sail to-night?" I asked of the agent. "Yes, in
all probability," he replied. "If the signal be seen

before three we shall do so.   If not, then not ; " and
so I returned to the hotel.

Smith had involuntarily shown signs of fatigue
during the journey, but yet he had borne up well
against it. I had never felt called on to grant any extra
indulgence as to time because the work was too much
for him.   But now he was a good deal knocked up,
and I was a little frightened, fearing that I had over-
driven him under the heat of the sun.   I was alarmed
lest he should have fever, and proposed to send for
the Jaffa doctor.   But this he utterly refused.   He
would shut himself for an hour or two in his room,
he said, and by that time he trusted the boat would
be in sight.   It was clear to me that he was very
anxious on the subject, fearing that his uncle would
be back upon his heels before he had started.

I ordered a serious breakfast for myself, for with
me, on such occasions, my appetite demands more
immediate attention than my limbs.   I also acknowledge that I become fatigued, and can lay myself at
length during such idle days and sleep from hour to
hour; but the desire to do so never comes till I have
well eaten and drunken. A bottle of French wine, three
or four cutlets of goats' flesh, an omelet made not of
the freshest eggs, and an enormous dish of oranges,
was the banquet set before me ; and though I might
have found fault with it in Paris or London, I thought
that it did well enough in Jaffa.   My poor friend
could not join me, but had a cup of coffee in his
room.   "At any rate take a little brandy in it," I

said to him, as I stood over his bed. "I could not swallow it," said he, looking at me with almost beseeching eyes. "Beshrew the fellow," I said to myself as I left him, carefully closing the door, so that the sound should not shake him; "He is little better than a woman, and yet I have become as fond of him as though he were my brother."

I went out at three, but up to that time the boat had not been signalled. "And we shall not get out to-night?" "No, not to-night," said the agent. "And at what time to-morrow?" "If she comes in this evening, you will start by daylight. But they so manage her departure from Beyrout, that she seldom is here in the evening." "It will be noon to-morrow then?" "Yes," the man said, "noon to-morrow." I calculated, however, that the old gentleman could not possibly be on our track by that time. He would not have reached Jerusalem till late in the day on which we saw him, and it would take him some time to obtain tidings of his nephew. But it might be possible that messengers sent by him should reach Jaffa by four or five on the day after his arrival. That would be this very day which we were now wasting at Jaffa. Having thus made my calculations, I returned to Smith to give him such consolation as it might be in my power to afford.

He seemed to be dreadfully afflicted by all this. "He will have traced me to Jerusalem, and then again away; and will follow me immediately."

"That is all very well," I said; "but let even a

young man do the best he can, and he will not get
from Jerusalem to Jaffa in less than twelve hours.
Your uncle is not a young man, and could not possibly do the journey under two days."

"But he will send. He will not mind what money
he spends."

"And if he does send, take off your hat to his
messengers, and bid them carry your compliments
back. You are not a felon whom he can arrest."

"No, he cannot arrest me ; but, ah ! you do not
understand ;" and then he sat up on the bed, and
seemed as though he were going to wring his hands
in despair.

I waited for some half hour in his room, thinking
that he would tell me this story of his. If he required that I should give him my aid in the presence
either of his uncle or of his uncle's myrmidons, I
must at any rate know what was likely to be the
dispute between them. But as he said nothing I
suggested that he should stroll out with me among
the orange-groves by which the town is surrounded.
In answer to this he looked up piteously into my
face as though begging me to be merciful to him.
"You are strong," said he, "and cannot understand
what it is to feel fatigue as I do." And yet he had
declared on commencing his journey that he would
not be found to complain ? Nor had he complained
by a single word till after that encounter with his
uncle. Nay he had borne up well till this news had
reached us of the boat being late. I felt convinced

that if the boat were at this moment lying in the harbour all that appearance of excessive weakness would soon vanish. What it was that he feared I could not guess; but it was manifest to me that some great terror almost overwhelmed him.

"My idea is," said I,—and I suppose that I spoke with something less of good-nature in my tone than I had assumed for the last day or two, "that no man should, under any circumstances, be so afraid of another man, as to tremble at his presence,—either at his presence or his expected presence."

"Ah, now you are angry with me; now you despise me!"

"Neither the one nor the other. But if I may take the liberty of a friend with you, I would advise you to combat this feeling of horror. If you do not, it will unman you. After all, what can your uncle do to you? He cannot rob you of your heart or soul. He cannot touch your inner self."

"You do not know," he said.

"Ah but, Smith, I do know that. Whatever may be this quarrel between you and him, you should not tremble at the thought of him; unless indeed——"

"Unless what?"

"Unless you had done aught that should make you tremble before every honest man." I own I had begun to have my doubts of him, and to fear that he had absolutely disgraced himself. Even in such case I,—I individually,—did not wish to be severe on him;

but I should be annoyed to find that I had opened my heart to a swindler or a practised knave.

"I will tell you all to-morrow," said he; "but I have been guilty of nothing of that sort."

In the evening he did come out, and sat with me as I smoked my cigar. The boat, he was told, would almost undoubtedly come in by daybreak on the following morning, and be off at nine; whereas it was very improbable that any arrival from Jerusalem would be so early as that. "Beside," I reminded him, "your uncle will hardly hurry down to Jaffa, because he will have no reason to think but what you have already started. There are no telegraphs here, you know."

In the evening he was still very sad, though the paroxysm of his terror seemed to have passed away. I would not bother him, as he had himself chosen the following morning for the telling of his story. So I sat and smoked, and talked to him about our past journey, and by degrees the power of speech came back to him, and I again felt that I loved him. Yes, loved him! I have not taken many such fancies into my head, at so short a notice; but I did love him, as though he were a younger brother. I felt a delight in serving him, and though I was almost old enough to be his father, I ministered to him as though he had been an old man, or a woman.

On the following morning we were stirring at daybreak, and found that the vessel was in sight. She would be in the roads off the town in two hours'

time, they said, and would start at eleven or twelve.
And then we walked round by the gate of the town,
and sauntered a quarter of a mile or so along the
way that leads towards Jerusalem. I could see that
his eye was anxiously turned down the road, but he
said nothing. We saw no cloud of dust, and then
we returned to breakfast.

"The steamer has come to anchor," said our dirty
Polish host to us in execrable English. "And we
may be off on board," said Smith. "Not yet," he
said; "they must put their cargo out first." I saw,
however, that Smith was uneasy, and I made up my
mind to go off to the vessel at once. When they
should see an English portmanteau making an offer
to come up the gangway, the Austrian sailors would
not stop it. So I called for the bill, and ordered
that the things should be taken down to the wretched
broken heap of rotten timber which they called a
quay. Smith had not told me his story, but no
doubt he would as soon as he was on board.

I was in the very act of squabbling with the Pole
over the last demand for piastres, when we heard a
noise in the gateway of the inn, and I saw Smith's
countenance become pale. It was an Englishman's
voice asking if there were any strangers there; so I
went into the courtyard, closing the door behind me,
and turning the key upon the landlord and Smith.
"Smith," said I to myself, "will keep the Pole quiet
if he have any wit left."

The man who had asked the question had the air

T

of an upper English servant, and I thought that I recognised one of those whom I had seen with the old gentleman on the road ; but the matter was soon put at rest by the appearance of that gentleman himself. He walked up into the courtyard, looked hard at me from under those bushy eyebrows, just raised his hat, and then said, "I believe I am speaking to Mr. Jones."

"Yes," said I, "I am Mr. Jones. Can I have the honour of serving you?"

There was something peculiarly unpleasant about this man's face. At the present moment I examined it closely, and could understand the great aversion which his nephew felt towards him. He looked like a gentleman and like a man of talent, nor was there anything of meanness in his face ; neither was he ill-looking, in the usual acceptation of the word ; but one could see that he was solemn, austere, and over-bearing ; that he would be incapable of any light enjoyment, and unforgiving towards all offences. I took him to be a man who, being old himself, could never remember that he had been young, and who, therefore, hated the levities of youth. To me such a character is specially odious ; for I would fain, if it be possible, be young even to my grave. Smith, if he were clever, might escape from the window of the room, which opened out upon a terrace, and still get down to the steamer. I would keep the old man in play for some time ; and, even though I lost my passage, would be true to my friend. There lay our

joint luggage at my feet in the yard. If Smith
would venture away without his portion of it, all
might yet be right.

"My name, sir, is Sir William Weston," he began.
I had heard of the name before, and knew him to be
a man of wealth, and family, and note. I took off
my hat, and said that I had much honour in meeting
Sir William Weston.

"And I presume you know the object with which
I am now here," he continued.

"Not exactly," said I. "Nor do I understand how
I possibly should know it, seeing that, up to this
moment, I did not even know your name, and have
heard nothing concerning either your movements or
your affairs."

"Sir," said he, "I have hitherto believed that I
might at any rate expect from you the truth."

"Sir," said I, "I am bold to think that you will
not dare to tell me, either now, or at any other
time, that you have received, or expect to receive,
from me anything that is not true."

He then stood still, looking at me for a moment
or two, and I beg to assert that I looked as fully at
him. There was, at any rate, no cause why I should
tremble before him. I was not his nephew, nor was
I responsible for his nephew's doings towards him.
Two of his servants were behind him, and on my side
there stood a boy and girl belonging to the inn.
They, however, could not understand a word of
English. I saw that he was hesitating, but at last

he spoke out. I confess, now, that his words, when they were spoken, did, at the first moment, make me tremble.

"I have to charge you," said he, "with eloping with my niece, and I demand of you to inform me where she is. You are perfectly aware that I am her guardian by law."

I did tremble;—not that I cared much for Sir William's guardianship, but I saw before me so terrible an embarrassment! And then I felt so thoroughly abashed in that I had allowed myself to be so deceived! It all came back upon me in a moment, and covered me with a shame that even made me blush. I had travelled through the desert with a woman for days, and had not discovered her, though she had given me a thousand signs. All those signs I remembered now, and I blushed painfully. When her hand was on my forehead I still thought that she was a man! I declare that at this moment I felt a stronger disinclination to face my late companion than I did to encounter her angry uncle.

"Your niece!" I said, speaking with a sheepish bewilderment which should have convinced him at once of my innocence. She had asked me, too, whether I was a married man, and I had denied it. How was I to escape from such a mess of misfortunes? I declare that I began to forget her troubles in my own.

"Yes, my niece,—Miss Julia Weston. The disgrace

which you have brought upon me must be wiped out; but my first duty is to save that unfortunate young woman from further misery."

"If it be as you say," I exclaimed, "by the honour of a gentleman——"

"I care nothing for the honour of a gentleman till I see it proved. Be good enough to inform me, sir, whether Miss Weston is in this house."

For a moment I hesitated; but I saw at once that I should make myself responsible for certain mischief, of which I was at any rate hitherto in truth innocent, if I allowed myself to become a party to concealing a young lady. Up to this period I could at any rate defend myself, whether my defence were believed or not believed. I still had a hope that the charming Julia might have escaped through the window, and a feeling that if she had done so I was not responsible. When I turned the lock I turned it on Smith.

For a moment I hesitated, and then walked slowly across the yard and opened the door. "Sir William," I said, as I did so, "I travelled here with a companion dressed as a man; and I believed him to be what he seemed till this minute."

"Sir!" said Sir William, with a look of scorn in his face which gave me the lie in my teeth as plainly as any words could do. And then he entered the room. The Pole was standing in one corner, apparently amazed at what was going on, and Smith,—I may as well call her Miss Weston at once, for the baronet's statement was true,—was sitting on a sort of divan in the corner of the chamber, hiding her face in her hands. She had made no attempt at an escape, and a full explanation was therefore indispensable. For myself I own that I felt ashamed of my part in the play,—ashamed even of my own innocency. Had I been less innocent I should certainly have contrived to appear much less guilty. Had it occurred to me on the banks of the Jordan that Smith was a lady, I should not have travelled with her in her gentleman's habiliments from Jerusalem to Jaffa. Had she consented to remain under my protection, she must have done so without a masquerade.

The uncle stood still and looked at his niece. He probably understood how thoroughly stern and disagreeable was his own face, and considered that he could punish the crime of his relative in no severer way than by looking at her. In this I think he was right. But at last there was a necessity for speaking. "Unfortunate young woman!" he said, and then paused.

"We had better get rid of the landlord," I said, "before we come to any explanation." And I motioned to the man to leave the room. This he did very unwillingly, but at last he was gone.

"I fear that it is needless to care on her account who may hear the story of her shame," said Sir William. I looked at Miss Weston, but she still sat hiding her face. However, if she did not defend herself, it was necessary that I should defend both her and me.

"I do not know how far I may be at liberty to speak with reference to the private matters of yourself or of your—your niece, Sir William Weston. I would not willingly interfere——"

"Sir," said he, "your interference has already taken place. Will you have the goodness to explain to me what are your intentions with regard to that lady?"

My intentions! Heaven help me! My intentions, of course, were to leave her in her uncle's hands. Indeed, I could hardly be said to have formed any intention since I had learned that I had been honoured by a lady's presence. At this moment I deeply regretted that I had thoughtlessly stated to her that I was an unmarried man. In doing so I had had no object. But at that time "Smith" had been quite a stranger to me, and I had not thought it necessary to declare my own private concerns. Since that I had talked so little of myself that the fact of my family at home had not been mentioned. "Will you have the goodness to explain what are your intentions with regard to that lady?" said the baronet.

"Oh, Uncle William!" exclaimed Miss Weston, now at length raising her head from her hands.

"Hold your peace, madam," said he. "When called upon to speak, you will find your words with difficulty enough. Sir, I am waiting for an answer from you."

"But, uncle, he is nothing to me ;—the gentleman is nothing to me!"

"By the heavens above us, he shall be something, or I will know the reason why! What! he has gone off with you ; he has travelled through the country with you, hiding you from your only natural friend ; he has been your companion for weeks——"

"Six days, sir," said I.

"Sir!" said the baronet, again giving me the lie. "And now," he continued, addressing his niece, "you tell me that he is nothing to you. He shall give me his promise that he will make you his wife at the consulate at Alexandria, or I will destroy him. I know who he is."

"If you know who I am," said I, "you must know——"

But he would not listen to me. "And as for you, madam, unless he makes me that promise——" And then he paused in his threat, and, turning round, looked me in the face. I saw that she also was looking at me, though not openly as he did ; and some flattering devil that was at work round my heart, would have persuaded that she also would have heard a certain answer given without dismay,—would even have received comfort in her agony from such answer. But the reader knows how completely that answer was out of my power.

"I have not the slightest ground for supposing," said I, "that the lady would accede to such an arrangement,—if it were possible. My acquaintance with her has been altogether confined to——. To tell the truth, I have not been in Miss Weston's confidence, and have taken her to be only that which she has seemed to be."

"Sir!" said the baronet, again looking at me as though he would wither me on the spot for my falsehood.

"It is true!" said Julia, getting up from her seat, and appealing with clasped hands to her uncle—"as true as Heaven."

"Madam!" said he, "do you both take me for a fool?"

"That you should take me for one," said I, "would be very natural. The facts are as we state to you. Miss Weston,—as I now learn that she is,—did me the honour of calling at my hotel, having heard——" And then it seemed to me as though I were attempting to screen myself by telling the story against her, so I was again silent. Never in my life had I been in a position of such extraordinary difficulty. The duty which I owed to Julia as a woman, and to Sir William as a guardian, and to myself as the father of a family, all clashed with each other. I was anxious to be generous, honest, and prudent, but it was impossible; so I made up my mind to say nothing further.

"Mr. Jones," said the baronet, "I have explained to you the only arrangement which under the present circumstances I can permit to pass without open exposure and condign punishment. That you are a gentleman by birth, education, and position I am aware,"—whereupon I raised my hat, and then he continued : "That lady has three hundred a year of her own——"

"And attractions, personal and mental, which are worth ten times the money," said I, and I bowed to my fair friend, who looked at me the while with sad beseeching eyes. I confess that the mistress of my bosom, had she known my thoughts at that one moment, might have had cause for anger.

"Very well," continued he. "Then the proposal which I name cannot, I imagine, but be satisfactory. If you will make to her and to me the only amends which it is in your power as a gentleman to afford, I will forgive all. Tell me that you will make her your wife on your arrival in Egypt."

I would have given anything not to have looked at Miss Weston at this moment, but I could not help it. I did turn my face half round to her before I answered, and then felt that I had been cruel in doing so. "Sir William," said I, "I have at home already a wife and family of my own."

"It is not true !" said he, retreating a step, and staring at me with amazement.

"There is something, sir," I replied, "in the unprecedented circumstances of this meeting, and in your position with regard to that lady, which, joined to your advanced age, will enable me to regard that useless insult as unspoken. I am a married man. There is the signature of my wife's last letter," and I handed him one which I had received as I was leaving Jerusalem.

But the coarse violent contradiction which Sir William had given me was as nothing compared with the reproach conveyed in Miss Weston's countenance. She looked at me as though all her anger were now turned against me.   And yet, methought, there was more of sorrow than of resentment in her countenance. But what cause was there for either?   Why should I be reproached, even by her look?   She did not remember at the moment that when I answered her chance question as to my domestic affairs, I had answered it as to a man who was a stranger to me, and not as to a beautiful woman, with whom I was about to pass certain days in close and intimate society.   To her, at the moment, it seemed as though I had cruelly deceived her.   In truth the one person really deceived had been myself.

And here I must explain, on behalf of the lady, that when she first joined me she had no other view than that of seeing the banks of the Jordan in that guise which she had chosen to assume, in order to escape from the solemnity and austerity of a disagreeable relative.   She had been very foolish, and that was all.   I take it that she had first left her uncle at Constantinople, but on this point I never got certain information.   Afterwards, while we were travelling together, the idea had come upon her, that she might go on as far as Alexandria with me.   And then——.
I know nothing further of the lady's intentions, but

I am certain that her wishes were good and pure. Her uncle had been intolerable to her, and she had fled from him. Such had been her offence, and no more.

"Then, sir," said the baronet, giving me back my letter, "you must be a double-dyed villain."

"And you, sir," said I——" But here Julia Weston interrupted me.

"Uncle, you altogether wrong this gentleman," she said. "He has been kind to me beyond my power of words to express; but, till told by you, he knew nothing of my secret. Nor would he have known it," she added, looking down upon the ground. As to that latter assertion, I was at liberty to believe as much as I pleased.

The Pole now came to the door, informing us that any who wished to start by the packet must go on board, and therefore, as the unreasonable old gentleman perceived, it was necessary that we should all make our arrangements. I cannot say that they were such as enable me to look back on them with satisfaction. He did seem now at last to believe that I had been an unconscious agent in his niece's stratagem, but he hardly on that account became civil to me. "It was absolutely necessary," he said, "that he and that unfortunate young woman," as he would call her, "should depart at once,—by this ship now going." To this proposition of course I made no opposition. "And you, Mr. Jones," he continued, "will at once perceive that you, as a gentleman, should allow us to proceed on our journey without the honour of your company."

This was very dreadful, but what could I say ; or, indeed, what could I do ? My most earnest desire in the matter was to save Miss Weston from annoyance ; and under existing circumstances my presence on board could not but be a burden to her. And then, if I went,—if I did go, in opposition to the wishes of the baronet, could I trust my own prudence ? It was better for all parties that I should remain.

"Sir William," said I, after a minute's consideration, "if you will apologise to me for the gross insults you have offered me, it shall be as you say."

"Mr. Jones," said Sir William, "I do apologise for the words which I used to you while I was labouring under a very natural misconception of the circumstances." I do not know that I was much the better for the apology, but at the moment I regarded it sufficient.

Their things were then hurried down to the strand, and I accompanied them to the ruined quay. I took off my hat to Sir William as he was first let down into the boat. He descended first, so that he might receive his niece,—for all Jaffa now knew that it was a lady,—and then I gave her my hand for the last time. "God bless you, Miss Weston," I said, pressing it closely. "God bless you, Mr. Jones," she replied. And from that day to this I have neither spoken to her nor seen her.

I waited a fortnight at Jaffa for the French boat,

eating cutlets of goats' flesh, and wandering among the orange groves. I certainly look back on that fortnight as the most miserable period of my life. I had been deceived, and had failed to discover the deceit, even though the deceiver had perhaps wished that I should do so. For that blindness I have never forgiven myself.

THE HOUSE OF HEINE BROTHERS, IN MUNICH.

———◆———

THE house of Heine Brothers, in Munich, was of good repute at the time of which I am about to tell, —a time not long ago; and is so still, I trust. It was of good repute in its own way, seeing that no man doubted the word or solvency of Heine Brothers; but they did not possess, as bankers, what would in England be considered a large or profitable business. The operations of English bankers are bewildering in their magnitude. Legions of clerks are employed. The senior book-keepers, though only salaried servants, are themselves great men; while the real partners are inscrutable, mysterious, opulent beyond measure, and altogether unknown to their customers. Take any firm at random,—Brown, Jones, and Cox, let us say;—the probability is that Jones has been dead these fifty years, that Brown is a Cabinet Minister, and that Cox is master of a pack of hounds in Leicestershire. But it was by no means so with the house of Heine Brothers, of Munich. There they were, the two elderly men, daily to be seen at their dingy office in the Schrannen Platz; and if any business was to be transacted requiring the interchange

of more than a word or two, it was the younger
brother with whom the customer was, as a matter of
course, brought into contact.   There were three clerks
in the establishment; an old man, namely, who sat
with the elder brother and had no personal dealings
with the public; a young Englishman, of whom we
shall anon hear more; and a boy who ran messages,
put the wood on to the stoves, and swept out the bank.
Truly the house of Heine Brothers was of no great
importance; but nevertheless it was of good repute.

The office, I have said, was in the Schrannen Platz,
or old Market-place.   Munich, as every one knows, is
chiefly to be noted as a new town,—so new that many
of the streets and most of the palaces look as though
they had been sent home last night from the builders,
and had only just been taken out of their bandboxes.
It is angular, methodical, unfinished, and palatial.
But there is an old town; and, though the old town
be not of surpassing interest, it is as dingy, crooked,
intricate, and dark as other old towns in Germany.
Here, in the old Market-place, up one long broad
staircase, were situated the two rooms in which was
held the bank of Heine Brothers.

Of the elder member of the firm we shall have
something to say before this story be completed.   He
was an old bachelor, and was possessed of a bachelor's
dwelling somewhere out in the suburbs of the city.
The junior brother was a married man, with a wife
some twenty years younger than himself, with two
daughters, the elder of whom was now one-and-

twenty, and one son. His name was Ernest Heine,
whereas the senior brother was known as Uncle Hatto.
Ernest Heine and his wife inhabited a portion of one
of those new palatial residences at the further end of
the Ludwigs Strasse ; but not because they thus lived
must it be considered that they were palatial people.
By no means let it be so thought, as such an idea
would altogether militate against whatever truth of
character painting there may be in this tale. They
were not palatial people, but the very reverse, living
in homely guise, pursuing homely duties, and satisfied with homely pleasures. Up two pairs of stairs,
however, in that street of palaces, they lived, having
there a commodious suite of large rooms, furnished,
after the manner of the Germans, somewhat gaudily as
regarded their best salon, and with somewhat meagre
comfort as regarded their other rooms. But, whether
in respect of that which was meagre, or whether in
respect of that which was gaudy, they were as well
off as their neighbours ; and this, as I take it, is the
point of excellence which is desirable.

Ernest Heine was at this time over sixty ; his wife
was past forty ; and his eldest daughter, as I have
said, was twenty-one years of age. His second child,
also a girl, was six years younger ; and their third
child, a boy, had not been born till another similar
interval had elapsed. He was named Hatto after his
uncle, and the two girls had been christened Isa and
Agnes. Such, in number and mode of life, was the
family of the Heines.

We English folk are apt to imagine that we are nearer akin to Germans than to our other continental neighbours. This may be so in blood, but, nevertheless, the difference in manners is so striking, that it could hardly be enhanced. An Englishman moving himself off to a city in the middle of Central America will find the customs to which he must adapt himself less strange to him there, than he would in many a German town. But in no degree of life is the difference more remarkable than among unmarried but marriagable young women. It is not my purpose at the present moment to attribute a superiority in this matter to either nationality. Each has its own charm, its own excellence, its own Heaven-given grace, whereby men are led up to purer thoughts and sweet desires ; and each may possibly have its own defect. I will not here describe the excellence or defect of either ; but will, if it be in my power, say a word as to this difference. The German girl of one-and-twenty,—our Isa's age,—is more sedate, more womanly, more meditative than her English sister. The world's work is more in her thoughts, and the world's amusements less so. She probably knows less of those things which women learn than the English girl, but that which she does know is nearer to her hand for use. She is not so much accustomed to society, but nevertheless she is more mistress of her own manner. She is not taught to think so much of those things which flurry and disturb the mind, and therefore she is seldom flurried and disturbed. To both of them,

love,—the idea of love,—must be the thought of all
the most absorbing ; for is it not fated for them that
the joys and sorrows of their future life must depend
upon it ? But the idea of the German girl is the more
realistic, and the less romantic. Poetry and fiction
she may have read, though of the latter sparingly ;
but they will not have imbued her with that hope
for some transcendental Paradise of affection which
so often fills and exalts the hearts of our daughters
here at home. She is moderate in her aspirations,
requiring less excitement than an English girl ; and
never forgetting the solid necessities of life,—as they
are so often forgotten here in England. In associating
with young men, an English girl will always remember that in each one she so meets she may find an
admirer whom she may possibly love, or an admirer
whom she may probably be called on to repel. She is
ever conscious of the fact of this position ; and a
romance is thus engendered which, if it may at times
be dangerous, is at any rate always charming. But
the German girl, in her simplicity, has no such consciousness. As you and I, my reader, might probably
become dear friends were we to meet and know each
other, so may the German girl learn to love the
fair-haired youth with whom chance has for a time
associated her ; but to her mind there occurs no
suggestive reason why it should be so,—no probability that ·the youth may regard her in such light,
because that chance has come to pass. She can
therefore give him her hand without trepidation, and

talk with him for half an hour, when called on to do so, as calmly as she might do with his sister.

Such a one was Isa Heine at the time of which I am writing. We English, in our passion for daily excitement, might call her phlegmatic, but we should call her so unjustly. Life to her was a serious matter, of which the daily duties and daily wants were sufficient to occupy her thoughts. She was her mother's companion, the instructress of both her brother and her sister, and the charm of her father's vacant hours. With such calls upon her time, and so many realities around her, her imagination did not teach her to look for joys beyond those of her present life and home. When love and marriage should come to her, as come they probably might, she would endeavour to attune herself to a new happiness and a new sphere of duties. In the meantime she was contented to keep her mother's accounts, and look after her brother and sister up two pair of stairs in the Ludwigs Strasse. But change would certainly come, we may prophesy; for Isa Heine was a beautiful girl, tall and graceful, comely to the eye, and fit in every way to be loved and cherished as the partner of a man's home.

I have said that an English clerk made a part of that small establishment in the dingy banking-office in the Schrannen Platz, and I must say a word or two of Herbert Onslow. In his early career he had not been fortunate. His father, with means sufficiently moderate, and with a family more than sufficiently large, had sent him to a public school at which he had been very idle, and then to one of the universities, at which he had run into debt, and had therefore left without a degree.   When this occurred, a family council of war had been held among the Onslows, and it was decided that Herbert should be sent off to the banking-house of Heines, at Munich, there being a cousinship between the families, and some existing connections of business. It was, therefore, so settled; and Herbert, willing enough to see the world,—as he considered he should do by going to Munich,—started for his German home, with injunctions, very tender from his mother, and very solemn from his aggrieved father.   But there was nothing bad at the heart about young Onslow, and if the solemn father had well considered it, he might perhaps have felt that those debts at Cambridge reflected more fault on him than on his son.   When Herbert arrived at Munich, his cousins, the Heines,—far-away cousins though they were,— behaved kindly to him.   They established him at first in lodgings, where he was boarded with many others, having heard somewhat of his early youth. But when Madame Heine, at the end of twelve months, perceived that he was punctual at the bank, and that his allowances, which, though moderate in England, were handsome in Munich, carried him on without debt, she opened her motherly arms and suggested to his mother and to himself, that he should live with them.   In this way he also was domiciled up two pairs of stairs in the palatial residence in the Ludwigs Strasse.

But all this happened long ago. Isa Heine had been only seventeen when her cousin had first come to Munich, and had made acquaintance with him rather as a child than as a woman. And when, as she ripened into womanhood, this young man came more closely among them, it did not strike her that the change would affect her more powerfully than it would the others. Her uncle and father, she knew, had approved of Herbert at the bank; and Herbert had shown that he could be steady; therefore he was to be taken into their family, paying his annual subsidy, instead of being left with strangers at the boarding-house. All this was very simple to her. She assisted in mending his linen, as she did her father's; she visited his room daily, as she visited all the others; she took notice of his likings and dislikings as touching their table arrangements,—but by no means such notice as she did of her father's; and without any flutter, inwardly in her imagination or outwardly as regarded the world, she made him one of the family. So things went on for a year,—nay, so things went on for two years with her, after Herbert Onslow had come to the Ludwigs Strasse.

But the matter had been regarded in a very different light by Herbert himself. When the proposition had been made to him, his first idea had been that so close a connection with a girl so very pretty would be delightful. He had blushed as he had given in his adhesion; but Madame Heine, when she saw the blush, had attributed it to anything but the true cause. When Isa had asked him as to his wants and wishes, he had blushed again, but she had been as ignorant as her mother. The father had merely stipulated that, as the young Englishman paid for his board, he should have the full value of his money, so that Isa and Agnes gave up their pretty front room, going into one that was inferior, and Hatto was put to sleep in the little closet that had been papa's own peculiar property. But nobody complained of this, for it was understood that the money was of service.

For the first year Herbert found that nothing especial happened. He always fancied that he was in love with Isa, and wrote some poetry about her. But the poetry was in English, and Isa could not read it, even had he dared to show it to her. During the second year he went home to England for three months, and by confessing a passion to one of his sisters, really brought himself to feel one. He returned to Munich resolved to tell Isa that the possibility of his remaining there depended upon her acceptance of his heart; but for months he did not find himself able to put his resolution in force. She was so sedate, so womanly, so attentive as regarded cousinly friendship, and so cold as regarded everything else, that he did not know how to speak to her. With an English girl whom he had met three times at a ball, he might have been much more able to make progress. He was alone with Isa frequently, for neither father, mother, nor Isa herself objected to such communion; but yet things so went between them that he could not take her by the hand and tell her that he loved her. And thus the third year of his life in Munich, and the second of his residence in the Ludwigs Strasse, went by him. So the years went by, and Isa was now past twenty. To Herbert, in his reveries, it seemed as though life, and the joys of life, were slipping away from him. But no such feeling disturbed any of the Heines. Life, of course, was slipping away; but then is it not the destiny of man that life should slip away? Their wants were all satisfied, and for them, that, together with their close family affection, was happiness enough.

At last, however, Herbert so spoke, or so looked, that both Isa and her mother knew that his heart was touched. He still declared to himself that he had made no sign, and that he was an oaf, an ass, a coward, in that he had not done so. But he had made some sign, and the sign had been read. There was no secret,—no necessity for a secret on the subject between the mother and daughter, but yet it was not spoken of all at once. There was some little increase of caution between them as Herbert's name was mentioned, so that gradually each knew what the other thought; but for weeks, that was all. Then at last the mother spoke out.

"Isa," she said, "I think that Herbert Onslow is becoming attached to you."

"He has never said so, mamma."

"No; I am sure he has not. Had he done so, you would have told me. Nevertheless, is it not true?"

"Well, mamma, I cannot say. It may be so. Such an idea has occurred to me, but I have abandoned it as needless. If he has anything to say he will say it."

"And if he were to speak, how should you answer him?"

"I should take time to think. I do not at all know what means he has for a separate establishment." Then the subject was dropped between them for that time, and Isa, in her communications with her cousin, was somewhat more reserved than she had been.

"Isa, are you in love with Herbert?" Agnes asked her, as they were together in their room one night.

"In love with him? No; why should I be in love with him?"

"I think he is in love with you," said Agnes.

"That is quite another thing," said Isa, laughing. But if so, he has not taken me into his confidence. Perhaps he has you."

"Oh no. He would not do that, I think. Not but what we are great friends, and I love him dearly. Would it not be nice for you and him to be betrothed?"

"That depends on many things, my dear."

"Oh yes, I know. Perhaps he has not got money enough. But you could live here, you know, and he has got some money, because he so often rides on horseback." And then the matter was dropped between the two sisters.

Herbert had given English lessons to the two girls, but the lessons had been found tedious, and had dwindled away. Isa, nevertheless, had kept up her exercises, duly translating German into English, and English into German; and occasionally she had shown them to her cousin. Now, however, she altogether gave over such showing of them, but, nevertheless, worked at the task with more energy than before.

"Isa," he said to her one day,—having with some difficulty found her alone in the parlour,—"Isa, why should not we go on with our English?"

"Because it is troublesome,—to you I mean."

"Troublesome. Well; yes; it is troublesome. Nothing good is to be had without trouble. But I should like it if you would not mind."

"You know how sick you were of it before;— besides, I shall never be able to speak it."

"I shall not get sick of it now, Isa."

"Oh yes you would ;—in two days."

"And I want you to speak it. I desire it especially."

"Why especially?" asked Isa. And even she, with all her tranquillity of demeanour, could hardly preserve her even tone and quiet look, as she asked the necessary question.

"I will tell you why," said Herbert; and as he spoke, he got up from his seat, and took a step or two over towards her, where she was sitting near the window. Isa, as she saw him, still continued her work, and strove hard to give to the stitches all that attention which they required. "I will tell you why I would wish you to talk my language. Because I love you, Isa, and would have you for my wife,—if that be possible."

She still continued her work, and the stitches, if not quite as perfect as usual, sufficed for their purpose.

"That is why I wish it. Now will you consent to learn from me again?"

"If I did, Herbert, that consent would include another."

"Yes ; certainly it would. That is what I intend. And now will you learn from me again?"

"That is,—you mean to ask, will I marry you?"

"Will you love me? Can you learn to love me? Oh, Isa, I have thought of this so long! But you have seemed so cold that I have not dared to speak. Isa, can you love me?" And he sat himself close beside her. Now that the ice was broken, he was quite prepared to become an ardent lover,—if she would allow of such ardour. But as he sat down she rose.

"I cannot answer such a question on the sudden," she said. "Give me till to-morrow, Herbert, and then I will make you a reply ;" whereupon she left him, and he stood alone in the room, having done the deed on which he had been meditating for the last two years. About half an hour afterwards he met her on the stairs as he was going to his chamber. "May I speak to your father about this," he said, hardly stopping her as he asked the question. "Oh yes; surely," she answered; and then again they parted. To him this last-accorded permission sounded as though it carried with it more weight than it in truth possessed. In his own country a reference to the lady's father is taken as indicating a full consent on the lady's part, should the stern paterfamilias raise no objection. But Isa had no such meaning. She had told him that she could not give her answer till the morrow. If, however, he chose to consult her father on the subject, she had no objection. It would probably be necessary that she should discuss the whole matter in family conclave, before she could bring herself to give any reply.

On that night, before he went to bed, he did speak to her father; and Isa also, before she went to rest, spoke to her mother. It was singular to him that there should appear to be so little privacy on the subject; that there should be held to be so little necessity for a secret. Had he made a suggestion that an extra room should be allotted to him at so much per annum, the proposition could not have been discussed with simpler ease. At last, after a three days' debate, the matter ended thus,—with by no means a sufficiency of romance for his taste. Isa had agreed to become his betrothed if certain pecuniary conditions should or could be fulfilled. It appeared now that Herbert's father had promised that some small modicum of capital should be forthcoming after a term of years, and that Heine Brothers had agreed that the Englishman should have a proportionate share in the bank when that promise should be brought to bear. Let it not be supposed that Herbert would thus become a millionnaire. If all went well, the best would be that some three hundred a year would accrue to him from the bank, instead of the quarter of that income which he at present received. But three hundred a year goes a long way at Munich, and Isa's parents were willing that she should be Herbert's wife if such an income should be forthcoming.

But even of this there was much doubt. Application to Herbert's father could not be judiciously made for some months. The earliest period at which, in accordance with old Hatto Heine's agreement, young Onslow might be admitted to the bank, was still distant by four years; and the present moment was thought to be inopportune for applying to him for any act of grace. Let them wait, said papa and mamma Heine,—at any rate till New Year's Day, then ten months distant. Isa quietly said that she would wait till New Year's Day. Herbert fretted, fumed, and declared that he was ill treated. But in the end he also agreed to wait. What else could he do?

" But we shall see each other daily, and be close

to each other," he said to Isa, looking tenderly into her eyes. "Yes," she replied, "we shall see each other daily—of course. But Herbert——"

Herbert looked up at her and paused for her to go on.

"I have promised mamma that there shall be no change between us,—in our manner to each other, I mean. We are not betrothed as yet, you know, and perhaps we may never be so."

"Isa!"

"It may not be possible, you know. And therefore we will go on as before. Of course we shall see each other, and of course we shall be friends."

Herbert Onslow again fretted and again fumed, but he did not have his way. He had looked forward to the ecstasies of a lover's life, but very few of those ecstasies were awarded to him. He rarely found himself alone with Isa, and when he did do so, her coldness overawed him. He could dare to scold her, and sometimes did do so, but he could not dare to take the slightest liberty. Once, on that night when the qualified consent of papa and mamma Heine had first been given, he had been allowed to touch her lips with his own; but since that day there had been for him no such delight as that. She would not even allow her hand to remain in his. When they all passed their evenings together in the beer-garden, she would studiously manage that his chair should not be close to her own. Occasionally she would walk with him, but not more frequently now than of yore.   Very few, indeed, of a lover's privileges did he enjoy.   And in this way the long year wore itself out, and Isa Heine was one-and-twenty.

All those family details which had made it inexpedient to apply either to old Hatto or to Herbert's father before the end of the year need not be specially explained.   Old Hatto, who had by far the greater share in the business, was a tyrant somewhat feared both by his brother and sister-in-law ; and the elder Onslow, as was known to them all, was a man straitened in circumstances.   But soon after New Year's Day the proposition was made in the Schrannen Platz, and the letter was written.   On this occasion Madame Heine went down to the bank, and, together with her husband, was closeted for an hour with old Hatto.   Uncle Hatto's verdict was not favourable.   As to the young people's marriage, that was his brother's affair, not his.   But as to the partnership, that was a serious matter.   Who ever heard of a partnership being given away merely because a man wanted to marry ?   He would keep to his promise, and if the stipulated moneys were forthcoming, Herbert Onslow should become a partner,—in four years.   Nor was the reply from England more favourable.   The alliance was regarded by all the Onslows very favourably.   Nothing could be nicer than such a marriage !   They already knew dear Isa so well by description !   But as for the money,—that could not in any way be forthcoming till the end of the stipulated period.

"And what shall we do?" said Herbert, to Papa Heine.

"You must wait," said he.

"For four years!" asked Herbert.

"You must wait,—as I did," said Papa Heine. "I was forty before I could marry." Papa Heine, however, should not have forgotten to say that his bride was only twenty, and that if he had waited, she had not.

"Isa," Herbert said to her when all this had been fully explained to her, "what do you say now?"

"Of course it is all over," said she, very calmly.

"Oh Isa, is that your love?"

"No, Herbert, that is not my love; that is my discretion;" and she even laughed with her mild low laughter, as she answered him. "You know you are too impatient to wait four years, and what else therefore can I say?"

"I wonder whether you love me?" said Herbert, with a grand look of injured sentiment.

"Well; in your sense of the word I do not think I do. I do not love you so that I need make every one around us unhappy because circumstances forbid me to marry you. That sort of love would be baneful."

"Ah no, you do not know what love means!"

"Not your boisterous, heartbreaking English love, Herbert. And, Herbert, sometimes I think you had better go home and look for a bride there. Though you fancy that you love me, in your heart you hardly approve of me."

"Fancy that I love you! Do you think, Isa, that a man can carry his heart round to one customer after another as the huckster carries his wares?"

"Yes; I think he can. I know that men do. What did your hero Waverley do with his heart in that grand English novel which you gave me to read? I am not Flora Mac Ivor, but you may find a Rose Bradwardine."

"And you really wish me to do so?"

"Look here, Herbert. It is bad to boast, but I will make this boast. I am so little selfish, that I desire above all that you should do that which may make you most happy and contented. I will be quite frank with you. I love you well enough to wait these four years with the hope of becoming your wife when they are over. But you will think but little of my love when I tell you that this waiting would not make me unhappy. I should go on as I do now, and be contented."

"Oh heavens!" sighed Herbert.

"But as I know that this would not suit you,—as I feel sure that such delay would gall you every day, as I doubt whether it would not make you sick of me long before the four years be over,—my advice is, that we should let this matter drop."

He now walked up to her and took her hand, and as he did so there was something in his gait and look and tone of voice that stirred her heart more sharply than it had yet been stirred. "And even that would not make you unhappy," he said.

She paused before she replied, leaving her hand in his, for he was contented to hold it without peculiar pressure. "I will not say so," she replied. "But, Herbert, I think that you press me too hard. Is it not enough that I leave you to be the arbiter of my destiny?"

"I would learn the very truth of your heart," he replied.

"I cannot tell you that truth more plainly. Methinks I have told it too plainly already. If you wish it, I will hold myself as engaged to you,—to be married to you when those four years are past. But, remember, I do not advise it. If you wish it, you shall have back your troth. And that I think will be the wiser course."

But neither alternative contented Herbert Onslow, and at the time he did not resolve on either. He had some little present income from home, some fifty pounds a year or so, and he would be satisfied to marry on that and on his salary as a clerk; but to this papa and mamma Heine would not consent; —neither would Isa.

"You are not a saving, close man," she said to him, when he boasted of his economies. "No Englishmen are. You could not live comfortably in two small rooms, and with bad dinners."

"I do not care a straw about my dinners."

"Not now that you are a lover, but you would do when you were a husband. And you change your linen almost every day."

" Bah ! "

" Yes ; bah, if you please.   But I know what these things cost.   You had better go to England and fetch a rich wife.   Then you will become a partner at once, and Uncle Hatto won't snub you.   And you will be a grand man, and have a horse to ride on."   Where-upon Herbert went away in disgust.   Nothing in all this made him so unhappy as the feeling that Isa, under all their joint privations, would not be unhappy herself.   As far as he could see, all this made no difference in Isa.

But, in truth, he had not yet read Isa's character very thoroughly.   She had spoken truly in saying that she knew nothing of that boisterous love which was now tormenting him and making him gloomy ; but nevertheless she loved him.   She, in her short life, had learnt many lessons of self-denial ; and now with reference to this half-promised husband she would again have practised such a lesson.   Had he agreed at once to go from her, she would have balanced her own account within her own breast, and have kept to herself all her sufferings.   There would have been no outward show of baffled love,—none even in the colour of her cheeks ; for such was the nature of her temperament.   But she did suffer for him.   Day by day she began to think that his love, though boisterous as she had at first called it, was more deep-seated than she had believed.   He made no slightest sign that he would accept any of those proffers which she had made him of release.   Though he said so loudly

that this waiting for four years was an impossibility,
he spoke of no course that would be more possible,—
except that evidently impossible course of an early
marriage. And thus, while he with redoubled vehe-
mence charged her with coldness and want of love,
her love waxed warmer and warmer, and his happiness became the chief object of her thoughts. What
could she do that he might no longer suffer ?

And then he took a step which was very strange to
them all. He banished himself altogether from the
house, going away again into lodgings. "No," he
said, on the morning of his departure, "I do not release you. I will never release you. You are mine,
and I have a right so to call you. If you choose to
release yourself, I cannot help it ; but in doing so you
will be forsworn."

"Nay, but, Herbert, I have sworn to nothing,"
said she, meaning that she had not been formally betrothed to him.

"You can do as you please ; it is a matter of conscience ; but I tell you what are my feelings. Here
I cannot stay, for I should go mad ; but I shall see
you occasionally ;—perhaps on Sundays."

"Oh, Herbert !"

"Well, what would you have ? If you really cared
to see me it would not be thus. All I ask of you
now is this, that if you decide,—absolutely decide on
throwing me over, you will tell me at once. Then I
shall leave Munich."

"Herbert, I will never throw you over." So

they parted, and Onslow went forth to his new lodgings.

Her promise that she would never throw him over was the warmest word of love that she had ever spoken, but even that was said in her own quiet, unimpassioned way. There was in it but very little show of love, though there might be an assurance of constancy. But her constancy he did not, in truth, much doubt. Four years,—fourteen,—or twenty-four, would be the same to her, he said, as he seated himself in the dull, cold room which he had chosen. While living in the Ludwigs Strasse he did not know how much had been daily done for his comfort by that hand which he had been so seldom allowed to press; but he knew that he was now cold and comfortless, and he wished himself back in the Ludwigs Strasse.

"Mamma," said Isa, when they were alone. "Is not Uncle Hatto rather hard on us? Papa said that he would ask this as a favour from his brother."

"So he did, my dear; and offered to give up more of his own time. But your Uncle Hatto is hard."

"He is rich, is he not?"

"Well; your father says not. Your father says that he spends all his income. Though he is hard and obstinate, he is not selfish. He is very good to the poor, but I believe he thinks that early marriages are very foolish."

"Mamma," said Isa again, when they had sat for some minutes in silence over their work.

" Well, my love ?"

" Have you spoken to Uncle Hatto about this ? "

"No, dear ; not since that day when your papa and I first went to him. To tell the truth, I am almost afraid to speak to him ; but, if you wish it, I will do so."

"I do wish it, mamma. But you must not think that I am discontented or impatient. I do not know that I have any right to ask my uncle for his money ; —for it comes to that."

" I suppose it does, my dear."

"And as for myself, I am happy here with you and papa. I do not think so much of these four years."

"You would still be young, Isa ;—quite young enough."

"And what if I were not young ? What does it matter ? But, mamma, there has been that between Herbert and me which makes me feel myself bound to think of him. As you and papa have sanctioned it, you are bound to think of him also. I know that he is unhappy, living there all alone."

" But why did he go, dear ? "

" I think he was right to go. I could understand his doing that. He is not like us, and would have been fretful here, wanting that which I could not give him. He became worse from day to day, and was silent and morose. I am glad he went. But, mamma, for his sake I wish that this could be shortened."

Madame Heine again told her daughter that she

would, if Isa wished it, herself go to the Schrannen Platz, and see what could be done by talking to Uncle Hatto. "But," she added, " I fear that no good will come of it."

" Can harm come, mamma ? "

" No, I do not think harm can come."

" I'll tell you what, mamma, I will go to Uncle Hatto myself, if you will let me. He is cross I know ; but I shall not be afraid of him. I feel that I ought to do something." And so the matter was settled, Madame Heine being by no means averse to escape a further personal visit to the Head of the banking establishment.

Madame Heine well understood what her daughter meant, when she said she ought to do something, though Isa feared that she had imperfectly expressed her meaning. When he, Herbert, was willing to do so much to prove his love,—when he was ready to sacrifice all the little comforts of comparative wealth to which he had been accustomed, in order that she might be his companion and wife,—did it not behove her to give some proof of her love also ? She could not be demonstrative as he was. Such exhibition of feeling would be quite contrary to her ideas of female delicacy, and to her very nature. But if called on to work for him, that she could do as long as strength remained to her. But there was no sacrifice which would be of service, nor any work which would avail. Therefore she was driven to think what she might do on his behalf, and at last she resolved to make her personal appeal to Uncle Hatto.

"Shall I tell papa?" Isa asked of her mother.

"I will do so," said Madame Heine. And then the younger member of the firm was informed as to the step which was to be taken; and he, though he said nothing to forbid the attempt, held out no hope that it would be successful.

Uncle Hatto was a little snuffy man, now full seventy years of age, who passed seven hours of every week-day of his life in the dark back chamber behind the banking-room of the firm, and he had so passed every week-day of his life for more years than any of the family could now remember. He had made the house what it was, and had taken his brother into partnership when that brother married. All the family were somewhat afraid of him, including even his partner. He rarely came to the apartments in the Ludwigs Strasse, as he himself lived in one of the older and shabbier suburbs on the other side of the town. Thither he always walked, starting punctually from the bank at four o'clock, and from thence he always walked in the morning, reaching the bank punctually at nine. His two nieces knew him well; for on certain stated days they were wont to attend on him at his lodgings, where they would be regaled with cakes, and afterwards go with him to some old-fashioned beer-garden in his neighbourhood. But these festivities were of a sombre kind; and if, on any occasion, circumstances prevented the fulfilment of the ceremony, neither of the girls would be loud in their lamentations.

In London, a visit paid by a niece to her uncle would, in all probability, be made at the uncle's private residence; but at Munich private and public matters were not so effectually divided. Isa therefore, having put on her hat and shawl, walked off by herself to the Schrannen Platz.

"Is Uncle Hatto inside?" she asked; and the answer was given to her by her own lover. Yes, he was within; but the old clerk was with him. Isa, however, signified her wish to see her uncle alone, and in a few minutes the ancient grey-haired servant of the house came out into the larger room.

"You can go in now, Miss Isa," he said. And Isa found herself in the presence of her uncle before she had been two minutes under the roof. In the mean time Ernest Heine, her father, had said not a word, and Herbert knew that something very special must be about to occur.

"Well, my bonny bird," said Uncle Hatto, "and what do you want at the bank?" Cheery words, such as these, were by no means uncommon with Uncle Hatto; but Isa knew very well that no presage could be drawn from them of any special good nature or temporary weakness on his part.

"Uncle Hatto," she began, rushing at once into the middle of her affair, "you know, I believe, that I am engaged to marry Herbert Onslow?"

"I know no such thing," said he. "I thought I understood your father specially to say that there had been no betrothal."

"No, Uncle Hatto, there has been no betrothal; that certainly is true; but, nevertheless, we are engaged to each other."

"Well," said Uncle Hatto, very sourly; and now there was no longer any cheery tone, or any calling of pretty names.

"Perhaps you may think all this very foolish," said Isa, who, in spite of her resolves to do so, was hardly able to look up gallantly into her uncle's face as she thus talked of her own love affairs.

"Yes, I do," said Uncle Hatto. "I do think it foolish for young people to hold themselves betrothed before they have got anything to live on, and so I have told your father. He answered me by saying that you were not betrothed."

"Nor are we. Papa is quite right in that."

"Then, my dear, I would advise you to tell the young man that, as neither of you have means of your own, the thing must be at an end. It is the only step for you to take. If you agreed to wait, one of you might die, or his money might never be forthcoming, or you might see somebody else that you liked better."

"I don't think I shall do that."

"You can't tell. And if you don't, the chances are ten to one that he will."

This little blow, which was intended to be severe, did not hit Isa at all hard. That plan of a Rose Bradwardine she herself had proposed in good faith, thinking that she could endure such a termination to

the affair without flinching. She was probably wrong
in this estimate of her power; but, nevertheless, her
present object was his release from unhappiness and
doubt, not her own.

"It might be so," she said.

"Take my word for it, it would. Look all around.
There was Adelaide Schropner,—but that was before
your time, and you won't remember." Considering
that Adelaide Schropner had been for many years a
grandmother, it was probable that Isa would not
remember.

"But, Uncle Hatto, you have not heard me. I
want to say something to you, if it will not take too
much of your time." In answer to which, uncle Hatto
muttered something which was unheeded, to signify
that Isa might speak.

"I also think that a long engagement is a foolish
thing, and so does Herbert."

"But he wants to marry at once."

"Yes, he wants to marry—perhaps not at once, but
soon."

"And I suppose you have come to say that you
want the same thing."

Isa blushed ever so faintly as she commenced her
answer. "Yes, uncle, I do wish the same thing.
What he wishes, I wish."

"Very likely,—very likely."

"Don't be scornful to me, uncle. When two people
love each other, it is natural that each should wish
that which the other earnestly desires."

"Oh, very natural, my dear, that you should wish to get married!"

"Uncle Hatto, I did not think that you would be unkind to me, though I knew that you would be stern."

"Well, go on. What have you to say? I am not stern; but I have no doubt you will think me unkind. People are always unkind who do not do what they are asked."

"Papa says that Herbert Onslow is some day to become a partner in the bank."

"That depends on certain circumstances. Neither I nor your papa can say whether he will or no."

But Isa went on as though she had not heard the last reply. "I have come to ask you to admit him as a partner at once."

"Ah, I supposed so;—just as you might ask me to give you a new ribbon."

"But, uncle, I never did ask you to give me a new ribbon. I never asked you to give me anything for myself; nor do I ask this for myself."

"Do you think that if I could do it,—which of course I can't,—I would not sooner do it for you, who are my own flesh and blood, than for him, who is a stranger?"

"Nay; he is no stranger. He has sat at your desk and obeyed your orders for nearly four years. Papa says that he has done well in the bank."

"Humph! If every clerk that does well,—pretty well, that is,—wanted a partnership, where should we be, my dear? No, my dear, go home and tell him when you see him in the evening that all this must be at an end. Men's places in the world are not given away so easily as that. They must either be earned or purchased. Herbert Onslow has as yet done neither, and therefore he is not entitled to take a wife. I should have been glad to have had a wife at his age,—at least I suppose I should, but at any rate I could not afford it."

But Isa had by means as yet done. So far the interview had progressed exactly as she had anticipated. She had never supposed it possible that her uncle would grant her so important a request as soon as she opened her mouth to ask it. She had not for a moment expected that things would go so easily with her. Indeed she had never expected that any success would attend her efforts; but, if any success were possible, the work which must achieve that success must now commence. It was necessary that she should first state her request plainly before she began to urge it with such eloquence as she had at her command.

"I can understand what you say, Uncle Hatto."

"I am glad of that, at any rate."

"And I know that I have no right to ask you for anything."

"I do not say that. Anything in reason, that a girl like you should ask of her old uncle, I would give you."

"I have no such reasonable request to make, uncle.

I have never wanted new ribbons from you or gay toys. Even from my own mother I have not wanted them ;—not wanted them faster than they seemed to come without any asking."

"No, no ; you have been a good girl."

"I have been a happy girl ; and quite happy with those I loved, and with what Providence had given me. I had nothing to ask for. But now I am no longer happy, nor can I be unless you do for me this which I ask of you. I have wanted nothing till now, and now in my need I come to you."

"And now you want a husband with a fortune !"

"No !" and that single word she spoke, not loudly, for her voice was low and soft, but with an accent which carried it sharply to his ear and to his brain. And then she rose from her seat as she went on. "Your scorn, uncle, is unjust,—unjust and untrue. I have ever acted maidenly, as has become my mother's daughter."

"Yes, yes, yes ;—I believe that."

"And I can say more than that for myself. My thoughts have been the same, nor have my wishes even, ever gone beyond them. And when this young man came to me, telling me of his feelings, I gave him no answer till I had consulted my mother."

"She should have bade you not to think of him."

"Ah, you are not a mother, and cannot know. Why should I not think of him when he was good and kind, honest and hard-working ? And then he had thought of me first. Why should I not think of him ? Did not mamma listen to my father when he came to her ?"

"But your father was forty years old, and had a business."

"You gave it him, Uncle Hatto. I have heard him say so."

"And therefore I am to do as much for you. And then next year Agnes will come to me ; and so before I die I shall see you all in want, with large families. No, Isa ; I will not scorn you, but this thing I cannot do."

"But I have not told you all yet. You say that I want a husband."

"Well, well ; I did not mean to say it harshly."

"I do want—to be married." And here her courage failed her a little, and for a moment her eye fell to the ground. "It is true, uncle. He has asked me whether I could love him, and I have told him I could. He has asked me whether I would be his wife, and I have given him a promise. After that, must not his happiness be my happiness, and his misery my misery ? Am I not his wife already before God ?"

"No, no," said Uncle Hatto loudly.

"Ah, but I am. None feel the strength of the bonds but those who are themselves bound. I know my duty to my father and mother, and with God's help I will do it, but I am not the less bound to him. Without their approval I will not stand with him at the altar ; but not the less is my lot joined to his

for this world. Nothing could release me from that
but his wish."

"And he will wish it in a month or two."

"Excuse me, Uncle Hatto, but in that I can only
judge for myself as best I may. He has loved me
now for two years——"

"Psha!"

"And, whether it be wise or foolish, I have sanctioned it. I cannot now go back with honour, even
if my own heart would let me. His welfare must be
my welfare, and his sorrow my sorrow. Therefore I
am bound to do for him anything that a girl may do
for the man she loves; and, as I knew of no other
resource, I come to you to help me."

"And he, sitting out there, knows what you are
saying."

"Most certainly not. He knows no more than that
he has seen me enter this room."

"I am glad of that, because I would not wish that
he should be disappointed. In this matter, my dear,
I cannot do anything for you."

"And that is your last answer, uncle?"

"Yes, indeed. When you come to think over this
some twenty years hence, you will know then
that I am right, and that your request was unreasonable.

"It may be so," she replied, "but I do not
think it."

"It will be so. Such favours as you now ask are
not granted in this world for light reasons."

" Light reasons ! Well, uncle, I have had my say, and will not take up your time longer."

" Good by, my dear. I am sorry that I cannot oblige you ;—that it is quite out of my power to oblige you."

Then she went, giving him her hand as she parted from him ; and he, as she left the room, looked anxiously at her, watching her countenance and her gait, and listening to the very fall of her footstep. " Ah !" he said to himself, when he was alone, " the young people have the best of it. The sun shines for them; but why should they have all ? Poor as he is, he is a happy dog,—a happy dog. But she is twice too good for him. Why did she not take to one of her own country ? "

Isa, as she passed through the bank, smiled sweetly on her father, and then smiled sweetly at her lover, nodding to him with a pleasant kindly nod. If he could have heard all that had passed at that interview, how much more he would have known of her than he now knew, and how proud he would have been of her love. No word was spoken as she went out, and then she walked home with even step, as she had walked thither. It can hardly be said that she was disappointed, as she had expected nothing. But people hope who do not expect, and though her step was even and her face calm, yet her heart was sad.

" Mamma," she said, " there is no hope from uncle Hatto."

" So I feared, my dear."

Y

"But I thought it right to try—for Herbert's sake."

"I hope it will not do him an injury in the bank."

"Oh, mamma, do not put that into my head. If that were added to it all, I should indeed be wretched."

"No; he is too just for that. Poor young man! Sometimes I almost think it would be better that he should go back to England."

"Mamma, if he did, I should—break my heart."

"Isa!"

"Well, mamma! But do not suppose that I mean to complain, whatever happens."

"But I had been so sure that you had constrained your feelings!"

"So I had,—till I knew myself. Mamma, I could wait for years, if he were contented to wait by my side. If I could see him happy, I could watch him and love him, and be happy also. I do not want to have him kneeling to me, and making sweet speeches; but it has gone too far now,—and I could not bear to lose him." And thus to her mother she confessed the truth.

There was nothing more said between Isa and her mother on the subject, and for two days the matter remained as it then stood. Madame Heine had been deeply grieved at hearing those last words which her daughter had spoken. To her also that state of quiescence which Isa had so long affected seemed to be the proper state to which a maiden's heart should stand till after her marriage vows had been pronounced. She had watched her Isa, and had approved of everything,—of everything till this last avowal had been made. But now, though she could not approve, she expressed no disapproval in words. She pressed her daughter's hand and sighed, and then the two said no more upon the matter. In this way, for two days, there was silence in the apartments in the Ludwigs Strasse; for even when the father returned from his work, the whole circle felt that their old family mirth was for the present necessarily laid aside.

On the morning of the third day, about noon, Madame Heine returned home from the market with Isa, and as they reached the landing, Agnes met them with a packet. "Fritz brought it from the bank," said Agnes. Now Fritz was the boy who ran messages and swept out the office, and Madame Heine put out her hand for the parcel, thinking, not unnaturally, that it was for her. But Agnes would not give it to her mother. "It is for you, Isa," she said. Then Isa, looking at the address, recognised the handwriting of her uncle. "Mamma," she said, "I will come to you directly;" and then she passed quickly away into her own room.

The parcel was soon opened, and contained a note from her uncle, and a stiff, large document, looking as though it had come from the hands of a lawyer. Isa glanced at the document, and read some few of the words on the outer fold, but they did not carry home to her mind any clear perception of their meaning. She was flurried at the moment, and the words, perhaps, were not very plain. Then she took up her note, and that was plain enough. It was very short, and ran as follows :—

"My dear Niece,

"You told me on Monday that I was stern, and harsh, and unjust. Perhaps I was. If so, I hope the enclosed will make amends, and that you will not think me such an old fool as I think myself. "Your affectionate uncle,

"HATTO HEINE.

"I have told nobody yet, and the enclosed will require my brother's signature ; but I suppose he will not object."

*   *   *   *   *

"But he does not know it, mamma," said Isa. "Who is to tell him? Oh mamma, you must tell him."

"Nay, my dear ; but it must be your own present to him."

"I could not give it him. It is uncle Hatto's present. Mamma, when I left him I thought that his eye was kind to me."

"His heart, at any rate, has been very kind." And then again they looked over the document, and talked of the wedding which must now be near at hand. But still they had not as yet decided how Herbert should be informed.

"At last Isa resolved that she herself would write to him. She did write, and this was her letter :—

"Dear Herbert,

"Mamma and I wish to see you, and beg that you will come up to us this evening. We have tidings for you which we hope you will receive with joy. I may as well tell you at once, as I do not wish to flurry you. Uncle Hatto has sent to us a document which admits you as a partner into the bank. If, therefore, you wish to go on with our engagement, I suppose there is nothing now to cause any very great delay.

Isa."

The letter was very simple, and Isa, when she had written it, subsided into all her customary quiescence. Indeed, when Herbert came to the Ludwigs Strasse, not in the evening as he was bidden to do, but instantly, leaving his own dinner uneaten, and coming upon the Heines in the midst of their dinner, she was more than usually tranquil. But his love was, as she had told him, boisterous. He could not contain himself, and embraced them all, and then scolded Isa because she was so calm.

"Why should I not be calm," said she, "now that I know you are happy?"

The house in the Schrannen Platz still goes by the name of Heine Brothers, but the mercantile world in Bavaria, and in some cities out of Bavaria, is well aware that the real pith and marrow of the business is derived from the energy of the young English partner.

THE MAN WHO KEPT HIS MONEY IN A BOX.

I FIRST saw the man who kept his money in a box in the midst of the ravine of the Via Mala. I interchanged a few words with him or with his wife at the hospice, at the top of the Splugen; and I became acquainted with him in the court-yard of Conradi's hotel at Chiavenna. It was, however, afterwards at Bellaggio, on the lake of Como, that that acquaintance ripened into intimacy. A good many years have rolled by since then, and I believe this little episode in his life may be told without pain to the feelings of any one.

His name was ——; let us for the present say that his name was Greene. How he learned that my name was Robinson I do not know, but I remember well that he addressed me by my name at Chiavenna. To go back, however, for a moment to the Via Mala;—I had been staying for a few days at the Golden Eagle at Tusis,—which, by the bye, I hold to be the best small inn in all Switzerland, and its hostess to be, or to have been, certainly the prettiest

landlady,—and on the day of my departure south-
wards, I had walked on, into the Via Mala, so that
the diligence might pick me up in the gorge. This
pass I regard as one of the grandest spots to which
my wandering steps have ever carried me, and though
I had already lingered about it for many hours, I
now walked thither again to take my last farewell of
its dark towering rocks, its narrow causeway and
roaring river, trusting to my friend the landlady to
see that my luggage was duly packed upon the diligence. I need hardly say that my friend did not
betray her trust.

As one goes out from Switzerland towards Italy,
the road through the Via Mala ascends somewhat
steeply, and passengers by the diligence may walk
from the inn at Tusis into the gorge, and make their
way through the greater part of the ravine before the
vehicle will overtake them. This, however, Mr.
Greene with his wife and daughter had omitted to
do. When the diligence passed me in the defile, the
horses trotting for a few yards over some level portion of the road, I saw a man's nose pressed close
against the glass of the coupé window. I saw more
of his nose than of any other part of his face, but
yet I could perceive that his neck was twisted and
his eye upturned, and that he was making a painful
effort to look upwards to the summit of the rocks
from his position inside the carriage.

There was such a roar of wind and waters at the
spot that it was not practicable to speak to him, but

I beckoned with my finger and then pointed to the road, indicating that he should have walked. He understood me, though I did not at the moment understand his answering gesture. It was subsequently, when I knew somewhat of his habits, that he explained to me that on pointing to his open mouth, he had intended to signify that he would be afraid of sore throat in exposing himself to the air of that damp and narrow passage.

I got up into the conductor's covered seat at the back of the diligence, and in this position encountered the drifting snow of the Splugen. I think it is coldest of all the passes. Near the top of the pass the diligence stops for awhile, and it is here, if I remember, that the Austrian officials demand the travellers' passports. At least in those days they did so. These officials have now retreated behind the Quadrilatère,—soon, as we hope, to make a further retreat,—and the district belongs to the kingdom of United Italy. There is a place of refreshment or hospice here, into which we all went for a few moments, and I then saw that my friend with the weak throat was accompanied by two ladies.

"You should not have missed the Via Mala," I said to him, as he stood warming his toes at the huge covered stove.

"We miss everything," said the elder of the two ladies, who, however, was very much younger than the gentleman, and not very much older than her companion.

"I saw it beautifully, mamma," said the younger one; whereupon mamma gave her head a toss, and made up her mind, as I thought, to take some little vengeance before long upon her step-daughter. I observed that Miss Greene always called her step-mother mamma on the first approach of any stranger, so that the nature of the connection between them might be understood. And I observed also that the elder lady always gave her head a toss when she was so addressed.

"We don't mean to enjoy ourselves till we get down to the Lake of Como," said Mr. Greene. As I looked at him cowering over the stove, and saw how oppressed he was with great coats and warm wrappings for his throat, I quite agreed with him that he had not begun to enjoy himself as yet. Then we all got into our places again, and I saw no more of the Greenes till we were standing huddled together in the large court-yard of Conradi's hotel at Chiavenna.

Chiavenna is the first Italian town which the tourist reaches by this route, and I know no town in the North of Italy which is so closely surrounded by beautiful scenery. The traveller as he falls down to it from the Splugen road is bewildered by the loveliness of the valleys,—that is to say, if he so arranges that he can see them without pressing his nose against the glass of a coach window. And then from the town itself there are walks of two, three, and four hours, which I think are unsurpassed for

wild and sometimes startling beauties. One gets
into little valleys, green as emeralds, and surrounded
on all sides by grey broken rocks, in which Italian
Rasselases might have lived in perfect bliss; and then
again one comes upon distant views up the river
courses, bounded far away by the spurs of the Alps,
which are perfect,—to which the fancy can add no
additional charm. Conradi's hotel also is by no
means bad; or was not in those days. For my part
I am inclined to think that Italian hotels have
received a worse name than they deserve; and I
must profess that, looking merely to creature comforts, I would much sooner stay a week at the Golden
Key at Chiavenna, than with mine host of the King's
Head in the thriving commercial town of Muddleboro,
on the borders of Yorkshire and Lancashire.

I am always rather keen about my room in travelling, and having secured a chamber looking out upon
the mountains, had returned to the court-yard to
collect my baggage before Mr. Greene had succeeded
in realising his position, or understanding that he had
to take upon himself the duties of settling his family
for the night in the hotel by which he was surrounded.
When I descended he was stripping off the outermost
of three great coats, and four waiters around him
were beseeching him to tell them what accommodation he would require. Mr. Greene was giving sundry
very urgent instructions to the conductor respecting
his boxes; but as these were given in English, I was
not surprised to find that they were not accurately

followed. The man, however, was much too courteous to say in any language that he did not understand
every word that was said to him. Miss Greene was
standing apart, doing nothing. As she was only
eighteen years of age, it was of course her business to
do nothing; and a very pretty little girl she was, by
no means ignorant of her own beauty, and possessed
of quite sufficient wit to enable her to make the most
of it.

Mr. Greene was very leisurely in his proceedings,
and the four waiters were almost reduced to despair.

"I want two bed-rooms, a dressing-room, and some
dinner," he said at last, speaking very slowly, and in
his own vernacular. I could not in the least assist
him by translating it into Italian, for I did not speak
a word of the language myself; but I suggested that
the man would understand French. The waiter, however, had understood English. Waiters do understand all languages with a facility that is marvellous;
and this one now suggested that Mrs. Greene should
follow him up-stairs. Mrs. Greene, however, would
not move till she had seen that her boxes were all
right; and as Mrs. Greene was also a pretty woman, I
found myself bound to apply myself to her assistance.

"Oh, thank you," said she. "The people are so
stupid that one can really do nothing with them.
And as for Mr. Greene, he is of no use at all. You
see that box, the smaller one. I have four hundred
pounds' worth of jewellery in that, and therefore I
am obliged to look after it."

"Indeed," said I, rather startled at this amount of confidence on rather a short acquaintance. "In that case I do not wonder at your being careful. But is it not rather rash, perhaps ——"

"I know what you are going to say. Well, perhaps it is rash. But when you are going to foreign courts, what are you to do? If you have got those sort of things you must wear them."

As I was not myself possessed of any thing of that sort, and had no intention of going to any foreign court, I could not argue the matter with her. But I assisted her in getting together an enormous pile of luggage, among which there were seven large boxes covered with canvas, such as ladies not uncommonly carry with them when travelling. That one which she represented as being smaller than the others, and as holding jewellery might be about a yard long by a foot and a half deep. Being ignorant in those matters, I should have thought it sufficient to carry all a lady's wardrobe for twelve months. When the boxes were collected together, she sat down upon the jewel-case and looked up into my face. She was a pretty woman, perhaps thirty years of age, with long light yellow hair, which she allowed to escape from her bonnet, knowing, perhaps, that it was not unbecoming to her when thus dishevelled. Her skin was very delicate, and her complexion good. Indeed her face would have been altogether prepossessing had there not been a want of gentleness in her eyes. Her hands, too, were soft and small, and on the whole she may be said to have been possessed of a strong battery of feminine attractions. She also well knew how to use them.

"Whisper," she said to me, with a peculiar but very proper aspiration on the h—"Wh-hisper," and both by the aspiration and the use of the word I knew at once from what island she had come. "Mr. Greene keeps all his money in this box also; so I never let it go out of my sight for a moment. But whatever you do, don't tell him that I told you so."

I laid my hand on my heart, and made a solemn asseveration that I would not divulge her secret. I need not, however, have troubled myself much on that head, for as I walked up stairs, keeping my eye upon the precious trunk, Mr. Greene addressed me.

"You are an Englishman, Mr. Robinson," said he. I acknowledged that I was.

"I am another. My wife, however, is Irish. My daughter,—by a former marriage,—is English also. You see that box there."

"Oh, yes," said I, "I see it." I began to be so fascinated by the box that I could not keep my eyes off it.

"I don't know whether or no it is prudent, but I keep all my money there; my money for travelling, I mean."

"If I were you, then," I answered, "I would not say anything about it to any one."

"Oh, no, of course not," said he; "I should not think of mentioning it. But those brigands in Italy always take away what you have about your person, but they don't meddle with the heavy luggage."

"Bills of exchange, or circular notes," I suggested.

"Ah, yes; and if you can't identify yourself, or happen to have a headache, you can't get them changed. I asked an old friend of mine, who has been connected with the Bank of England for the last fifty years, and he assured me that there was nothing like sovereigns."

"But you never get the value for them."

"Well, not quite. One loses a franc, or a franc and a half. But still, there's the certainty, and that's the great matter. An English sovereign will go anywhere," and he spoke these words with considerable triumph.

"Undoubtedly, if you consent to lose a shilling on each sovereign."

"At any rate, I have got three hundred and fifty in that box," he said. "I have them done up in rolls of twenty-five pounds each."

"I again recommended him to keep this arrangement of his as private as possible,—a piece of counsel which I confess seemed to me to be much needed,— and then I went away to my own room, having first accepted an invitation from Mrs. Greene to join their party at dinner. "Do," said she ; "we have been so dull, and it will be so pleasant."

I did not require to be much pressed to join myself to a party in which there was so pretty a girl as Miss Greene, and so attractive a woman as Mrs. Greene.

I therefore accepted the invitation readily, and went away to make my toilet. As I did so I passed the door of Mr. Greene's room, and saw the long file of boxes being borne into the centre of it.

I spent a pleasant evening, with, however, one or two slight drawbacks. As to old Greene himself, he was all that was amiable; but then he was nervous, full of cares, and somewhat apt to be a bore. He wanted information on a thousand points, and did not seem to understand that a young man might prefer the conversation of his daughter to his own. Not that he showed any solicitude to prevent conversation on the part of his daughter. I should have been perfectly at liberty to talk to either of the ladies had he not wished to engross all my attention to himself. He also had found it dull to be alone with his wife and daughter for the last six weeks.

He was a small spare man, probably over fifty years of age, who gave me to understand that he had lived in London all his life, and had made his own fortune in the city. What he had done in the city to make his fortune he did not say. Had I come across him there I should no doubt have found him to be a sharp man of business, quite competent to teach me many a useful lesson of which I was as ignorant as an infant. Had he caught me on the Exchange, or at Lloyd's, or in the big room of the Bank of England, I should have been compelled to ask him everything. Now, in this little town under the Alps, he was as much lost as I should have been in Lombard Street, and was ready enough to look to me for information. I was by no means chary in giving him my counsel, and imparting to him my ideas on things in general in that part of the world; —only I should have preferred to be allowed to make myself civil to his daughter.

In the course of conversation it was mentioned by him that they intended to stay a few days at Bellaggio, which, as all the world knows, is a central spot on the lake of Como, and a favourite resting-place for travellers. There are three lakes which all meet here, and to all of which we give the name of Como. They are properly called the lakes of Como, Colico, and Lecco; and Bellaggio is the spot at which their waters join each other. I had half made up my mind to sleep there one night on my road into Italy, and now, on hearing their purpose, I declared that such was my intention.

"How very pleasant," said Mrs. Greene. "It will be quite delightful to have some one to show us how to settle ourselves, for really——"

"My dear, I'm sure you can't say that you ever have much trouble."

"And who does then, Mr. Green? I am sure Sophonisba does not do much to help me."

"You won't let me," said Sophonisba, whose name I had not before heard. Her papa had called her Sophy in the yard of the inn. Sophonisba Greene! Sophonisba Robinson did not sound so badly in my ears, and I confess that I had tried the names

together. Her papa had mentioned to me that he
had no other child, and had mentioned also that he
had made his fortune.

And then there was a little family contest as to
the amount of travelling labour which fell to the lot
of each of the party, during which I retired to one of
the windows of the big front room in which we were
sitting. And how much of this labour there is inci-
dental to a tourist's pursuits! And how often these
little contests do arise upon a journey! Who has
ever travelled and not known them? I had taken
up such a position at the window as might, I
thought, have removed me out of hearing; but
nevertheless from time to time a word would catch
my ear about that precious box. "I have never
taken my eyes off it since I left England," said Mrs.
Greene, speaking quick, and with a considerable
brogue superinduced by her energy. "Where would
it have been at Basle if I had not been looking
afther it?" "Quite safe," said Sophonisba; "those
large things always are safe." "Are they, Miss?
That's all you know about it. I suppose your bonnet-
box was quite safe when I found it on the platform
at—at—I forget the name of the place?"

"Freidrichshafen," said Sophonisba, with almost
an unnecessary amount of Teutonic skill in her pro-
nunciation. "Well, mamma, you have told me of
that at least twenty times." Soon after that, the
ladies took them to their own rooms, weary with
the travelling of two days and a night, and Mr.

z

Greene went fast asleep in the very comfortless chair in which he was seated.

At four o'clock on the next morning we started on our journey.

> " Early to bed, and early to rise,
> Is the way to be healthy and wealthy and wise."

We all know that lesson, and many of us believe in it ; but if the lesson be true, the Italians ought to be the healthiest and wealthiest and wisest of all men and women. Three or four o'clock seems to them quite a natural hour for commencing the day's work. Why we should have started from Chiavenna at four o'clock in order that we might be kept waiting for the boat an hour and a half on the little quay at Colico, I don't know ; but such was our destiny. There we remained an hour and a half, Mrs. Greene sitting pertinaciously on the one important box. She had designated it as being smaller than the others, and, as all the seven were now ranged in a row, I had an opportunity of comparing them. It was something smaller,—perhaps an inch less high, and an inch and a half shorter. She was a sharp woman, and observed my scrutiny. "I always know it," she said in a loud whisper, "by this little hole in the canvas," and she put her finger on a slight rent on one of the ends. "As for Greene, if one of those Italian brigands were to walk off with it on his shoulders, before his eyes, he wouldn't be the wiser. How helpless you men are, Mr. Robinson!"

"It is well for us that we have women to look after us."

"But you have got no one to look after you;—or perhaps you have left her behind?"

"No, indeed. I'm all alone in the world as yet. But it's not my own fault. I have asked half a dozen."

"Now, Mr. Robinson!" And in this way the time passed on the quay at Colico, till the boat came and took us away. I should have preferred to pass my time in making myself agreeable to the younger lady; but the younger lady stood aloof, turning up her nose, as I thought, at her mamma.

I will not attempt to describe the scenery about Colico. The little town itself is one of the vilest places under the sun, having no accommodation for travellers, and being excessively unhealthy; but there is very little either north or south of the Alps,—and, perhaps I may add, very little elsewhere,—to beat the beauty of the mountains which cluster round the head of the lake. When we had sat upon those boxes that hour and a half, we were taken on board the steamer, which had been lying off a little way from the shore, and then we commenced our journey. Of course there was a good deal of exertion and care necessary in getting the packages off from the shore on to the boat, and I observed that any one with half an eye in his head might have seen that the mental anxiety expended on that one box which was marked by the small hole in the canvas far exceeded that which was extended to all the other six boxes. "They deserve that it should

z 2

be stolen," I said to myself, "for being such fools." And then we went down to breakfast in the cabin.'

"I suppose it must be safe," said Mrs. Greene to me, ignoring the fact that the cabin waiter understood English, although she had just ordered some veal cutlets in that language.

"As safe as a church," I replied, not wishing to give much apparent importance to the subject.

"They can't carry it off here," said Mr. Greene. But he was innocent of any attempt at a joke, and was looking at me with all his eyes.

"They might throw it overboard," said Sophonisba. I at once made up my mind that she could not be a good-natured girl. The moment that breakfast was over, Mrs. Greene returned again up-stairs, and I found her seated on one of the benches near the funnel, from which she could keep her eyes fixed upon the box. "When one is obliged to carry about one's jewels with one, one must be careful, Mr. Robinson," she said to me apologetically. But I was becoming tired of the box, and the funnel was hot and unpleasant, therefore I left her.

I had made up my mind that Sophonisba was ill-natured; but, nevertheless, she was pretty, and I now went through some little manœuvres with the object of getting into conversation with her. This I soon did, and was surprised by her frankness. "How tired you must be of mamma and her box," she said to me. To this I made some answer, declaring that I was rather interested than otherwise, in the safety of the precious trunk. "It makes me sick," said Sophonisba, "to hear her go on in that way to a perfect stranger. I heard what she said about her jewellery."

"It is natural she should be anxious," I said, "seeing that it contains so much that is valuable."

"Why did she bring them?" said Sophonisba. "She managed to live very well without jewels till papa married her, about a year since; and now she can't travel about for a month without lugging them with her everywhere. I should be so glad if some one would steal them."

"But all Mr. Greene's money is there also."

"I don't want papa to be bothered, but I declare I wish the box might be lost for a day or so. She is such a fool; don't you think so, Mr. Robinson?"

At this time it was just fourteen hours since I first had made their acquaintance in the yard of Conradi's hotel, and of those fourteen hours more than half had been passed in bed. I must confess that I looked upon Sophonisba as being almost more indiscreet than her mother-in-law. Nevertheless, she was not stupid, and I continued my conversation with her the greatest part of the way down the lake towards Bellaggio.

These steamers, which run up and down the lake of Como and the Lago Maggiore, put out their passengers at the towns on the banks of the water by means of small rowing-boats, and the persons who are about to disembark generally have their own articles ready to their hands when their turn comes for leaving the steamer. As we came near to Bellaggio, I looked up my own portmanteau, and, pointing to the beautiful wood-covered hill that stands at the fork of the waters, told my friend Greene that he was near his destination. "I am very glad to hear it," said he, complacently, but he did not at the moment busy himself about the boxes. Then the small boat ran up alongside the steamer, and the passengers for Como and Milan crowded up the side.

"We have to go in that boat," I said to Greene.

"Nonsense!" he exclaimed.

"Oh, but we have."

"What! put our boxes into that boat," said Mrs. Greene. "Oh dear! Here, boatman! there are seven of these boxes, all in white like this," and she pointed to the one that had the hole in the canvas. "Make haste. And there are two bags, and my dressing-case, and Mr. Greene's portmanteau. Mr. Greene, where is your portmanteau?"

The boatman whom she addressed, no doubt did not understand a word of English, but nevertheless he knew what she meant, and, being well accustomed to the work, got all the luggage together in an incredibly small number of moments.

"If you will get down into the boat," I said, "I will see that the luggage follows you before I leave the deck."

"I won't stir," she said, "till I see that box lifted

down. Take care; you'll let it fall into the lake. I know you will."

"I wish they would," Sophonisba whispered into my ear.

Mr. Greene said nothing, but I could see that his eyes were as anxiously fixed on what was going on, as were those of his wife. At last, however, the three Greenes were in the boat, as also were all the packages. Then I followed them, my portmanteau having gone down before me, and we pushed off for Bellaggio. Up to this period most of the attendants around us had understood a word or two of English, but now it would be well if we could find some one to whose ears French would not be unfamiliar. As regarded Mr. Greene and his wife, they, I found, must give up all conversation, as they knew nothing of any language but their own. Sophonisba could make herself understood in French, and was quite at home, as she assured me, in German. And then the boat was beached on the shore at Bellaggio, and we all had to go again to work with the object of getting ourselves lodged at the hotel which overlooks the water.

I had learned before that the Greenes were quite free from any trouble in this respect, for their rooms had been taken for them before they left England. Trusting to this, Mrs. Greene gave herself no inconsiderable airs the moment her foot was on the shore, and ordered the people about as though she were the Lady Paramount of Bellaggio. Italians, however, are used to this from travellers of a certain description. They never resent such conduct, but simply put it down in the bill with the other articles. Mrs. Greene's words on this occasion were innocent enough, seeing that they were English; but had I been that head waiter who came down to the beach with his nice black shiny hair, and his napkin under his arm, I should have thought her manner very insolent.

Indeed, as it was, I did think so, and was inclined to be angry with her. She was to remain for some time at Bellaggio, and therefore it behoved her, as she thought, to assume the character of the grand lady at once. Hitherto she had been willing enough to do the work, but now she began to order about Mr. Greene and Sophonisba; and, as it appeared to me, to order me about also. I did not quite enjoy this; so leaving her still among her luggage and satellites, I walked up to the hotel to see about my own bed-room. I had some seltzer water, stood at the window for three or four minutes, and then walked up and down the room. But still the Greenes were not there. As I had put in at Bellaggio solely with the object of seeing something more of Sophonisba, it would not do for me to quarrel with them, or to allow them so to settle themselves in their private sitting-room, that I should be excluded. Therefore I returned again to the road by which they must come up, and met the procession near the house.

Mrs. Greene was leading it with great majesty, the

waiter with the shiny hair walking by her side to
point out to her the way. Then came all the luggage,—each porter carrying a white canvas-covered
box. That which was so valuable no doubt was
carried next to Mrs. Greene, so that she might at a
moment's notice put her eye upon the well-known
valuable rent. I confess that I did not observe the
hole as the train passed by me, nor did I count the
number of the boxes. Seven boxes, all alike, are
very many ; and then they were followed by three
other men with the inferior articles,—Mr. Greene's
portmanteau, the carpet-bag, &c., &c. At the tail
of the line, I found Mr. Greene, and behind him
Sophonisba. "All your fatigues will be over now,"
I said to the gentleman, thinking it well not to be
too particular in my attentions to his daughter. He
was panting beneath a terrible great-coat, having
forgotten that the shores of an Italian lake are not
so cold as the summits of the Alps, and did not
answer me. "I'm sure I hope so," said Sophonisba.
"And I shall advise papa not to go any further unless he can persuade Mrs. Greene to send her jewels
home." "Sophy, my dear," he said, "for Heaven's
sake let us have a little peace since we are here."
From all which I gathered that Mr. Greene had not
been fortunate in his second matrimonial adventure.
We then made our way slowly up to the hotel, having
been altogether distanced by the porters, and when
we reached the house we found that the different
packages were already being carried away through

the house, some this way and some that. Mrs. Greene, the meanwhile, was talking loudly at the door of her own sitting-room.

"Mr. Greene," she said, as soon as she saw her heavily oppressed spouse,—for the noonday sun was up,—"Mr. Greene, where are you?"

"Here, my dear," and Mr. Greene threw himself panting into the corner of a sofa.

"A little seltzer water and brandy," I suggested. Mr. Greene's inmost heart leaped at the hint, and nothing that his remonstrant wife could say would induce him to move, until he had enjoyed the delicious draught. In the mean time the box with the hole in the canvas had been lost.

Yes; when we came to look into matters, to count the packages, and to find out where we were, the box with the hole in the canvas was not there. Or, at at any rate, Mrs. Greene said it was not there. I worked hard to look it up, and even went into Sophonisba's bed-room in my search. In Sophonisba's bed-room there was but one canvas-covered box. "That is my own," said she, "and it is all that I have, except this bag."

"Where on earth can it be?" said I, sitting down on the trunk in question. At the moment I almost thought that she had been instrumental in hiding it.

"How am I to know?" she answered; and I fancied that even she was dismayed. "What a fool that woman is!"

"The box must be in the house," I said.

"Do find it, for papa's sake ; there's a good fellow.
He will be so wretched without his money. I heard
him say that he had only two pounds in his purse."

"Oh, I can let him have money to go on with," I
answered grandly. And then I went off to prove
that I was a good fellow, and searched throughout the
house. Two white boxes had by order been left down-
stairs, as they would not be needed ; and these two
were in a large cupboard off the hall, which was used
expressly for stowing away luggage. And then there
were three in Mrs. Greene's bed-room, which had
been taken there as containing the wardrobe which
she would require while remaining at Bellaggio. I
searched every one of these myself to see if I could
find the hole in the canvas. But the hole in the
canvas was not there. And, let me count as I would,
I could make out only six. Now there certainly had
been seven on board the steamer, though I could not
swear that I had seen the seven put into the small
boat.

"Mr. Greene," said the lady, standing in the middle
of her remaining treasures, all of which were now
open, "you are worth nothing when travelling. Were
you not behind ?" But Mr. Greene's mind was full,
and he did not answer.

"It has been stolen before your very eyes," she
continued.

"Nonsense, mamma," said Sophonisba. "If ever
it came out of the steamer it certainly came into
the house."

"I saw it out of the steamer," said Mrs. Greene, "and it certainly is not in the house. Mr. Robinson, may I trouble you to send for the police?—at once, if you please, sir."

I had been at Bellaggio twice before, but nevertheless I was ignorant of their system of police. And then, again, I did not know what was the Italian for the word.

"I will speak to the landlord," I said.

"If you will have the goodness to send for the police at once, I will be obliged to you." And as she thus reiterated her command, she stamped with her foot upon the floor.

"There are no police at Bellaggio," said Sophonisba.

"What on earth shall I do for money to go on with?" said Mr. Greene, looking piteously up to the ceiling, and shaking both his hands.

And now the whole house was in an uproar, including not only the landlord, his wife and daughters, and all the servants, but also every other visitor at the hotel. Mrs. Greene was not a lady who hid either her glories or her griefs under a bushel, and, though she spoke only in English, she soon made her protestations sufficiently audible. She protested loudly that she had been robbed, and that she had been robbed since she left the steamer. The box had come on shore; of that she was quite certain. If the landlord had any regard either for his own character or for that of his house, he would ascertain before an hour was over where it was, and who had been the thief. She would give him an hour. And then she sat herself down; but in two minutes she was up again, vociferating her wrongs as loudly as ever. All this was filtered through me and Sophonisba to the waiter in French, and from the waiter to the landlord; but the lady's gestures required no translation to make them intelligible, and the state of her mind on the matter was, I believe, perfectly well understood.

Mr. Greene I really did pity. His feelings of dismay seemed to be quite as deep, but his sorrow and solicitude were repressed into more decorum. "What am I to do for money?" he said. "I have not a shilling to go on with!" And he still looked up at the ceiling.

"You must send to England," said Sophonisba.

"It will take a month," he replied.

"Mr. Robinson will let you have what you want at present," added Sophonisba. Now I certainly had said so, and had meant it at the time. But my whole travelling store did not exceed forty or fifty pounds, with which I was going on to Venice, and then back to England through the Tyrol. Waiting a month for Mr. Greene's money from England might be even more inconvenient to me than to him. Then it occurred to me that the wants of the Greene family would be numerous and expensive, and that my small stock would go but a little way among so many. And what also if there had been no money and no jewels in that accursed box! I confess that at the

moment such an idea did strike my mind. One hears
of sharpers on every side committing depredations by
means of most singular intrigues and contrivances.
Might it not be possible that the whole batch·of
Greenes belonged to this order of society. It was a
base idea, I own ; but I confess that I entertained it
for a moment.

I retired to my own room for a while that I might
think ·over all the circumstances. There certainly
had been seven boxes, and one had had a hole in the
canvas. All the seven had certainly been on board
the steamer. To so much I felt that I might safely
swear. I had not counted the seven into the small
boat, but on leaving the larger vessel I had looked
about the deck to see that none of the Greene trap-
pings were forgotten. If left on the steamer, it had
been so left through an intent on the part of some
one there employed. It was quite possible that the
contents of the box had been ascertained through
the imprudence of Mrs. Greene, and that it had been
conveyed away so that it might be rifled at Como.
As to Mrs. Greene's assertion that all the boxes had
been put into the small boat, I thought nothing of it.
The people at Bellaggio could not have known which
box to steal, nor had there been time to concoct the
plan in carrying the boxes up to the hotel. I came
at last to this conclusion, that the missing trunk had
either been purloined and carried on to Como,—in
which case it would be necessary to lose no time in
going after it ; or that it had been put out of sight

in some uncommonly clever way, by the Greenes themselves, as an excuse for borrowing as much money as they could raise and living without payment of their bills. With reference to the latter hypothesis, I declared to myself that Greene did not look like a swindler ; but as to Mrs. Greene— ! I confess that I did not feel so confident in regard to her.

Charity begins at home, so I proceeded to make myself comfortable in my room, feeling almost certain that I should not be able to leave Bellaggio on the following morning. I had opened my portmanteau when I first arrived, leaving it open on the floor, as is my wont. Some people are always being robbed, and are always locking up everything ; while others wander safe over the world and never lock up anything. For myself, I never turn a key anywhere, and no one ever purloins from me even a handkerchief. Cantabit vacuus—, and I am always sufficiently vacuus. Perhaps it is that I have not a handkerchief worth the stealing. It is your heavy-laden, suspicious, mal-adroit Greenes that the thieves attack. I now found that the accommodating Boots, who already knew my ways, had taken my travelling gear into a dark recess which was intended to do for a dressing-room, and had there spread my pormanteau open upon some table or stool in the corner. It was a convenient arrangement, and there I left it during the whole period of my sojourn.

Mrs. Greene had given the landlord an hour to find the box, and during that time the landlord, the

landlady, their three daughters, and all the servants
in the house certainly did exert themselves to the
utmost.   Half a dozen times they came to my door,
but I was luxuriating in a washing-tub, making up
for that four-o'clock start from Chiavenna.   I assured
them, however, that the box was not there, and so the
search passed by.   At the end of the hour I went
back to the Greenes according to promise, having
resolved that some one must be sent on to Como
to look after the missing article.

There was no necessity to knock at their sitting-
room door, for it was wide open.   I walked in, and found
Mrs. Greene still engaged in attacking the landlord,
while all the porters who had carried the luggage up
to the house were standing round.   Her voice was loud
above the others, but, luckily for them all, she was
speaking English.   The landlord, I saw, was becoming sulky.   He spoke in Italian, and we none of us
understood him, but I gathered that he was declining
to do anything further.   The box, he was certain, had
never come out of the steamer.   The Boots stood
by interpreting into French, and, acting as second
interpreter, I put it into English.

"Mr. Greene," said the lady, turning to her husband, "you must go at once to Como."

Mr. Greene, who was seated on the sofa, groaned
audibly, but said nothing.   Sophonisba, who was
sitting by him, beat upon the floor with both her
feet.

"Do you hear, Mr. Greene?" said she, turning to

him. "Do you mean to allow that vast amount of property to be lost without an effort? Are you prepared to replace my jewels?"

"Her jewels!" said Sophonisba, looking up into my face. "Papa had to pay the bill for every stitch she had when he married her." These last words were so spoken as to be audible only by me, but her first exclamation was loud enough. Were they people for whom it would be worth my while to delay my journey, and put myself to serious inconvenience with reference to money?

A few minutes afterwards I found myself with Greene on the terrace before the house. "What ought I to do?" said he.

"Go to Como," said I, "and look after your box. I will remain here and go on board the return steamer. It may perhaps be there."

"But I can't speak a word of Italian," said he.

"Take the Boots," said I.

"But I can't speak a word of French." And then it ended in my undertaking to go to Como. I swear that the thought struck me that I might as well take my portmanteau with me, and cut and run when I got there. The Greenes were nothing to me.

I did not, however, do this. I made the poor man a promise, and I kept it. I took merely a dressing-bag, for I knew that I must sleep at Como; and, thus resolving to disarrange all my plans, I started. I was in the midst of beautiful scenery, but I found it quite impossible to draw any enjoyment from it;—

from that or from anything around me. My whole mind was given up to anathemas against this odious box, as to which I had undoubtedly heavy cause of complaint. What was the box to me? I went to Como by the afternoon steamer, and spent a long dreary evening down on the steamboat quays searching everywhere, and searching in vain. The boat by which we had left Colico had gone back to Colico, but the people swore that nothing had been left on board it. It was just possible that such a box might have gone on to Milan with the luggage of other passengers.

I slept at Como, and on the following morning I went on to Milan. There was no trace of the box to be found in that city. I went round to every hotel and travelling office, but could hear nothing of it. Parties had gone to Venice, and Florence, and Bologna, and any of them might have taken the box. No one, however, remembered it; and I returned back to Como, and thence to Bellaggio, reaching the latter place at nine in the evening, disappointed, weary, and cross.

"Has Monsieur found the accursed trunk?" said the Bellaggio Boots, meeting me on the quay.

"In the name of the ——, no. Has it not turned up here?"

"Monsieur," said the Boots, "we shall all be mad soon. The poor master, he is mad already." And then I went up to the house.

"My jewels!" shouted Mrs. Greene, rushing to

me with her arms stretched out as soon as she heard my step in the corridor. I am sure that she would have embraced me had I found the box. I had not, however, earned any such reward. "I can hear nothing of the box either at Como or Milan," I said.

"Then what on earth am I to do for my money?" said Mr. Greene.

I had had neither dinner nor supper, but the elder Greenes did not care for that. Mr. Greene sat silent in despair, and Mrs. Greene stormed about the room in her anger. "I am afraid you are very tired," said Sophonisba.

"I am tired, and hungry, and thirsty," said I. I was beginning to get angry, and to think myself ill used. And that idea as to a family of swindlers became strong again. Greene had borrowed ten napoleons from me before I started for Como, and I had spent above four in my fruitless journey to that place and Milan. I was beginning to fear that my whole purpose as to Venice and the Tyrol would be destroyed; and I had promised to meet friends at Innspruck, who,—who were very much preferable to the Greenes. As events turned out, I did meet them. Had I failed in this, the present Mrs. Robinson would not have been sitting opposite to me.

I went to my room and dressed myself, and then Sophonisba presided over the tea-table for me. "What are we to do?" she asked me in a confidential whisper.

"Wait for money from England."

"But they will think we are all sharpers," she said; "and upon my word I do not wonder at it from the way in which that woman goes on." She then leaned forward, resting her elbow on the table and her face on her hand, and told me a long history of all their family discomforts. Her papa was a very good sort of man, only he had been made a fool of by that intriguing woman, who had been left without a sixpence with which to bless herself. And now they had nothing but quarrels and misery. Papa did not always get the worst of it;—papa could rouse himself sometimes; only now he was beaten down and cowed by the loss of his money. This whispering confidence was very nice in its way, seeing that Sophonisba was a pretty girl; but the whole matter seemed to be full of suspicion.

"If they did not want to take you in in one way, they did in another," said the present Mrs. Robinson, when I told the story to her at Innspruck. I beg that it may be understood that at the time of my meeting the Greenes I was not engaged to the present Mrs. Robinson, and was open to make any matrimonial engagement that might have been pleasing to me.

On the next morning, after breakfast, we held a council of war. I had been informed that Mr. Greene had made a fortune, and was justified in presuming him to be a rich man. It seemed to me, therefore, that his course was easy. Let him wait at Bellaggio for more money, and when he returned home, let him buy Mrs. Greene more jewels. A poor man always presumes that a rich man is indifferent about his money. But in truth a rich man never is indifferent about his money, and poor Greene looked very blank at my proposition.

" Do you mean to say that it's gone for ever ?" he asked.

" I'll not leave the country without knowing more about it," said Mrs. Greene.

"It certainly is very odd," said Sophonisba. Even Sophonisba seemed to think that I was too off-hand.

" It will be a month before I can get money, and my bill here will be something tremendous," said Greene.

" I wouldn't pay them a farthing till I got my box," said Mrs. Greene.

"That's nonsense," said Sophonisba. And so it was.

" Hold your tongue, Miss !" said the step-mother.

" Indeed, I shall not hold my tongue," said the step-daughter.

Poor Greene ! He had lost more than his box within the last twelve months; for, as I had learned in that whispered conversation over the tea-table with Sophonisba, this was in reality her papa's marriage trip.

Another day was now gone, and we all went to bed. Had I not been very foolish I should have had myself called at five in the morning, and have gone away by the early boat, leaving my ten napoleons behind me. But, unfortunately, Sophonisba had exacted a promise from me that I would not do this, and thus all chance of spending a day or two in Venice was lost to me. Moreover, I was thoroughly fatigued, and almost glad of any excuse which would allow me to lie in bed on the following morning. I did lie in bed till nine o'clock, and then found the Greenes at breakfast.

"Let us go and look at the Serbelloni Gardens," said I, as soon as the silent meal was over; "or take a boat over to the Sommariva Villa."

"I should like it so much," said Sophonisba.

"We will do nothing of the kind till I have found my property," said Mrs. Greene. "Mr. Robinson, what arrangement did you make yesterday with the police at Como?"

"The police at Como?" I said. "I did not go to the police."

"Not go to the police? And do you mean to say that I am to be robbed of my jewels and no efforts made for redress? Is there no such thing as a constable in this wretched country? Mr. Greene, I do insist upon it that you at once go to the nearest British consul."

"I suppose I had better write home for money," said he.

"And do you mean to say that you haven't written yet?" said I, probably with some acrimony in my voice.

"You needn't scold papa," said Sophonisba.

"I don't know what I am to do," said Mr. Greene,

and he began walking up and down the room; but still he did not call for pen and ink, and I began again to feel that he was a swindler. Was it possible that a man of business, who had made his fortune in London, should allow his wife to keep all her jewels in a box, and carry about his own money in the same?

"I don't see why you need be so very unhappy, papa," said Sophonisba. "Mr. Robinson, I'm sure, will let you have whatever money you may want at present." This was pleasant!

"And will Mr. Robinson return me my jewels, which were lost, I must say, in a great measure through his carelessness," said Mrs. Greene. This was pleasanter!

"Upon my word, Mrs. Greene, I must deny that," said I, jumping up. "What on earth could I have done more than I did do? I have been to Milan and nearly fagged myself to death."

"Why didn't you bring a policeman back with you?"

"You would tell everybody on board the boat what there was in it," said I.

"I told nobody but you," she answered.

"I suppose you mean to imply that I've taken the box," I rejoined. So that on this, the third or fourth day of our acquaintance, we did not go on together quite pleasantly.

But what annoyed me, perhaps, the most, was the confidence with which it seemed to be Mr. Greene's intention to lean upon my resources. He certainly had not written home yet, and had taken my ten napoleons, as one friend may take a few shillings from another when he finds that he has left his own silver on his dressing-table. What could he have wanted of ten napoleons? He had alleged the necessity of paying the porters, but the few francs he had had in his pocket would have been enough for that. And now Sophonisba was ever and again prompt in her assurances that he need not annoy himself about money, because I was at his right hand. I went up-stairs into my own room, and counting all my treasures, found that thirty-six pounds and some odd silver was the extent of my wealth. With that I had to go, at any rate, as far as Innspruck, and from thence back to London. It was quite impossible that I should make myself responsible for the Greenes' bill at Bellaggio.

We dined early, and after dinner, according to a promise made in the morning, Sophonisba ascended with me into the Serbelloni Gardens, and walked round the terraces on that beautiful hill which commands the view of the three lakes. When we started I confess that I would sooner have gone alone, for I was sick of the Greenes in my very soul. We had had a terrible day. The landlord had been sent for so often, that he refused to show himself again. The landlady—though Italians of that class are always courteous—had been so driven that she snapped her finger in Mrs. Greene's face. The three girls would not show themselves. The waiters kept out of the way as much as possible; and the Boots, in confidence, abused them to me behind their back. "Monsieur," said the Boots, "do you think there ever was such a box?" "Perhaps not," said I; and yet I knew that I had seen it.

I would, therefore, have preferred to walk without Sophonisba; but that now was impossible. So I determined that I would utilise the occasion by telling her of my present purpose. I had resolved to start on the following day, and it was now necessary to make my friends understand that it was not in my power to extend to them any further pecuniary assistance.

Sophonisba, when we were on the hill, seemed to have forgotten the box, and to be willing that I should forget it also. But this was impossible. When, therefore, she told me how sweet it was to escape from that terrible woman, and leaned on my arm with all the freedom of old acquaintance, I was obliged to cut short the pleasure of the moment.

"I hope your father has written that letter," said I.

"He means to write it from Milan. We know you want to get on, so we purpose to leave here the day after to-morrow."

"Oh!" said I, thinking of the bill immediately, and remembering that Mrs. Greene had insisted on having champagne for dinner.

"And if anything more is to be done about the nasty box, it may be done there," continued Sophonisba.

"But I must go to-morrow," said I, "at 5 A.M."

"Nonsense," said Sophonisba. "Go to-morrow, when I,—I mean we,—are going on the next day !"

"And I might as well explain," said I, gently dropping the hand that was on my arm, "that I find, —I find it will be impossible for me—to—to——"

"To what ?"

"To advance Mr. Greene any more money just at present." Then Sophonisba's arm dropped all at once, and she exclaimed, "Oh, Mr. Robinson !"

After all, there was a certain hard good sense about Miss Greene which would have protected her from my evil thoughts had I known all the truth. I found out afterwards that she was a considerable heiress, and, in spite of the opinion expressed by the present Mrs. Robinson when Miss Walker, I do not for a moment think she would have accepted me had I offered to her.

"You are quite right not to embarrass yourself," she said, when I explained to her my immediate circumstances; "but why did you make papa an offer which you cannot perform ? He must remain here now till he hears from England. Had you explained it all at first, the ten napoleons would have carried us to Milan." This was all true, and yet I thought it hard upon me.

It was evident to me now, that Sophonisba was prepared to join her step-mother in thinking that I had ill-treated them, and I had not much doubt that I should find Mr. Greene to be of the same opinion.

There was very little more said between us during the walk, and when we reached the hotel at seven or half-past seven o'clock, I merely remarked that I would go in and wish her father and mother good bye. "I suppose you will drink tea with us," said Sophonisba, and to this I assented.

I went into my own room, and put all my things into my portmanteau, for according to the custom, which is invariable in Italy when an early start is premeditated, the Boots was imperative in his demand that the luggage should be ready over night: I then went to the Greenes' sitting-room, and found that the whole party was now aware of my intentions.

"So you are going to desert us," said Mrs. Greene.

"I must go on upon my journey," I pleaded in a weak apologetic voice.

"Go on upon your journey, Sir!" said Mrs. Greene. "I would not for a moment have you put yourself to inconvenience on our account." And yet I had already lost fourteen napoleons, and given up all prospect of going to Venice !

"Mr. Robinson is certainly right not to break his engagement with Miss Walker," said Sophonisba. Now I had said not a word about an engagement with Miss Walker, having only mentioned incidentally that she would be one of the party at Innspruck. "But," continued she, "I think he should not have misled us." And in this way we enjoyed our evening meal.

I was just about to shake hands with them all, previous to my final departure from their presence, when the Boots came into the room.

"I'll leave the portmanteau till to-morrow morning," said he.

"All right," said I.

"Because," said he, "there will be such a crowd of things in the hall. The big trunk I will take away now."

"Big trunk,—what big trunk?"

"The trunk with your rug over it, on which your portmanteau stood."

I looked round at Mr., Mrs., and Miss Greene, and saw that they were all looking at me. I looked round at them, and as their eyes met mine I felt that I turned as red as fire. I immediately jumped up, and rushed away to my own room, hearing as I went that all their steps were following me. I rushed to the inner recess, pulled down the portmanteau, which still remained in its old place, tore away my own carpet rug which covered the support beneath it, and there saw——a white canvas-covered box, with a hole in the canvas on the side next to me!

"It is my box," said Mrs. Greene, pushing me away, as she hurried up and put her finger within the rent.

"It certainly does look like it," said Mr. Greene, peering over his wife's shoulder.

"There's no doubt about the box," said Sophonisba.

"Not the least in life," said I, trying to assume an indifferent look.

"Mon Dieu!" said the Boots.

"Corpo di Baccho!" exclaimed the landlord, who had now joined the party.

"Oh—h—h—h—!" screamed Mrs. Greene, and then she threw herself back on to my bed, and shrieked hysterically.

There was no doubt whatsoever about the fact. There was the lost box, and there it had been during all those tedious hours of unavailing search. While I was suffering all that fatigue in Milan, spending my précious zwanzigers in driving about from one hotel to another, the box had been safe, standing in my own room at Bellaggio, hidden by my own rug. And now that it was found everybody looked at me as though it were all my fault. Mrs. Greene's eyes, when she had done being hysterical, were terrible, and Sophonisba looked at me as though I were a convicted thief.

"Who put the box here?" I said, turning fiercely upon the Boots.

"I did," said the Boots, "by Monsieur's express order."

"By my order?" I exclaimed.

"Certainly," said the Boots.

"Corpo di Baccho!" said the landlord, and he also looked at me as though I were a thief. In the meantime the landlady and the three daughters had clustered round Mrs. Greene, administering to her all manner of Italian consolation. The box, and the money, and the jewels were after all a reality; and much incivility can be forgiven to a lady who has really lost her jewels, and has really found them again.

There and then there arose a hurly-burly among us as to the manner in which the odious trunk found its way into my room. Had anybody been just enough to consider the matter coolly, it must have been quite clear that I could not have ordered it there. When I entered the hotel, the boxes were already being lugged about, and I had spoken a word to no one concerning them. That traitorous Boots had done it,—no doubt without malice prepense; but he had done it; and now that the Greenes were once more known as moneyed people, he turned upon me, and told me to my face, that I had desired that box to be taken to my own room as part of my own luggage!

"My dear," said Mr. Greene, turning to his wife, "you should never mention the contents of your luggage to any one."

"I never will again," said Mrs. Greene, with a mock repentant air, "but I really thought——"

"One never can be sure of sharpers," said Mr. Greene.

"That's true," said Mrs. Greene.

"After all, it may have been accidental," said Sophonisba, on hearing which good-natured surmise both papa and mamma Greene shook their suspicious heads.

I was resolved to say nothing then. It was all but

impossible that they should really think that I had intended to steal their box ; nor, if they did think so, would it have become me to vindicate myself before the landlord and all his servants. I stood by therefore in silence, while two of the men raised the trunk, and joined the procession which followed it as it was carried out of my room into that of the legitimate owner. Everybody in the house was there by that time, and Mrs. Greene, enjoying her triumph, by no means grudged them the entrance into her sitting-room. She had felt that she was suspected, and now she was determined that the world of Bellaggio should know how much she was above suspicion. The box was put down upon two chairs, the supporters who had borne it retiring a pace each. Mrs. Greene then advanced proudly with the selected key, and Mr. Greene stood by at her right shoulder, ready to receive his portion of the hidden treasure. Sophonisba was now indifferent, and threw herself on the sofa, while I walked up and down the room thoughtfully,—meditating what words I should say when I took my last farewell of the Greenes.

But as I walked I could see what occurred. Mrs. Greene opened the box, and displayed to view the ample folds of a huge yellow woollen dressing-gown. I could fancy that she would not willingly have exhibited this article of her toilet, had she not felt that its existence would speedily be merged in the presence of the glories which were to follow. This had merely been the padding at the top of the box. Under that lay a long papier-maché case, and in that were all her treasures. "Ah, they are safe," she said, opening the lid and looking upon her tawdry pearls and carbuncles.

Mr. Greene, in the meantime, well knowing the passage for his hand, had dived down to the very bottom of the box, and seized hold of a small canvas bag. "It is here," said he, dragging it up, "and as far as I can tell, as yet, the knot has not been untied." Whereupon he sat himself down by Sophonisba, and employing her to assist him in holding them, began to count his rolls. "They are all right," said he; and he wiped the perspiration from his brow.

I had not yet made up my mind in what manner I might best utter my last words among them so as to maintain the dignity of my character, and now I was standing over against Mr. Greene with my arms folded on my breast. I had on my face a frown of displeasure, which I am able to assume upon occasions, but I had not yet determined what words I would use. After all, perhaps, it might be as well that I should leave them without any last words.

"Greene, my dear," said the lady, "pay the gentleman his ten napoleons."

"Oh yes, certainly;" whereupon Mr. Greene undid one of the rolls and extracted eight sovereigns. "I believe that will make it right, Sir," said he, handing them to me.

I took the gold, slipped it with an indifferent air

into my waistcoat pocket, and then refolded my arms across my breast.

"Papa," said Sophonisba, in a very audible whisper, "Mr. Robinson went for you to Como. Indeed, I believe he says he went to Milan."

"Do not let that be mentioned," said I.

"By all means pay him his expenses," said Mrs. Greene; "I would not owe him anything for worlds."

"He should be paid," said Sophonisba.

"Oh, certainly," said Mr. Greene. And he at once extracted another sovereign, and tendered it to me in the face of the assembled multitude.

This was too much! "Mr. Greene," said I, "I intended to be of service to you when I went to Milan, and you are very welcome to the benefit of my intentions. The expense of that journey, whatever may be its amount, is my own affair." And I remained standing with my closed arms.

"We will be under no obligation to him," said Mrs. Greene; "and I shall insist on his taking the money."

"The servant will put it on his dressing-table," said Sophonisba. And she handed the sovereign to the Boots, giving him instructions.

"Keep it yourself, Antonio," I said. Whereupon the man chucked it to the ceiling with his thumb, caught it as it fell, and with a well-satisfied air, dropped it into the recesses of his pocket. The air of the Greenes was also well satisfied, for they felt that they had paid me in full for all my services.

And now, with many obsequious bows and assurances of deep respect, the landlord and his family withdrew from the room. " Was there anything else they could do for Mrs. Greene ? " Mrs. Greene was all affability. She had shown her jewels to the girls, and allowed them to express their admiration in pretty Italian superlatives. There was nothing else she wanted to-night. She was very happy and liked Bellaggio. She would stay yet a week, and would make herself quite happy. And, though none of them understood a word that the other said, each understood that things were now rose-coloured, and so with scrapings, bows, and grinning smiles, the landlord and all his myrmidons withdrew. Mr. Greene was still counting his money, sovereign by sovereign, and I was still standing with my folded arms upon my bosom.

" I believe I may now go," said I.

" Good night," said Mrs. Greene.

" Adieu," said Sophonisba.

"I have the pleasure of wishing you good bye," said Mr. Greene.

And then I walked out of the room. After all, what was the use of saying anything ? And what could I say that would have done me any service ? If they were capable of thinking me a thief,—which they certainly did,—nothing that I could say would remove the impression. Nor, as I thought, was it suitable that I should defend myself from such an imputation. What were the Greenes to me ? So I walked slowly out of the room, and never again saw one of the family from that day to this.

As I stood upon the beach the next morning, while my portmanteau was being handed into the boat, I gave the Boots five zwanzigers. I was determined to show him that I did not condescend to feel anger against him.

He took the money, looked into my face, and then whispered to me, " Why did you not give me a word of notice beforehand ?" he said, and winked his eye. He was evidently a thief, and took me to be another ; —but what did it matter ?

I went thence to Milan, in which city I had no heart to look at anything ; thence to Verona, and so over the pass of the Brenner to Innspruck. When I once found myself near to my dear friends the Walkers I was again a happy man ; and I may safely declare that, though a portion of my journey was so troublesome and unfortunate, I look back upon that tour as the happiest and the luckiest epoch of my life.

THE END.

READ MORE IN PENGUIN

In every corner of the world, on every subject under the sun, Penguin represents quality and variety – the very best in publishing today.

For complete information about books available from Penguin – including Puffins, Penguin Classics and Arkana – and how to order them, write to us at the appropriate address below. Please note that for copyright reasons the selection of books varies from country to country.

In the United Kingdom: Please write to *Dept. JC, Penguin Books Ltd, FREEPOST, West Drayton, Middlesex UB7 OBR*

If you have any difficulty in obtaining a title, please send your order with the correct money, plus ten per cent for postage and packaging, to *PO Box No. 11, West Drayton, Middlesex UB7 OBR*

In the United States: Please write to *Penguin USA Inc., 375 Hudson Street, New York, NY 10014*

In Canada: Please write to *Penguin Books Canada Ltd, 10 Alcorn Avenue, Suite 300, Toronto, Ontario M4V 3B2*

In Australia: Please write to *Penguin Books Australia Ltd, 487 Maroondah Highway, Ringwood, Victoria 3134*

In New Zealand: Please write to *Penguin Books (NZ) Ltd, 182–190 Wairau Road, Private Bag, Takapuna, Auckland 9*

In India: Please write to *Penguin Books India Pvt Ltd, 706 Eros Apartments, 56 Nehru Place, New Delhi 110 019*

In the Netherlands: Please write to *Penguin Books Netherlands B.V., Keizersgracht 231 NL–1016 DV Amsterdam*

In Germany: Please write to *Penguin Books Deutschland GmbH, Friedrichstrasse 10–12, W–6000 Frankfurt/Main 1*

In Spain: Please write to *Penguin Books S. A., C. San Bernardo 117–6° E–28015 Madrid*

In Italy: Please write to *Penguin Italia s.r.l., Via Felice Casati 20, I–20124 Milano*

In France: Please write to *Penguin France S. A., 17 rue Lejeune, F–31000 Toulouse*

In Japan: Please write to *Penguin Books Japan, Ishikiribashi Building, 2–5–4, Suido, Tokyo 112*

In Greece: Please write to *Penguin Hellas Ltd, Dimocritou 3, GR–106 71 Athens*

In South Africa: Please write to *Longman Penguin Southern Africa (Pty) Ltd, Private Bag X08, Bertsham 2013*

READ MORE IN PENGUIN

GEORGE ELIOT – A SELECTION

Scenes of Clerical Life
Edited with an Introduction by David Lodge

Though *Scenes of Clerical Life* was published at a time when religious questions were hotly debated, George Eliot's choice of subject for her fictional début is, on the face of it, surprising, since she had lost her Christian belief long before and was closely associated with the progressive, free thinking opinion of her day. Yet her mature views were never simple ones, and under the surface orthodoxy of the *Scenes* we can detect signs of her search for a 'religion of Humanity'.

Romola
Edited with an Introduction by Andrew Sanders

In *Romola* George Eliot recreates the upheavals of fifteenth-century Florence. Living in the city-state at this time is the noble and courageous Romola, who finds herself increasingly disillusioned by Savonarola's career and repelled by her unscrupulous and self-indulgent husband, Tito Melema.

Middlemarch
Edited by W. J. Harvey

With sure and subtle touch, George Eliot paints a luminous and spacious landscape of life in a provincial town, interweaving her themes with a proliferation of characters. In her penetrating analysis of human nature she achieved what Dr Leavis called 'a Tolstoyan depth and reality'.

The Mill on the Floss
Edited with an Introduction by A. S. Byatt

The Mill on the Floss is one of George Eliot's best-loved works containing an affectionate and perceptive study of provincial life, a brilliant evocation of the complexities of human relationships and a heroine whose rebellious spirit closely resembles George Eliot's own.

READ MORE IN PENGUIN

JANE AUSTEN – A SELECTION

Sense and Sensibility
Edited with an Introduction by Tony Tanner

Sense and Sensibility has as its heroines two strikingly different sisters, Elinor and Marianne Dashwood. Elinor is reserved, tactful, self-controlled, Marianne impulsively emotional and demonstrative; but Jane Austen goes beyond this simple antithesis to explore with subtle precision the tension that exists in every community between the needs of the individual and the demands of society.

Pride and Prejudice
Edited with an Introduction by Tony Tanner

Much has been said of the light and sparkling side of *Pride and Prejudice* – the delicious social comedy, the unerring dialogue, the satisfying love stories and its enchanting and spirited heroine. Nonetheless, the novel is also about deeper issues in which Jane Austen demonstrates her belief that the truly civilized being maintains a proper balance between reason and energy.

Persuasion
Edited with an Introduction by D. W. Harding

Persuasion is a tale of love and marriage told with the irony, insight and just evaluation of human conduct which sets Jane Austen's novels apart. Anne Elliott and Captain Wentworth have met and separated years before. Their reunion forces a recognition of the false values that drove them apart.

Lady Susan/The Watsons/Sanditon
Edited with an Introduction by Margaret Drabble

Lady Susan is a sparkling melodrama which takes its tone from the outspoken and robust eighteenth century. *The Watsons* is a tantalizing and highly delightful story whose vitality and optimism centres on the marital prospects of the Watson sisters in a small provinicial town. *Sanditon* is set in a seaside town and its themes concern the new speculative consumer society and foreshadow the great social upheavals of the Industrial Revolution.

THE PENGUIN TROLLOPE

THE PENGUIN TROLLOPE